Praise for

BEYOND ALL REASONABLE DOUBT

"Chilling and complex. The truth in this story is a cracked mirror, changing at every angle. Giolito masterfully plumbs the nature of guilt or innocence until no character, nor even the reader, is left unscathed."
—Joanna Schaffhausen, author of *The Vanishing Season*

"Another breathtaking novel from Malin Persson Giolito! *Beyond All Reasonable Doubt* masterfully questions the role media and public opinion play in court. A deeply moving suspense novel that zeroes in on humanity's deepest flaws."
—Viveca Sten, author of *In the Heat of the Moment*

Praise for

QUICKSAND

"This is the evolution of Scandinavian crime, in more ways than one."
—Fredrik Backman, author of *A Man Called Ove*

"A remarkable new novel...Giolito...writes with exceptional skill...[*Quicksand* is] always smart and engrossing... Giolito keeps us guessing a long time and the outcome, when it arrives, is just as it should be." —*Washington Post*

"[*Quicksand*] provides a razor-sharp view of modern Sweden and its criminal justice system, yet is a tonic for readers who have had enough of the brooding, often-bloody 'Scandi-crime' that has been so popular in recent years."
—NPR, Best Books of the Year

"Astonishing...a dark exploration of the crumbling European social order and the psyche of rich Swedish teens... the incisive language that's on display here surely involves translation precision that's second to none."
—*Booklist* (starred review)

"[*Quicksand*] is structured as a courtroom procedural, yet it clearly has ambitions beyond that, addressing Sweden's underlying economic and racial tensions."
—*New York Times Book Review*

"Brilliantly conceived and executed, this extraordinary legal thriller is not to be missed."
—*Library Journal* (starred review)

"Haunting and immersive."   —*Publishers Weekly*

"Expert dialogue and irresistible momentum make an all-too-realistic story come breathing off the page...Part courtroom thriller, part introspection, *Quicksand* is pulled tight throughout by the suspense, not only of Maja's verdict, but of the elusive 'truth' of what really happened in the classroom that day."   —*Shelf Awareness*

"Sharp social commentary through the tragic story of a young woman's trial for mass murder...The rhythm, tone, and language are just right...a splendid work of fiction."
—*Kirkus Reviews*

"Persson Giolito's craft takes us on a psychological ride."
—*Huffington Post*

"A compelling, multilayered study of a terrible school shooting."   —*Boston Herald*

Also by Malin Persson Giolito

QUICKSAND

beyond all reasonable doubt

MALIN PERSSON GIOLITO

Translated from the Swedish by
RACHEL WILLSON-BROYLES

Other Press
New York

The quote on p. 372 is from *The Holy Bible*, The New Oxford Annotated Bible,
New Revised Standard Version, Fourth Edition, Luke 18:17.
New York: Oxford University Press, 2010.

Production editor: Yvonne E. Cárdenas
Text designer: Julie Fry
This book was set in Founders Grotesk and Presnsa
by Alpha Design & Composition of Pittsfield, NH

3 5 7 9 10 8 6 4

Library of Congress Cataloging-in-Publication Data

Names: Persson Giolito, Malin, 1969- author. | Willson-Broyles, Rachel, translator.
Title: Beyond all reasonable doubt : a novel / Malin Persson Giolito ;
translated from the Swedish by Rachel Willson-Broyles.
Other titles: Bortom allt rimligt tvivel. English
Description: New York : Other Press, [2019] | "Originally published in Swedish
by Piratförlaget as Bortom varje rimligt tvivel."
Identifiers: LCCN 2018049563 (print) | LCCN 2018055329 (ebook) |
ISBN 9781590519202 (ebook) | ISBN 9781590519196 (paperback)
Subjects: LCSH: Judicial error—Fiction. | Legal stories. | Murder—Investigation—Fiction.
Classification: LCC PT9877.26.E79 (ebook) | LCC PT9877.26.E79 B6713 2019 (print) |
DDC 839.73/8—dc23
LC record available at https://lccn.loc.gov/2018049563

Thank you, Åsa.

Katrin
1998

In the beginning, all is well. First she shaves her legs, carefully, using Dad's shaving cream. The bathtub ends up dotted with tiny bits of hair and her legs become satiny smooth. She applies a mask for oily, shiny skin and a hair treatment for split ends. The mirror fogs over and her bangs curl in the fresh air from the window she opens.

Then she paints her toenails and fingernails in a thin layer of pale pink. Mom's dress and necklace are hanging from a padded hanger, moving slowly with the warm draft. The stereo plays just loud enough and her perfume is brand-new. She sings softly without knowing the words, stands nude before the mirror and puts on her makeup: first powder, then eye shadow, mascara, and just a hint of blush. She and Carmen are the only ones at home. Mom and Dad are away for the weekend and she has all the time she needs.

All is well. Nothing bad could happen. There's no way anything can go wrong.

But then there's something she forgot to pick up at the store. She has to hurry, pulls the dress over her head and feels the nail polish sticking to the fabric. She runs to the store with Carmen in tow, skips the waste bags, yanking at the leash. The dog could spend hours sniffing. There is no time for that.

On the way home, Carmen stops short and refuses to budge. She plants her legs and pulls back and Katrin has to tug on the leash so hard that Carmen's collar rides up and gets stuck on her ears. Katrin has to drag the dog the last little way, through the gate and up the stairs.

By the time they're back in the house, Katrin is too hot. The stains will be visible on the dress once the sweat dries, salty deposits eating into the fabric, and she stinks. When she's nervous the sweating won't stop. Her body betrays her. She smells like yeast and sulfur, musty and dead.

But it'll be fine, she says. She repeats it several times. Whispering it into the mirror. Everything, everything, everything will work out for the very very best.

If only she hurries to wash herself properly. She gets back into the shower. Soaping her underarms, dabbing her sticky nails with acetone on a cotton ball. She pulls a washcloth between her thighs, where it already itches even though it's only been two days since she removed the hair there.

He doesn't like her pubic hair; her slimy fluids make it stick together and stiffen into curls. He hates it when that happens.

She washes again, and once more. Rubbing until she's covered with thick, white lather. But acid rises in her stomach and her mouth tastes sour. She clears her throat and brings up a bitter yellow glob. When she licks the back of her hand, she gets a whiff of bile and reflux. She's so incredibly disgusting. She reeks. She can smell it herself.

Her gums start to bleed after the third brushing. She gargles as long as she can without choking.

She inhales. Tries to breathe slowly. Deeply. One breath at a time. She dries off. Raises her arms. The deodorant needs time to dry; it has to dry all the way before she gets dressed. Then she runs naked up the stairs and borrows another dress from Mom, a white one that's a tiny bit tight across her chest. She balls up the other one and shoves it to the bottom of the hamper. She doesn't bother with perfume; it's too strong. Whorish, maybe, it was really cheap after all.

Breathe slowly. Shoulders down. The recipes are laid out in the kitchen. She's going to make salad for a starter, battered cod for the main course, and the sticky chocolate cake is already done. It took her almost an entire day to make up her mind; she spent ages lying on her bed, paging through Mom's glossy *All About Food*. There were too many options, and all the photos of salmon tartare, marbled steak, puréed soups, creamy sauces, and glistening vegetables gave her a headache. But in the end she managed to plan a whole menu, and it will all work out well. It really should. Right?

Everything is prepared, almost done, and the table is set. They're not going to sit out in the garden; he doesn't like to eat outside. Outdoor eating is so typically Swedish, as in grilled pork chops and home permanents, boxed wine and clogs. Not Swedish the good way, like everything that is right and proper and the only way to do things. They'll sit in the dining room instead, across from one another. With the napkins on the plates; it looks so overdone when you fold them and tuck them in the glasses.

Then he arrives too early. Crashing through the door, his steps a little off-center, he doesn't take off his shoes. Carmen barks and whines, cowering and putting her ears back.

There are stains on his shirt; his eyes are red and he's already eaten. He doesn't want salad anyway. It's nothing but rabbit food, obviously she should have thought of that.

What was she thinking? She should have casually asked him if he felt like pizza, not this housewife crap. Cookbooks, breadcrumbs, measuring cups, cringey. An ironed tablecloth, candles, and linen napkins — seriously, ridiculous.

Her cheeks get hot and she turns off the oven. He walks up the stairs and down again. Leans toward a painting, backs up, walks off, pulls the curtains. He turns off the stereo, doesn't choose something new. The room is silent. She can hear him breathing.

Katrin follows him around. But not too close. Maybe he wants something in particular; maybe he'll say something soon. She never should have turned on the stereo. Of course he doesn't like that music. Dad's music. Radio racket — she should have turned it off herself. How could he like it here?

"Carmen," she snaps. "Down!" But the dog is already flat on her stomach. She turns around again. He isn't looking at her. "Wouldn't you like to take a seat?" she asks. Like an old woman, she thinks, she's acting like a goddamn old lady. He can walk around as much as he likes, it's not her problem, is it?

But he sits down after all. On one of the kitchen chairs — and he pulls her over and draws her panties aside. He calls her baby and presses her close, sticking two fingers inside, stroking her lightly with his thumb. He pulls his fingers out again and looks her right in the eyes.

"I'll never get tired of you," he says. And then he kisses her.

That's like saying "I love you," she thinks. I'll never get tired of you. It's like he loves me for real, just not with those exact words. Of course he likes me. Of course everything will be fine.

He asks her to go into the master bedroom — not her room. He tells her to undress while he watches. She's happy to. Her nausea dies down. When he watches her. That gaze — it's sunshine on closed eyelids, an evening skinny-dip in a countryside lake. They could eat afterward. He might want the fish, after all? A little later. Or dessert. He must like chocolate, right? Of course he does, right?

It's going to be great, really great, like in a movie. She's sure of it. She knows what she'll do. Afterward. She'll borrow Mom's silk robe, tie it loosely, and feed him with one hand. "Taste this," she'll whisper. "Here you go."

She arches her back and her breasts lift and his eyes go foggy; he almost groans. He's sitting with his legs spread wide, drinking from the bottle he brought. He has undone his pants and he touches her roughly, one hand on her sex, using the neck of the bottle to stroke her nipples. They pucker. "You whore," he says softly. And then he strikes her. "You're always horny," he whispers. Then he pushes into her. With a single thrust, like a kick of his boot. She whimpers.

She tries to close her eyes. She tries to swallow. She tries to stay quiet and calm. She lies down and he leans over her. She bites her lip. As long as she doesn't say anything, turns her face away, it will be over soon. But it's as if her body can't obey. The tears come of their own accord. When she tries to get away, he pinches her nipples harder; when she whimpers, he pumps faster. When he uses the bottle instead she hears herself scream.

Time passes. Or does it stand still? Her head is bleeding. Then she opens her eyes. He has gone to get Carmen and is holding her by the scruff. The whites of Carmen's eyes are showing. How the fuck is he supposed to be able to come? How is he supposed to have a nice time while that fucking dog is skittering around on the parquet, staring at him? That overgrown rat. What kind of pet is that? What use could they have for this stupid thing?

Usually she never says no. But now. "Not the dog," she says, "please, not Carmen."

Carmen likes to sleep in bed with her, under the covers, at her waist. When Mom isn't looking Katrin lets Carmen drink milk from her breakfast glass. She knows sit and stay and paw, and lots more, but only does it if Katrin asks her to. Carmen is her dog. Just hers.

"No?" he laughs.

"Please," she begs again. "Please. What did you do to Carmen?"

"None of your business," he says, smiling. He holds the dog tighter, by the neck now. He slams Carmen's head against the foot of the bed. He's shouting. "You do not say a word to me. Just shut up. Is that so hard? To keep your mouth shut?"

He sucks at Katrin's nipples, drawing them out, pressing them back. He turns her over. Spreads her thighs; she squeezes her eyes closed again. It will never end. Won't it ever end?

"I'm sorry, Carmen," she whispers. Softly, into the pillow. "I'm sorry."

■ ■ ■

It's a neighbor who makes the emergency call. And it's not for Katrin's sake but because of the dog. Something must have happened to the dog. It sounds like it's gone insane.

The call is labeled low-priority. That's the term they use when the dispatcher has no intention of sending help; it's all perfectly routine. They cannot send out an emergency vehicle because someone next door forgot to take the dog out. There are more important alarms.

There's always someone dying in a big city. Those in better shape spend their time fighting. And they drink too much and swim very badly, often simultaneously. Neglected toddlers shove their sticky fists into canisters of lye and are found with burns around their mouths. Buildings are set on fire and banks are robbed of people's poorly invested savings. Families returning from the countryside crash head-on with oncoming trucks because they desperately want to make it home in time to watch a show. Disturbed teens cut their wrists in the hopes of feeling like a rock star, or at least feeling something. Lost souls call in to report homemade explosives they intend to place under the desk of their former boss. Someone has trouble breathing. Someone else is waving a knife.

Dangerous things happen all the time; serious events that demand acute intervention. Around the clock, all year long, no time off for vacations or holidays. But if your neighbor's dog is barking — you don't call the emergency line, you go next door to speak to the dog's owner.

The neighbor calls again. And again. When the fourth call comes in, there happens to be a patrol car nearby. They send it over.

By the time the two officers arrive, Carmen is hoarse. At first, they can barely hear her. As they approach the door she begins to howl. The door is closed, but not locked. As one of them opens it, the colleague puts a hand on his secured service weapon. Their bulletproof vests are back in the car. One of them has to shove the dog aside with his boot so they can enter the hall. The animal reels and her hind legs buckle but she gets up again, unsteadily, snapping at the air.

The dog's eyes are bulging and she wobbles and staggers; her matted sides heave like the gills of a freshly caught fish. The air is stifling with the smell from the excrement that has run from her rectum, it's still trickling out uncontrolled under her stiff, raised tail. She cowers, whines, and runs off, slipping in circles across the parquet.

The officers stand just inside the door for a moment. The dog's terror fills the narrow hall, creeping in under their clothes, trickling down their backs. The fear has barbs that hook into the officers' skin. They hesitate, calling out a few times without expecting any response. Their radios crackle and click.

One of the officers heads for the kitchen. The other walks in the opposite direction. A well-worn sofa is arranged before a silent TV. The dining room table has been set for two. Upstairs, three doors are wide open. The younger of the two officers stops in front of the first. It doesn't look like a young girl's room. He clears his throat and calls for his colleague. But his throat closes up, burning with bile. His voice hardly carries. He has to call out again.

I don't want to, he has time to think. He can hear the dog again, downstairs.

The white dress is laid neatly on a nearby chair, clean and whole. The quilt is on the floor and the curtains are drawn. His colleague comes up the stairs to stand beside him. He breathes heavily through his nose, his hand shakes, he has trouble unbuttoning the little case on his belt. At last it opens and he works the radio free and calls for help.

They go downstairs to wait. Soon the house will be teeming with officers, technicians, investigators. The dog has to go. They don't want to touch her. When they aim their boots near her, she lets herself out. She sits on the steps, shaking, her nose in the air, her jaws slightly parted.

Then she barks, one last time, into the early summer night.

ONE

1

"Why?" she asked. "Give me one good reason."

Stockholm's Nation was poorly insulated; the wind whistled through the moldings and sills of the student union. Sophia Weber, longtime attorney, and Professor Emeritus Hans Segerstad were sitting near one of the tall windows. Sophia was freezing. The stubborn wind outside had nearly reached gale force. Despite the window recesses and the velvet curtains, leftover curls of the storm found their way inside.

Sophia pulled her cardigan tighter and rubbed the back of her neck. *Just don't let this damn draft give me a crick*, she thought, and tried once more to get a reaction out of Hans Segerstad.

"Can you explain to me why you think I would want to work for Stig Ahlin?"

Because I need this case about as much as I need plantar warts and back taxes, Sophia thought, gazing around. Hans Segerstad still hadn't responded. Either his hearing was going bad or he hadn't bothered to listen.

The long, wide tables had been set with care and the glow of the candelabras hid the grime. The room was crowded and noisy, just the way Sophia recalled from her own student days. The sense of disorientation and arrogance, the plate full of leftovers going cold. Overcooked rice, watery chicken, and a couple of sad vegetables salted into obliteration — this was the very same food she had prepared back when she worked in the student union kitchen. It even smelled the same. The odor of unfulfilled dreams and the fear that this was all there was. Time stood still here.

A young man was sitting at the next table. Despite the dim lighting he was squinting as if the sun were shining in his eyes. *Wait, he's looking at me*, Sophia thought, nodding at him and smiling in fake recognition. The man's upper lip drew into a crooked smile and his eyes narrowed even more. Sophia's cheeks went hot.

Aside from Hans Segerstad, Sophia didn't know a soul in here. They only looked the same as they had when she was young, studying the same subjects and discussing the same topics. *Blah, blah, blah, exams, blah, blah, blah, he never calls, he never leaves me alone, did you get your student aid grants, what did she do to her hair?* Sophia didn't know them. But she knew exactly who they were.

A long time had passed since Sophia had been a student of Hans Segerstad's. Yet they had kept in touch. She was typically the one who called him, sometimes to ask for an expert opinion. But this time he had contacted her. She was flattered and hopped on a train up from Stockholm just a few hours later.

Segerstad rocked on his chair. The glass he was hold-ing tipped considerably to one side. He was on his second bottle of dry wine, the most expensive on the menu. Sophia herself was sober. She usually was, even back when she was a student. While her friends drank for release, she avoided alcohol to keep from losing control. She raised her voice. It was time to speak up. She would let him finish the last of the bottle, but before he could order another she would explain that this was definitely not a case for her. That he would have to find someone else.

"Stig Ahlin has been in prison for sixteen or seventeen years and he's already gone through four or five lawyers. Shouldn't he put in a request to get his life sentence converted to a time-limited one and get out the usual way?"

At last Hans Segerstad reacted. He stopped rocking on his chair and raised his glass in triumph.

"It's been thirteen years since he was put away. Almost to the day." He took a long drink. "You'll be his third lawyer and when you get him released you'll go down in legal history. No other Swede has sat in prison so long before being granted an appeal by the Supreme Court. No one."

Sophia shook her head.

"I started a seminar group about violence against women when I was at university. For the first few weeks we only had four members. When Stig Ahlin was indicted it became the most popular group that semester. Everyone wanted to show they were distancing themselves from...that they hated Stig Ahlin and everything he stands for."

Hans waved his hand in the air in annoyance.

"Stands for? Everything he stands for? Jeez. What kind of idealistic nonsense is that?"

At the time he was taken into custody, Stig Ahlin was a researcher in endocrinology and metabolism. He was employed by the Karolinska Institute. The newspapers referred to him as Professor Death. But he wasn't a professor, only a lecturer. He was also a thirty-five-year-old, recently divorced father with dark blue eyes and ash-blond hair. Sophia recalled the pictures of him in his white doctor's coat, standing before full lecture halls in front of screens that depicted internal organs. And in the company of a small child with curly hair and a blurred-out face. His daughter. The media loved those blond curls.

The photographs and horrifying stories about Stig Ahlin were not the sort of thing you were likely to forget. He had murdered a young girl, and it was so easy to write headlines about him that he should have been a professor.

"I'm only trying to explain," Sophia said, "why I don't feel like working for free."

Hans Segerstad leaned toward her.

"Do you plan to become minister of justice or a Supreme Court justice? Because in that case I understand why you're talking rubbish. In that case, you must not challenge the establishment. Anything but criticism. Anything but questions. In that case you have to emphasize that our country is unique. Why, here in Sweden, no innocent person could ever be falsely convicted."

"I have a hard time believing—" Hans cut her off.

"No, of course not! How could Stig Ahlin be innocent? Our police officers always tell the truth, our prosecutors are never careless, and the opinions of our judges never fail. Everything is perfect in our country. Anyone who claims otherwise only wants to harm our trust in the justice system. Right?" He stared at Sophia. "Right?"

Sophia wasn't about to tolerate insults.

"No," she said. As firmly as she could. "Not at all. What I'm trying to say is that I have a hard time believing there would be any point. This is a special situation. If Stig Ahlin had come to me thirteen years ago, I would have defended him. Sure, I was still a student at the time, but I defend alleged rapists and pedophiles and murderers, you know that. I always have."

And I'm good at it, she thought. *Even if I almost always lose.*

"But this man has gotten the counsel he wanted. More than once, evidently. Now he's a convicted criminal who can't pay. And that's the difference. If I'm going to work pro bono, which I do far too often, shouldn't I have the right to choose clients and causes I believe in? This Ahlin...I don't have time to defend every hopeless querulant who believes that...For all I care, he can stay where he is."

She stopped talking. Hans Segerstad was right. This was nothing but emotional babbling.

"And we're talking about an appeal to the Supreme Court for a retrial. My God, Hans. Those are hopeless. You know it as well as I do. We might as well launch a campaign to get Stig Ahlin the Nobel Peace Prize. Our chance of success would be about the same."

Hans Segerstad was no longer looking at her. He was digging through his bag. Music floated over from the bar. The dinner guests had begun to leave. Segerstad started by handing her a plastic folder of photographs.

"I didn't have the energy to scan these."

Sophia accepted the folder. Then Hans fished out two thumb drives. She took those too.

"Take this home, read it, and call me when you're done. You have to take this case. He needs help. Once you look at the material, you'll agree. The preliminary investigation was substandard, the indictment was ill-founded, and with a single exception the chain of evidence was horribly weak. He never should have been convicted. But it's going to take time and money to do anything about it. Naturally I have no problem finding a different attorney for Stig Ahlin. Most of your colleagues would piss themselves with excitement if they got the chance to be seen in this context. But I'm asking you."

Then he sat up straight and looked Sophia in the eye. She felt all her follow-up questions evaporate.

"Really, the problem isn't you. It's Ahlin," said Hans. "He hasn't had a lawyer in eight years — he hates them. To some extent, I sympathize. The vulture he started out with managed to get a man with no previous record thrown in prison for life in a case based on precarious circumstantial evidence. I have promised there will be no more mistakes of that nature. Which, between us, was an easy promise to make, because it can hardly get any worse than it already is. Not even with a self-righteous idealist like you."

Hans paused, sipping his wine and staring at Sophia over the rim of his glass. It was clear he thought it was her turn to speak.

"If you're trying to butter me up," Sophia said, "I'd like to point out that you're terrible at giving compliments."

"Eh. You don't need flattery. I just think Stig Ahlin needs a lawyer who doesn't scare easy. Who won't be frightened by him, or by what it might mean to represent him. That's why I'm giving you the chance. You see, I believe him. I believe he's innocent."

Wow, Sophia thought, reaching for her briefcase. *Who's the idealistic one now?*

"I'm way too nice," she said, putting the materials away.

Her attention was drawn once more to the man at the next table. Why was he scrunching up his face like that? Did he think it made him more attractive? But he was looking at her — he really was.

"I'll take a glance at it, Hans. That's all I'll commit to."

Innocent. Hans Segerstad was claiming that Stig Ahlin was innocent. She would need the peace and quiet of her office to decide how to formulate her refusal. Because she was not going to get involved with this, not on her life. Not Stig Ahlin — she would never sink so low. She glanced back at the dazzled man and closed her briefcase.

"But," she inquired again, "aside from all the idealistic and emotional and completely uninteresting reasons you've just presented…" The young man at the next table refused to take his narrowed eyes from her. Sophia straightened her back and shoulders. "Why should I do it?"

"Because you'll get him exonerated."

"Do I really want to do that?"

"It's worse than that. You will do anything to make it happen."

Katrin
1998

It was just past six in the morning. The crime-scene investigation would go on for another couple of hours, but Chief
Inspector Bertil Lundberg had seen enough. It was time to
start working on other matters. He had arranged to meet
with his colleagues in the third-floor conference room.

The prosecutor wouldn't arrive until nine. She had children to drop off at day care, or it might have been school.
Or else they were sick. It was always something with district prosecutor Petra Gren's children. *What does that
husband of hers do?* Bertil often wondered. But maybe she
didn't have one, what did he know?

He would have to arrange for a special briefing with
Gren when she showed up. That might be just as well. That
would allow him to postpone "becoming familiar with the
case," "dealing with the media," and "getting a handle on
the situation." Instead, he could concentrate on assigning
tasks. His headache would ease up if they could just get
started. If, in fact, that was why the inside of his skull was
droning so badly.

His palm against his chest, Bertil tried to force down his reflux. He hadn't been able to eat before leaving home. Typically, Sara would make oatmeal for him, with butter and whole milk. But when he left, she was still deep asleep. Snoring faintly, her upper lip sharp and her hand cupped over her round belly. Bertil had kissed the back of her neck, lingered a moment in her warm scent, before taking off. He had locked the deadlock with two turns of the key.

He'd thought it was too late, that he and Sara were both too old. But now they were going to be parents. Incredibly enough, he was going to be a dad. And he was almost happy; he'd stopped thinking about how old he'd be when his child finished school.

Bertil walked straight from the elevator to the conference room without a word; he took his place at the front of the room and leaned against the wall. He counted those in attendance. Everyone was on time — that was always something.

To start, the team consisted of fifteen or sixteen people. Not bad at all. But Bertil knew that high level of resources wouldn't last forever. He guessed he had three weeks to a month to wind this up before he had to say goodbye to half the force at Midsummer and admit failure.

Bertil rubbed his temples. He couldn't think that way. There was no reason to be so cynical. A fifteen-year-old, killed in her own home. It shouldn't be all that complicated.

If Bertil were to guess, and he was happy to, they would just need to track down Katrin's boyfriend. It was always the same sad song. The girl had met the wrong guy. She got it into her head that some real pig was sexier than James Dean. She fell in love with an idiot, a fool who had to hurt her to feel like a real man. And then it all went to shit.

Bertil took a step away from the wall. It was time to get started.

"Good morning," he managed. "Thanks for coming. A homicide, in case anyone somehow missed the news. Our victim's name is Katrin Björk. She was fifteen years old and home alone for the weekend. Her parents are in Skagen. I've spoken with Malmö, who in turn talked to the Danes, who woke Mom and Dad up in a room at Brøndums Hotel. So, we can be pretty sure it wasn't the dad." Bertil attempted a smile, forcing the corners of his lips to turn up. It didn't go well; his head was still buzzing, now even louder. He went on. "Or the mom."

One of his colleagues stood up and headed for the exit with his back hunched. At the door he turned around and brought an imaginary mug to his mouth.

What is he doing? Bertil thought. He shook his head in wonder. *Couldn't he have gotten coffee before the meeting?* Bertil frowned and turned to those who remained.

"The murder weapon? He really went at her. It's hard to tell, but he did use some sort of implement. We'll have to see what they say, but she doesn't appear to have been shot. I don't think he cut her with a knife. It didn't look like it, anyway. But did he strike her with something? We'll have to wait and see. Meanwhile, we'll start with the usual. The neighbor who called in underwent initial questioning on-site. He said the parents asked him to keep an eye on their daughter. To make sure she didn't throw any big parties. Naturally we'll have to talk to him again. Find out what he saw or didn't see. And check him out thoroughly. Eva, will you make sure to do that as soon as we're done here? Give him a vigorous workup. And you, Lena."

Bertil waved a hand at another of the women.

"You find out where Katrin attended school. I'll visit there on Monday morning. I may try to speak to her closest bereaved friends today. If we can identify them. We'll see what the parents say. As I'm sure you all understand, I'd really like to find a boyfriend. And fast. It looked like the victim had invited someone over for dinner. It's not as if this dinner guest is such a long shot. I want to know who he is. Preferably an hour ago. Because we'll be bringing him in. We have to talk to her friends. It's not out of the question it was someone who attends her same school."

Lena nodded.

"And don't be sloppy! Run every name that pops up. I want to know everything about everyone. If one of her teachers was hauled in for exposing himself in the park. If her mailman rents pornos at the same video store she goes to. I want you to find out if her neighbor looks into her windows with binoculars. You know what I mean. Eva, like I said: you stay here and do what needs doing on this end. And for God's sake, make sure to answer the phone if it rings. If I call, I don't want to end up with the operator because you're on a smoke break. Smoke at your damn desk if you have to. You must be reachable. Understand? Send someone out for your lunch. Pee in a cup. Just don't leave the goddamn phone."

Eva rubbed her eyes and nodded. Two others yawned.

"The parents are returning home this morning. They'll be driven straight here. I'll take care of them. Lena, you can come with me. I need someone to hold their hands and listen, if they need it. Danne and Klas, you go back to the house, knock on doors, talk to everyone you see in the vicinity. Someone must have seen him arrive. Or leave. Be sure you talk to everyone who lives there, not just the ones who happen to be at home and answer the door."

Another two colleagues stretched their jaws. Lena picked up one of the morning papers, leaned back, and began to read.

Bertil Lundberg looked around. No one was returning his gaze. The man who had left to get coffee had not come back. Eva was digging through her purse.

Lena turned a page in the paper. Bertil had already glanced through it in the car on the way to the station. There was nothing about last night's murder. TT, the news agency, had already put out an item about it, but a dead girl found at home was not the kind of story that would stop the press or force the news editor to redesign the day's front page. Not, at least, until it was clear that the girl hadn't taken her own life.

A dead fifteen-year-old girl. She would end up among the incident reports: a few lines in a column alongside crashed trucks, a wounded wolf, and a stable of neglected horses on Gotland. This was the seventh teenager found dead in their own home this year, and if you believed what was and was not in the papers there was no reason to get worked up. It wasn't even an honor killing in the suburbs. In some sense, it was a bagatelle. Just another number in the statistics.

Bertil yanked the paper away from his colleague. Lena looked up from her empty hands in surprise. Her cheeks turned pale pink. Everyone else did their best to pretend they hadn't seen what had just happened.

These prize idiots, Bertil thought, carefully rolling up the paper. His hands grazed over the thin newsprint. *They think I'm just nagging. That they've heard this a thousand times. That they already know it all. Exactly what to do and how to do it. Now they're sitting there rocking on their chairs. Tough as nails. Chewing gum and thinking about other things. Leaving their emotions at home, sure that a simple notepad and some polite attention can get rid of all the feelings.*

"I'm sorry," said Bertil, "you may find this boring. You think there's nothing exciting about a dead kid if the story doesn't end up on the front page. You're disappointed that Katrin wasn't found dismembered in the forest or on the steps of City Hall."

He had their attention now.

Suddenly Bertil had the urge to hit something. Throw a mug against the wall to watch it explode in a cloud of white porcelain shards. Or smack someone with the rolled-up newspaper. Instead he placed it on the table and took a seat.

His rage vanished as quickly as it had come. In its place came weariness, almost exhaustion. *Why would I go after them like that? They haven't had time to do anything, not yet. What do I know about what they're thinking?* His knees trembled. He made a fist and hit himself softly on the thigh. In just four months he would be a dad. In four months Sara would be a mom. A hundred and twenty days. A new life. A better future. The meaning of life?

After a moment, Bertil spoke again. His voice was low, almost a whisper.

"Our victim's name was Katrin Björk. She wasn't even sixteen. The only child of two parents who are sitting in a police car on their way here. The parents didn't do it and we didn't find any remorseful boyfriend on the front steps. As it stands now, the case is completely open. I would appreciate it if you made an effort. At least until Midsummer."

Someone scraped their chair on the floor.

"Can we agree on that? That we'll work this out. Whatever miserable little parts of it can be worked out."

Bertil looked up. Someone nodded cautiously.

"What I'm trying to say," he said at last, "is that I would appreciate if we did our very best."

2

Sophia woke up way too early. She lay with her cheek pressed to the wall, squeezed into a twin bed with a pine frame and a foam mattress. Next to her, on his back, lay the squinting man from the night before. She had no idea what his name was, Johan or Stefan or Mattias. He'd told her; she had forgotten.

She'd been dreaming. When she was little she used to dream of being given a pony. Dark brown, with a black mane and tail, brushed to glossiness, it pressed its silken nose against her neck, blew warm air into her hair, and snorted with happiness to see her. But then she woke up, every time, and had to go to school. After her last class she went straight to the stables and at most was allowed to pick the hooves of Prince, who refused to stand still. Instead he turned around and bit her with his chattering yellow teeth. The same thing was happening now.

In her dream she had slept with someone else. With him. She really shouldn't, she thought, even in her dreams, but she couldn't help it. He was big, bigger than she remembered. Almost grotesque. Thick and long, he pressed into her, one hand around her neck, kissing her, and she never wanted to wake up. But she did. As usual. Right before she came, relentlessly, because one arm was asleep.

Sophia managed to turn over by pushing the bed away from the wall a few inches. She wriggled her way out, cautiously — she didn't want Johan-Stefan-Mattias to wake up. If he did she would have to call him something. To whisper in her morning voice: Good morning, Stefan-Mattias-or-maybe-Fredrik. There was no way. She would be forced to call him "honey." And she really wasn't prepared to take things that far.

Sophia wrangled her way into her panties and shirt, then grabbed her purse, briefcase, and the rest of the clothes that were folded on the desk. Her arms full, she sneaked to the bathroom. The man in the twin bed was in his third year of legal studies. She recalled him having said that much. Which had to mean he was at least twenty-two, right? Or twenty-three. That was pretty much an adult.

She dug a painkiller out of her purse, swallowed it, and avoided any further thoughts of the day before. How she had squeezed both her eyes and her genitals closed when he entered her. How his squinting eyes suddenly went perfectly round and his mouth became a rectangle with the strain. How she had come fast, faster than him, and how it had felt like scratching an already bleeding mosquito bite. She washed up as fast as she could, peed without flushing, and walked into the hall and down the stairs carrying her shoes. Not until she had crossed the street and reached the cemetery did she tie her shoelaces and button her coat. The moon was high over the cathedral, lemon yellow against the inky blue. It would be at least two hours before night loosened its grip, and no snow in the air yet.

At least I didn't get a stiff neck, she thought, winding her scarf around her throat an extra time.

Yesterday's wind had died down a bit. She turned onto Trädgårdsgatan and walked down to the swan pond. It smelled like baked goods there: saffron, cinnamon, melted butter. Sophia knew where to knock when the place was closed, and just one minute later she was holding a paper bag, all greasy from hot buttercream. With the bag in hand, she ran down toward Kungsgatan and Central Station.

Outside the main entrance a young man was sitting on some unfolded newspapers having a smoke. Sophia made eye contact with him; he was still a teenager. Her determined pace, which was meant to take her away from there, faltered. Like the man she had left on Studentvägen just now, this beggar resembled someone she knew, or had known, or should know. She stopped, fumbling through her purse, and found a five-hundred-krona bill. It was a ridiculous amount, but now it was too late so she handed it to him.

I should pat him on the shoulder, she thought. *I could say something casual about the weather, the morning, the darkness — or anything at all. Would he want my pastry?*

"Thanks," he said, swiping his hair from his forehead to keep from having to look at her, and she felt even more ashamed. He didn't even seem surprised, just folded the bill and stuffed it in his pocket.

Sophia fled. Only ten yards on did she become angry. *Five hundred kronor. How could I be so stupid? Am I trying to*

buy my way out of this cold sweat? And if that is what I'm try-
ing to do, shouldn't I pay the right person?

Her heart pounded in her chest. *Should I have left a bill*
on the nightstand back at Magnus-Mattias-Johan-Anders's? Is
that what I should have done? Or should I have looked at his
door to find out his name?

The train would leave at four minutes past six; Sophia
stepped onto the station stairs nine minutes early. She
bought a ticket from the machine on the platform, used
some hand sanitizer, climbed aboard, sat down, and placed
her briefcase on her lap. Then she took out the folder of
photographs. The seats around her were empty, so she
didn't have to worry that someone might notice what she
was reading.

She rested her temple against the cold windowpane
and stared at the first photograph in her hand. It was an
enlargement, printed in color on a sheet of A4. The crime
scene. The victim was in the center, naked and with one
leg drawn up slightly to the side, her arm at an impossible angle. Her mouth was agape. Her eyes were open too,
veiled by a pale yellow film. Her clothes were folded up on
a chair.

Nothing about the room where the girl lay seemed to fit
what had happened to her. It was too neat. She must have
disrobed voluntarily; Sophia recalled the newspapers having reported as much.

The second photo was a close-up. Sophia glanced
around quickly; she was still alone in the train car. Sixteen
years old, or had she been fifteen? It was impossible to tell.

Her heart rate began to slow. Sophia sank deeper into the seat. Her hands stopped trembling.

Naturally she would look through the file, even if she wouldn't take the case. It couldn't hurt — it was an exciting case. Back when the crime occurred, she had read everything she could get her hands on. The papers had written about it as though they expected this to be the last homicide they would ever get to cover. There were stories about the dead girl, her parents, her interests, her friends, her teachers, and her school. About her good grades and her short life, a little girl's dreams and a young woman's plans for her life. About the end-of-term ceremony at her school just a few days after her death. And about the sick doctor who had taken her life.

Above all, they had written about him, the doctor. Sophia had devoured every story, ravenously, intently.

Of course she would go through the documents Hans had given her. The misfortunes of others were much easier to deal with. But only the sort that were written down on paper. Not the kind of misery that sat on chilly front steps, holding out a hand.

She opened her laptop, inserted one of the thumb drives, and opened the folder marked "FöU Supplements 1–30." The preliminary investigation. It took a moment for the documents to load, and as she waited she really felt her exhaustion. It was always that same feeling, the same dizziness. Her failing will as she faced a new assignment.

This isn't a new assignment, she thought. *I don't need to get to know this man; I don't have to steel myself. I can* empathize with the victim or simply ignore her if I want to. I don't have to protect the perpetrator or explain why. He isn't my responsibility and whatever he's done it can't rub off on me.

It doesn't have to mean anything to me. These people are nothing to me. Nothing at all.

Her heart fluttered. And then she began to read.

Katrin
1998

Katrin Björk's parents were staying with good friends. They had to make do with the overnight bags they had brought to Skagen. Their house would be off limits for another few days before the technicians finished their work.

Chief Inspector Bertil Lundberg had asked what they wanted to do about the dog. The neighbor had said he couldn't take it, but they couldn't leave it up at the house, either. A friend of the family, the same one the parents were staying with, had dropped by to pick it up. A woman. She had gathered the animal into her arms, stumbled back to the hastily parked car, and driven off.

Bertil had noticed her prolonged glances at the house. At the blue-and-white police tape waving in the summer breeze. Those glances told the story of what had happened. The house where Katrin had grown up was no longer a home. Just the scene of a murder.

Now Bertil was up at Katrin's school. He was sitting in one of the rooms near the principal's office. It was rather reminiscent of his own bosses' offices. For some reason, this surprised him. With the exception of a short visit to a teachers' lounge, he had never been behind the scenes of a high school before.

Once, many years ago, Bertil had responded to a call about a teacher who had hanged himself. But the hanging had taken place in the boys' locker room, not in the secret spaces that belonged only to the teachers. That teacher might have wanted to make sure that the students under-stood what he had done, that his misery would not be hid-den away in the administrative area.

Bertil was only familiar with the students' everyday routines, which hadn't changed much since his own school days: lockers, bathrooms full of graffiti, gymnasiums that reeked of sour sweat and nonslip gym socks, classrooms that smelled like pencil lead and dust, the noisy cafeterias where kids stuck their sandwiches to the undersides of the tables, butter side up.

This was the second day he was spending at Katrin's school. He had spoken to no fewer than six different teary-eyed teachers, one school nurse, two janitors, and four girls who all claimed to have been Katrin's best friend. Now, he was interviewing a girl the nurse had suggested he talk to. Katrin and this girl had been friends at one point. For rea-sons the nurse wasn't privy to, they had broken off contact.

The school nurse had also said that the young woman sometimes seemed hostile, that she had "problems," but that Bertil should try to look past her nose ring, clunky shoes, and odd makeup.

I'd love to, he thought. *I'd love to see past everything. If only she would say something. Hostile or otherwise. Then I could be as understanding and open as anything.*

"You were friends with Katrin?" he tried.

The girl shook her head.

"You weren't friends with Katrin?"

She shook her head again.

Bertil sighed and tapped his pen against his notebook. He took a tissue from his pocket and handed it to her. Her tears had snaked trails through her thick white makeup. The girl clenched her hand around the tissue and looked him straight in the eye.

Blow your nose, Bertil thought, looking down. *For God's sake, blow your nose.*

"I'm afraid you'll have to explain that to me," he said. "I'm having trouble understanding what you mean. Did you have a fight? Did something happen?"

A guy? Someone she'd just broken up with? Or who had just broken up with her?

"Eh!" The girl blew her nose.

Finally, Bertil thought.

"How the hell should I know?" she said. "She didn't talk to me anymore. She hated me." The tears intensified. "She didn't want to hang out with me."

Bertil couldn't help but shake his head. He had spoken to Katrin's teacher, Katrin's parents, Katrin's riding teacher, Katrin's best friend — that is, the best friend her mother considered to be her best friend. And that friend's parents. And now this kid. At quarter past eight this morning he had met the first in a line of criers. Now it was past four. The school day was over. The students had gone home. All but this one. He should let her go too. This was going nowhere.

"I was the only one who...and she didn't want to, she didn't want to see me."

Her crying turned to sobbing.

Bertil hummed. He waited for her to calm down.

"Is there anything you could tell me about Katrin? Like did she have a boyfriend?"

"A boyfriend?" The girl was sounding hysterical. "A fucking boyfriend? Is that what you think? You think it's that fucking easy?"

Bertil made a vague motion with his head. *There's easy, and there's easy,* he thought.

The heavily made-up child across from him blew her nose again. A lone booger was left dangling from her nose ring. Bertil waved dejectedly at his own nose to encourage her to wipe her face. But it didn't work.

"Katrin hated the guys at school," she sniffled. "Hated them. She didn't want a boyfriend. She didn't...it didn't... that's not how it was."

Bertil paged through his notes to keep from looking at her.

"Well, then tell me how it really was. I can't guess. Can you tell me about Katrin and her relationships with guys? The ones she liked and the ones she didn't? Which ones liked her? And their names, if you know them?"

Because he really wanted to know. Who Katrin had been with. And with any luck, he would also find out if she had been unfaithful to any of them, who had been upset with whom, and so on and so forth for all eternity.

"What guys?" She blew her nose again. This time it was into the sleeve of her black sweater, which was way too long. The booger got stuck there instead. "You don't get it. Why the hell would I tell you that? How am I supposed to know? Katrin had tons of guys. Shit, I don't have time to sit here all damn day. I have to go home. I want to go home."

"I'm a fast writer. Tell me everything you know. Let me decide whether it's important or not."

But it didn't take all day. It didn't even take four minutes. She couldn't give him any names; apparently it wouldn't matter how many times he asked. It seemed she didn't know anything. Then she blew her nose a few times more, swore, and was out the door.

Once the girl was gone, Bertil looked through his notes one last time and listened to parts of the recorded material. He made additional notes where he felt it was necessary. Soon he would have to go up to the station and form an overview of everyone's work. He would have to come back another day. If she would only calm down, he could imagine talking to this girl again. Once things were more in balance, once the shock had worn off.

Bertil looked at the clock. He had better call the crime scene guys to see how far they had come. If he had any extra time he could head over and check it out for himself.

It wouldn't be long before the parents demanded to be allowed back home. Not to move back in, just to look. Try to move that cog in the gear that might one day let them comprehend what had happened. One tick forward.

Bertil didn't want Katrin's mother and father to be allowed in too early. He couldn't quite put his finger on why that was. It probably didn't have anything to do with his investigation. He wanted to spare them something.

His colleagues often said the worst thing about their job was giving news of a death. Telling a mother her child had died — nothing could be more difficult. Bertil didn't agree. The shock that hit those who received such news could be dealt with just like a cut to a major artery. You had to concentrate solely on the acute situation, on putting pressure on the open wound. There was screaming and panic. Doctors were called in, pills shaken out and swallowed, syringes filled and injected. It could be handled.

It was worse later on. Once the agony had turned to sorrow. When you came back, when you had to talk to them again. When the pills were gone and life went on. Bertil thought this was infinitely harder to handle. The sadness and resignation. The hatred and despair. The emptiness and knowledge.

Let them rest in this stage of initial shock, when nothing was real. He supposed that was what he wanted to do. Let Katrin Björk's parents put off coming home, put off seeing what couldn't be cleaned away: the fact that it wasn't their home anymore. That beyond the blue-and-white tape, nothing would ever go back to the way it had been.

3

Stockholm Central Station was dimly lit, the morning still pitch black. The few commuters waiting on the platform were standing around with eyes downcast, necks bent, breathing into their scarves. "O Holy Night" was buzzing through the loudspeakers.

Sophia Weber went straight from the station to Fjärils-gården. An evergreen wreath hung on the door that led from the hallway into the assisted-living apartment. After a cautious knock she let herself in with her own key. When she opened the bedroom door, the old man looked up from what he was reading.

"What if I'd had a visitor? What if I had been brightening my morning by amusing myself with something other than the arts-and-culture section of *Dagens Nyheter*? What would you have done then?"

Sophia slipped to his bedside and put her arms around him.

"Dearest Grandpa. Obviously, I would have heard what was up back in the parking lot and turned straight around to go home. You've never liked quiet women, have you?"

Sture Weber gave her a small, reluctant smile.

"Hmm. You're almost right. You would have. Heard the screams." He cautiously wriggled out from under the covers and lowered his feet to the floor where his slippers were waiting. When Sophia placed her hand on his arm he pushed it away. "But I have nothing against a quiet nature. It's just that with me, even the most reserved ones get loud." He smoothed the ruffled hair on his crown and stretched. "Could my little girl fix a cup of coffee for her old grandpa? And a decent breakfast, perhaps?"

He patted her hand and she took his and squeezed it. She held on to it for a moment before he pulled it back and started to walk the short distance to his wardrobe.

His hands were all that was left of what he had once been. They were as large as when she was a little girl and he could lift her up with one hand around her waist. The rest of him had shrunk. Those blue eyes had grown watery. His chest had become sunken. His legs were twisted in a serious mutation.

Sophia went to the kitchen and filled the espresso maker with water and freshly ground coffee, screwed the two parts together, and set the contraption on the stove. Then she opened the fridge and took out eggs and bacon, a few tomatoes, and cream. She whisked the cream into the eggs, melted extra-salted butter in one frying pan, and laid the bacon in the other.

She had long since stopped interfering in what Sture ate. He was old enough to make his own decisions about that sort of thing. What was more, she thought his weight loss was much more concerning than the specter of high cholesterol. Her grandfather had lived a good life — he deserved to enjoy bacon for breakfast in the years he had left. That was what Grandma had always made him, and that was what he wanted to eat.

Sophia heard Sture close and lock the bathroom door. The sound of the Mora clock's swinging pendulum was in the background, like a shadow of what their life had once been like in the run-down villa in Djursholm. The open fireplace, the swollen window casings, overloaded bookcases in every room, and black specks of mold in the basement. As the bathwater flowed and Sture got into and out of the handicap-accessible bathtub, Sophia set the table with Grandpa and Grandma's wedding china.

Sture hadn't kept much from the house. Sophia had a few things in her apartment: a set of teacups, a bureau with a bulging belly and brass fittings, a pair of threadbare rugs, a display case with warped glass, and Grandpa's desk. Grandpa had been surprisingly unsentimental. He seemed relieved when the house was sold. The desk was the only thing he'd had trouble leaving behind. He was so happy when she said she would love to have it, and now it was in her bedroom. It was ridiculously large, but that didn't matter. Every time Grandpa came over he would stand by the old desk and stroke its scratched surface. His fingers lingered on the lines in the wood.

Sture came into the kitchen in his robe and slippers and caught his breath before sitting down across from Sophia, then picked up his glass and drank all of the freshly squeezed orange juice at once. When he noticed that Sophia had frothed milk he smiled in satisfaction and portioned it into the two ceramic mugs of coffee she'd set on the table.

"I've been asked to handle Stig Ahlin's petition for a new trial."

"I'll be damned." Sture took a cautious sip of his coffee and cut a strip of bacon in half. He had just shaved, so his wrinkled cheek was silky soft. With the bacon speared on his fork, he went on. "That bastard. Stig Ahlin. Isn't he tired of trying to get his appeal?"

"You'd think so." Sophia finished chewing. "But he's actually never appealed to the Supreme Court before. Hans Segerstad has got it into his head that Ahlin is innocent and he wants me to help him."

"Segerstad." Sture nodded in amusement. "How is that whippersnapper? Still just as lazy and unkempt, I assume. I'm sure if you asked him he'd say he's doing you a favor, and not the other way around."

Sophia nodded.

"So what are you going to do?" Sture wondered.

"I don't know. I started reading on the train from Uppsala. I'm not going to lie, I'm not particularly tempted. But I have to look at the material first. Before I say no."

Sture coughed and set down his silverware.

"Little Fia." He sank his thumb surprisingly deep into one nostril and scratched his nose thoroughly. "You'll never get Stig Ahlin a new trial." Sture withdrew his thumb, wiped it on his robe, and shook his head. He smiled as if she were too young to understand. "Put your efforts into trying to get his sentence time-limited," he said. "If you feel like you absolutely must help that man."

"Thanks," said Sophia. "For those encouraging words."

She tried to smile, tried to tamp it down, but it was so hard to fend off. As always, it hatched somewhere under her skin. Swarming, crawling: the feeling that he never thought she was good enough, that he didn't believe in her.

"And stop pretending you're going to say no to Hans Segerstad. We both know you'd never do that." Sture shoved his plate away. "You've never been able to say no to older men. Father complex and all that. It's because you have this special relationship to me." Sture patted Sophia's hand. "And because you never met your dad. And because your mom never cared enough. How is she, by the way? How is your miserable mother?"

"I have no idea how Mom is," Sophia said curtly, pulling her hand away and ratcheting up her anger instead. That was easier to deal with. "But thanks for the lecture. I would guess she's fine. If you're so sure I can't manage it, then what do you think I should do about Stig Ahlin's appeal? Shouldn't I say no and hand the job over to someone more capable than I am? What should I tell Hans Segerstad? He thinks I can be of use, anyway. It's not as if he's completely clueless about my qualities as a lawyer. But you think Hans Segerstad is mistaken? He's only considered to be one of Sweden's best procedural law experts of all time."

"According to whom? Besides Segerstad himself?" Sture shook his head. "And do you really think I would be so stupid as to tell you what to do? I have no desire to be responsible for your mistakes. But once you've accepted the job, you'll keep me updated, right? Call it consulting. As you know, when it's little Sophiasson doing the asking, my services are free, and besides, I've always been fascinated by that case. We could go out to eat. You and me and that professor. Hans Segerstad likes that. Being invited to a restaurant that he can't pay for with his miserable salary."

The color rose in Sture's face and he reached for a napkin. He seemed to have abandoned his meal.

For a moment, there was silence. Sophia waited for him to continue.

"It was a hell of a thing, that no one looped me in back when it was all happening. I would have loved to take a look at that Stig Ahlin. Seldom have so many journalists assigned so many diagnoses of 'psychopath' to a single man. Who was later found to be perfectly normal when the actual investigation was over. Perfectly normal, Sophia. Do you hear what I'm saying?" Sture pinched his nose and managed to fend off a sneeze. "Not only was he healthy enough to be sent to prison, they didn't even find a hint of a single personality disorder. That's extremely unusual when it comes to that type of violent crime. Of course, one might ask if there's anyone in our two circles of acquaintances who doesn't suffer from a tasteful amount of narcissism. Not everyone is in as bad shape as your friend Segerstad. But still."

Sophia shook her head in resignation.

"I want you to know that being diagnosed as perfectly normal is extremely abnormal," Sture went on. "There weren't even any signs of substance abuse, if I recall correctly. If you ask me, the people who investigated him were screwups. Around that time, it was starting to be old-fashioned to assign diagnoses. At least to criminals. Because then you would have to spend money on caring for them. Depressing. Awfully depressing."

He began to cough. Sophia's stomach twisted. She hated that cough; it never faded. It came on suddenly and wouldn't let up. In the middle of a sentence or just before Sture fell asleep. It was persistent — he couldn't even speak when it was at its worst. The doctors said it had to do with his heart. His body couldn't manage to get rid of fluids properly, so they collected in his lungs and made him hack.

"Why do you think it would be a mistake to represent him?"

Sture took out a handkerchief.

"Are you listening to yourself? When did I say it would be a mistake? I'm not getting involved. But you should probably prepare yourself — you'll have to take a lot of crap. From people you don't know and hopefully don't care about. Because it may have been years since Stig Ahlin was convicted, but people have hardly forgotten him. People like Professor Death are never forgotten — they only get more and more famous. And people, whoever they are, they hate him and anyone who's on his side. No matter why they're there. There will be a hell of a fuss. Especially if you do a good job. Whether you want to or not."

He left his plate on the table and walked back to his bedroom, his legs stiff.

"Will you clean up, honey?" he called from the doorway. "I need to lie down for a bit. I'm getting a cold."

The bedroom door closed.

He always does this. Sophia began to load the dishwasher. *How the hell does he manage it? Every time. He makes me feel as if I've already failed. I haven't even done anything yet. I haven't had time. So how come he already knows I'm going to make a mistake?*

She closed the dishwasher with a bang. Sture's snores were already coming the bedroom; he sounded like a panting animal, his breathing irregular and aggressive. She felt like she had been pounded black-and-blue.

He falls asleep too fast, she thought. *It's not normal to drop off so quickly.*

Katrin
1998

I shouldn't be driving, thought Chief Inspector Bertil Lundberg.

He parked outside Stortorp rehab facility. Just over a hundred hours had passed since Katrin Björk was murdered. In that time he had gotten nineteen or twenty hours of sleep. On the way over he had nodded off in the car, only waking when he swerved onto the wrong side of the road. He couldn't keep going like this.

It felt as if they were stuck. The overwhelming help they'd received from the general public since the press coverage started wasn't helping. Because in this investigation, everything else was missing. The witness statements were vague, contradictory, and unreliable. The crime scene investigation had turned up very little, if anything. The investigation wasn't over yet, of course, but Katrin hardly seemed to have resisted. Yes, there were some defensive wounds, but there was no skin under her nails, no pulled-out hair in the girl's clenched fists, nothing they could use.

He climbed out of the car and stretched his neck; it crackled. Stortorp was a peaceful place. Beautiful, even. Katrin had had a side job in one of the units and Bertil was there to speak with her coworkers.

We can't lose momentum, he thought. *The days are just flying by. And I have nothing to go on.*

He let his eyes wander over the avenue he'd just passed. Knotty trunks and pale green crowns. The water was in the other direction, pale blue and still.

The building greeted him with corridors full of freshly ironed cotton curtains, flowers in shiny vases, rooms that drew the mind more to a manor house hotel than illness. It was lovely in a way you would hardly connect to health care or teenagers being brutally murdered.

It must be hard to get a spot here, he thought. *To be allowed to lie here and rest up on the taxpayer's dime.*

A few conversations later, he had only a few scattered notes in his book. Katrin had been popular with her colleagues. They had considered her a responsible girl, quiet but kindhearted, sweet and good with the patients.

Kindhearted, Bertil thought as he gathered his belongings. *Now there's a word people only use about the dead.*

But beyond how everyone had spoken as if they were in a turn-of-the-century novel about virtue and conscience, it was clear that this tragedy was only growing more incomprehensible. Katrin had exemplary grades, her bedroom was plastered with rosettes for jumping and dressage, and she always helped her mother empty the dishwasher when asked. As if that wasn't enough, she had also worked part-time wiping the bottoms of the elderly.

She really was kindhearted, damn it, Bertil thought with a sigh.

On his way back down the hall he was stopped by a straight-backed man in his thirties.

"Excuse me," the man said tersely. "I don't want to be a bother, but I'm a doctor — well, not here in this facility, but my mother is one of the patients and I heard Katrin died, I heard you're talking to people who knew her..."

The man placed a hand on Bertil's shoulder. Bertil turned his head to look at it. The man pulled it back.

"It's such a tragedy," he said. He spoke through his nose. "Katrin was sweet. She gave my mother fantastic support. They were close. Did the staff tell you...?"

"Kindhearted," Bertil mumbled, shaking his head.

How should I know if the staff mentioned your mother? You haven't even told me her name.

"Anyway." The man cleared his throat. "Katrin became a good friend to my mother. I suppose when it comes right down to it, my mother shouldn't even have gotten a spot here. She's hardly a candidate for rehab. But I pulled some strings, and..." He gave a curt laugh. "What wouldn't you do, to keep your mother out of the usual three-to-a-room nursing home situation?"

Bertil couldn't help but sneak a look at his watch. Why couldn't the people he ran into ever be normal? Normal people must be out there. The sensible, plainspoken ones.

Who got to the point without first talking about themselves for half an hour.

Bertil blinked and allowed himself an intense moment of longing for Sara and their shared bed. The bed most of all.

He wanted to get out of there. There was a chance he would have to return to Katrin's school, question her friends again. And the parents. He was still looking for a boyfriend, and someone must know something. Katrin had set the table for two, and naturally it would have been a boyfriend she invited over when her parents were away on vacation. It was crystal clear.

The doctor droned on. Evidently he had got the idea that Bertil wanted to know how he'd found an opening here for his mother, who had dementia. There was some board he was on, or a committee he was chairman of, a good friend and an acquaintance, another good friend, and the director of the foundation that ran the home.

What did this guy want? To seem important? Or get something off his chest? In that case he should have turned to the hospital therapist. Or the hospital chaplain. Those people were paid to listen. *My salary*, Bertil thought, *is not generous enough for me to have to tolerate this rubbish.*

"It may sound strange," the man said, his eyes fixed on a point beyond Bertil's shoulder, "that my mother can't remember her name every day, but she can still make good friends with the staff. But I'm not just saying this. Mom is easily frightened, that's part of her illness. And of course, you know, they weren't good friends in the traditional way. It was more that Katrin made Mom feel safe. And some days are better than others. She has small windows of clarity. But they typically blow shut rather quickly. That's also part of the pattern of her illness."

Bertil glanced at his watch again. There was no getting rid of his irritation. *What was this person going on about now? That Katrin had cared for his mother? Why would I need to know that? His mom was a patient; Katrin had worked here. Wouldn't it then be par for the course for Katrin to spend time with her now and again? And I don't give a crap if he's a doctor. Do I look sick? Do I look like I need a prescription? Because if he doesn't stop talking soon I'll probably need something. Something to calm me down.*

"Mom really took to her. And when Katrin was here, she had to shoulder much of the responsibility for her. But I don't want to..."

He sounded firm now, as if Bertil were a dim-witted student who refused to listen.

"I want to make sure you don't disturb Mom. It would be an incredibly bad idea to question her. She would become very anxious if you went into her room and began talking about death. You have to leave Mom alone. I can assure you that the senior physician here at Stortorp agrees with this assessment. It would not be healthy for her. Definitely not."

Bertil's forehead creased. This was only getting stranger. *How did this man get it into his head that I'm going to interrogate his mother? A woman with dementia, an old lady, out of all the patients whose bottoms Katrin wiped. It seems extremely unlikely that she would have anything to tell me. Why does this guy think I would be interested in her?*

The man cleared his throat again. His arm flew into the air, but he seemed to stop it mid-gesture. Then he looked at his hand. It was as if he didn't quite know where to put it now that it couldn't land on Bertil's shoulder. He lowered his arm again.

"The long and short of it is, there's no reason to upset my mother. I don't want her to wander out of her room at night. It's happened before. For the time being she's in a period of relative calm and I want it to stay that way. She's already forgotten who Katrin was. Certainly it comes in waves, what she does and does not remember, but she's a very unreliable witness."

Witness? Bertil Lundberg sought the man's eyes, but they suddenly flickered away. Something flitted over the man's face. He crossed his arms, then brought them down again and let them hang at his sides. *What a strange word to choose.*

"Mom can easily become anxious. Over nothing, really. And she misunderstands things."

Oh, does she, Bertil thought.

"I truly hope," the man said, softer now, "that you find the monster who committed this heinous crime."

"I'm sure we will." Bertil nodded slowly and extended his hand. "I don't believe I caught your name."

The man hurried to reciprocate his gesture. Bertil squeezed the man's broad palm with care.

I'll be needing your personal identification number as well, he thought, smiling. The man smiled back. Thin lips. The smile didn't reach his eyes.

"Stig Ahlin is the name," he said. He cleared his throat twice. "Stig Ahlin."

4

Only silence awaited her. Her coffee cup was still in the entryway. On the hall table, exactly where she'd left it a little over twenty-four hours earlier. Sophia Weber stared at it, almost in surprise. Well, why shouldn't it be there? Who would have moved it?

She took it with her to the kitchen and placed it in the sink. There was already a small plate, a butter knife, and a fork in there. The frying pan was on the cold stove, full of water. The grease had solidified into a layer on top and glistened in the light.

Just as she'd left it.

There was no point in using the dishwasher anymore. It took so long to fill it up that the whole apartment started smelling sour before it was time to run it.

She stood there for a moment, rubbing her arms. It was cold and damp — she had left the kitchen window ajar again. The chill crept under her skin. She turned on the hot tap and the water sputtered out. The sink quickly filled with suds.

Suddenly she felt uncertain. What was it she was about to do? The dishes, sure, but then what? She turned off the tap, took a bottle of cleaning spray from the cabinet under the sink, and began to spray all the surfaces in the kitchen. Not because they were dirty, but because it smelled good.

When she was done she went to her bedroom, crawled into the unmade bed, and pulled a bundle of papers from her briefcase. She was representing a young man who had been denied entry into a pub in downtown Stockholm. When the man asked why, the bouncers responded by lifting him up and depositing him in a trash can. Her client claimed he was a victim of racism, that the guards had treated him badly because they didn't like "people like him." Sophia wasn't looking forward to trying to convince the court that this medium-blond Swede of Walloon descent was right. Especially since he had climbed back out of the trash can unharmed and gone back with two empty bottles which he broke against the forehead of one of the two dark-skinned bouncers.

Later, she thought, dropping the file on the floor. The thumb drives from Hans Segerstad were at the bottom of one of the interior compartments. She closed her hand around them. *It doesn't mean I'm going to take this on. I'm just going to read a little, the parts I would want to read anyway.*

Sophia turned on her computer, inserted one thumb drive, and began to scroll through the documents. She clicked her way through various situation reports and case notes drawn up by the lead investigator during the first few days after the murder.

The tips that had come in from the public were the usual kind: all over the place, made up and unlikely. Four of the most detailed sightings of a very much alive Katrin even took place after she was found dead.

Katrin had been seen on a beach outside Mölle, at a bar in Gothenburg, at a bus stop in Sundsvall. She and a masked man had purchased cigarettes at a gas station in the vicinity of Karlstad, and along with four female friends she had robbed a bank in downtown Stockholm. An older woman called her local police precinct to report that she had been drinking her afternoon coffee on the balcony when she saw Katrin dragged into a white van, yes, she insisted, it really was a white van. The man yanking at her was wearing a black balaclava, yes, she insisted, it really was a black balaclava. One of Katrin's classmates, a teenager described in the notes as a "girl with serious social issues, many absences from school, and frequent encounters with both social and legal authorities," had said Katrin had a number of boyfriends.

Sophia took out her cell phone and opened her note-taking app. "Find out the classmate's name," she tried to type. Autocorrect changed "classmate" to "classified." "Find out the classified name." She tried to fix it: "Classmate? Interrogate?" Her phone changed it to "Classified? Interrupt?" She added "Boyfriends?" Her phone wrote "Boycott?" It was hopeless. Instead she pulled up her secretary's number. Then she remembered it was Saturday.

I should take a nap, she thought. *Rest a little. I can't work all the time. I need my rest too.* She put her phone aside entirely and closed her eyes. *Think about something else. Sleep for a while.*

She immediately thought about him.

There was no task that could take her mind off him. Her thoughts were so intense that they became physical.

They clawed their way into her flesh and got caught there. She closed her eyes and there he was, standing right next to her. And her body responded as it always had in reality. Her pulse increased, her throat constricted, her palms grew damp. It was like her muscles got the flu. Her thoughts of him were like a thunderstorm. She couldn't control them.

She swallowed, scratched at her eyes, and pressed her hand to her chest. *It hurts so much,* she thought. *What if I'm having an aneurysm? Does that make your heart hurt?*

Just minutes later, she was asleep.

■ ■ ■

Detective Inspector Adam Sahla was eating breakfast. His wife Norah was in her usual spot at the sink. Her face was almost gray and her hair looked dirty. He wondered if she was getting sick but decided not to ask. She would only take it as an insult. Or a chance to inform him that he didn't help out enough, always did things wrong, and never lived up to expectations.

Norah had crossed her arms. She hadn't even made herself coffee. She never did anything for herself as long as the children were still eating. Anyone as sensitive to low blood sugar as Norah was should have food even before getting out of bed. But the worst thing he could do was suggest she should eat, because somehow it was always his fault she didn't have time, because he sat down to eat while her headache got worse.

"You remember she has a ballet recital today?"

His wife did still talk, in a monotone, about things that had to be done. About things she expected him to do. But she seldom looked at him anymore.

Norah left the sink and retrieved a hairbrush and two hair ties from one of the drawers under the stove. She had a special drawer for items she needed for getting the kids ready each morning. Extra toothbrushes, bandages, their son's schedule. Adam had no idea what-all she stuck in that drawer. Nor could he understand how it could be so inconceivably difficult to brush the children's teeth in the bathroom that such a drawer was necessary; it was less than thirty feet from the kitchen to the bathroom. But he seldom bothered to point this out either.

"I've already flagged my afternoon for flex time. They know I have to go."

She didn't have to say a thing. It was Saturday; Adam already knew what she was thinking, what she was always thinking when he left her with the children, when she thought he should be off duty, should take responsibility. But she wasn't saying anything, at least. And she wasn't looking at him. *I even remembered to change the batteries in the video camera,* he thought.

"Promise you'll come, Dad? Do you one hundred percent promise?"

Adam bent down to his daughter and swept her up. She was so light, a string bean, and she wound her skinny arms around his neck. He closed his eyes and nuzzled his nose into her collarbone. *I'll be there. And I plan to sit in the very first row of that stuffy auditorium with the camera in front of me like a safety net to save me from free-falling through time.*

He had to fix things with Norah. They should be able to find a therapist they could talk to, someone who could help them.

Hopefully, it would get better over Christmas break. He'd given notice that he would be taking two weeks off. With any luck he wouldn't have to drop by the office more than one afternoon. That would surely help. They could find their way back — it hadn't always been like this. He swallowed and whispered in his daughter's ear.

"Of course I'm coming."

When his daughter was younger, so little she could hardly walk, maybe a year old, she would steal his phone when he came home from work. She always hid it; each day she found a new hiding place. Adam had once found it vibrating, its battery almost drained, in a paper bag full of empty bottles waiting to be returned. Back then she had been convinced it was the telephone that took him away, that made her mom clench her teeth so hard you could see the muscles in her jaw. It was no wonder his daughter tried to do what she could to avoid that.

He'd never known how he was expected to react, not that time either. But they had recently purchased their row house, and Norah was working from home and earning only a fraction of her former salary.

The only other option besides working more to make ends meet would have been to move to another suburb, but no one wanted their children to grow up in those parts of the city. And even though Norah wouldn't have admitted it, she didn't either. So why should he feel guilty for making sure they had enough to live well?

But Adam thought it had gotten better since then. They were living in the city again, and he didn't have to work overtime as often. These days he didn't come home as late and he wasn't gone every weekend. Once a week he was the one to pick the kids up at day care. At least, the weeks when nothing unexpected happened. He truly didn't need to have a guilty conscience anymore.

"Sweetheart."

Adam cupped his hand around his daughter's head, stroked the bridge of her nose with his index finger, and looked deep into her eyes without blinking.

"My darling baby. Of course I'm coming. I promise."

. . .

The box of Christmas decorations was in the basement storage area. Along with a rolled-up yoga mat that had gone stiff, a pair of hiking poles, and four pairs of jogging shoes Sophia no longer used.

She would bring the decorations up to the apartment. She was planning to convince Grandpa to come stay with her over Christmas. He could sleep in her bed and she would take the sofa. If he refused, he could take the mobility service back home at night, but at least her place would look nice for Christmas Eve.

I should invite Mom too, she thought before she could

stop herself. There was no reason to ask Grandpa; it was a given that they would be together. But her mother needed those formalities. The polite questions that kept a lid on their many conflicts.

Sophia extended invitations. Her mother said no. The year before she had blamed taxi services. It would be too difficult to come, she'd said. It was impossible to book a taxi on Christmas Eve, not to mention expensive.

As politely as she could, Sophia had said she understood. She hadn't pointed out that Grandpa had already booked a taxi there and back. This would have been to abandon their agreement. Nor had Sophia offered up her bed. And her mother hadn't said that she could sleep on the sofa. Or on a mattress on the floor.

They both knew that their lies depended on not questioning each other. But it also required each to leave space for the other to lie. The potential for a theoretical truth had to remain, or else the facade would crack. That was how they got through their relationship.

I'll call her next week, Sophia thought. *Otherwise it will be too far in advance. No one would buy that it's impossible to get a taxi if you call and order one three weeks before Christmas. I'll have to apologize for not calling sooner. I can blame work. Say I didn't have time.*

Back up in her apartment she looked at the bed. The photographs and her notes had spilled across the messy bedspread.

I could ask Adam for help, she thought. *He could help me with information, with contacts, with asking around. What would it matter? A phone call doesn't mean anything. I need to be able to talk to him. He's a good contact to have. Better than most, actually. Or an email. I could email him. It's not the end of the world. If he was anyone else I would call.*

Sophia pressed her palm to her forehead.

He doesn't think about you that way. Not anymore. Probably he never did. It was a mistake, something we did because we were sad and drunk. He's still with his family, there's no reason for me to write him an email.

But he could help me. I could ask him to unearth old documents that might be useful. That's it. I'm sure he'll want to help me. He knows he can trust me. We could meet. If we keep it professional. Talk about work. Just work.

■ ■ ■

Adam's last interrogation for the day started early, at one o'clock. He should have had eons of time. To bring it to a close, to consider all the many ways events could have unfolded. As a detective inspector, Adam Sahla was a special investigator for the Stockholm police in cases that involved children. One of his tasks was to question children who were suspected of having been victims of a crime. It was a delicate undertaking and didn't have much in common with typical interrogations.

The girl had been removed from her home and placed with a foster family a few weeks prior. This wasn't the first time her family was under investigation, but she had never been taken from her parents before. She had only been six months old when Social Services received the first report about her and her brother. Now she was six and she didn't want to say much about what had happened, if anything *had* happened. This was only the second time Adam had met her and they were still getting to know each other.

How could Adam have predicted that she would suddenly start to talk? That he would hardly make it into the interrogation room before she climbed into his lap, grabbed his index finger, and told the story, hardly stopping to take a breath?

It was a unique breakthrough; it would probably never happen again. An opportunity like this would make it possible for the courts to save the girl's life. To create a new, more secure future for her and her siblings.

Adam's boss met him in the stairwell when the interrogation was over. They were waiting for a prosecutor to give the order that would allow them to pick up the father. His boss paced back and forth in front of the elevator.

"You stay with that kid. Understood? Have some juice with her, offer her cookies, as many as she wants. That kid isn't leaving here until we know we've got that bastard behind bars where he belongs."

Adam didn't protest the sentiment. But he wasn't the only one who could eat cookies and drink juice.

His boss tried to keep his voice under control.

"I shouldn't need to explain myself here. That girl feels safe with you. We have to allow her to feel safe. Do whatever you want, but do not leave. Well done, by the way.

That was a damn good job. You're the best we've got for this stuff. You have to stay. You know how important it is. Order in lunch. McDonald's? All kids like hamburgers. Ice cream? Does McDonald's have ice cream? Can ice cream be delivered?"

Adam didn't bother to point out that both he and the girl had eaten lunch before the interrogation began. He also chose not to point out that there was hardly money for ice cream delivery in the budget.

"It's not enough if I just link the phone to my cell?"

"No, that's not enough." By now his boss was speaking so loudly he was almost shouting. "For Christ's sake, Adam. That kid will have no more...that child must not be subjected to any more...anything we can avoid subjecting her to. It's not enough for the caseworker to stay, and it's not enough for you to take off and bring your cell, because if that was enough, I would have said so."

∎ ∎ ∎

Adam stepped into the auditorium just as a group of jazz dancers in neon legwarmers were receiving their applause. His daughter was already in the audience, still wearing her tutu and stage makeup. She didn't say a word when Adam arrived; instead she slid off her mother's lap and sat as far away as she could, cross-legged on the floor in front of the first row.

For the first time that day, Adam's wife made eye contact with him; she didn't blink once. Her blue eyes were dark, but she didn't say a thing. And Adam felt a sudden rush of anger.

I need you now. I need your help to make her understand that I didn't do this on purpose. You know how hard it is. You know it as well as I do, and if you're not on my side our kids will never understand that I'm not deserting them. I'm not off playing golf with bank buddies. I'm not standing there trying to pick out a matching tie in the morning instead of taking my kids to school. I'm doing my job because it would be unthinkable for me not to do it. And you know that. I need your help.

But Adam didn't say a word either. Instead they watched the performance. A hazy mass of children dancing to a hazy piece of music with no melody. They were the wrong kids; it was the wrong music. Adam wasn't listening and couldn't focus his gaze. He looked at his daughter's straight back; her tight bun revealed her skinny neck. She was too far away for him to pull her close. Hug her until she could no longer protest. He stood up and walked out. He had only gotten as far as the stairs before he noticed a text had come in.

It wasn't from her. It was never from her. He had given up hope. So many times he had tried to get in touch. He had called, written, gone to her work. She didn't want to; she never wanted to talk; she didn't even want to tell him why not.

Almost. He had almost given up hope that it would be her.

Katrin
1998

Chief Inspector Bertil Lundberg was sitting in Stig Ahlin's mother's room at Stortorp rehab facility. The woman had dozed off again. As he waited for her to wake up, he paged through some papers that had been on her nightstand. It looked like a curriculum. Could it be something Stig Ahlin had left behind at his last visit?

A mediocre dissertation is nearly always a result of the researcher making up their mind too quickly. When you wish to find a particular outcome you become blind to alternative explanations. This does not necessarily happen consciously, but it is still devastating to the research. To obtain optimal results you must maintain an initial phase of open-minded investigation. Only after certain factors have been identified and confirmed can you begin to formulate your thesis.

Bertil put the document back. The text actually reminded him of his own work. An investigation demanded caution. And a fine-tuned sense of intuition. It could be devastating in the end to settle on any conclusions too rapidly.

He drummed his fingers on the edge of the mattress.

Should I wake the old lady? he wondered. *Will she be frightened if I do?*

Bertil had not made up his mind. There was nothing to make up his mind about. So far it was easy to keep his eyes up, because there was nothing to focus on. But he had to do this. He had to question an old woman with dementia who fell asleep every five minutes. Anything else would have been a breach of duty.

Because there was something odd about Stig Ahlin. That much was clear. He had tracked down Bertil to reassure himself they wouldn't speak with his mother. But why?

Bertil had to admit it was slow going, though, interrogating this old lady. When he asked about Stig, she only remembered who he was half the time. If he reminded her that Stig was her son, her forehead wrinkled in concern. Once she had picked up the framed photo on her nightstand.

"Yes," Bertil said encouragingly, waiting for her to continue. Then she patted the photo a few times, placed it on her chest, and fell asleep. The name Katrin only gave rise to an extremely foggy gaze and nervous picking at the hem of the bedspread.

Bertil intended to leave soon. He'd found it necessary to come, to give it a shot. But he couldn't spend his whole day here; he had other things to do. He should go home and sleep. "Take the chance when it comes," his colleagues liked to say. "Sleep while you can, because you're not likely to get much later." At least there was one part of parenting he was already prepared for, he liked to think.

The old woman had awoken. She looked him straight in the eye. Her eyes were cloudy, a shade of brown like spilled coffee. Her eyelashes were short and stubby, and her skin was like yellowed parchment. Suddenly, she smiled wide.

"Dear little Katrin! Of course, I remember her. Katrin takes very good care of me. She washes my hair, picks out my clothes, and helps me trim my nails. Sometimes she paints them too."

The woman extended one hand to show him.

"We talk to each other, that little girl and me. She asks about me and then she tells me everything. About her young life. It's not always easy to be young. You don't realize how happy you were until later. How could I forget Katrin? She's very lovely. Once she kissed my son. I think they're in love."

5

Sophia had no more than seven Christmas presents to buy, maybe eight. Two for Grandpa, one for her secretary, and something for Anna's kids. She usually tried not to bother with a present for her mother, but she always bought something in the end. It was never particularly well received. The clothes Sophia chose made her mother feel fat; the perfumes Sophia thought smelled nice gave her mother a headache. She had no idea what kinds of books her mom liked. They never talked about that sort of thing.

Anna picked Sophia up at Skeppsbron. The winter sun was slanting through the windshield and the leather seat creaked as Sophia got in. She peered into the backseat.

"Is there a cap on how much cleaning is tax-deductible? Is that why you don't let the maid do the car?"

Anna glared at her and pulled onto the street. An empty juice box slid across the top of the dashboard and landed in Sophia's lap. Anna had a minor army of people to help her with everything from cleaning, gardening, and pool maintenance to child care and everything else Anna felt like she should have been able to manage on her own, since her own mother always had. It didn't ease her guilty conscience that her mother had not been responsible for her own firm with twenty employees. Rather the opposite.

Now Anna was going in the wrong direction.

"We're not going this way," Sophia said. "You need to turn around. The other way."

Once — she must have been twelve or thirteen — she had joined Anna and Anna's mother on their annual Christmas shopping day. They'd gone to NK, the fancy department store. When it was time for lunch they each had a shrimp sandwich at the café on the top floor. In line for the register Anna's mother had brushed the hair from the back of Anna's neck and kissed her just behind the ear. Anna had sighed, craned her neck away, and rolled her eyes. But Sophia had slowed down and stopped just beside them to wait. And when Anna's mom did the same to her, she didn't pull away. Instead she felt a pleasant warmth spread through her body. When they were done eating, Anna's mom ordered coffee for all three of them. Anna and Sophia stirred so much sugar into their cups that the liquid turned dirty yellow, but Anna's mother didn't say a word; she just smiled and let them get refills.

Later they looked at the shop windows all done up for Christmas and tried out perfumes. When one of the shop assistants wondered if Anna's mom would like to buy a bottle — they would be happy to wrap it up — she just shook her head as her cheeks turned pink. The assistant didn't say a word, only turned around and said something to a colleague. When the colleague rolled her eyes, Anna stalked up, sneered something about their ugly-as-shit aprons and German hairstyles and dragged her mother and Sophia away.

Anna's mother hadn't chastised her daughter. She didn't tell her not to curse. Instead she linked arms with both girls, left the department store, and headed for the subway. But her cheeks didn't cool until they were back home again.

One week later, Sophia had gone back to NK. She bought a bottle of Chanel No. 5 and had it wrapped in white paper with red ribbon and a sticker with the NK logo on it. Her plan was to give it to Anna's mother, but the package remained in Sophia's school bag. She hadn't been able to bring herself to take it out; hadn't dared to hand it over. She was afraid of embarrassing Anna's mom even more.

Instead, she gave the perfume to her grandmother. Which was only fair, given that it was her grandmother's money she'd stolen to buy it. Grandma had thanked her, but on Christmas Eve she crawled into Sophia's bed and scratched her back, as she usually did when Sophia had trouble falling asleep. Grandma had whispered that Sophia didn't need to buy expensive gifts; she already knew they loved each other.

The next year, Anna and her mother bought their Christmas presents at Åhléns. And Sophia was invited too.

Swearing, Anna made a U-turn across the solid lines of the lane.

"How are my kids?" Sophia wondered. "I mean, your kids?"

Sophia received the usual response. An incoherent tirade about lice, piano lessons, math homework, and how even though they had two hundred children's shoes in various sizes, there was never a single child who managed to find a pair that fit both their feet and the season. Anna had four children; the oldest would soon be thirteen and the youngest was almost four. When she talked about them, it sounded like there were fourteen of them.

Sophia tried to laugh in the right places, nod sympathetically or indignantly, sigh or protest, depending on what seemed right. Then she squeezed Anna's hand, which was resting on the gear shift. That familiar warmth spread through her body.

"I miss those kids," she said. "It's been way too long since I saw them."

When Sophia's phone rang, she picked it up, looked at the screen, and turned off the ringer. It didn't say who was calling. But it didn't matter. This was social time. With Anna, who was Sophia's sister in every way that counted. They wouldn't be going to the perfume counter at NK.

Katrin
1998

"You're asking what I believe happened?"

Bertil shrugged. Red splotches were spreading across District Prosecutor Petra Gren's neck. She had stepped into his office, closed the door behind her, and explained that she wanted to "discuss the state of the investigation." So Bertil had asked her a question, for a change. It didn't make her happy. Instead, the district prosecutor seemed to have caught a case of severe restlessness. She stood up and sat back down, crossed her right leg over her left, uncrossed it, and started over again. Up and down, again and again, never stopping. Bertil had settled for watching. Now she was up, legs planted wide, presumably to keep from tipping over on her high heels.

"You want to know what I think happened?" The district prosecutor's voice wavered. "How would I know? The only thing I know is this: I'm going to scream if we don't get somewhere soon. Give me a new view, a fresh idea, or at least a cinnamon roll. Stop asking stupid questions I can't answer."

Bertil didn't think his question had been stupid. They were on day sixteen, and he just wanted to find out what the head of his preliminary investigation could bring to the table. Something constructive, for a change. Because the only thing she'd done so far was make demands. Demands that he pull a simple solution out of thin air, along with air-tight evidence and preferably a believable confession. She wanted a tidy indictment, packaged in glossy paper with colorful, curly wrapping ribbon. And now she was raising her voice.

"If you want answers no one has, you'll have to turn to the county police commissioner. He knows everything. Especially about things he's never actually tried working on. Unfortunately, he's not in charge of the preliminary investigation in this case. That's me. And you know, I have neither a crystal ball in my office nor feminine intuition, if that's what you were hoping. And I'm truly sorry to disappoint you."

Bertil looked down at the table. *A cinnamon roll, hmm?* he thought. *Pastries and cakes seem to be her thing. Could she be one of those secret bulimics?*

When Bertil had returned ten days ago and reported that a woman at the rehab facility where Katrin worked said her thirty-five-year-old son had been with Katrin, Petra Gren certainly had become agitated. She had brought a pink princess cake to the briefing. Sure, she said there might not be much to celebrate, but she thought they deserved a treat anyway. She had eaten two pieces. But the sugar high hadn't lasted long. Petra Gren had not allowed herself to be swayed by the interrogation of Stig Ahlin's mother.

"Do you really want me to trust an old woman with dementia?" Petra Gren had asked. "She doesn't remember who her son is, but you think she knows who he's sleeping with? Stig Ahlin is a respected physician and university lecturer — we can't just run around spreading rumors about someone like that willy-nilly."

Bertil hadn't bothered to respond.

Petra Gren had been the one to bring cake. Not him. He was well aware of how bad off they were. Because the crime-scene investigation was a catastrophe. They hadn't found any trace of semen, no blood that didn't belong to the victim. Nothing to match to a potential perpetrator. Certainly they were still waiting for other test results, but they weren't going to get any breakthrough. They had no boyfriend gone bad, no father who refused to watch his daughter grow up for real. No neighbor on furlough from serving time for a violent crime. Nothing.

If something didn't happen soon, Petra Gren would dial down their resources. And in about a week they would have to scale back the team. She would allow them to plod on through another summer vacation month, but then the case would end up on the desk of some part-time chick with small children. And by Christmas the investigation would be completely forgotten. But Petra Gren would place responsibility for the bungled investigation squarely on him. That was always the way. In the end, it was always Bertil's fault.

At last Petra Gren calmed down. She sank into her chair,

brought her hands to her forehead, and leaned on Bertil's desktop.

"I don't want to mess this up," she whispered. "Katrin deserves better."

Right. It was a struggle for Bertil not to snort aloud, *Poor you. Having to bear this on your drooping shoulders.*

There was a knock at the door. One of the rookies, hair shorn close and his thick neck stuffed into the collar of his uniform, stood in the doorway and cleared his throat.

"Something came up. Am I interrupting?"

That depends, Bertil thought. *Do you want to ask how to get paid overtime? Whether it's okay to show autopsy photos to your girlfriend, or sell them to the evening papers? Because that would be interrupting.*

"Does it have to do with Katrin?"

The rookie nodded eagerly. He ran his hand over his scalp and stepped in.

"So, Stig Ahlin..." The rookie cleared his throat.

I can't handle this. Bertil failed to muffle a sigh. *If you're coming by to get a gold star, I'll toss you out.* Bertil sneaked a look at Petra. She had raised her head from his desk and was looking intently at the young man. It looked like she was smiling. *And I've forgotten your name. But I can't help it. You all look the same.*

"I asked, umm, our colleague," Bertil began. Might as well speed this story up. "I asked him to check around and see if Ahlin's name popped up anywhere."

The recruit nodded and waved a few documents. Bertil quashed a sigh. He knew how terribly long it usually took new recruits to give a report on their findings, however insignificant and meaningless they might be.

"Our colleagues at City had heard of Ahlin," Bertil said. "Apparently he's an early bird. Stig Ahlin is one of those who likes to stop by Jungfrugatan around six-thirty in the morning. On his way to work."

Petra tore her eyes from the trainee cop and turned to Bertil.

"Why hadn't I been informed of this?"

"Don't get excited for no reason, Gren," Bertil sighed. *If you came to our daily briefings you would already know.* "It's old news. Didn't lead anywhere. This Stig seems to be a certain type of doctor. And we'll continue to check up on him. But I can't devote resources to investigating his relationships with hookers. It's not illegal to buy whores."

"Yet," Petra snapped. "Soon. Soon things will be different in that arena."

"Quite possibly," Bertil said curtly. *As if anything would change in practice.* He turned to the rookie. "What were you going to say?"

"I got another hit on him this morning," he smiled.

"This morning? What do you mean, this morning?" Bertil rose. The rookie took a half step back. His smile froze. "It's past three o'clock. Have you been farting around under a barbell in the gym all day or something?"

"Uh...," the recruit attempted. "Stig Ahlin is the subject of another investigation."

"Did he try to rape and beat another demure schoolgirl to death?" Bertil walked toward the rookie to take the documents from him. "Because if you're about to say Stig Ahlin has repeatedly been nabbed doing thirty in a twenty zone, I'm sending you to the customs force. You can start strip-searching tourists coming in on direct flights from Schiphol."

The rookie put out his hand. Before Bertil could react, Petra had taken the document from him. As she read, the young man cleared his throat.

"His ex-wife has accused him of sexually abusing their daughter," he said. "They were brought in for questioning last week. I read the material, the interrogation of his wife, and well, I don't know, I don't think it's exactly something we can use. But the guy sure seems sexually disturbed..., couldn't that, couldn't that suggest, doesn't that make him pretty interesting for us?"

Bertil tore the paper from Petra's hand. He glanced through the text. When he was done, he looked up at Petra, and she gazed back. All they could hear was the buzz of the coffee machine in the hallway. The double-paned windows didn't let in a sound from the busy street outside.

Bertil noticed that the blotches on Petra's neck were returning. They were an even angrier color now.

The young man's gaze flicked back and forth.

Simon, that's his name, Bertil thought. *Simon, of course. How could I forget?*

"And, I mean, I wasn't able to find out...," Simon began tentatively. "The mother reported Stig Ahlin just a few weeks ago, a month, maybe, and I found out yesterday, last night, no, this morning. And, well, I mean, I was looking for you, Bertil, before, earlier, I tried to find you this morning, but you weren't here and I didn't want to just leave a note, and I had —"

"Let's calm down here," Bertil interrupted. He had raised both arms. He, too, spoke in a low tone. Almost to himself.

Bertil closed the door to the hallway and placed one hand on the rookie's shoulder. Simon looked down at Bertil. He must have been four or five inches taller than his boss.

"This thing," Bertil said, "it might not, it doesn't necessarily...it doesn't have to mean anything at all. We have to keep a cool head."

Petra Gren waved her hand dismissively. She seemed to have something caught in her throat.

Suddenly Bertil wanted to laugh. His blood rushed through his body, warm with confidence.

"But that's good, Simon. Really great. Finally something's happening." He nodded at him. "Well done! Nice. Now we have to make sure we do things in the right order. Get involved in this incest investigation. Every last detail. Stig Ahlin. I want to know everything about him. What kind of doctor is he? What are our prostitute contacts? Talk to the hookers. And talk to a psychologist, one of those profilers. Does Stig fit the mold? They may be able to tell us something about our murderer we don't already know."

At last Petra Gren opened her mouth.

"Don't bring him in yet." Her legs were perfectly still now, and her skin had cooled. "Don't let him suspect anything. But concentrate on him. Start with the wife."

6

Sophia was sitting in a two-person booth, trying to lean against a poorly designed backrest. She had a view of the whole restaurant. It was full. They'd had to wait ten minutes for a table, and that was about fifteen minutes too long. She and Anna were both about to faint with hunger. In addition, it was far too warm in here. The radiator beside their table sputtered and hot, dry air settled over the restaurant. Sophia could feel the sweat trickling down her back. Her blouse stuck to her skin. At least she had finished her Christmas shopping. Everything fit in a bag she'd left in the coat check along with her outerwear.

Anna hadn't checked her belongings. Her shopping bags were crammed into the booth next to Sophia, and the four or five that didn't fit were spread across the floor. Anna would keep going after lunch. And no doubt every free moment all the way up to Christmas.

"Stig Ahlin. No way."

Anna picked up the menu and shook it, possibly to find out if the small sheet would suddenly list more than just organic corn-fed chicken, farmed cod, fair-trade bulgur, locally grown vegetables, and carrot soup that hadn't been heated beyond 107 degrees and could thus be marked with a special carrot symbol that, according to the key in the margin, stood for "raw food."

"Is there anything to suggest the conviction was improper?"

"Yes." Sophia tugged at her blouse, trying to air herself out. The underwires of her bra were chafing. "Or Hans Segerstad thinks so, anyway. He has objections to just about every part of the ruling."

"But you're not convinced?"

"I honestly don't know. There are parts I think should...So far I haven't had time to read much, but there's almost always a reason to question the accuracy of a case based on circumstantial evidence."

"So, you think it's weak." Anna wrestled out of her coat and tossed it on the mountain of bags beside Sophia.

"Yes. I guess I do. Weaker than I remember. And there are a few things that feel...I don't know, but I don't quite buy that this well-bred young girl got together with Stig Ahlin. Or, more accurately, that he got together with her. The more I think about it, the stranger it gets. You remember, don't you?"

Anna nodded angrily. "Hard to forget."

"Liked prostitutes," Sophia said, almost to herself. "Some sort of sadistic sexual tendencies. And that part about the daughter. I know he testified that he slept with Katrin, but there should be something more there, something no one has noticed. Even if it's only that Katrin was outwardly sexually mature. His daughter was only a few years old. How does that fit? Although he was never charged with the incest, of course. And he had been married to a perfectly adult woman. But still. No, this isn't for me. I'm going to turn it down. Why would I spend a lot of time on such a pointless case? I'm sure you're aware too, how tiny the chances are of getting a life-sentence conviction overturned?"

Anna nodded. There was a deep crease on her forehead.

"Stig Ahlin has a better chance of winning the lottery," she said. "Hopefully there's no reason for me to worry, that pig is staying behind bars."

"What do you mean, 'hopefully'?" asked Sophia.

"Isn't it obvious what I mean? Excuse me, but Earth to Sophia, can you hear me? It sounds like you're thinking of accepting the case. Why else would we be talking about it? We don't usually talk about stuff you don't care about. And I'm sorry, Sophia, but I honestly don't get it. Stig Ahlin is Professor Death. He is."

Anna shoved the bags on the floor out of the way to make more room for her feet. A few guests on their way out stepped pointedly over them, lifting their knees high. Anna didn't notice.

"Why would you take him on just because you think the indictment was weak? And what was wrong with Katrin? Why are you talking about her? I don't get it — are you blaming her? She was fifteen years old and he killed her. Probably because he thought she was starting to turn into an old lady. He prefers them without pubic hair, doesn't he?"

"I'm not going to blame Katrin." Sophia rolled her eyes. "How stupid do you think I am? But it's still important to know how she lived her life. There's hardly anything about her in the investigation. That's sloppy. It's my job to notice stuff like that. And what do you mean, Professor Death? How do you know? Have you even read the decision?"

"I don't have to read it to know that Stig Ahlin is a pig."

Anna put the menu back down and turned around, her hand in the air. There were no servers nearby. She kept waving, her index finger pointing at the ceiling.

"I know he was never found guilty for the part about his daughter. I'm sure whatever she said wasn't enough, that poor kid. People always tell them they have to speak up, but when they do they find out it doesn't matter, it doesn't help, because who would believe a four-year-old? But a man who...Jesus, Sophia, do you even remember that murder? It seems like you've forgotten."

"I haven't forgotten. But there's a big difference between what was in the papers and what the preliminary investigation showed. And they closed the incest investigation before he was charged with homicide."

"I know. That's not what I'm saying. But I also remember...Did you look at the interrogation with the daughter?"

Sophia nodded. She no longer had the energy to protest. They had to eat before this conversation went off the rails.

"You should let that police officer you like, you should let him look at the transcript with the daughter," Anna said. "He's a specialist, you can say that's why. I'm sure he can tell you what sort of guy that Stig is. And how children feel when they've been subjected to the kind of stuff Stig Ahlin gets off on. He could explain to you why you shouldn't be thinking about mistakes in Stig Ahlin's conviction but should stay far, far away from that whole case. If you're really, really nice to him. Because you should be. Really, really nice to Adam."

Sophia shook her head. Was there really no one working at this place? Someone who could give them something to nibble on, a raw turnip, a bunch of warm dandelion leaves, anything? Anna's energy was undiminished as she spoke.

"God, you're so irritating, Sophia. Don't give me that look. You know exactly what I mean. Forget about Adam, then. It might make you happy to be with someone you like. And we can't have that." Anna took a breath. "Shit, I'm hungry. I have to eat."

Anna got up. Hardly a minute later, she returned with a young server in tow. He was carrying a basket with at least four different kinds of bread. When they were done ordering and had each spread a piece of bread with butter, Anna went on. She chewed as she spoke.

"What was I saying? Why do I think you should let him rot in his way too big and far too comfortable cell?" She swallowed. "Because Stig Ahlin makes me believe in the death penalty. People like him shouldn't be allowed to live. And if some mistake was made in the formalities, I hope to God you don't get him out on a technicality. Because of some legal mumbo jumbo that has nothing to do with truth and justice. Because if you do, I don't know if you can be the godmother of my children anymore."

Anna spread a thick layer of butter on another piece of bread and shoved it into her mouth.

"Anna," said Sophia. "Calm down. He was never convicted of what his wife said he did. How many times do I have to say it? He wasn't even charged."

"It doesn't matter. Katrin was a child too."

"The fact that he slept with Katrin doesn't make him a pedophile."

"Are you serious?" Anna sprayed a cloud of crumbs from her mouth. "How can you say that? A fifteen-year-old is a child. Jesus, she was only, like, two years older than Emil when she died. Do you think Emil is an adult? He still builds forts and wants to run away from home when I ask him to make his bed."

"The courts say so too." Sophia wiped her cheek. Most of Anna's half-chewed bread had landed there. "Our legal system says so. Katrin had reached the age of consent and she was sexually active."

"Doesn't matter. She was fifteen; he was the age we are now. That equals a pedophile. Even if you can't go to jail for it." Anna took a piece of *knäckebröd* and broke it in two, stacked the pieces, and put them in her mouth. "And everyone who's normal thinks so, Sophia. Stig Ahlin visited prostitutes. He liked little girls. And when he could no longer use his own daughter more than every other weekend, he slept with Katrin. Whom he murdered."

Anna took the last piece of bread from the basket. The butter was gone. She played with the bread for a moment before decisively starting to chew on it, slower this time.

"If you want to convince me, or anyone else for that matter, that he's not guilty, first you'll have to convince me that he never abused his daughter." Anna took a large sip of water and looked Sophia in the eye.

"But I can't appeal or request a new trial for something he wasn't even charged for."

"I'm not talking about a retrial here."

Sophia nodded. It was all she could do. There was no point in trying to have a discussion with Anna when she was like this.

"You may be right."

"I'm always right."

Sure, Sophia thought. *And you're not self-absorbed in the least.*

"If I take this client on," Sophia said, "it will be because I think it's so important I can't help myself. And in that case I will do my job. No matter what Grandpa thinks. Defend the interests of my client. Because that's what I do. Especially when no one else believes him."

"So, he's your client now?" Anna sounded tired. She leaned back. She suddenly looked sad.

"I didn't say that. I don't know. I haven't made up my mind yet."

The server arrived with the food. Anna listlessly picked up her fork and poked at her meat.

She's stuffed, Sophia thought.

"And when it comes to Adam, you need to understand something. I have no desire to have an affair with a married man. You may think that's not very romantic, but I think it's…Why would he leave his wife and kids after one night with me? Why would I want to subject myself to the humiliation of being satisfied with whatever's left over?"

Sophia chewed slowly. It was a struggle not to raise her voice.

"But I want you to know," said Sophia, "that there's a big difference between what Stig Ahlin's daughter said to the police and what was reported later in the newspapers. What the papers printed was what Stig Ahlin's ex-wife told the journalists. She was behind all the sordid details."

"Sordid? Sordid!?"

Anna put down her silverware. She looked at Sophia in silence; it must have lasted three seconds.

"Sometimes I just can't wrap my mind around you, Sophia. What is so sordid about saying that you've been the victim of a crime? About turning to the media if you think it might help? Her daughter was sexually abused by her own father. She had a child with a man she loved, and he…Do you have any idea what Stig Ahlin's wife must have gone through? I don't think —"

Don't say it, Sophia thought. *Just don't say it.*

"— I'm sorry, but if you had kids you would understand. It's the worst thing that could happen to a mother. In that situation, you would do anything to keep it from happening again. Anything."

Ida

1998

The hallway of Vitsippan Day Care smelled like wet socks. With all the children and harried parents gone, it seemed shabby. Marianne was sitting on a very low wooden bench under the row of coat hooks. She didn't want to arrive too early. She touched the picture of a kitten that marked her daughter Ida's cubby. The photo was peeling at the edges, and someone had colored the kitten's tongue green with a marker. Ida's rain gear was on the floor. When Marianne hung it up again, dried mud rained down. There were lone socks everywhere. Ida's winter hat had been left behind on the shelf.

It was twenty past seven. Marianne quashed the impulse to call and make sure Stig had given her a bath. Ida needed her routines. She had to go to bed soon or else she would be impossible to wake up in the morning. But he knew that. She'd told him at least a thousand times.

Marianne paused by the container of shoe protectors. Did she need to put on a pair now? Even though the day care was closed for the day and all the children had gone home? She pulled off her shoes and entered the room in sock feet.

"It's very kind of you to come in on such short notice."

Marianne ran a hand over her hair.

"You said it was important. So of course I came in. Stig was able to watch Ida. It's not his week, but he said it was okay. And that was lucky. Unusual, but lucky. Definitely. As long as he helps out, I have no problem... Well, it could get better now, who knows. I'm sure it will get better."

She tried to laugh, but it mostly sounded like a cough.

Why am I always like this? Why do I always try to explain why Stig does the things he does? Marianne gave a tentative smile.

The director of Vitsippan Day Care didn't smile back.

"Let's have a seat," she said.

Marianne felt the knot in her belly tighten as she stepped into the teachers' lounge. What was this? She'd assumed it would just be the two of them. Instead, there were already five people in the room. Ida's day care teachers, all three of them. Plus, a man in his fifties who introduced himself as a social worker and a woman who was a child care assistant. Why were there so many of them?

"I thought... Is this, does this have anything to do with what happened last week?"

Marianne felt her cheeks go hot. She had asked already. They'd said it didn't. And she had trusted them. She'd thought they were done discussing that incident, that she wouldn't have to talk about it anymore. But it was just as she'd suspected. They were still upset. And she would have to defend herself again.

It wasn't as if she didn't understand. She'd been upset too, but she hadn't blown it out of proportion. The boy's parents had gone crazy. They'd taken him to the recently opened Astrid Lindgren Children's Hospital where he had needed three stitches to stop the bleeding. Of course it had been unfortunate, but he would recover completely, no long-term effects at all. And what was Marianne supposed to do? How do you tell a four-year-old that you can't bite your friends on the genitals? On the wee-wee. Still, Marianne had tried several times to talk to Ida, to try to understand. But she couldn't keep nagging at her daughter forever. In addition, as she'd already told the staff, she would really like to know whose idea it had been to play such a strange game. It had to be the boys; surely the boys were the ones who wanted to experiment. They must have seen something they shouldn't have, on TV, or at home when the parents thought the kids were asleep. It wasn't necessarily all Ida's fault. She may have been trying to defend herself against an idea her friends had come up with.

I should have left my shoes on, Marianne thought.

Hadn't they been through enough? If she'd known she was about to be dragged in front of some type of jury, to be judged as a mother, she would have asked Stig to come along. This was his responsibility too.

To be honest, she thought it would be a good thing for them to talk to him instead. Take him to task. Because really, he was the problem. He refused to listen; he refused to take Marianne seriously. He refused to take Ida seriously, or at least the demands that came with having a child. It had always been that way, ever since Ida was a baby. It would be nice if someone besides Marianne told him to be involved.

Stig had hardly touched Ida when she was an infant. He fled to his job, called home to say he would be working all night and sleeping at the office. Marianne was left to parent all on her own. When they separated, Stig had never once put his own daughter to bed. His first time doing so was when she was staying overnight at his house. By then she was two and a half and Marianne had never dared to ask how long Ida had cried before falling asleep.

Before their separation, Marianne was the one who did day care drop-off and pickup, who made breakfast, who knew how warm the bottle of milk should be for Ida to drink it. Always, no exceptions. Stig had never bathed Ida, never clipped her nails, and honestly believed that a two-year-old could brush her own teeth. Ida was seven months old when Stig changed her diaper for the first time. At some dinner they'd had for a visiting researcher from Illinois and two doctoral candidates, he'd been met by laughter from their guests when he said he thought it was too intimate, that those tasks should be the job of the mother. Stig refused to dress her; he "couldn't choose" the right clothes, he said. He "could never find anything" in her closet. It was unthinkable that he should go to parent-teacher conferences or pack a lunch or buy new rain pants when the old ones were too small. Stig wasn't an absent father who refused to take responsibility. It was far worse. In Marianne's opinion, Stig shouldn't be allowed to call himself Ida's dad. He'd never earned the name.

I should have demanded that Stig come along, Marianne thought. *He should be the one sitting here, not me.*

"I've done my best to talk to Ida," Marianne said. "I think she understands now, that it was wrong, that you can't do that to your friends."

The director shook her head. No. This wasn't about the time Ida bit her friend. That's not why they had asked Marianne to come in, at least not the main reason. They wanted to talk about something else, something very alarming, very sensitive, and they could only have this discussion with Marianne. Because they were concerned. Very concerned.

They were sitting all in a row, the teachers and everyone else. On the same side of the table. Marianne was across from them. She tried to find a comfortable position on the hard chair. It wasn't easy. And there were so many of them. Marianne couldn't decide whom to focus on. They were all looking at her intently. All but Ida's youngest teacher, who was carefully inspecting her own hands, twisting and turning her fingers, picking at her cuticles, sticking one finger at a time in her mouth, then taking it out and eyeing it again.

To Marianne it felt like their seats were a foot or two above her own.

She didn't understand what they were talking about.

Concerned? She pulled her feet in under her chair and wound her arms around her waist. What did they mean?

Ida was a kind child, very cuddly and warm, considerate and funny. If you just got to know her, she wasn't a problem at all. Why were they worried? What right did they have to be worried about Ida? What right did they have to call Marianne into question? And Ida.

She didn't understand.

The director cleared her throat. She glanced at the other participants. The social worker nodded. It was as if he were giving her the go-ahead to start.

Then the director began to speak. When she was done, Ida's two older teachers took over. As soon as anyone paused for breath or to blow their nose, the social worker jumped in.

There wasn't a moment of silence. Someone was always speaking. Always telling. Their voices were a roar in Marianne's ears.

No, no one blamed her. It wasn't Ida's fault, not something she was responsible for. But they had to talk about this. About their concern. The reason Marianne had been asked to come in on such short notice.

And without waiting for Marianne to catch a breath, they said a little more. One by one — about inexplicable accidents, games that scared the other children, the diapers Ida refused to stop using, Ida's swollen vaginal opening. And about odd things Ida had said. About stories she'd told. About her dad.

Marianne looked at them. Their lips were moving. She could hear the sounds; she listened to the words coming from their mouths.

But she didn't understand.

After twenty minutes, Marianne stood up. Her knees were shaking. She slipped on the freshly polished floor and raised one hand.

They have to stop, she thought. *They have to stop. I can't take it anymore.*

"You have to stop," she said. "You have to stop talking now."

It was quarter to eight. They'd asked her to come in at this hour. She'd arranged to leave Ida at Stig's place and come on her own. It was so late at night. It was quarter to eight.

At seven-thirty Ida wanted to listen to a bedtime story. She wanted someone to stay with her in the bed, scratch her back gently, under her nightgown, stroke her forehead until her eyes began to close.

Ida didn't like being alone at night; she was too scared. She wanted someone to blow on the back of her neck so she wouldn't get too warm. She wanted someone to say, "Go to sleep, sweetheart, see you in the morning."

"I have to go," Marianne whispered at last. She wasn't sure anyone could hear her. "I have to go."

So she went. She left the room and quickly closed the door behind her. The director rose to stop her. "Wait," she heard from the other side of the door. Then Marianne hurried into the hallway and stepped into her shoes, walked through the exit with her shoelaces untied and her coat over her arm. She ran down the stairs, across the street; she ran so fast her mouth tasted like iron.

She couldn't stay. It was quarter to eight. She had to pick up Ida. She had to pick up her daughter right away.

7

Sophia hadn't wanted a ride home when they were done eating. Instead she strolled down to Norrmalmstorg. The sky was leaden and the air heavy with the promise of rain. She had eaten too much.

When she arrived at Norrmalmstorg she glanced up at the big clock. The Norrmalmstorg hostage crisis had taken place in the basement of that building, the legendary bank robbery that ended with staff being taken hostage, the incident that introduced the world to Stockholm syndrome. Sophia had been born that same week. When she was little, Grandpa used to talk about the dramatic days before the hostages were released and she was born. Her sixteen-year-old mother's labor pains had set in right around the same time as a policeman was shot in the face by one of the hostage takers, shot with a submachine gun through a hole the police themselves had drilled through the ceiling. The Norrmalmstorg hostage crisis was Sophia's favorite of the bedtime stories Sture could tell without reading from a book.

There was no bank in that building anymore, only clothing shops and a hotel. A few floors up, Sophia had gone to one of her first job interviews, just after passing exams.

One of Sweden's biggest law firms had had offices there at the time. But they had eventually moved out as well.

She had been offered another position three days earlier but wanted to serve at the district court instead. That big business—law firm life wasn't for her. Not because she was against earning money in principle, but that was never enough of a drive for her. What was more, there had been something about the interview she didn't like; it had felt like they were inviting her to join a cult. The partner who spoke to her had spent a little too much time talking about how they only hired the very best, the elite. And there was something about the room itself, the oil paintings of older, retired partners and the antique carpet under the oval conference table.

The law isn't all contract review and stock quotes, she recalled thinking, with that upright posture and steadfast conviction she'd had at twenty-two.

Sophia turned onto Birger Jarlsgatan. What time had the clock shown? The National Library was probably still open and it was more or less on her way home. She could pop in and peek at some microfilm, read the articles that had been published about Katrin's murder. Sophia liked to do that when she needed to quickly acquaint herself with a major case. It afforded her some distance from all the official reports. Typically, she did her research online, but this time it wasn't possible — the case was too old.

The more she read of the preliminary investigation, the more she felt she needed to know. Her mental image of the crime was different from what was in the file. Sophia wanted to form a clearer understanding of how wide that gap was, the gap between what the evidence showed and what had been shared with the public.

She walked through the main entrance of the National Library and stowed her outerwear in one of the lockers off to the right. About a dozen people were in the reading room; two of them were bent over their books, fast asleep. Sophia smiled at her memories of coming here on the weekends, when she was home from Uppsala and needed somewhere to study. She headed for the Annex and took the stairs down to the microfilm room.

Apart from the faint hum of the HVAC system, it was quiet. Few carrels were in use as Sophia found her way to the information desk. A man who appeared to have defied every rule about retirement managed, with some difficulty, to get out of his chair.

"It's organized alphabetically and chronologically," he muttered, gesturing at the shelves. "Let me know when you've found what you need. Then I'll show you how it works."

As he shuffled toward the carrel Sophia had chosen he glanced sidelong at the boxes she'd selected — she had around thirty of them, all from the same time period: the week before the murder up until the trial.

"Professor Death," he remembered. "Are you one of those anti-progressives? Who think computers give off harmful rays?"

Sophia shook her head, bewildered. "I'm afraid I don't understand."

"Almost all the newspapers and magazines from the late nineties have been digitized. If you visit our databases, you can search by keyword. That ought to be much faster than this Stone Age method."

"I was planning to do that later," Sophia said, embarrassed, looking hesitantly at the box she'd intended to start with. She turned it over a few times, looking for a tab that would open it. The librarian groaned and took the box from her hands. He opened it, turned on the machine, and inserted the end of the roll.

"You spool it forward with this knob. And look at this screen. The reading you can do on your own, I hope."

Stig Ahlin had been the subject of two different investigations: one into the abuse of his daughter and one into the murder of Katrin. In the first few weeks after the murder, nothing appeared on the front pages, but Sophia found a few articles buried further inside the papers. Though it was a tragic death, they gave only vague updates about the police work.

At first, nothing was written at all about the other investigation. That was just as it should be. A woman suspected that her ex-husband had sexually abused their daughter. She had, with support from the daughter's day care, filed a report. The parents were also in the midst of a custody battle and, because of the situation, she was demanding more child support. Newspapers scrupulously avoided writing about that sort of case. Especially when the investigation didn't lead to charges filed.

Everything changed when the two investigations were suddenly linked. When the lead suspect in the murder of Katrin Björk, age fifteen, turned out to be a thirty-five-year-old doctor who was also under suspicion of sexually violating his four-year-old daughter, the press coverage exploded.

There was tons of material to read. The leaks from within the investigation must have been more like a waterfall than a calm trickle. Sophia Weber paged through article after article on the dim screen. Wherever she looked, she found something new to read about the murder of Katrin Björk.

She'd searched the library's two largest databases. But it was a very special feeling to track down the articles and see them as they'd looked when they were published, to see the entire paper, page through it, notice where the article had been placed, how much space had been devoted to it. To skim through other articles: Frank Sinatra's funeral, the Spice Girls on tour, Saab investing over a billion kronor in a new factory in Trollhättan, downtown condos fetching record prices. Sophia pressed the spool button and pages flickered by.

At regular intervals she moved to a different carrel, where the screen was hooked up to a printer. She was on her third copy card; soon she would have to buy yet another. But first she wanted to read something very specific.

The worst thing that can happen to a mother. That's what Anna had said.

Sophia was browsing through one of the biggest evening papers. When she arrived at a date not long after Stig Ahlin was taken into custody, she found an interview with the mother of Stig Ahlin's daughter. It was three pages long. The photograph on the black-and-white microfilm screen showed the back of a woman sitting on a sofa with her legs curled up.

The headline was a quote. In the woman's lap was her daughter, who was peering at the photographer over her mother's shoulder. The girl's face was blurred out. The woman's hair was up in a bun; her head was bowed.

IT'S MY FAULT. I SHOULD HAVE DONE A BETTER JOB OF PROTECTING MY DAUGHTER.

Katrin
1998

The mood at the station was explosive. Everyone had put their lives on hold; all that existed was the investigation. They didn't pick their kids up from day care; the grandparents took care of that. They didn't call in sick; they took double doses of Tylenol and forced themselves to the station. The cots on their unit were full; no one in their work group wanted to leave the others. Only one thing mattered: resolving this investigation. Because they were about to break it open, they could all feel it. And everyone was thinking the same thing.

A goddamn doctor. It was a goddamn fucking evil thirty-five-year-old doctor who had beaten, slashed, and raped little Katrin. He was polished and handsome, spoke like an encyclopedia, and sneered when you didn't look at him with enough respect. He was the one who had ingratiated himself with fifteen-year-old Katrin, made her fall in love; he was the one who had fucked her and killed her.

He had called two days ago. Stig had called Bertil's direct line. The conversation lasted six minutes. Stig had no more than that to tell. About their liaison, as he called it. The brief liaison Stig had with Katrin — he wanted to inform the police about it because he realized it might be of interest to the investigation.

Stig Ahlin wanted to inform the police. He realized it might be of interest.

Twenty-nine hours had passed since they'd hung up, and Bertil was still so enraged that he literally had white spots dancing in his vision.

He couldn't comprehend what had happened. How Stig Ahlin could be so callous as to call up Bertil. Without even trying to lie. He wanted to brag. Show what an irresistible man he was. No woman could say no to him. He believed he was untouchable. Beyond suspicion. So superior that he could never be considered a suspect.

As a result, the first interview, which they'd actually been planning to postpone, was held with no drama whatsoever on Stig Ahlin's own initiative. The next day. With no lawyer present. For informational purposes only.

It all would have been much easier to deal with if the killer had been Katrin's age, Bertil thought. Someone with whom she'd had a typical teenage relationship. With the sort of problems you couldn't do anything about anyway.

Any teenager can fall in love with the wrong guy, someone from the wrong side of the tracks. That's the sort of thing you can warn them about. But how can you warn a teenager against falling in love with a full-grown doctor, a successful man, the father of a little kid? Someone who thought he was entitled to her. There was no protecting yourself against that sort of evil. It was impossible to anticipate.

Stig Ahlin had been allowed to leave the station and go home after his interview. They had shaken hands when he left. Stig had an appointment to keep.

"Call if there's any other way I can be of help." That's what he'd said.

"We'll do that," Bertil had responded.

Two of his colleagues were assigned to watch Stig Ahlin. And just as Petra Gren had requested, they brought in Stig's ex-wife Marianne.

Bertil was the one who'd spoken with her. At first, she hadn't seemed surprised. But then he'd asked if Marianne knew a Katrin Björk. She didn't. She'd assumed he wanted to talk about her daughter, Ida.

Katrin Björk was fifteen years old, Bertil told her, and had worked at the rehab facility where Stig's mother lived. At this, Marianne's face had turned even paler; she had seemed to grow absent. She recognized the girl's name now, she was the one who was murdered, the one they'd written about in the papers. But she still didn't understand why Bertil was talking about her. Marianne hadn't known that Katrin knew Stig's mother. Marianne herself hadn't seen Stig's mother for a very long time. They'd never been close, and Marianne had not visited her former mother-in-law since separating from Stig. She just never got around to it.

Stig hadn't mentioned any Katrin, Marianne said. No, she explained, they didn't talk much unless they had to. Stig had never mentioned other women aside from colleagues or the wives of acquaintances. This hadn't changed after they separated. Why would it? Marianne had never wished to know if he'd met someone new. Surely no one ever did?

Did she know he visited prostitutes? No. Did she know how he'd gotten to know this Katrin? No. Did she know he had gone to the porno theater on Birger Jarlsgatan? No. Did she know? No. She knew nothing.

"I don't know him," she said. Several times. "I don't know him. I don't know anything. This has to be some other man, not the one I was married to. Are you absolutely certain?"

"This has to be a bad dream," she said too. "A mistake." It had to be, because she couldn't take it anymore. But it never ended. She hardly had time to think *this has to be over now* before falling even farther into the abyss. The realization that had robbed her of her whole reality, everything she knew to be true, was not the last lie she would have to make fit into her new life.

"Can you explain?" she asked. "Can you tell me how it happened?"

Then Bertil asked if Stig had ever bitten her. Marianne didn't understand that question either, not at first. It was just as absurd as everything else they wanted her to react to.

"No," she said. At first. And then it was as if the blood drained from her body, as if she were having an out-of-body experience. Only then did she realize what Bertil was getting at. Or what had happened. Suddenly, so many pieces fell into place.

"I can't think about it," she said then. "Don't make me."

Because one Monday, when she picked Ida up from day care, after a weekend at Stig's, her daughter had had a bite mark on her shoulder.

"I assumed she'd gotten it at day care," she said. "Lots of kids are biters at that age. It's common. It really is. And I know I talked to the day care about it. I wanted to make sure they knew that Ida's not the only one who does things she shouldn't. But they insisted it hadn't happened at day care. Or at least that they hadn't noticed it. She must have gotten it somewhere else. But where would that have been? That's what I said to them. Ida didn't want to talk about it. She said it was a secret. Oh my God. She said it was a secret."

And then Marianne began to cry again. Quietly. Distanced, somehow, as if this tragedy were happening to someone else, on a movie screen or in a made-up story.

When she finally started talking, Stig's ex-wife Marianne had a lot to say. About how Stig Ahlin had treated those he loved most. How he woke up before anyone else, went on his usual six-mile run, and then waited for Marianne and their daughter to wake up. How he complained — he started as soon as they got up. The dishwasher hadn't been loaded the right way, the butter had been left out to go bad overnight, the laundry was in a growing mountain in front of the TV in the living room, and he couldn't understand why he was expected to deal with it, even though he was the one who took care of everything else in their family, including earning every last krona the family spent.

He was never satisfied. He shouted. When Ida got scared and started crying, he shouted even louder.

Stig thought Marianne ate too much, and at the wrong times and in the wrong ways. That she made meals when he wasn't hungry and that she never bought food he wanted to eat. She made too much food at once and not enough when it was actually needed. She dressed oddly and either used too much makeup or not enough. And no matter how hard she tried to stay one step ahead of him, he always found new reasons to criticize her. She held the clutch down too long when she drove, she pulled too hard on the cold-water tap, she used too much hot water, she forgot to turn off the lights when she left a room, she forgot to air their place out in the morning and turn off the radiators before doing so.

She hadn't been the one to ask for a divorce; he had. But now, finally, after a year, she was starting to see things in a different light. Her mental health had improved these days. Or, it had been better. Until she'd listened to those first questions from the day care staff.

What had they said? In concrete terms? They thought Ida was acting strangely. She scratched her genitals, wanted to "play sex" with the teachers, and told extremely alarming stories about her dad's pee. Ida's genitals were often red; she masturbated during story time and used her tongue whenever she wanted to give a kiss.

The investigation was still ongoing. It had just begun. Marianne had petitioned for sole custody for the duration.

Marianne cried when she spoke about her daughter. Sometimes so hard that they had to take a break. And yes, there had been times when Stig bit her during sexual inter-course. Hard. Hard enough to leave marks. Did he do that? Surely, he had. Once or twice, anyway.

One time, Bertil had taken Marianne's hand. He'd wanted to comfort her. To explain that it wasn't her fault.

"You're saving your daughter now," he'd said. "Thanks to you, things will be different. Thanks to you, he will never again be able to hurt her."

Bertil had regretted it immediately. *You can't say that sort of thing,* he'd thought. *I can't put the onus on her.* But he'd so badly wanted to say something. Wanted to relieve her pain, assure her that it would get better. In all likeli-hood, he was really just trying to comfort himself. But it hadn't helped.

His own daughter. And a fifteen-year-old girl. A god-damn doctor.

That's what Bertil was thinking as he brought the inter-view to a close. For which time in a row? He couldn't keep track. Little Ida. Little Katrin.

And that bastard of a doctor had called Bertil to brag about it.

8

Despite the cramped entryway and moisture damage, Sophia Weber loved her office in Gamla Stan. The alley, the ill-conceived floor plans, their poor finances, and her hardworking colleagues. There were four of them in total, including her, five when they took on an intern. And although her colleagues didn't feel like family, the office felt as natural as if it were her actual home. And she didn't think this was pathetic in the least. She was proud of the law firm of Gustafsson & Weber. She enjoyed her life there.

In reality, she couldn't afford to help Stig Ahlin. All her time should be devoted to clients who paid their bills. She knew that. Yet she couldn't help herself.

It'll only be for this weekend, she'd tried to convince herself while reading the case file over breakfast. *I'll just find a tidy way to get out of this,* she thought as she put the file in her briefcase. *I'm allowed to do whatever I want on weekends,* she said to herself as she plodded with it up Skeppsbron on her way to the office, where she planned to read even more about Stig Ahlin.

The firm of Gustafsson & Weber was located on the top floor, but they had access to the courtyard, where rays of the sun sometimes found their way in, and where a valiant but stunted little birch grew. When she needed a break, Sophia liked to sit in a plastic chair she'd put there and breathe different air than that in her office. There was a crack in the plastic, and her nylons always snagged on it. But she didn't have the energy to get a new chair, so she kept using it year-round, no matter the weather, to drink her coffee and gaze at the ashtray that no one ever emptied. Everyone knew Anna-Maria was the one who filled it with nasty butts, but since she refused to admit she smoked, and since no one else wanted to deal with the dirty job, the ashtray and its evidence remained. It had been full for a long time, now.

Sophia Weber opened the door to Gustafsson & Weber and deactivated the alarm. She went to her office without turning on the lights; there she sat down in her chair and started up her computer. Both long walls of the small room were lined with low bookcases, where she kept her textbooks, her collection of case summaries, and the preparatory materials she used regularly. Four filing cabinets were crowded on either side of the desk. The tops of the cabinets and shelves were covered in files that hadn't fit anywhere else. It looked like a mess, but Sophia knew exactly what was where. A document that couldn't be located within two minutes — that was a lost document.

Hanging on the wall behind her desk was a watercolor she'd received as a gift from Grandma and Grandpa when she passed her Master of Laws degree. Beside it she kept three framed drawings Anna's children had made for her.

On the desk stood a single photograph of her, Grandma, and Grandpa. They'd been on vacation in Paris. Two weeks after they came home, Grandma had learned she had cancer.

Sophia looked down at her briefcase. Suddenly it felt insurmountable. Why was she subjecting herself to this? Why did she always end up at work? Every Sunday. No exceptions. She looked at her watch. A present from Grandpa. In a few hours, she and Grandpa would make dinner together. They did so every Sunday these days, ever since things had ended between her and Peter.

At least I have plans for dinner, she thought. *I can't stay at the office all day, so that's good. And I can just as well read the newspapers here as at home. Plus there are cookies in the pantry. And food in the freezer, I can warm it up for lunch.*

She started out on the love seat in the reception area, reading through the paper backward. When she was done, she picked up her laptop from the floor and started clicking through the documents. She wanted to get an overview of what they contained. And what was missing. She wanted to know what wasn't there.

In the middle of the list of documents, she stopped short. It was too much. She put down the laptop again and closed her eyes.

There were other people she could talk to. Other searches. In her office was a list of phone numbers, direct lines to all the police officers she'd worked with, even those she'd removed from her cell phone.

He would know whom I should talk to, she thought. *I could ask. That's all. Nothing more.* Sophia got up and found the list of numbers. She browsed through it until she found Adam Sahla's. She had a direct number for his workplace and another for his cell. Without thinking, she dialed the cell number. It rang on the other end, again and again. No one answered. When the voicemail picked up, she ended the call. But first she listened to his voice. Then she called again. Just once more.

■ ■ ■

Adam had forgotten his cell phone at home. He couldn't bring himself to wait for Norah to get ready, to do whatever it was she needed to finish up before she could even think of going out. So he had left, taking the bundled-up kids with him. Not until they reached the park did he realize he had left without his phone.

Now Norah wouldn't be able to call and find out where they had gone.

He sighed. He would deal with that problem later. Right now, he had to distract his daughter, who was sprawled on the ground, sobbing. Another kid was using the park tricycle she'd wanted to ride. She was actually too big for a trike, and there were about a dozen other bikes available, but she didn't want any of those.

His son had sat down on a bench. There was no doubt what he thought of being forced to join this outing. His back was hunched, he was resting his chin on his hands, and his eyes looked like they were about to trickle out of his skull.

Adam tried to suppress his anger. Smother his irritation. The feeling that it wasn't the park that was the problem here — it was that his son never thought anything was fun. That his son never moved voluntarily.

I always have to prod him, Adam thought. *Jog behind him and nudge him on. When I was little, I wouldn't have been able to sit still in a place like this. Mom had to let me out after dinner, so I could run the energy off, or else I couldn't fall asleep. I certainly would have thought up something to do. There's tons of stuff to play with here.*

Adam righted his daughter, who immediately ran off for the slide.

But my son just sits there gaping. He never shows interest. Unless it's happening on a computer screen or is covered in chocolate.

Adam sat down next to the boy and placed a hand on his head. His earlobes were ice cold.

Or he's sad, Adam thought. *A kid with no spring in his step. Is he unhappy, something's going on at school? Or at home? He lives with us, after all. With our issues, and with me. A dad who never comes home in time for dinner because there are far too many other kids who are worse off.*

Adam put his arm around the boy and squeezed him as hard as he dared.

"We won't stay long, I promise."

His son groaned.

"Then what do you want to do? Tell me! Please. I'd really like to know what you want. I can't guess, but I'd be happy to do something you would enjoy too."

"Where's Mom?"

"At home."

"I want to go home."

"We're here for now. For a while. It's not so bad. I'm sure we can find something to do. Are you sure there's nothing you would enjoy? Want to play ball for a while? Or go in and check out badminton rackets? We could play badminton."

"Can I play on your phone?"

Adam stood up just as he saw Norah walking toward them. He shouldn't have worried. Of course, Norah had realized they had gone to the park. Adam walked over to meet her.

Norah had let down her hair and gave him a small smile as he picked up his daughter from the ground, where she had once again thrown herself after some defeat Adam hadn't yet managed to identify. Norah's coat was open. Underneath she was wearing a white T-shirt and blue jeans. He smiled back and tossed his daughter over his shoulder. His daughter began to laugh. Like a bird: bright tones, cascades of sunshine.

"You forgot your phone," Norah said, kissing him on the cheek. He took her hand and pulled her close. She smelled as if she'd just gotten out of the shower. His daughter slid down into his arms; he held her between the two of them for a brief moment. She looked up at them.

"Mama," she said. "You're the prettiest mom in the world. Prettier than Sleeping Beauty and Snow White put together."

Then they let go of each other. Norah went over to their son and Adam looked at his phone. Two missed calls. He brought up the number. Hidden. No message.

Must not have been important, he thought, then turned off the phone and stuck it in his pocket. *Not important enough, at any rate.* He took his wife's hand. It was cool. She turned to him with a tentative smile.

We could go to Nordiska Museet, he thought. *Everyone always thinks the museum is fun.*

■ ■ ■

Three hundred and forty-three pages — that's how much Sophia had copied from the microfilm archive at the National Library. It had cost her 1,390 kronor and she had taken the money from her private account. This wasn't her case yet, so she didn't want to treat it as a work expense. Because she hadn't said yes.

Now she was trying to sort the articles into a binder to keep them from getting lost and so she would know what she had copied.

No one talked about this. Not at law school, not at the Swedish Bar Association, and especially not when you happened to run into a colleague out and about. The eternal sorting of documents, shuffling papers. All the hours spent stapling, copying, browsing, hole-punching, putting in binders.

Sophia had wanted to divide the articles into those about the murder, those about the incest allegations, and those about Katrin Björk. It hadn't gone well. She'd had to put them in chronological order instead. Too often the articles dealt with everything all at once, especially the murder and the incest allegations.

But at least she had managed to produce one separate category. She marked it with a tabbed divider and put it at the very back: a section of articles on Katrin. The preliminary investigation didn't contain much about her, other than what came out of the interviews with Katrin's parents, friends, and teachers. Sophia had hoped the media could give her a more nuanced picture. Information that would help her understand what sort of person Katrin had been. Up to now, she hadn't found what she was looking for. Quite the opposite. Not a single negative word seemed to have been written about Katrin. Good grades in school, clever, pleasant, kind, and conscientious.

Sophia punched holes in yet another article, an interview with Katrin's riding instructor, crying in front of the horse they said was Katrin's favorite. She inserted it into the binder and closed the metal rings as gently as she could.

The next article in the stack was no more than half a page long. Some male journalist had spoken to an anonymous friend of Katrin's. Sophia glanced through the text. This one would also end up behind the divider. She read the ending more thoroughly and felt her forehead crease. The article certainly didn't say anything expressly out of the ordinary, but it had been written in a different sort of tone.

She started over from the beginning. There was something there. A hint that it wasn't always sunshine and rainbows in the suburb where Katrin grew up. That Katrin's grades hadn't been as good as the year before, that she was often absent, and that her riding instructor hadn't seen her in four months; that there were a lot of parties at school and that Katrin typically attended them. The journalist ended with a paragraph about a school psychologist who talked, in general terms, about how easy it was to make mistakes as a teenager.

Sophia took a yellow sticky tab and affixed it to the page, then got a pen and circled the journalist's name. It was never hard to get in touch with members of the press. She took out her phone and looked at the screen.

Shit, she was going to be late to see Grandpa. They'd agreed to prepare dinner together, but she would never make it now, not if Sture was going to eat at his usual hour. He hated it when she was late. An inability to be on time was a sign of weakness. He also considered it evidence of disrespect. In some ways, the failure to respect Sture's time as a retired person seemed worse than any other fault.

Sophia called a cab. As the phone rang, she scooped up the papers on the floor, placed them loosely in the binder, and put the binder on the desk. *The journalist*, she thought. *I have to remember to call that journalist.*

Katrin
1997

When Stig stepped into his mother's room that day, a young woman was stroking her wrinkled, silky-skinned hand with its ridged nails and liver spots.

The woman was holding the hand he used to hold. The hand that had patted him, clipped his sharp baby nails, washed his own hands before meals, and wrestled his little fingers into gloves when it was cold out. She was warming the hands that had touched him long before he was old enough to remember.

Stig paused in the doorway, stood at the threshold, didn't want to step in. Instead he watched as his mother smiled happily at a memory, one she didn't, in that moment, need to anchor to anything else. It felt strangely intimate.

The young woman stood up and he straightened his back and put out his hand. Katrin was her name; she worked there. They spoke for a moment. Katrin said something about his mother, that the power had gone out earlier that day. That Katrin had propped the doors open so she could hear in case any of the patients needed help. And in doing so, she'd heard Stig Ahlin's mother crying in her room.

Stig nodded. Her illness was merciless that way, he said. It allowed his mother to remember the war and the years surrounding it, when she was a little girl, but closed off everything that had happened since. Her memory had capsized, had become a place filled with cloudy water and swampy ground.

Katrin kept talking and Stig looked at her. Black tights, ballerina flats, a freshly ironed white shirt under the scrub jacket all staff wore over their street clothes. Katrin hadn't buttoned her jacket, and her shirt was open at the collar; it cast a shadow on the thin skin at her collarbone.

Then she moved on. She had other patients to see to. Stig followed her with his gaze; she'd left the door open.

When he left the facility an hour later, Katrin was standing just down the road, waiting for the bus. The bus didn't come very frequently, this far off the main roads. There was no reason to let Katrin stand around waiting. Stig picked her up; it was no trouble for him to give her a ride. No trouble at all.

Katrin took off her jacket before getting into the car. She laid it over her lap and fiddled with her purse. She had put on fresh makeup; her hair was down now, and she had brushed it out of her face. Stig drove her to Sergels Torg, where she said she had an errand to run. When he stopped at a red light, she unbuckled her seatbelt.

"Thanks for the ride," she said before getting out. Less nervous now. Stig was holding the gearshift; she turned toward him and placed her cool hand over his. Her index finger found its way in and brushed his palm. He could feel her blunt fingernail. Then she was gone.

9

Sture was almost done making dinner when Sophia arrived at Fjärilsgården.

"You're late."

Forty minutes. That was all. And we never said an exact time. I said I'd try to come early. Try. I never promised anything.

"Sorry."

She slipped off her jacket, hung it up, and rinsed her hands.

"You can set the table."

Sophia quickly gathered plates, glasses, and silverware. She looked around to see if anything else needed doing. But the potatoes were already boiling. The meat was seasoned and lying on a wooden cutting board. Sture lifted the lid and stuck a knife into one of the spuds.

"They're done," he snapped. "You can drain them."

Sophia accepted the pot and glanced around for the lid. Sture was still holding it as he sampled the sauce. When the butter stopped hissing in the frying pan he put the lid down on the other side of the stove, took the meat, and set it to fry. It sputtered. Sture turned on the fan. Sophia took one of the forks from the table instead. She held the potatoes in with it while she drained the water.

Three of the potatoes ended up in the sink. She picked them up, burning her fingers. Then she set them on the table and took a package of tomatoes from the fridge.

"I don't want any goddamn tomatoes," Sture said. "Sit down. Eat while it's hot."

For all my life, she thought. *At least it used to be both Grandma and me. Back then we could deal with these overreactions together. Exchange glances in understanding.*

Sophia placed the tomatoes on a plate. They glistened.

These days I just sit here alone with my questions. Tiptoeing my way quietly around them to keep from making things worse. To wait for the right time. To wait for the professor's mood to improve.

Suddenly her rage was upon her. She angrily took a big gulp of the wine Sture had poured. *Well, now is a good time for me.* She didn't even need to collect herself first.

"There were a few things I wanted to ask you about."

"Hmm."

"Are you listening?"

Sture chewed his food.

"If I can get hold of Stig Ahlin's daughter, and I can convince her to talk to me..."

Sophia tried to catch Sture's eye. He was looking down at his plate, mashing his potatoes into the gravy and cutting his steak.

"If I can get her to answer my questions about the incest allegations her mother made against Stig, can I trust that whatever she tells me is the truth? What does she remember for real, and what will be stuff she's learned from her mother, the newspapers, the investigation?"

Hello, she wanted to cry out. *Listen to me. I'm talking.*

"How should I know?" Sture said.

Sophia fell silent. She felt tears burning in her eyes. Fucking tears. How come she could never tamp down her anger? Why did it always betray her? She was so angry at him, for so many things. If she could just keep from crying, she could have told him so. She could have spoken up. *How should you know? Because it was your job. You are better versed in the human psyche than anyone I know.*

But Sophia didn't say anything. What was the point of starting a fight? Grandpa would just end up upset as well. Instead she took another bite and tried to swallow down the words that wanted out.

You always say it, she thought. *Let me know if you need help. Do you want some money? Do you need anything? Anything at all? I would do anything for you. But you never do anything, Grandpa. You never do anything. When I really need you, you won't even listen.*

She cleared her throat.

"Stig's daughter was four years old. I've read the interviews with her and as far as I can tell, she never said flat out that her dad abused her. I'd like to ask her whether he did. But I'm not sure she'll remember. What really happened. Will she? Remember it?"

When I was four, Grandpa. Do you remember what that was like? Because I think you do. A little bit, anyway. I remember the hall in our apartment, the one we had before we moved to Djursholm. I couldn't have been very old then. It might be my very first memory. Was I three? Or four? It's not a real memory; it's more like a photograph, a blurry image. A felt rug, a hall, a brown velvet chair.

But I remember how it felt when you looked at me. I must have been awfully small, I remember I had to reach up high, for you to hold my hand. It made my arm stiff. And I remember you helping me balance, I don't know what I was walking on, but you held both my hands way up over my head and still I stumbled. Water ran into my boots, you laughed and picked me up.

You carried me home, the whole way, with water sloshing around my feet. All the way home to Grandma, who put both my socks and the boots on the radiator. That radiator, I can still picture it, remember what it sounded like, how the water gurgled in the pipes when Grandma turned it on. I remember that, I think. I want you to help me, to tell me if those memories are real. It has to be a real memory, doesn't it? But why do I remember that, and nothing else?

I want you to explain, to help me understand if what I think I remember comes from something you told me or if it comes from something that happened to me. I want you to explain if it is the same for Stig's daughter.

Or is it different with trauma? Do you remember the really bad stuff, but not the okay parts? Or do you repress it? Why do I remember so little of Mom, why do I remember her hair but not her eyes? Have I repressed the things she did, or was she never there?

Sture still wasn't speaking. Sophia cut a piece of meat and ate it. The tomatoes on her plate were greasy, swimming in gravy and butter. She'd meant to make a salad, with garlic and parsley. Grandpa usually liked that. Even if he was bad at eating vegetables. She stuck the tomato into her mouth whole.

She cut the next one in two and ate it with potatoes and gravy. Grandpa was glaring down at his plate. He refilled his glass of wine and pushed the bottle across to Sophia. She ignored it.

Grandpa ran his thumb over his plate to capture the last of the gravy.

"Are you going to eat that?" He pointed at Sophia's meat.

"Go ahead."

Sture pierced the half piece of steak with his fork and shoved it in his mouth. He kept chewing as he went to the den.

Sophia ate two potatoes and the last tomato. Then she hand-washed and dried the china and put everything back in the small cabinets.

"Are you leaving already?" Grandpa wondered from the sofa. Unconcerned now. His voice was bright again.

"I have to work," Sophia said. *Next time*, she thought. *I can't deal with this right now. I'll bring it up with him on another day.* She went over to the sofa to bend down and kiss his cheek.

Sture took her hand and pointed at the armchair right next to him.

"What kind of foolishness is that, little Fia? You shouldn't spend all your time working. What is this non-sense? It's Sunday, and you should take care of yourself. Have a seat and stare at the television with your old grand-father. Have a little more wine. Keep me company for a while. We can have a chat. How's it going with your sex offender? Have you decided what to do? Are you going to make sure he's released so he can violate more young girls? There was something you wanted to ask me about. Better ask now, before I fall asleep."

Just leave instead, she thought. *Get out of here. He needs to understand that he can't just treat you any way he pleases.* But she sat down. Sture gave a small smile, took her hand, and placed it against his skinny chest. Somewhere in there his heart was beating.

"We should talk another time, I think," she said at last, pulling up her feet and tucking them underneath her. Sture tossed her a folded blanket. It landed on her head. He cleared his throat, turned off the TV, and set the remote aside.

"So Stig Ahlin's daughter Ida was four when her dad went to prison?"

"Yes."

Sture leaned back.

"Four is a complex age. There's a lot going on. We start to get a grip on the world around us. Many of us have our first memories from that age. But memories are always tricky, especially the ones we make when we're really small."

Sophia turned toward Sture and spread the blanket over her lap.

"In her case, it's even thornier than for the great majority of people," he said. "I have a hard time believing that this kid — she's eighteen? — I imagine she's done whatever she could to find out all about her father. That she has looked up articles, requested documents, read everything she could get her hands on."

"Hmm."

"Does she have contact with Stig Ahlin?" Sture pulled an impressively long booger out of his nose, observed it for a moment, and then rolled it into a hard ball between his fingers.

"No. He forced his way to a couple of supervised visits during the first few years. But then I suppose he got tired of demanding them."

"Was it the mother who accused him of incest?" Sture flicked the booger ball away.

"Yes."

"The loyalty aspect makes it more complicated. So, no. God knows."

"What are you talking about? What do you mean by 'no'?"

"Isn't that what you wanted to know?" Sture rubbed his palm beneath his nose. "If you were to ask her today what really happened. I don't think you'd get a sound answer. If I were you, I wouldn't bother asking. Plus, it doesn't matter. It's not as if it has anything to do with the murder."

Sture leaned forward and took the remote from the table.

"No," said Sophia. "But you remember what you want to remember, isn't that what they say?"

"Right." Sture violently blew his nose into his sleeve. "And repressed memories result in bodily, physical reactions that can only be managed through invasive psychotherapy to bring the dark-eyed trolls into the light?"

"Yes. Don't you agree on that?"

Sture turned on the TV.

"Sometimes you're exhausting, Sophia. It's not that hard to realize that what we experience as children can affect us later in life. But that's not what you asked me. You want to know whether the daughter recalls what happened to her, what her dad did, now that she's grown."

"Yes. Something along those lines."

"It's almost impossible to say. Maybe. Maybe not. But what's worse, there'd be no way for you to know if she's telling the truth, even if she did want to talk to you. The best you can do is go back to what they said when they were little. Although in principle you can get a kid to say anything. And what's more, they often express themselves so strangely that we can interpret their stories just about however we like." Sture sighed so deeply that he got short of breath and began to cough. "How should I know about her situation? What is her agenda today? Why would you want to dig around in that? Charges were never brought against him for those accusations."

But it still feels important. I don't quite know why, but I would like to know.

"If you like, I can take a quick glance at those old inter-rogations. I can find out whether it was an idiot who inter-viewed the kid, or someone who knew what he was doing. If you want my help, all you have to do is ask, you know that. I'm happy to be of service." He turned up the volume. "But right now, I want to watch this. We'll deal with it later."

What if I don't want to know after all? Sophia thought. *What I need to know has to do with Katrin Björk and Stig Ahlin. I should not allow myself to be swayed by stuff that has nothing to do with them.*

Katrin
1998

The water came from Lake Magelungen by way of the Fors River. It rushed through crayfish traps and zander nets, striking the canoes that were resting ashore, bellies up. The bay filled from many lakes: Flaten, Dammträsk, Lissman, and Kvarnsjön. Its outflow went through the streams toward Lake Ådran; it made its way through Gudö River, through Gammelströmmen and Nyfors, all the way out to the Kalvfjärden inlet and the Baltic Sea.

Yet Lake Drevviken was perfectly still. The breeze moved gently through the tops of the pines and the tufted branches of the juniper bushes. Moss and boulders took over at the forest's edge. Where the moss stopped growing, the slabs of stone plunged straight down to the water.

A hundred yards away, in the park outside the convalescent home, Stig Ahlin was out for a stroll with his mother. Her legs were still strong, and she liked to take walks, even if she couldn't remember where she was going or who was holding her arm. Stig walked slowly. He was in no rush. Now and then he made a comment about the impressive view. But otherwise, the two of them were quiet.

Then he saw her. She was a little farther on, walking down the raked gravel path. Pushing a wheelchair in front of her. Stig took a firmer grip on his mother's forearm, guiding them in her direction. When they got closer, she looked up at him with a smile.

Katrin sat down on a bench, turning the wheelchair toward the view and her gaze toward Stig.

"Wouldn't you like to rest for a minute?" she wondered.

He was used to this. The attention. They wanted him. It had always been that way, especially with the ones who knew he was a doctor. The younger ones were the most persistent. After lectures they stood around in clumps, asking questions they already knew the answer to. Laughing at everything he said. They came to his office, with their lips gently moistened and with expectations he didn't have the energy to fulfill. But they were around in other contexts as well. On the train. At the corner store. When he went out to restaurants. The women were always nearby. With their warm skin and darting eyes, their nervous odors and forbidden desires.

Stig helped his mother onto the bench and sat down next to her. Close — he brushed against Katrin. She was startled and drew a hasty breath. But she didn't move. She just sat a bit straighter.

■ ■ ■

Stig picked Katrin up at the bus stop. The bus was right behind him, but still she took off her jacket and got in his car. Just like the first time. This time she had put on lipstick. She rubbed her lips together, breathed with her mouth open, let her legs slip apart.

He took her home with him. Afterward he wouldn't remember if he'd asked first — it was obvious what was about to happen. She took off her shoes in the hall. He kept his on and didn't have to tell her where to go. She walked into his bedroom, stepped out of her pants, lay on her back, and helped him take off her panties. He left her shirt on but pulled it up along with her bra so he could get to her breasts. They flattened out, but she didn't say much. She brought her groin up to meet him, pressed it hard against him. Toward the end she braced her heels against the mattress. He penetrated her deeply. Hard. She was tight. Her shirt was over her face when he came, when he ejaculated all over her flat stomach.

10

On Monday morning, when Sophia stepped into the office, Gustafsson & Weber's secretary Anna-Maria Sandström was in her spot behind the wide, tall, half-moon-shaped reception desk.

Anna-Maria gave her a cheerful nod. Her hands were laced around a teacup the size of a goldfish bowl and her mouth was full of gummy candy. She'd wiggled her feet out of her flats and propped them up on a chair. She was seven months' pregnant and would work for another four weeks. The sprout-, bean-, and soy-based diet she usually pretended to adhere to had gone out the window. Sophia suspected that her secretary had been chewing on a licorice whip even as she peed on the fateful stick. And that she had grilled up half a Belgian cow to celebrate the positive result. For the past twenty-seven weeks, Anna-Maria's nutritional intake was based on refined white sugar and crispy bacon instead of locally grown ancient grains. But she still washed down all her food with tea that smelled like a manure pile. Hence the enormous cup.

"They caudd fum corth..." Anna-Maria chewed frantically, swallowed, and started over. "They called from court.

That thing you had scheduled for eleven today has been canceled."

Sophia shook her head. She'd blocked off her whole day for a pretrial hearing and had hoped the judge's instructions would finally make it possible for them to leave this messy, drawn-out case behind them.

"Did they bother to give any sort of explanation?"

Anna-Maria shook her head. Her mouth was full again.

Sophia fetched her mail and went to her office. The rain was rushing through the gutters alongside the tilted skylight. She turned on the ceiling light and sat down in front of her computer. For one fluttery second, she felt the urge to get up and leave, to use this pocket of breathing room on something other than work.

But there was always something to do. If nothing else, the pile of unread legal magazines, judgments, and opinions waited at her door, everything she should keep up to date on but never had the energy to deal with.

She ignored the looming tower of paper and took her briefcase from the floor. She would work. What else could she do? Museums were closed on Mondays, and it seemed far-fetched that she would go to the movies.

Stig Ahlin's papers were on top. They were the last thing she'd read the night before, and they would be the first thing she read today.

If I take this on, this is how it'll be. Every free moment. I'll spend all the time I don't really have on him.

She inserted the first thumb drive into the computer.

The screen filled with a list of documents.

She was tired. She could admit that, at least. Of reading, of trying to understand, of trying to sense the real story behind the files. It would take weeks to read through it all. She couldn't devote more time to it if she would only turn down the case in the end. There were shortcuts she could take, quicker and much simpler ways to come up with an excuse.

Sophia went back to the lobby. Anna-Maria had dozed off in her chair. She slowly opened her eyes, wiped her mouth, and looked at Sophia. She nodded a few times and rubbed her palms on the legs of her pants, as if to show she was ready for any assignment. Sugar glittered on her chin.

"Could you call Emla Prison?" Sophia said. "Ask them to see to it that Stig Ahlin calls me as soon as possible. You'll have to give them my number and explain that I'm an attorney, calling at the request of Hans Segerstad. I'm going out for breakfast. Give them my cell."

Katrin
1998

It was Monday morning at the institute, and Stig Ahlin was giving a lecture. The hall was half-full. The lecture had been delayed; the projector was hard to get working. One of the younger students had climbed up onstage, tinkering, pushing buttons, turning it off and on again until at last he brought up the correct image and could adjust the focus. The projector was always having issues; none of the instructors understood how it worked.

The hall was dark when they stepped in, the only light came from the screen and the students' reading lamps. The custodian, a bowlegged woman wearing way too many clothes, jangled in with her keys and two men with wide stances, black leather jackets, and shoulder belts. They turned on the lights. Everyone in the hall could tell that they were police officers.

At first, Stig Ahlin was annoyed. He asked if they would consider waiting outside. When they didn't respond, he explained that he was almost finished, that they could have a seat and wait.

They didn't. They rocked from side to side, and one of them brought a hand to his hip. It looked as though he didn't quite know what to do with his limbs.

"Stig Ahlin?" they asked. As though they didn't already know.

Stig Ahlin nodded. But the lecture wasn't scheduled to end for another ten minutes, and these students would be sitting for exams before the month was out. So he turned back around. He tried to finish up as fast as he could.

Then both men took a step forward. They could have touched Stig. But they didn't.

"We have a warrant for your arrest. You may come with us."

Stig Ahlin noticed this, how they said "may." He wondered why. It seemed absurd, when it was clear he didn't have a choice. But he was convinced he knew what was going on; this was Marianne's fault.

His attorney — he already had one — agreed with Stig that it was crucial he keep his cool. Once Marianne calmed down, as soon as the investigation was complete, life would go back to normal.

Stig thought he understood what was going on. And still, he was surprised. *I've already submitted to questioning,* he thought. *Four times in two weeks, without protest. I always arrived on time. My behavior has been impeccable. So what's this? An arrest? Picked up by the police?*

"There must be some mistake," said Stig. The officers didn't respond.

Stig remained where he was. With his sleeves rolled up and his lecture notes in hand. He thought the incomprehensible had already happened. But this, at least, had to be a mistake. There was no other option.

"What is this about?" he wondered. It came out automatically. It was probably what he was expected to say. But because he thought he already knew the answer, he cursed himself for asking. He didn't want his students to know about his ex-wife's accusations.

"You'll have to ask our colleagues in the violent crimes unit," said one officer. "All we know is that you need to come in for questioning."

That's all they said. The students heard. The violent crimes unit. Stig himself didn't react very strongly. He still thought he knew what it was all about.

Stig Ahlin was not permitted to fetch his coat. They took him straight out to the car, one man in front of him and one behind, all through the building. Nor was he allowed to exit through the revolving door; the man at his back took his forearm and herded him out through the regular door, the one to the side that was used by people in wheelchairs.

The dim morning light still hung over the hospital campus. As Stig Ahlin got into the backseat of the patrol car, he looked up at the redbrick facades and the faint lights. Forensic Medicine was just a five-minute walk away.

Stig expected a crowd of curious onlookers. But there was almost no one there. Not even the custodian saw him vanish. Everything was oddly deserted, empty, dark and cold. As the engine started, the car doors locked. The officers asked Stig to fasten his seat belt. He wiped his hands on his pant legs and cleared his throat a few times in succession.

The trip took fifteen minutes. They didn't speak during the journey. If Stig had had a cell phone, he might have taken it out to make a call. To his attorney. He would have liked to have something to do. But he didn't have his phone; it was in his coat pocket.

They took Stig in the elevator straight from the parking garage to the jail, and once there he had to strip naked. He was forced to wait for a few minutes, his hands cupped over his crotch, before he was duly searched and instructed to put on the jail uniform. The waistband of the briefs was so stretched out that they slipped down and bared half his buttocks.

Stig asked for new briefs but his request was ignored. Then he was shown to his cell. Sixty-five square feet. Half an hour later, the door opened.

"You can ring the bell if you need to go to the john. Lunch is in a few hours. We'll start tomorrow."

Stig Ahlin didn't know what would start. But he was still convinced this was about Marianne and Ida.

He didn't know that his arrest had been planned since the previous Thursday, by an entirely different police division than the one that had investigated Marianne's accusations. That the decision had been made by a district prosecutor and that the chief district prosecutor had signed off on two orders, one for the arrest and another for a search warrant. He had no idea that even as he stood there with his hands over his dick, freezing as he awaited his impending body search, two police officers were going through his office at work. Nor did he know that his car had been transported to the forensic technicians, and that four other officers, along with the investigation leader and chief inspector Bertil Lundberg, were searching every square inch of his four-room home on the island of Kungsholm in central Stockholm.

. . .

Chief Inspector Bertil Lundberg was not a fan of executing search warrants. There was this feeling. It typically showed up as he waited beside a locked door without knowing what he would find on the other side.

It wasn't that he expected mutilated corpses. All it took was the usual odors: grime, clothes, leftover food, an unflushed toilet. Going through another person's belong-ings: boxes, cabinets, the mail. It always made him feel vaguely seasick. Even when he was left to work in peace.

Everything had been carefully planned and prepared. The apartment was empty. His colleagues had picked up Stig Ahlin. But they rang the bell anyway, before allow-ing the locksmith to open the door. It took three minutes. Then they could begin.

The chance to work undisturbed was an important pre-requisite for a successful search. And it was nice not to have to deal with the suspect. Not to have to show care, explain the legalities in a pedagogical manner, and look whoever answered in the eye, gaze into shrinking pupils. Not to have to deal with drunks, violent people, crazies. To avoid the rush of adrenaline, the sudden sweat, the fear that something would go wrong.

It would take some time to go through the four rooms. Bertil Lundberg was in charge of how to divide up the task.

They'd had their initial run-through the Friday before, but since they didn't know how the apartment was furnished Bertil had decided to hold off on detailed instructions until they were on-site.

They wanted to find the clothes Stig Ahlin had been wearing when the crime was committed. Clean or dirty. Or some other item with traces of blood. They would also be looking for correspondence or photographs or another type of documentation that could link the victim to the suspect. Beyond this, their instructions were of a more general nature.

A general nature. But meticulously drawn up. This was a well-planned search. They were prepared. More than usual. Plus, they would be left in peace. They could take all day if they wanted to. And the next day too, if it proved necessary.

But Bertil knew. It was always difficult, every time you stood there. As you stood there with your unbiased instructions in front of an open cabinet or an open drawer, staring at the pill bottle full of sedatives, an economy pack of condoms, vacation pictures and unsorted bills, parking receipts and pub receipts and taxi receipts.

In fact, it was impossible to know what was relevant and what should be left behind to keep the preliminary investigation file from becoming unmanageably large. But it had to be done. And he was the one responsible for making sure it was done right.

. . .

The next morning, Stig Ahlin had to eat his breakfast in his cell. A cup of cold coffee and a plastic-wrapped cheese sandwich with margarine. They were out of everything else, the guard informed him.

Around the same time Stig was munching on his roll, a journalist from the TT news bureau was making the rounds of police headquarters to collect tips for stories. This was routine. The journalist ran into Chief Inspector Bertil Lundberg in the hall. Lundberg was on his way to the jail to interrogate Stig Ahlin. The journalist knew what types of cases Lundberg dealt with. So he asked a few questions.

Stig Ahlin was brought to the interview room at eight o'clock. He'd already been asked whom he would like as a defense attorney. He'd given the name of the lawyer who had handled his divorce.

They'd had trouble getting hold of him, said the officer who was transporting him. It would be some time until he arrived. There was no question it would be best to start anyway. They couldn't just wait for the lawyer forever.

Then the officer left, and Stig was alone in the interview room. At 8:04, the first article was published on TT's teleprinter network. Stig's colleagues at Karolinska heard the first reports in the break room around nine.

"A doctor in his thirties has been apprehended as a suspect in the murder of fifteen-year-old Katrin Björk, who was found dead in early June of this year in her home in Enskede outside Stockholm. The man is also suspected of having sexually abused his four-year-old daughter and was arrested at his workplace in the Stockholm area."

During the first interrogation, they didn't talk about the murder. Instead they discussed the investigation about Ida. This was what Stig expected; he didn't find it strange. What was their relationship like? How did Stig think the divorce had affected Ida? Did he think their relationship had become strained since he moved out? What did he have to say about the investigation?

Stig Ahlin tried to guide the discussion toward Marianne. They should talk more about her. Stig thought it was important that they understand what sort of person she was. The police didn't seem interested.

They'd put Stig in a low easy chair. It reminded him of one of those psychotherapist couches from a Woody Allen film. Stig wondered if they thought it would help him relax, become talkative. Or if they just wanted to annoy him.

To keep from half reclining, Stig sat on the edge and leaned forward. The two officers were a yard or so away, in regular, upright chairs. Between them was a low, round table that held a carafe of water and three glasses. At some point, Stig picked up the wrong glass. Then he stopped drinking entirely.

Chief Inspector Bertil Lundberg wasn't working alone. He conducted the interrogation along with a colleague. Stig answered all their questions and tried to make eye contact with them to ensure they understood what he was saying. As Stig spoke, Bertil's colleague jostled his leg as though he had poor circulation or was trying to dislodge a forgotten pair of briefs from his pants leg.

Stig Ahlin despised the police. They were jumpy. Unintelligent, with all the character of room-temperature butter. Stig thought Bertil Lundberg seemed unfocused. He kept grabbing his own clean-shaven chin each time Stig answered a question. It felt like Bertil Lundberg only wanted to get the interrogation over with, as if he already knew everything he needed to know and had to be somewhere else.

Stig Ahlin looked at the two of them as he struggled to comprehend what was happening. Lundberg with his hand on his chin, and the other guy, with the epileptic leg. Were they conducting this interrogation according to some tactic they'd learned at an expensive seminar? Five hours later, Stig Ahlin was allowed to return to his cell. The interrogation would resume the next morning, when Stig's lawyer would also be present.

■ ■ ■

What was this all about? he had asked. But in fact, he wanted answers to a different set of questions. How long will I be here? What are you going to do? What am I expected to do? What's going on?

He didn't understand. Reality lost its shape, its stability. He had been transported. Searched. Dressed in someone else's clothes. He slept. Woke. Ate.

What is going on? The panic would ease if only he received an answer. If only someone would explain. But no one did.

Each time the door closed, he started over. Like a fly on the hunt for a place to die, he moved around the cell. Sat down. Stood up. Sat down.

When would the door open next? What would happen then? When would this end?

He never asked.

11

At Emla Prison there was no graffiti. No discarded, empty bottles on the side of the driveway, no tunnel stinking of urine that visitors must pass through with their hearts in their throats. There were neither sheer cliffs nor a ferocious sea around the prison. There was no sniper at the ready. There were only row houses, managed forests, and fallow fields. The Emla facility was centrally located, in among baby carriages, pets, and apple trees. When Sophia got off the bus and began to walk toward the building, she found herself in the company of a man with a Rollator. He was out for a walk and looked at her as she glanced toward the prison: at the perimeter fence, the lawn, the security wall, the spotlights, the palisade fence, and the security cameras. Nothing was visible of the world inside.

Sophia approached the wooden security booth, feeling oddly cheerful for such an errand, and pressed the button to state her business. A dull metallic pop from the gate let her know that she could enter. The same pop echoed from every door. Even as she lifted her hand to touch the handle, it buzzed. Someone was watching her and knew when she was ready to open it. There was no need to wait.

The visiting room was empty when Sophia stepped in. She sat on the chair, leaving the sofa for Stig. While she waited for him to arrive she armed herself as usual, with a pen and notepad. She had jotted down a number of questions beforehand. But in fact, she was most interested in what Stig Ahlin would tell her about his expectations, should she take up his cause. And what she could expect from him.

A few minutes later he came through the door. He didn't look like the man Sophia remembered. During the trial his hair had seemed unnaturally thick, and his teeth ridiculously white. But that was all gone. What was left was a sinewy man with his gray hair cut so short it hardly covered his scalp.

They said hello. Sophia tried to squeeze his hand with the perfect amount of pressure, then sat down again, a bit too quickly, and ran her hand over her notepad a few times.

She cleared her throat. Stig Ahlin said nothing. His hands rested against his thighs, still, his palms upturned. It looked like a meditation pose. He looked at her without smiling, absently. Neither spoke.

Sophia cleared her throat again. She would have to be the one to begin.

"Well," she said. "You know why I'm here."

Stig Ahlin threw out his hands, then returned them to his legs and smiled stiffly. "And here I am."

Sophia didn't say anything for a moment, waiting for more words that never came.

I could stand up and leave, she thought. *I don't have to stay.*

"Right. Well," she said. "I need to know why you want me to work with you, if that is in fact what you want."

"Hans Segerstad recommended you. And so far, that's enough. For me."

"Thank you for your confidence," she managed to say. She opened her notepad and looked down at it. *Thirteen years he's been behind bars. And yet he manages to look as if I'm the one who came here to bother him. As if he's spending his precious time on me, and not vice versa. I suppose I should count to ten. To keep from saying something I might regret.*

"How can I help, counselor?"

One, two, three, four, Sophia thought. *Five, six, seven, eight. Nine. Ten.*

"You can tell me what you want. How you feel about this. Whether you truly want me to take this on. As I'm sure you know, it is very unusual to be granted a new trial. It would be simpler to apply to have your sentence converted to time-limited. The chances of that happening are much higher. And that doesn't rule out... You could petition for a retrial from the outside."

"I'm not interested in having my sentence converted." Stig's voice sliced through the room. "As long as I remain convicted, there is no reason for me to get out. I can't work, I have no family, I have no life. That's all been taken from me. In here, at least I'm somewhat safe."

He fell silent and returned to staring at her.

"Safe?" Sophia asked. "You know, there are ways to... If you get out, you can apply for protected identity."

Stig Ahlin shrugged.

"Then how do you think I can help you?" she asked.

Stig Ahlin remained silent. His hands were motionless on his legs. She tried again.

"If I'm going to help you, you need to help me." Sophia looked at her wrist. It was bare. She'd had to leave her watch at the security checkpoint. "I'm not a mind reader. Tell me something I haven't read in the papers. Or in the case file. I assume you've had time to take a look at it. Could you tell me what you think of what's in there? Anything, really."

"So that's it," said Stig. "You want to know who I am. Get to know me?" Even though they were sitting less than three feet apart, Stig managed not to look at her. "What an empathetic person you are, I'm impressed."

Sophia didn't respond.

"Are you looking for a good reason to say no?" he asked.

Sophia still didn't respond.

"Naturally you don't believe I'm innocent. But you don't want to admit that's the reason you don't want to represent me. A pretty little lawyer like you. It won't do to gain a reputation as squeamish." Stig lowered his voice. "Is it money? Is that the problem? That's usually the reason people like you say no to people like me. Or lack of time? Do you have too many clients already? Probably. And yet here you are. You need more, something you can tell Hans. Something he'll have to accept but doesn't cause him to lose respect for you. You don't want to blame it on having too much to do, because it's important for Segerstad to believe you can take on any amount of work. Did you come here to annoy me? A difficult working relationship would be a splendid excuse. Put the blame at my feet. The best thing for everyone involved, of course, would be for me to make the decision for you. 'Stig Ahlin doesn't want me to represent him.' Because then you can say your hands are tied, that there's nothing you can do."

Stig Ahlin turned to the closed door. The room had no real windows, but just below the ceiling was a rectangular opening. Sophia leaned back. One of Stig Ahlin's hands twitched.

"How do I convince you?" he snapped. A drop of saliva landed on the table. "What do I need to say to make you want to work to get me freed? Do I have to tell you about my unhappy childhood? How I was beaten as a boy, and lost my father at an early age? Or would you rather hear about something that happened later on? How I was a victim of prejudice? How the papers designated me a symbol of patriarchal oppression? How my ex-wife made sure to get me convicted of one crime by accusing me of another? You're already sure that this is how I managed to convince Hans Segerstad. By taking that tack. Segerstad has a weakness for those who've been subjected to unfair treatment by women. Naturally, you're already aware of that."

He fell silent.

The window opening was barred on the outside. It was an inexplicable precaution. Even if someone did manage to squeeze through the eight-inch gap, it didn't lead anywhere. The opening might as well have been an unlocked sliding door — it still wouldn't have been possible to use it to escape.

You're not relaxed and calm, Sophia thought. *You're nervous. Afraid of being turned down. You hate that you have to talk to me. For thirteen years you've been locked up, but you've never gotten used to depending on others.*

"Nothing I say can make you change your mind," Stig Ahlin said at last. "You can pretend as much as you want, but you believe I killed Katrin Björk and you have no desire to get your hands dirty with that sort of case. I'm sitting here because everyone thinks I'm guilty of killing a woman when I didn't. But why should I expect you to believe that?"

Stig gestured around the visiting room. It was so cramped that, in doing so, he almost touched Sophia. He ran his other hand over his buzz cut.

"So, if that's all..." Stig Ahlin rose and bent his head in a deliberate nod.

A woman, Sophia thought. *So, you call Katrin a woman.*

Katrin
1998

The night before his detention hearing, Stig Ahlin had to sleep directly on the plastic cover that was sewn onto the mattress. His bedding had been taken away. The suicide risk was deemed too high. Once every thirty minutes, the guards checked on Stig to make sure he was still alive. They kicked the door, stuck their heads in, and shouted. "Stand up!"

It was a different person every time. Each of them shouted. Stig never recognized the person who'd woken him. Because he did wake up. Every time. And he stood up. Only once did he not bother. That time, he was yanked up off the bed and shoved against the wall. "Stand up! Do you hear me?"

The next morning, Stig's lawyer said there wasn't much to be done about it. This would all soon be over anyway. Filing a complaint would only disrupt the process. It really wasn't in Stig's best interest to disrupt the process. And what was more, the wake-ups were done for Stig's own safety rather than to disturb his sleep. It was forbidden in Sweden to wake someone up just to discombobulate them — in fact, it was forbidden in all civil societies, so naturally it would never happen in a jail. And least of all Sweden.

But it wasn't over soon. The court approved the prosecutor's detention request. Stig Ahlin was suspected with probable cause of taking Katrin Björk's life. He was considered a risk; he might abscond, continue to commit crimes, or interfere with the investigation. Thus, he would continue to be held in jail. He was remanded.

Just over four months later, the preliminary investigation was concluded, and charges were filed. Stig was still in jail. Only then was he allowed to read the newspaper and watch TV again, since he could no longer obstruct the investigation. He had, of course, asked his lawyers to fight the restrictions long before they were lifted, but once they were gone he almost regretted it. At least, in isolation, there had been a strange calm. After he was remanded in custody, they'd stopped waking him up at night. He was taken out for breaks. They gave him food. He could ring the bell to use the bathroom. This was a type of security. Stig had gotten used to it — just as he had the urine odor in his cell.

Stig's lawyer tried to persuade him not to read the papers. He told him to avoid the TV news. Half of what the media said wasn't even in the preliminary investigation file and was thus not worth getting worked up over. That's how the lawyer put it. Stig shouldn't get worked up. His lawyer thought Stig should ignore what the world knew. But the guards left the evening papers out. Gave them to him. They wanted Stig to know.

The hearing at the district court lasted six days in total. A few days after the arguments were finished, it was decided that Stig would undergo a forensic-psychiatric evaluation. For five weeks Stig was relocated and had to live in a closed psychiatric facility. It was not a good sign that the court wanted his mental health examined, since it implied they planned to hand down a conviction. But Stig Ahlin didn't absorb the implications. Instead he felt oddly relieved.

Sure, he was still locked up, but on the psych ward he was locked up in a familiar environment. The people he met were colleagues. They spoke the same language. The sheets on the beds were the same old county council ones he knew from the hospital. He'd slept on them often during his internship. It almost made him feel safe. He also had the idea that it would be to his advantage if the court understood that he wasn't mentally ill. They would change their minds, he thought. They had to.

When it was time for the ruling to be announced, Stig Ahlin was moved back to the jail.

All in all, he had spent almost six months at the jail when one of the guards opened the door and said he was to call his lawyer. The thick mattress with its red plastic cover creaked as he rose. Stig called from a pay phone that was attached to the wall, with a steel-clad cord and a coin slot.

"We'll appeal," said his lawyer.

It was the first thing he said, and Stig didn't protest. Then the lawyer read a few sentences aloud from the decision. The words floated out, blending with the voices from the jail corridor. The vocabulary seemed unfamiliar, as if it came from a different language.

"It will arrive any minute, if you haven't already received it. It's important that you take time to read it in peace and quiet. We can talk again later." So his attorney said. He was probably trying to flatter Stig.

His attorney was an idiot. It was no special perk to get to read your ruling in peace and quiet; everyone had that right. Stig had allowed himself to be defended by a second-rater. The realization made his jaw clench and his chest constrict.

"Good," Stig responded.

A few minutes later, the guard arrived with the district court ruling. It was seventeen pages long; the staff had put it in a brown envelope with Stig's name handwritten on the front. The ruling found Stig Ahlin guilty of homicide. But nine days would pass before Stig read it.

"It was a show trial," said his lawyer when they spoke on the phone. The lawyer was always trying out various outraged phrases, saying them two or three times in different tones of voice. Stig could tell he was preparing himself to speak to the media. "A show trial," he repeated.

It's all over, Stig thought. And that was more or less how it began.

12

Stig Ahlin was back in his room. He had a window, but he kept the black roller blinds down so the room wouldn't become unbearably hot. He lay down on the bed.

Sophia Weber had asked him to tell her about himself. They did the same thing in the treatment program.

They wanted him to feel remorse. Only then could the therapists, lawyers, caregivers, other prisoners, and guards slot him neatly him into their own well-ordered lives. But he refused. Because they wanted to use his memories. Interpret them in a manner that had already been determined by what they thought they knew. Take control of the part of his life that wasn't behind bars.

The fact that his dad had collected junk and claimed he used the garage as a workshop, even though he'd never even touched a sheet of 220 sandpaper, much less a saw or a screwdriver — why should a memory like that be important? What could it mean, that he had no siblings? Or that his father had died three weeks before Stig turned eighteen? Meaningless details were magnified by the very act of uttering them. The row house his mother scrubbed on her knees, his father's TV chair no one else ever sat in, not even after he died. If he told these stories, they would be used to transform him into someone he wasn't. Sophia Weber would believe he had turned out a particular way because he had lost his virginity to a classmate in a sleeping bag that smelled like sweaty feet and stale beer. Because he used a condom that made his penis itch and because he gave the girl four hickeys so they would have something to show off the next day. She would decide that events like these explained why some things happened and why others never did.

Stig didn't want to talk about it. He didn't even want to think about it. Because if you spent enough time pondering life, your imagination would take over. You would start seeing connections and explanations. Ones that didn't truly exist, and yet you couldn't keep yourself from spotting them, filling in information and adding more color. It hadn't been a happy childhood. But it certainly hadn't been unhappy either.

Stig Ahlin looked at his blinds. He typically didn't open them until nighttime. He could glimpse a piece of sky outside. Next to the window was an air vent. It was fitted with a metal covering, but it wasn't airtight. On some cold winter days, he could occasionally feel the oxygen forcing its way in. The colder air. One breath later, it was gone. Then he would press his mouth to the opening. It didn't help.

From his window Stig could see a narrow strip of grass and the inner wall that enclosed the sex crimes isolation unit. But that was as far as his view extended, because that wall was even higher than the one beyond it.

The sex crimes unit at Emla Prison was no moss-covered ruin that afforded scope for boyish dreams about spectacular escapes. The roof wasn't made of copper and would never turn green with age. There was no wood paneling flaking in the wind, no stone steps turning porous in the salty sea breeze, no rusty, creaky hinges on settling doors. Here the building materials were dead, covered in graffiti, and fire-proof. Straight lines, easy to clean and well laid out.

Stig spent as little time as possible dwelling on what had once been. But certain memories lingered in his body. A gentle reminder that life had been different. Good, maybe. Summer memories. A dad tossing his son into the sea, taking him by one wrist and ankle and spinning him around, then letting go, light as a fishing net on the smooth surface. Stig didn't want to remember. Not the unhappy parts, and even less so the bliss. He tried to stick to the present. And remembering the good threatened to cast him over the edge.

His childhood had been neither difficult nor simple. But thoughts of his upbringing led to the most forbidden thoughts. The ones he must not entertain. What it had been like for his own daughter. Whether anyone had made her laugh, or tossed her into the water in his place.

Stig Ahlin didn't talk about himself. If he could help it, he didn't think about himself either. Especially not about his daughter. The thoughts of Ida were the worst ones.

■ ■ ■

The December air, refrigerator-cold, struck Sophia as she stepped through the door at the prison lobby and into the courtyard where the prison's transport vehicles arrived.

She walked back the way she'd come and stood at the bus stop. Thirty-two minutes before the bus would arrive to pick her up. For exactly twenty-five minutes she did a Sudoku. Then she made up her mind and called Hans Segerstad.

He answered immediately. He began talking before she could even say hello. He must have been sitting by the phone and waiting for her call.

"I know he's unpleasant," he was quick to say. "But it's not like you have to marry him. Don't let yourself be frightened off. I guess he's never been the ingratiating type, and I suspect anyone would end up a little grumpy after spending thirteen years in that place. I hope you'll allow me to explain something before you — "

Sophia interrupted him. "Don't worry. I'm calling to tell you why I've decided to help with Ahlin's petition for a new trial."

Hans laughed. "That sounds good. That sounds really good."

Sophia pictured Hans in her mind, holding his ancient cell phone in one hand — it was the same model her grand-father insisted on using — and slowly clenching his other hand into a fist, victorious. The phone already smeared with moisture and warmth.

"There are three reasons I want to work on this," she said. "The first and most important one: it makes me fuck-ing suspicious that all these fuckers are so fucking sure of everything."

"My, Sophia, that's a lot of swearing."

"Why is that? In a case based on circumstantial evidence? Two unanimous courts of law convicted him. Not until they appealed to the Supreme Court did anyone even quake in their well-shined lawyer shoes. One single justice wanted to grant him certiorari. Everyone else was dead certain he was guilty and saw no reason to review the case. The police, the prosecutors, the district court, the court of appeals. Not to mention the all-knowing general public. It's been fourteen years since Katrin Björk died; people hardly remember who they were married to fourteen years ago, but they remember that this man is guiltier than Judas. And the first reaction is always that this must be because he is guilty. It was my first reaction too. But that was before I started reading the case materials."

"I see you've noticed the discrepancies between the public image of Stig Ahlin and what actually emerged in the criminal investigation."

"Yes." Sophia nodded at her phone. "I have. And it's strange. I've certainly seen circumstantial evidence cases before. But one based on shakier grounds would be hard to find."

Hans chuckled in satisfaction.

"Second, I think it's too simple. A conscientious, successful doctor with no criminal record beats a little girl to death. I refuse to accept it. Not even his wife — and she accused Stig of doing the greatest evil one can imagine in real life — not even she claimed he was violent. More the opposite. But the fact that he gave her hickeys, that makes him some sort of vampire. I don't believe Stig Ahlin is the type to suddenly see red, or that everything just went black all of a sudden, or however people usually explain it. I can't put it together. Not even if he freaked out when he realized how young she was, or because she demanded more from him than he wanted to give. I can't make it work. That's my second reason."

Sophia was totally out of breath; she paused to recover. "But I'll only help you on one condition."

"What's the third reason?"

"Oh, right. The third reason, okay. Hold on. Hmm. What was I thinking? Oh!" Sophia threw her free hand into the air. "Forget the third reason. That's why I want to help you. Or, well, him."

"Thanks."

Sophia was thrown off balance. Hans, saying thanks?

Hans Segerstad had thanked her. It had been important to him that she accept the case, that she, and not just anyone, should be the one to help. He was admitting as much. She hadn't expected that.

"You're welcome. But there are a few things I want you to know. I have one condition. Because God have mercy if you're wrong. I'm not helping you with this case because you want to change case law about the evaluation of evidence. It's not a technicality, not for me, and I'll refuse to take part if you're planning a trick like that. You have to promise me. I'm far from convinced that he's innocent. You are sure, and I've found enough red flags that I'll trust you on it. And I'll continue to help you as long as I do. But if that changes, you'll have to fly solo again. Because we're going to do something positive now. I feel like doing something positive. Yeah, there it is! That's my third reason. I want to do something positive."

"I do too, Sophia." Hans Segerstad sounded serious now. "It's not a familiar feeling, I'll tell you that. But I feel the same way. And besides, we'll never be granted a new trial just based on some technicality."

"If I come to find he's as guilty as everyone thinks, I'm out. I don't give a shit if you think it's ethical or not. I'm out, right away. If that happens, I don't have time for this anymore. Here comes my bus."

And I want to get that retrial, Sophia thought as she boarded the bus. *That's my fourth reason. Get an innocent man freed, that was my dream once upon a time. It should still be my dream. That dream never starred a friendly, charming type who already had the world on his side. The dream was never about an easy case.*

She took a window seat. It was the same driver she'd had on the way there. At the back of the bus sat a woman with a child in her arms. When the bus turned back toward the main road again, she saw the outermost fence of the facility she'd just left.

She had once had to visit a client's room in a housing barracks. There had been fighting among the inmates and all the visiting rooms were being used as temporary isolation cells. They couldn't forbid visits from attorneys, so she had been escorted out of the main building, past the workshops, through the exercise yard, and into the corridor where her client was kept. When she arrived at her client's room they unlocked the door for her, allowed her to step in, and then closed the door behind her.

The air had been heavy with the sour odors of her client, and the blinds had been down. Her client was on his bed, and there he had to stay or else there wouldn't be room for them both. It had felt like being locked in a closet with someone she didn't know.

Sixty-five square feet. One twin bed bolted to the wall. At the foot of the bed was a TV; it too was mounted on the wall. Next to the bed was a narrow desk; above the bed was a bookshelf. All the furniture was bolted down, impossible to budge.

Stig Ahlin didn't want her to petition for his sentence to be time-limited.

"I'm somewhat safe in here."

So he'd said.

Sophia rested her forehead against the cool windowpane. She had met many people who were serving life sentences; she'd looked into their eyes, listened to their pleas. Heard them beg her to do something, anything, as long as someone did something, as long as something happened. As long as she broke the tedium.

One time, one of her clients asked her to petition for a new trial in a case of manslaughter he'd never confessed to. When she asked what new facts she could present, he'd said he wanted to confess. He was prepared to do anything, if only she could get him out of the routine life he was forced to follow. If only something would happen.

The bus slowly got up to speed. She was leaving Emla Prison and its surrounding community behind. Fields and managed forests flew past the window.

Stig Ahlin, though, he hadn't asked her for anything. He'd never asked anyone for help, not even Hans Segerstad. On the day his verdict took effect, he had stopped asking the system for help. Had he adapted? Did he accept what had happened? Could a man who claimed to be innocent still come to terms with a life sentence?

That smothering, restrictive boredom. No one had painted the building, no one had put up wallpaper; there was no budget for renovations and replacements. And the guys he had for company didn't do being supportive friends or sitting in circles and holding hands. In the kitchen where the prisoners could prepare food, all the knives had been dulled and their handles chained to the work surface. Stig Ahlin should want to get out of there. That should have been his greatest wish. It was inconceivable that he felt safer behind bars.

"I didn't murder Katrin Björk."

That was what he said. But he hadn't asked Sophia to believe him.

13

Every day but Sunday, for an hour each session, Stig Ahlin ran. Altogether he went between forty-five and fifty miles per week. It wasn't as if he took a day of rest because of his religious beliefs. He didn't have any. There were fewer staff around on Sundays, so there was no one to take him to the gym and watch him while he ran.

He knew he should be grateful. It was an almost bafflingly generous privilege that they opened his door an hour earlier than anyone else's, just so he could run. He also knew that it was a privilege that could be taken away at any time. And then he would have to settle for running during exercise time, along with everyone else, the people he shared his life with. The common wife killers, rapists, and whore fuckers. The ones who would get on the treadmill and walk slowly for an hour, just to keep him from using it. The ones who shouldn't even be there. They were the ones who had kicked the weight racks until it was decreed that free weights would no longer be allowed at prison gyms. Who grabbed a handle on one of the machines and wound it aimlessly in different directions before letting go. Who would shove a pencil into the mechanism, to break it, just so he couldn't run.

For the first few years, Stig Ahlin had been assigned to run in the exercise yard. The sex crimes isolation unit's yard was forty-five by sixty-five yards. He had run around and around, leaning slightly inward, with those unbearable fools standing and walking in the center, staring until their eyes bulged out of their skulls. He had tired them out. His hamster-wheel circus made them dizzy and the unit director had decided he could have an hour, not all on his own, of course, but almost.

Now he was allowed to work out across the yard, in the gym. The guards were all the same — sitting on a chair, reading the paper and checking their phones as if waiting for an important message.

It was never quiet. The HVAC system hummed. The treadmill rumbled. Stig landed with his whole weight. Sometimes he increased the incline to keep from running into the handles in front of him. The guard's radio squeaked and growled.

Stig had no music; he didn't do interval training. He just ran as fast as he could until he could taste iron. He fixed his eyes on the wall in front of him. For the first few years there had been a mirror there. It had vanished along with all the free weights. All that was left was the rectangle of darker paint that showed where it had been.

The room thundered when Stig Ahlin ran. And each booming step on the rubber belt was a reminder of what it wasn't, what it could never be.

Over 4,700 days without the sounds of rubber soles on gravel, grass, asphalt or sand, moss, dirt, or rock. Hour upon hour without his own time or control of his own movements. The belt relentlessly moved his feet back, forcing his muscles to counter with forward motion.

The belt could be angled upward, and he could regulate its speed himself. But there was nothing he could do to get the sensation of truly running. It was impossible to produce, even as a distant mirage. The sound got in the way.

Still he ran. He ran because they let him, but also because he didn't have to. And for one minute — he never knew ahead of time when it would happen — the sound might disappear, into the pain of aching muscles, when his brain let go out of exhaustion. Then everything went silent. Then his brain could rest.

He ran almost every morning. Every evening at quarter to eight, his door was locked from the outside.

The days went by. That was about it.

TWO

14

"Any new cases?" Lars Gustafsson, founder of Gustafsson & Weber and its oldest staff member, gazed around sleepily.

It was the Friday before the week of Christmas, and Sophia and her colleagues had decided to have a brief meeting before heading off for their annual Christmas luncheon. The entire staff was present in the conference room. Everyone was drinking black coffee except Anna-Maria, who was drinking two liters of chai with soy milk.

They would be dining at the Veranda at Grand Hôtel. Sophia had prepared by skipping breakfast and walking to work. She suspected most of her colleagues had done the same, and that they were dreaming of all the food they would soon get to eat as they sat there. Jansson's Temptation, little meatballs fried dark brown, six different kinds of ham, gravlax, and generously stuffed lamb sausage. Freshly baked sourdough and *knäckebröd* from a brick oven. Cheeseboards, egg-and-anchovy salad, truffle omelets, salmon pudding, Västerbotten quiche, lutefisk, fingerling potatoes, and soused herring with sour cream and fresh chives. Cheesecake, angel food pudding, fruit crumbles, *ris à la malta*, almond cream tarts, saffron bread, fruit salad, raspberry mousse, dream cookies, and French chocolate cake with whipped cream. Perhaps Lars Gustafsson wasn't tired at all. His mind was just elsewhere.

"I have to be at county court at ten tomorrow morning." Björn Skiller, the firm's youngest partner, hardly looked like he was thinking about food. "A deportation verdict. The enforcement part. A family. Two kids, ages three and two. The mother is pregnant."

"What country?" Anna-Maria had stopped typing on her phone.

"Afghanistan."

Everyone fell silent. There was nothing to say. Anna-Maria went back to her phone.

"Does anyone have good news to share?" Lars wondered.

Sophia took a deep breath. "I've decided to help Stig Ahlin petition for a new trial."

Sophia tentatively looked around. Anna-Maria was shaking her head in dismay. Lars raised his eyebrows.

"Of course you have," Björn mumbled.

Sophia had expected Anna-Maria to be upset. But that didn't matter much. Anna-Maria was always getting upset. Sophia was, however, a bit anxious about what her fellow partners would say. Their finances were strained. Helping out on a case like this was pure loss.

"Do you have time for that?" Lars had crossed his arms.

"I really want to do this." Sophia cleared her throat.

I want to, she thought. *It's been a long time since I had such strong feelings about a case.*

"You're going to like it." It took effort to keep from looking like she was asking permission. "When I've gotten a little farther I'll brief you. You might not think it's a good idea right now. But you'll change your minds when you know more."

Lars aimed a faint smile at Sophia. She thought he seemed annoyed. *I should have talked to him earlier,* she thought. *I should have told him a different way.*

"It sounds like something you could entertain us with over lunch. We can get a little tipsy and pretend that we're still idealists who believe in the system and our role within it."

Björn snorted. It was meant to be a laugh. Sophia nodded, and Anna-Maria excused herself and left. It had been half an hour since she'd used the bathroom.

Lars and Björn, too, stood up and headed for their offices. Sophia went to the reception desk to see if she could find any fruit. Just as she was sinking her teeth into a wrinkled apple, Lars stuck his head out of his office and called down the short hallway.

"Do you have a spare minute?"

Sophia nodded. Apple in hand, she took a seat in the chair before Lars's desk. She frantically finished chewing so she could defend herself.

"It's not going to affect our other cases," she said at last.

She knew she didn't truly need to make excuses. She could do as she pleased, and work on whatever she thought was important. But Lars had the right to ask. If she couldn't cover her share of the rent, his practice would be on the line as well.

Lars waved her off.

"I don't doubt that for a second. In fact, I think it's an important case. Well done, Sophia. Well done. We'll always make it through. Let me know if you need help, because we can certainly bring on an intern. You know I like interns."

Sophia felt her throat close up. She swallowed.

"I know you do." She swallowed again. "I hate interns. Especially the young chicks you choose."

Lars grinned. "I don't choose only female interns. Although they do work better. They know how to prioritize. Not like those millennial guys. You have no idea how many baffling things men today have to make the time for in order to self-actualize. Learn to play guitar, go to the gym, hang out with their girlfriends. I met a twenty-four-year-old recently who told me he liked to go mushroom-picking." Lars shook his head in misgiving. "Just when you think you've heard everything, you meet a man who likes mushroom-picking."

Sophia smiled. "Mushrooms are delicious."

Lars snorted. "Sure. Of course. But why waste a gifted mind like that? Anyway. Intern or no. You can always ask me for help, right?"

"Watch out. I might take you at your word."

"That's the idea." Lars looked Sophia in the eye. "I'm happy to help. Seriously. I don't know if I've ever seen a homicide case botched as badly as Stig Ahlin's. Ever. What did you do to get in on it? I thought he hated lawyers."

Sophia nodded. Relief spread through her body. It shouldn't come as a surprise that Lars was the first to believe she was doing the right thing.

"I know. And Stig Ahlin does his utmost to make lawyers hate him right back. Segerstad basically gave me the job."

"But Stig Ahlin accepted you. You're his attorney, not Hans Segerstad. And I'm jealous as hell. I wish I'd had the chance, myself."

"You're the first one I've talked to who doesn't think I'm nuts."

Lars laughed. "You spend too much time with the wrong people and not enough with me. People are stupid. I've known that for a long time. But that's not why I wanted to have a word with you. I wanted to warn you. I know how you are when you get going on a case. You want to do absolutely everything on your own." Lars stroked his tie. "Accept help, Sophia. Get protection, if you want to. You don't have to take the whole blow yourself. Because people are going to come after you, unpleasant people. You realize that, right? You have no idea how many people spend time hating folks they don't even know. Some of them can be truly nasty. You've only seen the tip of the iceberg so far. Once it gets out that you're Stig Ahlin's attorney, you'll learn stuff about hatred you never knew before. But remember, the whole firm is behind you. You're not alone."

"Thanks," Sophia said. "I appreciate it."

"Have you gotten any reactions yet?"

Sophia thought of Anna's anger. Her voice that would hardly hold, her eyes accusing Sophia of betrayal. Grandpa's scorn and condescending comments. Anna-Maria's disgust. The way the guards at Emla had looked at her. How they had taken an extra-long time to go through her bag, how she had been subjected to a body search. A quick one, of course, nothing more serious than a pat-down outside her clothes, but she had never been searched like that at a prison before. Not even when she was visiting her clients there on drug charges. She hadn't reacted at the time, at Emla, but now her colleague's question made her think about it.

Had she gotten any reactions? Yes. And not just from people she knew. The same day she visited Stig at the prison, just before eight in the evening, she'd received a couple of anonymous emails from someone, or several someones, who clearly knew she had agreed to be Stig Ahlin's attorney just a few hours earlier.

It was strange, but Sophia hadn't found it frightening. That sort of thing happened every week. She worked to help asylum seekers stay in the country; she represented women and children who'd been victims of crimes, and she defended men who were accused of rape. All of these things riled up people who wanted to share with the rest of the world what they considered to be rightful rage. It was typically worst when she expressed her opinions to the media — any opinion at all. She'd spoken about this with colleagues, and they all said the same thing: women who expressed opinions in public had to learn to tolerate those anonymous emails.

Most of them were about sex. From men who wrote that they hated her or wanted to fuck her. If only Sophia got some dick, she would change her mind, that was the general sentiment. Sometimes they said she should be sterilized, to keep the world from ending up with any more people like her. Very rarely they said she should just be beaten black and blue, but even those emails were usually based on the idea that she needed to be punished, that's what she must want most of all, it made her horny. That she said things she shouldn't because no one had ever truly filled her up.

The emails she'd received since deciding to work with Stig Ahlin weren't dangerous. They didn't say she needed cock; they said nothing about sex, violence, or forced sterilization. Sophia hadn't been scared when she received them. Only surprised that they'd arrived so soon after her visit to Emla.

Sophia rose from Lars's visitor's chair. It was noon, time to head over to Grand. It would take no more than ten minutes if they walked.

"No," she said at last. Insignificant emails from anonymous jokesters were not the sort of reaction Lars was referring to.

"None at all?" Lars sounded unconvinced.

"I'm not worried about Internet trolls. Those dudes just sit around clattering their hate into a keyboard. It's never any worse than that."

Lars Gustafsson nodded slowly.

"Okay," he said reluctantly. "You know best. Just promise you'll ask for help when you need it."

15

Hans Segerstad still kept an office in the law school building at Uppsala. No one had wanted to take it from him. In addition, he continued to serve as an adviser to a few of the research students he'd taken on before his retirement. He needed a place to meet with them.

Sophia arrived at his building twenty minutes before their appointment, and instead of waiting she decided to try the door code they'd used back when she was a student. Ten sixty-six, the Battle of Hastings. It still worked. She went straight up to Segerstad's office. It, too, looked as it always had. Shelves full of books, crammed in every which way, stacked on the floor. The wastebaskets were overflowing, and crumpled pieces of paper lay on the worn, dingy Persian rug.

Segerstad had always forbidden the janitors from entering his office when he wasn't there to make sure nothing would be disturbed. He was worried that his incomprehensible arrangement would be ruined if it came in contact with cleaning agents. Sophia guessed that large parts of his office hadn't been cleaned since he moved in.

In any case, her old professor was well prepared for their meeting. The conference table, with space for six, was covered in binders and documents: the case file.

Three rows of stacked papers, and the top one was the preliminary investigation. Interviews, notes, protocols, phone records, photographs, and forms gathered in binders and plastic folders, held together with black binder clips. The stacks in the next row were even taller. This was the slush pile, the leftovers: page after page of extra information that didn't belong in the material that had laid the ground for the charges.

The bottom row was the least comprehensive. It contained the two rulings, the one from the district court and the one from the appeals court, and the appeal that had been sent to the Supreme Court. There were also a number of other decisions concerning Stig Ahlin's time in prison and one pile Sophia wasn't sure about.

"What's this?" She tapped the top sheet of paper, then picked it up and began to read.

"Various medical records. Stig Ahlin has seen a number of his former colleagues in recent years. He's given me access to those as well."

"What do you want to do? Where should we start?"

The professor took half a step back as if to consider his work. He seemed satisfied. Despite the apparent chaos in his office, he was famous for his sense of order. This was one of the reasons they worked so well together. As a lawyer, Sophia had learned that half the battle was already won if you were more familiar with the file than your opponent was. The case file was the only reality you needed to care about when you were preparing for a hearing. Certainly, the principle of orality was in play: nothing except what was presented to the court during the hearing could be used to reach the final decision. But everyone who'd worked at a court or with court proceedings knew that this was where the secret lay. It was crucial to know the written material so well that you were the one who guided what came up in oral arguments and how it was presented.

In a case like this, when the challenge was to try to prove that a decision had been wrong, and so off the mark that the Supreme Court would be forced to rip it up, you had to go back. Find that one thing everyone else had missed. Or what had been buried under other information, most likely by the person who had been more familiar with the file.

"How much have you had time to read?"

Hans Segerstad had taken a seat in his desk chair. He looked at Sophia, who was still standing by the stacks of documents.

"The rulings, of course, and most of the preliminary investigation. I've still got quite a bit of the slush pile left, but I'll be done with that soon."

Sophia noticed the creases on Hans's forehead. He didn't believe her.

"I didn't have much to do last week."

Hans nodded slowly. He knew it was a lie.

"So, if I asked you what Katrin Björk had eaten for

dinner on the night of the murder, you would be able to account for —"

"The dinner was standing untouched in her parents' home. Fish, salad, and a freshly baked chocolate cake. The autopsy showed that she had sampled the batter. Quite a bit, I assume, given that some of it was still in her stomach. And she had eaten something else a few hours before the murder, I think it was yogurt and a sandwich. Something along those lines. You don't need to test me, I'm a fast reader. You know I am."

Hans gave a reluctant smile. "Well then. Okay, if you had to limit yourself to three things, where would you start digging?"

"Where would I start? I'd keep away from what you've done already."

Hans Segerstad laughed appreciatively. "Smart. What's going on? Are you getting so old you're starting to show respect for your even older colleagues? Have you stopped believing I'm always wrong?"

"Hardly." Sophia had picked up one of the documents she hadn't seen before. "I'd stay away because I don't think what you've already written — about the evaluation of evidence and the need to create precedent in this particular arena — I don't think that's going to get us our new trial. Not a chance. We need something entirely different."

Segerstad snorted. "So, what I've done is completely worthless?"

"Yes. Or, not completely."

"Thanks."

"But it will be worthless if we don't come up with the other part. The part that will get us a new trial."

"And naturally, you'll be the one to figure that out. May I ask what it is?"

"You wanted three things, you said? Because good things come in threes?"

"Because no one has time for anything beyond that."

"Then we should start with the rulings. And the way I see it, there really were exactly three factors that got Stig Ahlin convicted, and three things we need to show are incorrect. If we're going to convince the Supreme Court to grant a new trial."

"I'm listening."

Sophia smiled. It was always like this, no matter what they were discussing. He sat down, settled in comfortably, posed questions and assessed her answers, graded her. She stood up and presented what she'd learned. He told her whether she was right or wrong. It was like ballroom dancing. They knew the steps.

"First of all, there's what isn't in the decisions. The demonization of Stig Ahlin. The fact that he was depicted as the worst person imaginable. When he confessed to not only knowing Katrin Björk, but also having had a sexual relationship with her, it appeared extremely improbable that she would have known someone equally horrible, or possibly even more horrible. We have to change that image. The findings rule out alternative perpetrators. We must show that to be wrong. And by that I don't mean we have to solve the mystery, that we have to find whoever did it.

We only have to open up the possibility that he exists. Not finger someone and give his name and description, just open that door. In order to do that we need to get to know Katrin better. I don't believe in saints. I don't believe that Katrin Björk was one. Hell. Surely not even Mother Teresa could have been a saint as a teenager, right?"

"How will you do it? Did you find something in the preliminary investigation?"

"Yes. Something we can start with, anyway. There's an interview with an old friend of Katrin's that caught my attention. She claimed Katrin had a lot of boyfriends. And that she hated the guys at school. I'd like to talk to her again."

"Do you think you'll learn anything new that way?"

"I don't know. But I'm not ruling it out. Because the investigation contains next to nothing about Katrin. And far too little about the life she lived. They did some routine work at first, but then...it's as if everything ground to a halt when Stig Ahlin came onto the scene. Once he showed up, they focused entirely on him. They were so overjoyed that they dropped everything else. And Katrin could have had another boyfriend. I think it's unpardonably sloppy that there's nothing else in the file. Surely that can't have been it? Surely there's no way Stig Ahlin was her first and only guy. A fifteen-year-old doesn't go from grooming the prettiest pony in the stables to jumping in bed with a thirty-five-year-old doctor who likes hookers. At least not without stopping somewhere else along the way."

Hans nodded slowly.

"Good. Find out as much as you can about Katrin and her male acquaintances. We'll need that. About her problems. Her parents. What was her home life like? I've always thought it was remarkable that a responsible girl like her slept with Stig Ahlin. But I'm sure you know nothing about that stuff, right? I assume you were hardly the rebellious type. You were probably conscientious through and through."

"Yep," said Sophia.

"And there are experts on this kind of thing too, these days. We know more than we did in 1998. About the destructive behaviors of young girls. You know — when they cut themselves or burn themselves with cigarettes. A sweet girl sleeping with a thirty-five-year-old doctor who likes hookers. Why would she do that? Who can explain it? Do you know anyone?"

Yes, I do, she thought. *But he's with his family, putting up Christmas decorations and buying presents for his wife so she'll forgive him for working too much.*

"I'll give some thought to who we could ask," she said. "Someone who would know. But I'll start with the friend. That will give me an idea."

That journalist. The one who'd written the article about Katrin. The one that didn't simply heap praise. She'd already called him, but he hadn't answered. *I have to try again. He might have something important to tell me.*

"What else? What's the second part?"

"The incest allegations. Those are a huge problem, even if he was never charged. Because they colored everything else. The image of Stig Ahlin. That's not going to get us our new trial either, but if we can prove that the investigation was lacking in that area, it might help us along the way. Since the Supreme Court is already aware of all the problems with incest cases in the nineties, it's as if they're already limbered up for it. I think they'll listen to what we have to say on that front."

Hans Segerstad poked his tongue into his cheek. He leaned forward.

"I don't think you should dig around in that. I hear you, and I might even agree that you have a point. But as you said yourself, it's no cause for a new trial. The incest allegations didn't play a role in the case, nor will they be part of our petition. Let that go."

"But they were a big part of the public image of 'that monster Stig Ahlin.'"

"We're not appealing to the public, we're dealing with the Supreme Court. Let it go, I said. Not even you will have time to deal with everything. What's the final piece in your trinity?"

Hans Segerstad was smiling again. He knew very well what it was.

"Stig Ahlin confessed that he knew Katrin, that he had a relationship with her. That was a big mistake. If I may say so. But the strongest evidence that he was present at the scene of the homicide was the part about the bite marks. Tooth prints? That it was his particular set of teeth. Tooth prints, is that the phrase?"

Hans shrugged. "The marks left by a bite. Bite marks. Go on," he urged.

"Those are a very big problem," she declared. "They're why he was convicted. Without them, he would have been acquitted."

Hans Segerstad nodded.

"The prosecutor submits an opinion that says the bite marks are...I don't recall the exact numbers...that with some degree of certainty, they came from Stig."

Hans Segerstad rose, took a document from the table, and read it aloud.

"'Can, with certainty, be said to correspond to...'"

"Right." Sophia gave a deep sigh. "And on that basis, the court claims it's proven that the marks came from Stig's teeth, and that it is proven beyond all reasonable doubt that Stig Ahlin caused those wounds when he murdered her. They rule out the possibility that Stig bit her, but someone else killed her."

Hans put the document back down and resumed his spot behind his desk.

"You disagree?"

"I'm not as convinced that this opinion is God's word, carved into an incontestable stone tablet and handed down, with no middleman and no room for alternate interpretations, to Moses or the judge at court."

"Do I understand correctly that you're not a fan of *CSI*?" Hans spun in his chair.

"No. You know I'm not. I am sick to death of how the courts are overpopulated with people who've gotten the idea that forensic medicine is an exact science."

Hans Segerstad chuckled in satisfaction.

"Still, there's one part you have to agree with," he said. "If Stig did bite her, then it's reasonable to say he also killed her. On that point, at least, I agree with the judges. We have to do something about that analysis. Because the court believed it."

"That is definitely our biggest problem. But we can't settle for just calling the methodology into question in a general sense. That happened at both district court and appeals court. We need to demonstrate that the results were in error. The prosecutor doesn't want to send the samples for new, official testing. We'll have to do that on our own. And those tests must show, plain and simple, that those were not Stig Ahlin's teeth. If we can prove that, the Supreme Court must grant a new trial."

Sophia and Hans fell silent. They considered this for a moment. There wasn't much more to say. Really, nothing could be certain. It was far from a given that the Supreme Court would grant a new trial just because they managed to produce new test results that contradicted the old ones. The Supreme Court very seldom granted new trials. New information wouldn't be enough. It would also have to be sensational. And not even then could they be certain to get a retrial. It was close to impossible.

"But how will we do it?" Hans Segerstad had made a tent of his hands and was looking at Sophia. "What can they test now, after all these years?"

"I don't know. But we have to try."

They fell silent again. Hans rocked on his chair. Sophia looked around for somewhere to sit.

"I hope Stig Ahlin isn't expecting a quick solution. That he's prepared to wait."

"Well, he doesn't seem to be dying of stress, anyway." Hans Segerstad clasped his hands behind his neck.

"But if the truth is, he's stuck in prison for no good reason...," Sophia trailed off.

Hans's jaw tensed. "Then we'd better get to work."

Sophia took a seat in one of the chairs at the conference table. She lay her hand on top of one stack of papers and looked at the sea of documents. At all the files that had amounted to Stig Ahlin's fate. The piles that were his only hope for a future beyond the one the courts had decided for him. Thousands of documents, and no one but the two of them looking for an answer. It was up to her and Hans Segerstad. If there was something there, they would find it. They had to find it. There was no other option. Otherwise the answer would remain hidden.

16

"I've never written this kind of letter before." They all started out that way. No one had ever written that she often penned this sort of letter, that this was just one of many. Stig Ahlin had once even received two letters from the same woman, with identical opening lines: "I've never written this kind of letter before. This is the first time."

It was pathetic. They were pathetic. But these letter writers should get a bonus from the post office, Stig thought. Because no one else sent actual letters anymore. Only prison groupies and people who wanted him to die. And the only people who received handwritten letters in the mail anymore were people like him.

The women always wanted to tell him the same things. That they understood him. That they wanted him. They'd seen something in him that no one else had. For reasons they couldn't quite explain, Stig was the one they'd been looking for all their lives. Some described in detail what they wanted him to do to them, sexually. Some enclosed photographs. Those photos didn't always make it through inspection — Stig assumed they took the nudes and pinned them up in the guards' office — but he kept the ones he was allowed in one of his two desk drawers. Or else he got rid of them, so he wouldn't exceed the allowed prison limit of fifty postcards or photographs.

Among his own pictures, there was one of Stig and his family, the way they were before everything fell apart. It was an awful photo, taken indoors in their old apartment. Stig no longer recalled who the photographer had been — maybe he'd taken it himself with the timer function. Ida was blurry, in the center of the image; someone had brushed her hair out of her face, making it look like she had side bangs. She wasn't looking at the camera, but off to the right. The only one who was looking was her mother, Marianne, who had red-eye from the flash. Stig was sitting with his back to the others, as if he had already left them. He often thought he had.

The lens didn't capture the rest, what he recalled but wasn't in the shot: the green-glazed tile oven that leaked smoke into the room; the dining table they never used; their gazes that never met. The accusations, arguments so loud their next-door neighbors could listen in.

On the back of the photo, Stig had written "February 1996." Ida was two. Outside, the snow had been shoveled into tall piles. Two months later, he moved out. Later on, his wife would have reason to tell the newspapers she had kicked him out. That, naturally, was made up. He was the one who left them. He couldn't stay. He'd felt trapped. As if he'd known what being trapped really felt like.

The women who wrote to him said they understood how wronged he had been, and that they would fix him, repair what had broken. That they would teach him to trust again. That he could depend on them, even though he had been hurt by so many women.

Had he? Maybe. Maybe not. Stina, the first girl he got to kiss, had been twelve. They had skinny-dipped once, and she had downy fuzz between her legs and smelled like sweat. She stuck the tip of her tongue in his ear and said that was what people did. He opened his mouth against hers and sucked on her lower lip. His stomach fluttered, and he thought, *I'm in love.*

They played together all the time that summer. They were the only ones who hadn't gone to a summer cabin or a charter swimming pool. There was a phone booth on the platform for the train to Stockholm. You could buy candy in a kiosk right outside: Kexchoklad, Emser, Nickel, AKO toffees, and Zig Zags. They played there at the station — either they lay in the ditch and threw gravel at passing cars or they earned money. The sky hung over them, those fluffy clouds in blue skies that childhoods are meant to be full of. Stig no longer recalled who came up with the idea, but it turned out to be a lucrative one. It was the phone booth. A tiny opening, large enough for two or three grown-up fingers, and it wasn't hard to dig out the change that fell down at the end of a phone call, or that came back after using a one-krona coin to pay for a call that only cost twenty-five öre. They folded a small piece of cardboard to look like a box without a lid, then stuffed it up in that opening. Each day they ran to the train station, waited for a suitably unguarded moment, and emptied the phone of coins.

If only they could have gotten along, they would have become rich. Because each time they checked, there was money. One day they found eleven kronor and ten öre in the phone booth. It was remarkable that the piece of cardboard didn't fall out under the weight of the coins.

The day they became enemies began with a prank-call session from the phone booth. Stina would make prank calls until she went hoarse, but she seldom let Stig talk. There was no point, she thought. Stig was so bad at it that they would be found out right away. So, as Stina used a squeaky voice to talk to someone at city hall about flowers and allergies, Stig used a retracted ballpoint pen to carve things on the booth. Now and then he tugged at the cord; he wanted a turn too. But Stina just shoved him away.

Stig got bored. So he thrust his hand into Stina's bag and took out a photograph she always carried with her. It was of her mother — or at least that's what Stina said. But no one knew what Stina's mom looked like; she had left when Stina was a baby. Stig took the ragged bit of paper, which was yellowed and square. His laughter bubbling in his throat, he stepped out of the telephone booth, waving it at Stina.

She went bananas. She slammed the receiver onto its hook and ran at Stig, ran and ran and shoved him off the platform. Over the edge you were supposed to stay back from, the edge of the tracks where the train would arrive to pick up everyone going to Gothenburg or even to Stockholm, with its Gröna Lund amusement park and subways and the royal palace.

Stig fell. He screamed. But not very loudly; he even landed on his feet. Then he sat down with his legs folded beneath him and waited for death. At this, a man climbed stoically down onto the tracks and heaved Stig up with a strength that might have come from a life of manual labor. The whole adventure lasted somewhere between thirty and forty-five seconds.

Stig wasn't the one who had thrown his best friend down toward the millions of lethal volts that could have fried him to death. Stig was the one who believed he would smell like burned meat and that he would be buried in chunks, sliced up and grilled like the chicken he ate on days Mom didn't feel like cooking. Yet Stig was the one who got the blame. Quick as lightning, and without anyone bothering to ask what had really happened. Stina dashed off while he was being lifted to the platform, and when she came home she said he had done terrible things. She'd had to shove him, although she didn't mean for him to end up on the tracks. No one was interested in Stig's version of events. He simply had no shame. Plus, he was a thief. Because the second thing Stina did after she closed the door behind her was tattle about the phone booth. Stig was the only one to be punished for that too. Stina was given an ice cream. *Say you're sorry*, the grown-ups demanded. And then came the autumn leaves.

The women who wrote to Stig wanted him to get his sentence converted to time-limited. Attorney Sophia Weber wanted the same thing. The prison therapists talked about remorse. They wanted him to start over, have a new life. A different life. He could give in, improve himself. They would fix what was broken. *Say you're sorry*. He didn't understand what they meant.

17

Sophia was sitting on the floor of the living room, a long roll of paper before her: nine pages of A4 graph paper, taped together. On it she had drawn a timeline of the investigation into Katrin Björk's homicide.

There was a cold draft on the parquet. Nocturnal city sounds lay like a backdrop beyond the window.

Sophia had begun this practice back when she was studying the history of law. She would cover one wall of her student housing room with sheets of paper and fill in, using four different colors, the various events that marked legal milestones in current-day society. She hadn't removed the papers until exams were over and she was about to move out. Then, after much hesitation, she crumpled them up and threw them away. But if she closed her eyes, she could still picture that timeline: The Östgöta Law, 1290. King Magnus IV's Country Law, 1350. The Civil Code of 1734. The Criminal Code of 1864. The Constitution Act of 1974. She couldn't recall that these had in fact been helpful in preparing for exams, and yet they were what she remembered best of what she'd learned in her law school days. And she had come to realize it was a fantastic method to get an overview of a truly complicated case.

Now it was not Swedish legal history that she must memorize, but all the most important documents from the investigation of Katrin Björk's murder. She would locate them on the timeline. She didn't expect to finish in one evening, but she wanted to get started. Yet when she spread all the papers out on the floor of her apartment, she realized it would be best to get as far as she could before packing it all up again. And the hours had flown by. There was plenty to fill in. She was no longer aware of the time; she just wanted to finish up and go to bed.

Beyond getting a sense of the material, Sophia wanted to demonstrate that the investigation had changed direction when Stig Ahlin showed up. She had a feeling this was true, but there was no point in saying so unless she could give specific examples of the investigation's substandard quality and show that it had not been sufficiently unbiased, that they had been sloppy with much of the evidence.

During the first twenty-four hours after Katrin Björk's body was discovered, a number of documents had been drawn up, and almost as many were prepared in the following days. Only after a few weeks did new memos appear less frequently.

The first thing Sophia had drawn onto her overview was the emergency call. At 00:16, Katrin Björk's neighbor had called emergency dispatch. One hour and fourteen minutes later, the first police officers arrived on the scene.

Katrin's body had been delivered to the Solna offices of the National Board of Forensic Medicine less than twenty-four hours after she was killed. The initial examination of her body was performed there.

A great many of the samples harvested there were later sent to the city of Linköping to be analyzed at SKL, the National Laboratory of Forensic Science. The results from these tests bore various dates. Some test results were ready quickly; others took time. Other, additional analyses were only ordered after the investigation sparked new questions.

Sophia took notes by hand. She filled page after page of her timeline with new information. She wrote on every available surface; words climbed along the edges of the pages, onto the other side, and sometimes she had to tape on extra notes to have room for everything.

This is too messy to be useful, she thought. *Lars's intern will have to copy down a clean version for me.*

Sophia picked up a document from the floor: the preliminary investigation leader's request that the marks on Katrin's body be examined. It had been addressed to the forensic odontologist in Solna, and according to the date it fit into Sophia's timeline just after Stig Ahlin was questioned for the first time. She moistened her fingertip and paged through the piles of paper. Where was the answer? When had the results come back?

That dentist really took his sweet time, Sophia thought. *So much time.*

She browsed on. Anna-Maria hadn't yet printed out all the documents from the file. But Sophia had brought all

the test results home, she was sure. It had to be somewhere in there.

Being a scientist could be the dream job for eighties kids,
she thought. *Hanging out in the Mushroom Kingdom. Doing
crosswords while you wait for your bacterial cultures to grow.
Watering them once a day, or whatever it is you do to get bacteria to reproduce. Not exactly super stressful. Although an
odontologist doesn't grow bacteria, right? Then why did it take
so long?*

Bingo. There it was. Sophia took the paper from the
floor and frowned. She looked at the request from the
investigation leader once more. It had been addressed to
the National Board of Forensic Medicine. But the results
had come from a lab in Great Britain.

An ambulance went by on the street outside. The morning paper dropped onto the rug and the mail slot closed
with a bang. Sophia was startled. It was still pitch black
outside. She looked at the clock; she'd worked for much
longer than intended. Way, way too long. In five hours, she
had to meet a client at the office. She needed to spend at
least a few of those sleeping.

Sophia put down the documents and gathered them into
a neat stack. She tried to fold up the timeline, so she could
take it to work and tack it up in her office. There wasn't
much room, but she would make it work. She wanted to
gaze at it so often that she saw it when she closed her eyes.

*The interview with Stig Ahlin's mother is what made them
suspect Stig,* she thought. *It's not unusual that the prosecutor would have requested an analysis of the bites only once Stig*

Ahlin was a suspect. Before then, they didn't have any teeth to compare the marks to. And isn't it perfectly logical that they would have turned to the forensic odontologist in Solna?

Sophia gathered the rest of the papers that were spread across her living room floor and put them into the file as well. Before she closed it, she took out the analysis again. The stamp in the upper right corner said that the document was a translation from an original in English. She hadn't been surprised to find that it was a foreign report; those were done regularly. And she had already compared the translation to the English version. It seemed perfectly correct. What she had overlooked the first time was the addressee on the prosecutor's request. It hadn't sparked a reaction before. But it should have.

Now it was time to sleep. She had to sleep. But after the meeting tomorrow she would take another look at the slush pile. Because something was off. If the prosecutor had sent a request to the National Board of Forensic Medicine, why had the results come back from a different lab?

18

Tech support. Sophia and her colleagues forked over tons of money for it each month. She had no idea why, because no one ever actually offered support. But Sophia tried to get some anyway.

She'd called tech support because she wanted help turning the digital materials she'd received from Hans Segerstad into searchable text. Then she would be able to identify what came from the National Board of Forensic Medicine or the National Laboratory of Forensic Science, make a list of search terms, and weed out some of the enormous amounts of scanned material.

After more than thirty minutes on hold and thirty-five minutes in dialogue with a man who gave instructions she couldn't understand and chewed her out when her computer screen showed messages that didn't match what "should have" been there, she gave up. She hung up the phone and went back to picking through the slush manually.

Not a single file was date-stamped. Nor did the file names provide any hint of their contents. Rarely, a document was numbered. But what that number meant was impossible to know before you opened it. Sometimes it was a case number; sometimes it was an abbreviation of the date. In a few instances, it seemed the number had to do with a classification system used by the police.

Sophia found she simply had to open each file and start reading until she knew what it was about, at which point she could close it and move on to the next one. It was an extremely tedious task.

Once every half hour, she stood up, jumped up and down in place a few times, and rubbed her eyes. Then she went back to clicking and reading, closing and scrolling. But she didn't give up. It was there. It had to be there.

And she was right. It had taken over nine hours, but there it was in front of her. Just what she was looking for. Something she would have found in minutes if the material had been searchable. Sophia expanded the document so it filled her screen. Then she leaned back. It was a relatively large file and contained several individual documents.

Sophia read it. She looked at the photographs. Once, twice. The date. When she scrolled down, she also found the prosecutor's handwritten notes on the file. They were attached to the analysis and had been scanned at the same time. District Prosecutor Petra Gren had written, in her upright cursive: "The forensic odontologist's analysis does not provide useful results. Nor can SKL's analysis bring anything of value to the investigation."

Sophia raised her arms over her head in a lonely gesture of victory. She clenched her fists and smiled.

She really would have liked to share this with someone, laugh out loud, say *I swear it's true,* have a celebratory beer. But her colleagues had gone home; she was the only one left at the office. She couldn't even call Hans Segerstad. Even he should be asleep at this hour.

No useful results, she thought, shaking her head. *How did that damn prosecutor get away with it? For thirteen years.* Sophia clicked the Print button. *But it's all over now. Because I'm going to show her just how useful it is.*

Katrin
1998

It had been ten days since Stig Ahlin contacted investigation headquarters to report his relationship with Katrin Björk. Bertil and district prosecutor Petra Gren had withdrawn from the rest of the investigation team. They were holed up in Gren's office to review the state of their investigation.

"I want to bring him in now." Bertil stood up and opened the door into the hallway. It was stuffy in there. He could hardly breathe. "I want to lock him up. Tear apart his goddamn apartment and his goddamn car and his goddamn office."

"You may want to," Petra Gren cut him off. "But you can't. Surely you can see that for yourself."

Bertil turned to his colleague. She was sitting down, not even looking at him — she was inspecting her own nails, meticulously and attentively, as if they were her greatest concern in life.

"Why should I see it?" Bertil could tell he was speaking far too loudly. But it didn't matter. He didn't care if the whole department could hear him, if only Petra would listen, because this was important. "We need to shift into higher gear. Not only is it past time to bring him in, it's absolutely necessary. We're talking about an acute situation here. You have to get us a search warrant. You have to. Now. Immediately."

Petra Gren looked up. "Explain to me why I have to do that." She was spitting the words. "Explain yourself!" She raised one hand and pointed at him. "You're the one, you told me that Stig Ahlin is on guard because of the other investigation. Otherwise he wouldn't have called us. Ahlin has had all the time in the world to clean up. To think everything through. You see, Bertil Lundberg, I don't have to do anything. Because if we aren't certain that we can keep Stig Ahlin once we've got him, if we're not careful...we'll end up finding nothing and we'll have to release him, and then...if that happens, this investigation will be DOA. We might sabotage everything, and I want you to understand that."

Bertil just stared at her. At Petra and her extended index finger. He could hardly believe this was really happening. She was sitting there pointing at him. Raising her righteous finger and shaking it at him as if he were her little boy. What was wrong with her? That damn woman must be crazy. Where should he start?

"It's not too soon," he managed to say as she slowly lowered her hand. "Not a minute too soon. And I have no intention of sabotaging this. If only the office of the prosecutor would be so kind as to help out for a change. What are you waiting for? A divine revelation? We don't have anything more. This is it. You have to let me put some pressure on him. Perform a search. Let him sweat in jail. Because my colleagues sure aren't helping. No ma'am. They're handling him with kid gloves and hardly asking any questions about all the shit he's subjected his daughter to."

Bertil bit back the rest. He shoved his fist into his pocket and clenched his teeth, holding in everything he might have said about her ever-unreasonable demands that they must find what didn't exist. His team had been working around the clock ever since the night of the murder. Around the clock, for a month. But District Prosecutor Petra Gren got to pick up her kids from day care at five o'clock and stay home to wipe their snotty noses one week a month, basically.

"Put pressure on him?" Petra Gren snorted. She stuck her index finger in her mouth and began to gnaw at her nail polish, which was already half chipped off. "Do you seriously think your refined interrogation techniques are going to fix this for us? That you'll get Stig Ahlin to break down like a half-alcoholic wife beater? Get him to confess? Forget it. It's not happening. And what do you think you'll find if you search his apartment? A video of the crime that he kept to jerk off to at night? Her bloody bra in a shrine in the bathroom?"

Instead of responding, Bertil turned around and closed the door into the hallway again. Then he fell back into the visitor's chair and rubbed his eyes. They stung; his eyelids were scratchy as sandpaper.

"Stig Ahlin is no dummy," Petra continued. "He does absolutely everything right. He's cooperative, but only because it's to his advantage. He talks, but he doesn't say anything we don't already know. Obviously, he will have gotten rid of anything that might help us in the investigation."

There's no point, Bertil thought. *There's no point in trying to explain. She'll never understand what I mean.*

Petra had started paging through the documents on the desk in front of her.

"There's no sperm, no blood, and no DNA we can use, no fingerprints we can't explain — they're sure of that?"

Bertil sank farther into his chair. All he could do was shake his head. They'd discussed the test results a thousand times. They'd already been around that track. Several times. He refused to go back to square one. If Petra wanted to collect tickets for that ride, she could do it on her own.

"What about this forensic odontologist?" Petra was still going through the documents. "What is there to say about him?"

"Yes, what is there to say about that?" Bertil looked at Petra. "I called him. Explained the situation. That we have a victim with half-moon-shaped wounds on her body and a woman who says our main suspect bit her and their daughter both. That we have hookers who can testify that Stig Ahlin likes to get his teeth into the people he has sex with. What do you want me to say about that goddamn dentist? It should have been great for us. If only he'd done his job."

Bertil leaned forward and buried his head in his hands. He massaged his temples. Now it was Petra's turn to be silent. Bertil went on.

"I don't know why I'm jumping on you like this," he said. "You'll have to excuse me. I'm so tired. But that damn snob...I was as clear as could be. Compare the marks on Katrin's body with Stig Ahlin's teeth. Thanks. How hard can it be? But you know how they are. That smartass took half an hour to explain to me how busy he was. And a few days later, he came back with...with that." Bertil gestured at the papers on Petra's desk. "Couldn't he have given us something? They're usually so good at wrapping it up in scientific gobbledygook so they don't have to say anything for sure. But no siree Bob. Not when we really need it. I suppose he was terrified of saying anything that might help us, because then he might have to drag himself away from his work to explain what he means in a crowded courtroom. And answer brand-new follow-up questions. And how would he have time for that? What a goddamn coward."

Petra smiled faintly. It didn't reach her eyes. She had stopped chewing on her nails.

"It's not about cowardice," she said.

"I know." Bertil nodded.

"I want to see Ahlin locked up too. Just as much as you do. I keep lying awake at night thinking about her. Seeing that little girl...but I have to be able to charge him, get him convicted. And what we have isn't enough."

"I know." Bertil's head kept moving for another few seconds, up and down. Deep down, he knew she was right. It wasn't enough.

When he had stopped nodding he stared instead, resigned, at the forensic odontologist's report, which was still lying there between them on Petra's desk. It was unusable. Neither of them said the word out loud, but both of them were thinking it. Resolved by the police; no charges filed. The worst kind of failure: to know who the guilty party was but with no way of doing anything about it. That was where they were headed.

"I've been thinking about her too," said Bertil. "And about Ahlin's daughter. Does that goddamn odontologist know who pays his salary? Does he understand why he has that job in the first place?"

The prosecutor didn't respond. Instead she picked up the document and examined it. Read it.

She must have read it more than a hundred times, Bertil thought, just as he had. Searching for something between the lines, something they could use to justify a new request for a supplementary statement. An adjustment. A rewording.

A wrinkle deep as a slash from a knife ran between Petra Gren's eyebrows. The skin around her mouth was slack.

She's starting to look old, he thought. *Older than just a few months ago.* Then Petra began to speak in a different tone of voice.

"I met a British forensic odontologist at a conference in Berlin a while ago. He seemed very knowledgeable. And..." — it took her a second to think of the right word — "...pragmatic in a way we're hardly spoiled enough to see here in Sweden. He spoke like a real investigator, if you know what I mean. Considered himself part of the crime-fighting authority. He spoke about responsibility quite a bit."

Bertil nodded again. More slowly this time. He could feel a warmth spreading through his belly.

"We need people who feel responsible," he said. "Pragmatists. People who know how investigations work."

"You will be able to bring in Stig Ahlin. And I'll get you your search warrant. But I'm going to do something else as well. We're going to send those bite marks to a forensic odontologist who is better able to perform the sort of analysis we're after. They're more advanced in Great Britain than we are, on a number of fronts. It's not as if our National Board of Forensic Medicine are the only ones who can do forensic dentistry. And their experts are far from the most sophisticated."

"That sounds like a good idea," he said. "One of your better ones. And while you're doing your thing, I'll have a serious talk with Stig Ahlin. And go through his damn apartment with my very own fine-tooth comb. We'll find something."

"Then that's that," said Petra Gren. She stood up and came around her desk. "And once you've brought him in we'll get a proper dental impression. Make a good cast we can send to the foreign expert. That ought to make his job easier."

They shook hands. Petra's was perfectly dry, and her grip was firm. Bertil smiled, and Petra smiled back. Something had come to life in her eyes.

"Thanks," said Bertil. "Thanks a hell of a lot."

19

They were all out of wrapping paper. Norah had asked Adam to buy five rolls, but they'd already used it up. Of the last one there was only a four-inch scrap of unevenly cut red paper with a silver moose pattern. It wasn't enough to wrap Thumbkin. Much less the items he'd actually purchased.

He pulled out the kids' craft drawer. At the very bottom, among dried glue sticks, blunt scissors, and glitter sand, was a sheet of blue construction paper. It could work to wrap one of his two presents for Norah. He'd bought her a flannel nightgown and a bottle of perfume, the same kind he'd bought last year — he assumed she would have used it up by now. If this didn't work, he'd have to go to the twenty-four-hour shop on the corner to see if they had any wrapping paper. He could scarcely wrap his wife's Christmas presents in old newspaper.

He gazed sadly at the drooping bag with the newly purchased nightgown and turned the plastic-encased perfume bottle over a few times. What a lack of imagination. But Norah hadn't asked for anything. What was he supposed to do?

"It doesn't matter," she'd replied when he asked. And he knew what she was thinking. That everything turned out wrong in the end anyway. There was no point in trying; she was always disappointed by his gifts.

Naturally, Norah had taken care of the kids' presents on her own. She knew precisely what they wanted: the exact brands of jeans her son should have, the exact name of the latest tiny plastic animal with high-heeled shoes their daughter collected. Norah was in the know on everything. The Christmas list that was changed three times per day, which things they needed and which ones they wanted, which weeks Legos were in and when they suddenly became hopelessly out. He left her to it. Because he had no clue.

Every year, Adam asked for the same thing. One single thing. Fewer Christmas presents. But Norah wouldn't listen. Instead he ended up feeling like Ebenezer Scrooge, sitting there swearing over plastic packaging that protected the kids' toys as if they had been constructed of Chinese porcelain rather than by Chinese children.

This year would be just as repellent. Even the kids had to think this was too much. The apartment would fill to bursting with trash. All that paper Norah spent hours wrapping around the presents would be torn to shreds in a matter of seconds. The tiny plastic animals would be buried under mountains of empty packaging from stuff the kids had already forgotten they'd received.

Adam tried to fold the sheet of paper around the perfume bottle. It didn't work. Clearly, he should have asked them to gift wrap it back at the store. But the line had been so long that he didn't feel like waiting. And he'd assumed, given how much wrapping paper he had bought, that there would be a roll left.

He put the paper back in the craft drawer and went out in the hall. There was no helping it; he would have to do more shopping. And he had to calm down before tomorrow. He had to be in a good mood. He had to be cheerful. Anyway, it was too late to do anything about Norah's Christmas shopping and he didn't want them to fight on Christmas Eve too.

The whole family would gather. Adam's brother would be coming over with his kids. Adam's dad would fall asleep on the couch with a box of Aladdin chocolates in his lap. Norah's mom would start washing the dishes before they were done eating. Adam would give his presents to Norah. Norah would lean over the coffee table and let him kiss her cheek. Adam's mom wouldn't leave Norah in peace in her own kitchen, and Norah would be happy when the kids opened their presents and shrieked in excitement over what only she knew they wished for above anything else. It would be annoying and tense, cozy and pleasant. It would be as it always was. They just had to keep from fighting.

I should go to a real store, Adam thought. *Buy a decent present for Norah. A pair of earrings. Or a necklace. She would like that.*

Tomorrow was Christmas Eve. And in three days he would head to the trash-sorting station with their holiday garbage. Then everything would go back to normal. But tomorrow he had to be cheerful. Decently horny, extremely cheerful, and very grateful. Or at least considerate.

Why didn't he know what sort of present his wife wanted? After all these years? Why couldn't he figure out how to make her happy?

20

"What will you and Sherlock be starting off with?"

Sture was lying on his side on the sofa. The TV was blaring in the background. The Christmas tree was all lit up in its corner. Sophia had bought it the day before, had dragged it home from Östermalmstorg. She'd cut off the lowest branches to hang on the front door. The Christmas star, the red paper one that had hung in Grandpa and Grandma's kitchen when she was little, was aglow in her kitchen window and all four cream-colored Advent candles were lit.

Sophia's mother would not be making an appearance. She'd called the evening before to say she was sick. She would be staying home for Sture's sake; she didn't want to spread her germs to her father. Only after she hung up did it occur to Sophia that her mother had never mentioned what was ailing her. But it certainly hadn't sounded like she had a cold.

The remains of their lunch were on the kitchen table. It was just past four o'clock; it was dark out, and they would eat the same meal for dinner. And for breakfast tomorrow. If they ever felt like eating again. Sophia had brought a pillow from her bed and was lying on the floor. In her mouth was a fresh piece of toffee with the paper still on. It was the only way she could get the candy loose.

"What do you mean, starting off? What are you talking about?" Sophia spit a sticky glob into her hand. A wet chunk of paper had adhered to her tongue and another was stuck in a molar filling.

"Stig Ahlin's petition. The one that's going to put an eternal shine on your name and end up listed under its own special heading in the National Encyclopedia. Along with your photograph. There you sit, Sophia Weber, Attorney at Law, leaning slightly over your grandfather's mahogany desk, sword in one hand and tiny gold scale in the other. Where are you going to start, you and that disaster Segerstad? By dragging Katrin Björk through the mud?"

Sophia put down the candy dish and flipped onto her side. She wrangled the button of her pants free and pulled her shirt down as best she could. She had to stop eating.

"The bite marks. The ones that were found on Katrin's body and matched Stig's teeth."

Sture chuckled. "Is that so? And what will you do about them? Claim that he bit her in a friendly way, rather lovingly, a few minutes before some other random guy showed up to do her in?"

"It wasn't the National Board in Solna who did the tests," Sophia mumbled. "It was a different lab. They sent the whole thing abroad. And besides, this type of test is extremely questionable."

"Aha! Of course. A conspiracy." Sture raised his eyebrows. "I should have guessed. Naturally you can't petition for a new trial without some conspiracy theory in your back pocket. I'm starting to see where you're planning to go with this. You intend to prove that the bone fragments in the fire pit are really burned plastic."

"Unfortunately, it's not the same lab as in the Thomas Quick case. We didn't get that lucky."

Sture laughed even louder. He heaved himself off the sofa and headed for the kitchen, snorting.

"The brandy's in the pantry."

Sture returned with two glasses and a bottle clamped under his arm. Sophia shook her head when he handed one of the half-full glasses to her. He poured the contents into his own and sat back down on the sofa.

"And what will you noble, honest soldiers do about Ahlin's bite marks? It's going to be difficult to do any new tests on poor Katrin. Or will you march down to her young grave, backs straight and proud, shovels over your shoulders? Demand she be exhumed?" Sture took a considerable gulp of brandy. "Haven't you got some other pointless task to keep busy with? Didn't you ever learn to knit?"

"No," Sophia said. She bit back the rest of her reply. "I never learned to knit."

"What are you thinking, little Sophia? Are you thinking?"

Sophia lay where she was, hesitating. It was usually best to let it be. Refuse to let him provoke her. She didn't want to fight. At worst she would start to cry; at best she would fly into a rage and lose her temper. And that would upset Sture. It was Christmas Eve, and she didn't want to upset him. She picked up another piece of toffee but changed her mind and put it back. Then she stood up and left the room. She didn't feel like being ridiculed.

Two minutes later, she returned with a dark blue plastic folder. She placed it on the coffee table and took out a bundle of photographs, a few forms, and a piece of paper that looked like a drawing. She handed one of the forms to Sture.

"The test results presented during the trial were not the only ones produced during the investigation. They weren't even the first ones. The court wasn't privy to the original. Those results — which you can see there — said that it was impossible to state conclusively that the marks on the body were in fact bite marks."

Sophia pointed to a box near the bottom of the form. Sture took his reading glasses from his shirt pocket and read it. After a few seconds, he pushed the glasses down his nose and looked at Sophia.

"What do you mean, the court wasn't privy to this?"

Sophia cleared her throat.

"Just that. The original tests were done by a forensic odontologist with the National Board. But they are not included in the preliminary investigation. Why Stig's former lawyers didn't bring this up during the trial is a mystery. No one will ever be able to explain that to me. I found those test results in the slush pile."

"The slush pile?"

Sophia nodded. "The slush is what we call everything that doesn't end up in the material the prosecutor bases their charges on. The leftovers, you could say. All the extra stuff."

"I know what the slush pile is, Sophia, there's no need to educate your grandfather."

"I'm sorry, of course you know. Right. So, what was the court able to look at? Not the forensic odontologist's report, anyway, because it was considered unusable. Instead photographs of Katrin's body and a cast of Stig's teeth were sent to a lab in Great Britain. Those were the results that were presented in court later on. And people put faith in those tests. One hundred percent. Because Swedish courts automatically think anything done in Great Britain is of superior quality to what we do here. The only thing that makes a bigger impression than tests ordered by Scotland Yard are American tests. Because in the United States they know everything and a little more, as all Swedish lay judges have seen on *CSI*."

Sophia pulled over Sture's glass of brandy and took a sip. She made a face.

"And I know what that goddamn prosecutor is going to say when I call to ask why it wasn't included in the indictment. She'll say it didn't contribute anything. Because that's what people like her always say. As if they can't comprehend that it could possibly be of significance when they don't find anything. As if it's a surprise that a lack of findings can be absolutely critical for the defendant's argument. The prosecutor should have allowed this to remain in the material that was presented at court."

Sture nodded thoughtfully. He let Sophia continue.

"A conspiracy, you say? Unfortunately, you're wrong. It's no conspiracy, that's just how Swedish prosecutors work. I think they would just call it 'procedure.' But the fact that Ahlin's former lawyers didn't find this, that's just beyond inexcusable. But it's also typical. Most lawyers can't be bothered to look through the slush. I suppose they don't think that it's part of their job. They don't have time, because they have a golf handicap to improve, a Rotary meeting to attend. They don't want to get their delicate little fingers dirty by digging through it. Or they don't have time. Because God knows, meticulous and time-consuming work is seldom compensated."

Sture wiped his nose with his wrist. "There's nothing wrong with Rotary."

Sophia ignored him.

"I asked Hans to take a closer look at that lab in England. And how they reached their conclusions. Not that I believe he did it himself, I'm sure he ordered some poor research assistant to do it, but he was able to report back that the odontologist they used no longer has official status in Great Britain. He lost his job moonlighting for Scotland Yard and now he works exclusively with fixing teeth."

Sophia handed the second form to Sture. His eyes narrowed as he read.

"And as you can see, this Englishman compared images of Katrin's body with a cast of Stig's teeth. That is a horribly questionable method of analysis. Just one year after Ahlin was convicted, there was a major study in the United States where ten experts were asked to look at pictures and try to match them with dental casts. They were wrong over 60 percent of the time. Unfortunately, this by itself is unlikely to get us our new trial. Because it was one of the studies that was sent in to the Supreme Court back when they requested certiorari."

Sture leaned across the coffee table and looked at the photographs Sophia had laid out. They were close-ups of marks on various parts of Katrin's body: spots, specks, bruises, wounds.

"And this is how they decided it was his teeth," Sophia said. "You can see here. Or, sorry, they decided..." She took the form back and read aloud from the translation: "'The analysis shows with certainty that an unquestionable link exists between the dental impressions that were found'...blah blah blah...'and the mold of Stig Ahlin's teeth.'"

Sture looked at the analysis. The prints that were deemed to match Stig Ahlin's mouth map were marked with numbers and arrows. There were also photographs of Stig's dental cast in close proximity to the various close-ups of marks on Katrin's body.

"Now, it's true that I can't make heads or tails of those test results," Sophia went on, "but I might be the stupid one here. Because I think the courts act as if anyone who knows their multiplication tables by heart has supernatural powers. But still. If you pause briefly from your habitual dissing of everything I do, you would have to agree that this is hard to understand. Or at least that it seems odd. That SKL, or, excuse me, the forensic odontologist, didn't get anywhere, but that the other guy, the British amateur, did, easy as pie. And…" — she pointed to the drawing in Sture's hand — "…what was more, he concluded that 'with certainty' there was an 'unquestionable link.' In legal terms, you can't be any more convinced than that. This is what got Stig Ahlin convicted of homicide. He's been locked up for over thirteen years because of this."

Sture didn't say anything. He sipped his brandy, his hand cupping the glass. He put it down and looked once more at the papers spread over the coffee table, one by one. He compared the photographs to the drawing. Then he put it aside, gathering up the documents and tucking them into the plastic folder, and picked up the remote instead. Sture looked as if Sophia's account had hit him square in the chin, and now he was hanging on the ropes. He had no desire to expose himself and let her win with a knockout. Instead of saying anything, he turned on the TV.

Sophia had sat back down on the floor. As Sture flipped between channels she tried in vain to remove the paper from another piece of toffee.

"I never learned to knit," she said, "but I've always got that shovel over my shoulder. I dig up bodies. That's my goddamn job. And I do it well, I want you to know. Your little Fialotta is happy to play gravedigger. Because each and every skull had a tongue in it and could sing once."

Sture had settled on a channel that was showing a duet between a man singing an opera in Italian and a woman singing pop music in English. Without taking his eyes from the screen, Sture cleared his throat and swallowed.

"Don't use quotes you don't understand," he muttered. "That skull had a tongue in it. The gravediggers didn't say that; it was Hamlet. The gravediggers were clowns. And how are you supposed to afford new tests? Who will perform them?"

"I don't know," Sophia admitted. "Segerstad has already requested, three times, that the prosecutor order new tests, but he's been rejected. Every time. And if you want to know what I think, I think that's just as well. That prosecutor isn't going to help us. No prosecutor will. Why would they? And anyway, we all know the answers depend on how you ask the questions. I want to be the one asking the questions, if any new tests are done. I don't want any help from the office of the prosecutor. Anything else just puts us at risk of ending up even worse off. We're in the process of compiling a list of everything we want to compare. Hans has found a dentist to talk to, and I've arranged a meeting with Sweden's only forensic odontologist in early January. We're planning to request the dental casts that were used for the analysis and ask someone else to compare them with the photographs — what do I know? One of those methods they use. Anything to give us more sophisticated results than that..." Sophia pointed at the lab report. "I'm going to try to convince the odontologist to take a look at it. Where we send it after that depends on what she says. Most of all, I want her to write us a report. I have no idea where we'll get the money for new tests from. But we have to be able to afford it. Because we can't just let this go."

"Hmm."

Sture turned back to the TV. His glass was empty.

After just a short time, it seemed he was tired. It wasn't easy for him to get up off the sofa. When Sophia offered her hand, he waved it away.

He stood up and went to Sophia's bedroom. He turned around at the door.

"This is a petition for a retrial you're dealing with. If memory serves, you need to provide evidence of new facts in order to have the right to a fresh review." Sture cleared his throat. "If that first report got caught up in red tape, or was buried in the slush pile, then it is a new fact in and of itself." Sophia nodded. Sture went on. "But I don't think you should expect it to be enough."

Sophia shook her head. She knew this. Far too well.

He closed the door behind him, but then opened it again.

"How many years has that lazy bastard Segerstad been paging through the files without ever noticing that? Answer me that. How long did it take you? A few weeks. Christ, Segerstad is the laziest goddamn academic I've ever heard of. And the competition in his field is cutthroat. Pass that on from me, would you? What a clown." He turned around again. She could hear him speaking, still, on the other side of the door. "And I need to sleep for a while."

Sophia turned to the TV and pulled over the dish of candy. It was time for an ad break. She picked up a piece of toffee. The paper slid off neatly. Nothing got stuck.

She considered the shiny candy before sticking it in her mouth. It tasted divine.

All of a sudden, there it is, she thought. *All of a sudden, it's really happening.*

Katrin

1999

The evening before the district court hearing, after nightfall but just before the late news, the nonpartisan organization Women Against Violence held a torchlight demonstration. Eleven hundred men, women, and children marched with representatives from three TV channels and the rest of the press corps through downtown Stockholm, from Hötorget to Sergels Torg. A leading female politician with the Social Democrats headed up the procession, arm in arm with a well-known member of the Liberals. Behind them walked one of Sweden's most popular pop stars, beside one of the Green Party spokespeople.

They didn't sing any songs or chant any slogans. But when they arrived at the sunken square, they gathered around a stage and, torches held toward the dark January sky, listened to six short speeches about patriarchal oppression. Officially, the demonstration wasn't about Stig Ahlin but demands for more effective laws surrounding prostitution, changes to standards of evidence in sex crimes, and greater allocations to Sweden's women's shelters.

Five of the speakers began by talking about the murder of Katrin. Stig Ahlin's ex-wife Marianne Sörensson marched in the third row, and at Sergels Torg she was given a spot at the very front. Ida was in her stroller with a pacifier in her mouth and her teddy in her arms; near the end of the march she dozed off and the pacifier dropped from her mouth and got caught in the open neck of her snowsuit.

Once the last speaker had finished, the final part of the demonstration began as the activists' torches were dropped into five enormous fire baskets. One by one, the torches were handed forward; thousands of burning pieces mixed and the flames grew wilder. Then the baskets were hoisted by cranes and the last few minutes of the news showed a live feed from the square, a violent sea of fire. As the demonstrators turned home, their torches burned high against the black sky, for the dream of a future free of oppression from men.

■ ■ ■

The lead judge, the notary, and the three lay judges were seated in the courtroom before the main doors were opened. The prosecutor and Stig Ahlin's counsel had also been allowed in ahead of time. They greeted the bench briefly and took their places to wait. No other case was on the docket that day: a necessary decision for reasons of security. Only then did the lead judge announce that the district court doors could be opened so people could start to file in.

Of the 212 seats in the gallery, 150 had been reserved for the media. Sixty-two of the audience members were ordinary people who had lined up outside the entrance, some of them since the night before. They had rolled up their sleeping bags, received visitor's badges, and were allowed in by the security officers.

Everyone, journalist or otherwise, had to leave their outerwear, bags, and other belongings in a neighboring courtroom. It would be used as a coat check for the duration of the trial, and it was guarded by armed police in uniform. Then, those who wished to observe the trial had to undergo a patdown and walk through a metal detector that had been purchased by the district court and used only twice previously.

Stig Ahlin arrived last of all. He was escorted to the courthouse under armed guard and brought in through the loading dock. He had no hoodie to hide under, no jacket to pull up in front of his face. It was too late for such measures. Instead he was wearing a chalk stripe suit, a white shirt, and a pale blue tie. He'd been allowed to change before leaving the jail. The clothes were his own.

He was led to the seat next to his counsel. They shook hands and he sat down. The room was dead silent, aside from the sound of a pen quickly scrawling across paper. Someone in the first row had a notepad on their lap, had been sent from the biggest morning paper to sketch the defendant. No photography was allowed in the courtroom. The ladies in the third row had their knitting needles confiscated at security, but they'd been allowed to keep their crossword books.

When Stig Ahlin took his seat, the lead judge did a roll call. Everyone was present.

■ ■ ■

The search had resulted in ninety-seven confiscated objects. Six of them were presented during the trial: a roll of electrical tape, a human skull, two videotapes with crudely pornographic contents, and two objects — a dog's leash and a riding crop — that were described as "sex toys." The defendant owned neither a dog nor a horse.

Stig Ahlin's attorney maintained that the court should not consider these objects to have any bearing on the case. The skull was from the research department at Karolinska Hospital. Stig had borrowed it with the aim of using it in his work. He often worked on his research at home. The electrical tape couldn't be linked to the victim; the videotapes and sex toys were irrelevant. The attorney also objected to the very classification of the objects as sex toys.

One of the witnesses called by the prosecution was a prostitute who had identified Stig Ahlin as a regular client. The idea was that she could attest that Stig Ahlin had shown sexually violent behavior. The prostitute could testify that Stig had wanted to tie her up, that he had bitten her during intercourse on a number of occasions, and that he had frequently wanted to use a variety of sadomasochistic implements.

Stig's attorney pointed out that Stig Ahlin had not been charged with any crime in conjunction with his previous sexual relationship with this witness. Thus, the woman's testimony was irrelevant to the case. Furthermore, there was nothing about the woman's story to suggest that Stig had forced her to participate in sexual acts against her will.

At last, Stig's ex-wife Marianne was examined. She began by testifying that she had found bite marks on her daughter's shoulder a few months before the murder.

When the prosecutor asked Marianne to explain how she could be so sure Stig Ahlin was the one who had bitten her daughter, Ahlin's lawyer interrupted. In a loud voice, his hand moving in angry circles, he objected that the examination of Marianne must be considered to fall outside the narrow scope of what the prosecutor aimed to prove, that it simply had nothing to do with the case at hand. The lead judge nodded reluctantly and said that the prosecutor must refrain from posing questions about the investigation that had been closed. He did not need to further specify what he was referring to. Everyone present in the courtroom had read about that other investigation in the papers.

When the prosecution was finished, Stig's attorney asked Marianne to tell the court how long she had been divorced from Stig. He asked her to confirm that she had initiated a parental-rights case against Stig Ahlin, in which she demanded sole custody of their daughter. When he asked if she hoped Stig Ahlin would be sentenced to prison, Marianne began to cry.

"I hope so many things," she said. And already, Stig Ahlin's attorney realized that he never should have asked.

But before he could stop her, she went on. "Most of all, I hope he can never hurt another little girl."

Katrin's parents were listening from the front row. They were dressed in dark colors, and the rest of the audience was watching them intently, as intently as if this were Katrin Björk's funeral. When the prosecutor showed photographs from the crime scene, Katrin's father stood up and left the room. Her mother remained seated; she wasn't crying. Her hands were clenched tightly in her lap, and at the end of the day they left together, through the back door. Not once during the whole trial did they respond to questions from the media.

The British forensic odontologist who had analyzed the bite marks on Katrin Björk's body was interrogated by video link. His face was projected onto a large screen that was brand-new, used in only three previous trials. The caretaker had attended a class to learn how it worked. The technology ran perfectly during Stig Ahlin's trial.

The interrogation was recorded, and the expert was interrupted at regular intervals, to let the interpreter speak. But the odontologist's English was well articulated and easy to understand.

The prosecutor and Stig's counsel both asked their questions. By way of conclusion, the judge leaned toward his live microphone. He had a question for the expert as well.

"Could you be wrong?" he wondered.

The odontologist smiled faintly and leaned toward the camera.

"Caligula's sister and Nero's mother, the violent-natured

Agrippina, sent her soldiers to kill Caligula's wife Lollia Paulina," he said in a measured tone. "The soldiers were instructed to bring back the corpse's head to prove that she was dead. But the head was badly defiled, and Agrippina was forced to lift its upper lip and look at the discolored front teeth to be certain it was really Lollia Paulina. This was back in AD 66. We have been using teeth for identification purposes for a very long time. We have analyzed both dead material and skin. A person's teeth are unique. There are no two people with identical sets. In this way, the use of dental impressions in forensics is like that of fingerprints."

The British expert paused. He could be seen, on the big screen, sipping a glass of water. He allowed the interpreter to catch up.

"But there's one thing that sets them apart from simple fingerprints," he said. "If you go to a woman's house for dinner, you'll leave any number of fingerprints all over, without necessarily being involved in anything violent. But you won't accidentally bite her arm, breast, or genitals. Only a bite mark proves violent intent. And we've known this for many years too — it's nothing new. The fact that violently inclined people may bite their victims has been a source of fascination for many researchers. We have a great deal of experience with this."

The odontologist's smile had grown wider. He leaned back and ran his hand down his faintly patterned tie.

"You wonder if I might be wrong, Your Honor. I consider it to be out of the question."

21

They'd put up a Christmas tree in the common room of the sex crimes unit. It was fake. Decorations made of potential allergens were banned, but someone had tossed tinsel on it and hung a dozen red balls. It even had lights. The ornaments on the tree were the only glass decorations in the unit. For some reason these had passed the inspection that typically forbade everything from real basketballs to metal silverware and china plates.

Stig Ahlin wasn't alone. A few of his fellow prisoners were eating in the kitchen area. Others were in their rooms, watching TV. The doors were open; lockup wasn't for a while yet.

One of the two guards who worked at the sex crimes unit had gone off to the staff room. He'd said he was going to get a newspaper but seemed to have ended up staying there. The TV was on and the little light on the security camera was glowing.

Three of Stig's fellow prisoners had been allowed to leave the facility. One of the ones whose request had been denied was in the family barracks, where he would spend two days with his wife and kids. He had one year left to serve and still wasn't divorced.

Stig hadn't even requested a furlough. There was no one on the outside who would agree to celebrate Christmas with him. He had no invitations.

In the early years, he'd made a couple of halfhearted attempts. He had always been denied. Ida's sixth birthday. Denied. Christmas, New Year's, Midsummer. Denied. Dentist's appointment. Denied. The barber. Denied. But in his third year, two weeks before Christmas, two days after he'd sent off his application, he had been granted furlough. He would be allowed to watch his mother die.

He had to be under guard during his leave, so Stig was driven to the hospital in a patrol car. Since he was considered violent he had to wear handcuffs in the car. Not until they arrived at the hospital were the cuffs removed. Stig had to take the elevator and walk down three long corridors accompanied by two guards in uniform. They walked on either side of him, trailing slightly behind, so close they all brushed against each other when they went around a corner or had to open a door.

Despite the guards, it wasn't difficult for Stig to remember what it had once been like in hallways like this. Doing rounds, his back straight, his role clear.

Stig Ahlin's mother was alone in her room. She had an IV for saline and morphine; beyond that, all the machines were unhooked. Someone had been by with flowers. But there were no cards, and Stig couldn't figure out who would want to give his mother flowers. Her friends were dead. Her illness had made new acquaintances impossible. The staff could have brought in bouquets left behind by another patient.

He considered it out of the question that Ida would have been allowed to visit her grandmother. Ida's mother didn't put in any effort for Stig's mother's sake. She thought it was pointless. Or it was a way to punish him.

But the flowers still reminded him of when Ida met her grandmother for the first time. How his mother held the baby without becoming frightened, even when Ida began to cry. It was as if it were ingrained in his mother's body: the memory of how to hold, how to comfort.

Stig lifted the vase; it smelled musty. The water had turned to slime. It was death, smiling scornfully at them both, masquerading as wilting petals. Stig set the vase out in the hallway.

This was the only furlough he'd ever had. He'd been allowed to stay at the hospital for two days. He sat by the bed, listening to his mother's uneven breaths, stroking her swollen face, eating in the cafeteria, sleeping on an extra bed the staff pulled in for him. And still she didn't die, not for another four days. One of the guards came to his room after lockup. Opened the door, gave him the news, and locked him back in again. Two turns of the key.

The Christmas tree at Emla Prison didn't smell like anything. He had spent thirteen Christmases more or less the same way. This was a day like any other. Stig changed the channel on the TV. A portly man in a folk costume was solemnly lighting a red candle.

"From all of us…," the man groaned as the candle went out and he had to start over. "From all of us to all of you, a very, very merry Christmas."

22

Adam woke up just after four. Norah was asleep. The streetlights outside glowed through the window; they'd forgotten
to pull the blinds and the light fell in stripes across her naked
body. He lay there listening to her breathing.

All the doors in the apartment were open. They hadn't
yet cleaned up after the meal. When the kids fell asleep,
their teeth unbrushed and their hands sticky with chocolate, he had carried them to bed, pulled off their pants
and heavy Christmas-present sweaters, and smoothed the
covers over them. The relatives were heading home; they
exchanged kisses in the hall, running back and forth with
forgotten bags, clothes, and presents. Norah and Adam
made them take some leftovers and said goodbye one last
time. When the front door swung shut again, they stood in
the hall in silence. The smell of warm bodies, Adam's dad's
aftershave, and just-snuffed candles hung in the air.

Adam had pulled Norah close; she'd laid her head on his
shoulder.

"We can clean up tomorrow," he had said. And she had
nodded, no disagreement; she had taken his hand and gone
to the bedroom.

Afterward she had lain on her side beside him, tucking her hands under her cheek and looking at him. He'd done the same, and they had talked.

"Do you remember...," she had said, and told him what she was thinking of. He'd laughed and put his arms around her, pulling her close and holding her for a moment. Then she had cupped his cheeks, letting her fingers slide back and up through his shaggy hair. She had kissed him, and he'd thought, *I don't even need to say I remember, because she already knows.*

Now she was sleeping. He gently drew the covers over her and moved closer, pressing against her back and tucking his hand under her breasts. Their children were in the next room.

He closed his eyes, nuzzled his nose against his wife's neck, drew in her scent, and thought, *This, nothing but this. This is all I want.*

23

Even before she stepped into Åhléns, Sophia regretted the shopping trip. But she needed a new jacket and a new pair of pants. Clothes she could wear in court. Her old suit was worn thin in the crotch and she hadn't been able to find someone who could patch it up. It seemed like overkill to hire a seamstress, and the dry cleaners said they didn't fix holes that large.

Hitting the post-Christmas sales had seemed like a good idea. She could do as she'd been admonished by the magazine she'd read last time she was at the salon: buy good quality, invest in something more expensive. That would even be environmentally friendly. Grabbing a few garments at H&M without trying them on first — no more of that. This would be the start of her new, more glamorous life. She would at least procure herself some proper work clothes, without paying a fortune.

As Sophia approached the entrance she allowed herself to be swept up. By the current — that's how it felt. A compact mass of bodies all moving in the same direction, away from depression and the cards that were maxed out for Christmas, and toward quality or something that might feel like a great deal.

As she stood on the escalator, she felt her phone vibrating in her pocket. She wrangled it out and looked at the screen, but she didn't recognize the number. She hesitated. Sale shopping was not her favorite activity, but she was even less eager to visit the jail because an old client had spent the Christmas holiday beating up his wife or getting caught red-handed as he tried to break into someone else's home. She stared at the glowing number through four rings, then answered. If it was one of her clients, there was no point in trying to hide. She would only have to call back later.

"Hello!" It was a male voice. He seemed far away. "Can you hear me? Tor Bengtsson here!"

"Okay," Sophia responded hesitantly. She had no idea who this man was. Bengtsson? She had an old client named Bengtsson, but it didn't sound like him.

"You called me on the twenty-second," said Tor Bengtsson. "I'm sorry I didn't get back to you earlier, but I'm in Thailand. Just got your message. You wanted to talk about Stig Ahlin."

"Oh, right!"

As his identity finally dawned on her, Sophia found herself standing at the end of the escalator. A stroller hit her in the back, and she stepped sideways toward the kitchen section and stood beside the cupcake tins. She held her free hand over her ear to hear better. Tor Bengtsson was the journalist who had written the odd article about Katrin

Björk. She'd called him a few days before Christmas and had already managed to forget.

"Now I know who you are. I'm sorry."

"What do you want?"

Straight to the point, Sophia observed. *Naturally. It's expensive to call from Thailand, even if the evening paper picks up the bill.*

"I actually want to talk about Katrin Björk, not Stig Ahlin. You wrote a brief article about her years ago, and it sounded like you knew some things about her that weren't in the article."

"Why are you asking?" He sounded cross.

"Didn't I say? I'm Stig Ahlin's attorney, I'm helping him petition for a new trial. And I need to know more about Katrin Björk." Silence. Sophia wondered if they had been cut off. "Hello?"

"Does Stig Ahlin want to sit down for an interview?"

Sophia sighed. She should have guessed. "No. He doesn't."

"How do you know? You can't know. Have you asked?"

"Can't you just answer my question? We'll deal with all of that later. Do you remember the article you wrote?"

"Of course, I remember it," he replied. "It's not the sort of thing you'd forget. But you need to realize something. If Stig Ahlin is ready to talk, I'm ready to listen."

"I understand."

"Can you promise me an interview, then?"

"No. But I can promise that if Stig Ahlin decides to give an interview, I will tell him that you very much want to be the one who interviews him. And if you give us something we can use, something that helps us, then he might not hate you as much as he hates all the other journalists who wrote about the murder. But I can't make any promises. Because he hates you all. And that's not likely to change any time soon."

"Does he want money?"

"He doesn't need any money. Not so badly that he's about to beg you, in any case. He has no way to use it. His meals and lodging are free, he hasn't got any expensive hobbies, and he has enough money to buy new shoes."

"Okay. Good to know. You want to know more about Katrin Björk? Can you tell me anything about the petition?"

"Give it up."

"There must be *something* you can tell me."

"I can confirm that I'm working on a petition for an appeal for retrial on behalf of Stig Ahlin. Why don't we meet when you're back in Stockholm? We can discuss the petition. Not in detail, but in brief. How's that?"

"Good. I'll be back on January fourth. I'll give you a call then. When Katrin was killed — no, actually, when it became known that Stig Ahlin was a suspect in the murder of a fifteen-year-old girl, I was assigned to cover both stories. The murder wasn't really a sensation, but Stig Ahlin was. I was...I was twenty-four at the time, Jesus, time flies, and naturally I wasn't the lead on the stories, but I got to meet with the people our more senior reporter hadn't already talked to."

The line was crackling more.

"Can you hear me?"

"I can hear you again. You said you weren't alone on the coverage."

"No. Of course not. I was the little puppy of the team. Cute, but not housebroken. But I met some of her old friends. I was barely older than that gang. They talked to me. And what I learned didn't fit the angle the editorial team was going for. It simply wasn't their story. The article you're talking about — I only got it through because someone was subbing over Midsummer. But when the boss came back, that was the end of that. Plus, I got a whole lot of shit for it. I was damn proud of that psychologist's statement. I thought I'd really laid some good groundwork for the follow-up article that would have come later."

"But there was no follow-up."

"No. We weren't to breathe a word that Katrin could have been anything but top of her class, the teacher's pet, and her mother's pride and joy. At the editorial offices, we...well, there had been a serious debate about victim-blaming and, you know, we didn't have the cleanest consciences in the world. It wasn't the right time to start talking about whether Katrin's skirt had been too short, if you know what I mean."

"But her skirt was too short?"

"Yeah. Or, well..., it wasn't quite that simple. I got the feeling that she'd had a rough time. She lived it up a little, despite her top-of-the-class reputation. And she'd had to be driven home from some school dance because she got too drunk. Some of the guys talked about her, that she put out. The kind of girl whose name you can read in bathroom stalls. I met six different guys who claimed they'd slept with her. But, I mean, I don't know if it was true, they might have said that to impress me, teenage boys are weird. And sometimes it passes. And why would we write about that? She could sleep with as many people as she wanted, right? It didn't make the whole thing any less sad. I met her parents too. My colleague brought me along when he interviewed them, the only time they spoke to the media. We never would have gotten to talk to them if we'd written crap about Katrin. And also, Katrin was their only child. You knew that, right? She was an only child."

Sophia hummed a confirmation.

"It was so fucking sad. In hindsight, I guess I think it was the right decision, not to go after Katrin. You don't have to write about everything, you're allowed to show mercy, even if you're a journalist. But back then I was hotheaded. Everything I knew I wanted to put straight in the paper. I couldn't handle even a comma being struck in what I wrote. I took it as evidence of a conspiracy among the editors if they asked me to spend an afternoon on the tip line. I've gotten over that now."

The line crackled for a moment. When it was clear again, Tor Bengtsson went on.

"That goddamn Stig Ahlin...How is he doing? I remember him as a...well, not that I ever met him, but it's hard to imagine a more loathsome guy. Some of us went out to celebrate when he was convicted."

"I see." Sophia pressed her finger into her free ear, to hear better. "You did? You celebrated?"

"Don't hold it against me. Young and dumb. If he decides he'll give an interview, I would do just about anything to get it."

"You said that already. Do you have any material left from back then? Notes? Is there anyone I should talk to? Who can tell me more about Katrin?"

"I doubt it. But you should take a look at her old classmates. As I recall, everyone knew what she was up to. Now, all these years later, I don't imagine they'd have any problem discussing it. Or they would. People can be awfully strange. You can always give it a shot."

They fell silent. Sophia was about to end the call when she heard his voice again. It was crackly.

"Have you spoken with his ex-wife? Or his daughter? Do you have anything new from the daughter? She must be grown up by now, right?"

The call dropped.

Sophia stayed put for a moment, watching the people welling up off the escalator. An endless stream of people with purses hugged to their chests and eyes on the ground. There would be no new suit for her today. Why would she buy one? Blazers and skirts, blazers and dresses — she had plenty of those. They would tide her over for quite some time. Anyway, she could afford a suit even when it wasn't on sale. That way she could skip the crowds.

She walked around to the down escalator. This was a good day to go to the office. A really good day.

Lars Gustafsson was already there when Sophia stepped through the door. He was standing behind the reception desk and sorting the mail. He was wearing jeans and a very strange T-shirt. It took a moment for Sophia to realize it was a child's drawing. Someone, probably one of Lars's grandkids, had drawn a giant head with legs next to something that looked like a cross between a flower and a sun.

"It's me and my wife," he said. "Isn't it fantastic? He's only four. I got it for Christmas. We're playing soccer, I think. In the drawing, that is."

"Fantastic," Sophia agreed.

She glanced toward the offices. Björn Skiller appeared to be there as well. She shouldn't have been surprised. Christmas break, Midsummer, the day after Easter — the best time to be productive for a law firm. The phones were quiet; the courts were closed. The lawyers could write briefs, contracts, or, if nothing else, articles.

"What are you doing here?" Lars handed her a glossy ad brochure and two window envelopes. She accepted them and put the brochure straight in the wastebasket.

"Stig Ahlin. I wanted to try to get as much done as possible before the Christmas holidays are over."

"Smart. When are you planning to submit it?"

"Well, there's no point in submitting it if we don't have anything to present."

"But you do?"

Sophia gave a tiny smile. "Maybe. I'm going to give it another month. Then we'll try. He's already waited too long."

"What about the media? How is that going?"

"I'm sure it will work itself out."

She went to the kitchen. The coffeepot was half full; she picked it up and sniffed its contents. Lars and Björn must not have been here for long; it seemed fresh. And it was hot too. She poured a cup, went to her office, closed the door, and sat down at her desk.

Always the same ritual, and she never got tired of it. Something happened to her. Her heartbeat slowed, her breathing calmed. How could she have thought shopping was a good idea, when she could be at work?

Her computer whirred to life. She brought up the folder where she'd started sorting the case materials to make it easier to find what she was looking for. There were no more than forty documents in the interrogation folder, and she knew exactly which one she needed.

First, she wrote a name on a notepad: Eija Nurmilehto — not exactly a common one. Not in exclusive Djursholm, anyway. Sophia hoped Eija hadn't married and changed her name. If she had, it would slow Sophia down; she would have to wait for the Swedish authorities to finish up their celebration of the birth of Jesus. But if she was in luck, this woman wasn't the marrying kind.

A search of the name on hitta.se brought up four hits. But only one had the same birthday as the woman who'd been interviewed in the investigation into Katrin Björk's murder. Her birthday was listed right there online, in a box next to her address and phone number, in the event Sophia wanted to send flowers. Sophia could also click on a link to a satellite image of the woman's home. Maybe to find out what sort of flowers she had in her window.

Sophia ignored the satellite images and drank the last of her coffee. It had taken under ten minutes to find the woman. She pulled over the phone and dialed the number. The woman answered on the third ring. With her full name, to be safe. She still used her maiden name. It was unclear whether she was married. But it was obvious she had children — Sophia could hear them in the background.

24

It took forty-five minutes by public transport to get from Östermalmstorg to the suburb where Eija Nurmilehto lived.

When Sophia called, Eija had said that Sophia could come to her house. Eija herself never went into the city. Especially not during the Christmas sale days. Anyone who went downtown on December twenty-ninth must be awfully stupid, as Eija had informed her. And she wasn't, she'd added. Awfully stupid, that is.

Sophia had nothing against going the other direction, although she did find herself hesitating at the entrance to the subway. The cold had suddenly arrived, and her thin leather boots felt slippery. There was a neat line of taxis right next to the stairs. But there was no money for such extravagances, not for this case.

In the stairwell, Sophia regretted having dressed up. It didn't exactly look as if Eija had cleaned up in anticipation of a guest. She lived on the first floor. The balcony, visible from the street, was overloaded with pizza boxes, other boxes, ad circulars, broken toys, and a bike with one tire.

As Sophia stepped through the door, Eija was removing a big pile of window envelopes that had been lying unopened under the mail slot. The apartment smelled stuffy. Sophia tried to say hello to a boy in his early teens who crowded past her and through the door. He didn't return her greeting.

Eija Nurmilehto had been in Katrin's class when Katrin was murdered. Only one year later she had dropped out of school to set out on the journey that crash-landed her in this apartment. Naturally, since she was the same age as Katrin would have been, almost to the day, Eija Nurmilehto was younger than Sophia. Yet she seemed older.

Eija and Sophia found themselves standing in the hall. A half-decorated Christmas tree was visible in the living room; ornaments had been hung only on its lower branches. The typical day care ornaments, a couple of Christmas crackers, cardboard snowflakes, a green tissue-paper tree.

This was how it usually looked in the homes of her child clients who had been forcibly removed from their parents' care, Sophia thought. A tree decorated by little kids. And they could never reach high enough.

Sophia was about to wonder aloud if she would have to ask her questions in the hall when Eija dropped her arms to her sides, turned around, and went to the kitchen. The table was set: a mug each. Breakfast hadn't been cleared away, just shoved off to the side. A dirty butter knife, a half-full bowl of soggy chocolate flakes. A sweaty rind of cheese. *I should have brought a cake*, Sophia thought.

"I don't have anything to offer," Eija said, reaching for the coffeepot, "besides coffee. Do you want some? I don't have any milk. Or soy milk."

"Please," said Sophia. "I'd love some coffee."

She sat down and accepted her mug.

"As you understand, I read your interview."

"That's strange," said Eija. "I thought they'd tossed those."

"No. That sort of thing isn't thrown away. What led you to believe otherwise?"

Silence. Eija stood up. She removed the cheese from the table, threw it in the garbage, and put the breakfast dishes in the sink. She picked up Sophia's cup and wiped the table with a Wettex cloth that actually seemed clean. Then she sat back down.

"I read your interview," Sophia said again. "It seemed to me you wanted to say something about Katrin, but you weren't given the chance. I suppose the officer had planned to question you again, but then Stig Ahlin showed up and you were forgotten. I'd like you to tell me what you know."

"Bullshit."

"Why do you say that?"

"Because it's bullshit. People like that cop, he didn't listen to me. He didn't want to know. Because it didn't fit, what I had to say. It didn't fit in. He didn't want to listen to what I knew. They weren't planning to come back. No way."

"What do you mean?"

In fact, she knew exactly. The police officer had taken one look at Eija Nurmilehto and made up his mind about who she was. She was a hysterical teenager with extremely apparent issues. Eija had nothing in common with well-mannered

Katrin, with her single-family home and private riding lessons. But Sophia couldn't exactly say so. She needed to find out what this girl knew. And she would remain polite and obliging until she succeeded.

The coffee was ice-cold. Sophia drank it without feeling it. She rested her elbows on the table and tried to sound friendly.

"How did you and Katrin become friends? Couldn't you start by telling that story?"

Eija glared at Sophia.

I know what you think of me, Sophia thought. *But give me a chance. You want to tell your story. I can tell. You never would have said I could come here if you didn't long to talk about what you know. Ever since Katrin died, you've been waiting for someone to listen. Well, here I am. I beg you to start talking.*

Eija seemed to brace herself. At first it looked like she was about to stand up and ask Sophia to leave. But then she changed her mind.

"It just happened."

"What do you mean?"

"Katrin was the prettiest girl in the class," said Eija. "One night we ended up sitting next to each other on the bus. Or she came to sit next to me. And we started chatting. I don't know if you get how weird that was."

"I spoke to a journalist who said Katrin was having a tough time. That no one wrote about it, because she was dead, and they didn't want to make things even harder on her parents."

Eija's eyes narrowed slightly. She was listening.

"I'm not interested in piling a bunch of crap on Katrin," Sophia said. "But I want to know about her life, because if I don't know...I'm trying to find out what it was really like."

"I don't know if it's a good idea for me to tell you."

"Why not?"

Eija didn't respond. She turned her face away. Tears flowed from her eyes, but she didn't seem to register the fact. She let them trickle down to her throat without wiping them away.

"It's too late now."

"Try me," Sophia implored her. "I'm listening."

Katrin
1997

Katrin stopped visiting the stables. It wasn't fun any-more, just annoying. The mucking, the grooming, the hoof-picking, the lists, the constant competition, the constant posturing. Who will get to handle the privately owned horses? Who can get Dove on the bit? Where did you find that jacket? Who can do three flying changes down one long side of the ring? Get him in the corner, use your legs, look at the obstacle, heels down, shoulders back, soft hands. Isn't it time to consider buying your own pair of white breeches, and stop borrowing from the other girls? Do you always ride with spurs?

In the past she could sit in the stall for hours, but now she felt antsy after just a few minutes.

She told Dad it had gotten to be too much, with school and everything. He understood; he didn't think this was odd at all. Horses were something you grew out of. The stables were for little girls, and now she was big. And any-way, it was a pain to drive her back and forth all the time. She nodded. It had certainly been a long time since Dad had to give her a ride — she usually took the bus. But she nodded. Yes. She had a lot of other stuff going on. It was just as well. She would do something else.

Katrin stopped returning Sara's and Lina's calls. They called a lot. Each evening they left messages: "Call me back as soon as you can." Sure, Katrin said, but she didn't feel like talking to them. They wanted to babble for hours, preferably all three of them, on a party line, just press star, and then they would talk over each other, someone thought she was cute, someone had lost a ton of weight, ohmigod she was so skinny, she had to be bulimic, and someone might have had an abortion, and someone was always talking shit, who did she think she was?

"Say I'm in the shower and I'll call later." She mimed it: *No, not now, I'm not home. I'll call later, in a while, in just a minute.*

Did you have a fight? Dad wondered once. No, she said. Definitely not. They're my best friends. I just want to watch TV for a while, I have to do my homework, finish this chapter, iron this blouse.

Those times they did talk after all, Katrin lay on her bed, on her back, looking up at the ceiling and letting them babble. She agreed with what they said; she laughed when they laughed. But it was annoying to listen; there was so much else.

Katrin always went to school. She attended all her classes and was never tardy. But she didn't sit in front anymore. It wasn't a big deal, she could sit wherever she liked, and she was still the smartest in her class, so why should she have to raise her hand just because she knew the answer? The important thing was that she did her lessons. And she handed in all her homework and always got the best grades on tests, or at least almost the best. It wasn't hard — she studied and memorized and didn't even feel it. As long as she didn't have to sit in front. She couldn't handle sitting there anymore.

Her friends went to concerts and movies, went shopping. There was a café in the city where everyone liked to go. Katrin didn't join them. She didn't have time.

She didn't quit basketball. Not entirely. She went to games, but why should she attend practice? She still made her baskets. When they changed clothes afterward, she took long showers so everyone else was almost done by the time she got out. She never put on makeup while everyone else was crowded around the mirror, borrowing each other's mascara. And she took the bus home.

Eija Nurmilehto was different. She didn't ride, she didn't play basketball, she didn't listen to Pearl Jam. She only used makeup to make herself uglier than she already was, and she smelled like a gym bag that had been left in a locker too long, like the swimsuit Katrin had forgotten to hang to dry. Everyone knew she shoplifted from ICA, and Eija's phone number was scratched into the bus stop outside school. "Wanna fuck?" it said next to it. Everyone knew it was the right number, that it went to Eija's house, because everyone had tried calling it only to hang up when someone answered.

When Katrin walked up to Eija on the bus that day, it was just a random occurrence. She wasn't thinking *I want to talk to that girl*, but when she sat down and started talking it felt like she would never be able to stop. She followed Eija home, lay on the floor in her room in the middle of all that dust and staleness, and talked and talked. She stayed until Eija said, "You have to leave now, because my mom will be home soon."

Eija never told Katrin anything, never called to ask if she thought some guy was into her. Eija only said hello if Katrin greeted her first, and she listened without saying anything back. Eija was just there. And Katrin told her everything she never said to anyone else.

The guys she had gotten to know at a party. Upper-secondary school guys who'd come by to check out the younger girls. The ones who would soon be starting at their school, who would soon be legal. That's what they'd said; Katrin had been standing with Sara and Lina, and they laughed. She didn't. But one guy, the one with curly hair falling over his forehead, he stood behind the others, looking at her. They started talking, he came home with her, made sure she got all the way home without falling down and passing out somewhere. They made out and he got her number.

That was six months ago. He'd gotten a haircut since then. And they never hung out together with her friends, only his.

Sometimes he was the one who called, but often it was one of his friends. In the middle of the night. Katrin knew; she always kept the phone under her pillow. Just in case. If her dad woke up and answered first, they hung up. Dad typically didn't ask any questions, he just went back to bed. An hour or so later they'd call back. And she would answer when the phone clicked, even before the first ring.

But Dad was hardly ever the one who answered. She was too quick.

They wanted her to come out. By herself. No one else from her school was there. She was special. The only one of the young girls to be invited. The only one her age. It's a party. Wicked cool. A fucking rager. Come on. Don't be such a drag. Wear whatever. Doesn't matter. Hell, come naked. Ha ha ha.

There were night buses. There were taxis she could call to pick her up on the corner. She took the money from Dad. Sometimes the guys said they could come pick her up. There was always someone with a moped. Sometimes they "borrowed" a car. With or without a license. Never totally sober. There were always ways. Dad never suspected a thing.

Many times she just danced. She liked that. The music. When they played the music so loud it thumped in her chest. Everything else disappeared. She closed her eyes and danced; they watched. Sometimes that was all. Sometimes she just gave someone a blow job. She didn't have sex with anyone but him. He often made out with someone else. Sometimes it all went to shit. Those times, she did things she'd claimed she'd never do.

When she got home, she put on two sweaters. Slept in her clothes. Usually she would unplug the phone. And put it back in its spot. She wouldn't plug it in again until she had gotten up, showered, and eaten breakfast.

It started with him, with his buddies, but it didn't stop there. She felt them looking; she could see in their eyes what they thought of her. She understood how they talked to her; it was there in their voices, what they meant. They wanted her — she should have been the one with power over them. But that wasn't the case, and it was unbearable. Dad didn't notice a thing.

25

Eija blew her nose.

"Do you know who the guys were?"

She nodded. "More or less."

"And she was in love with one of them?"

"That, I'm not totally sure. In some ways, maybe. But he...she wanted to. She knew he didn't really want her, and then she tried to...it's hard to explain, there was so much going on. So many guys."

"Do you remember his name?"

Eija shook her head.

"Was she in love with Stig Ahlin?"

Eija shook her head again. She snorted; it almost sounded like a laugh.

"I mean, she told me about a guy she met at work, that happened once. I didn't realize it was him at first, but later on I thought it must have been. But she talked about a lot of different people. Stig Ahlin was no one." She shook her head harder. "She wasn't in love with Stig Ahlin, not a chance. He was one of the creeps, yeah, Christ, that's what we called them. She met a few of those. Quite a few. Stig

Ahlin was a fucking pig, she never would have fallen in love with him."

But sleep with him, Sophia thought. *That she wanted to do.*

"What do you mean when you say Stig Ahlin was no one?"

"That he wasn't important."

"He was a thirty-five-year-old doctor who slept with her. She was fifteen. That was 'nothing'?"

"Yeah."

Sophia didn't say anything. There was nothing to say.

"You don't get it," Eija declared. "I knew you wouldn't get it. How could you?"

I don't need this, Sophia thought. *It's enough that I know.*

"Then what happened?"

"I told her she had to talk to her parents, or else I would tell the school nurse. She had to stop. I was worried about her."

"What did she do?"

Eija gazed out the window. A young boy was frantically waving his arms over his head; Eija waved back and nodded. Her son, Sophia thought. Eija smiled.

"I'm watching," she mumbled, toward the window. Without taking her eyes from the boy, she said, "I worked as a maid in a hotel for a few years. A halfway sleazy one downtown. I was supposed to clean twenty rooms per day. On Sundays and Thursdays, when there were a lot of checkouts, it was rough. Lots of crap to clean up, you know? You have no idea the things people leave in their rooms. Out in the open, totally visible, even though they know someone has to...I've seen a lot. Streaks of shit in the toilet, tied-up condoms, bloody underwear, used pads left on the bathroom floor, sex toys. You think they were ashamed? The hell they were. Because the only person who would see was the maid. And who could I complain to, what the hell was I supposed to say? Pick up your own fucking shit? The maid doesn't exist. I didn't exist. I'm not a real person."

Eija aimed a thumbs-up at the window and smiled. The boy out in the yard had finished his show. She brought her hands together in silent applause and kept talking without looking at Sophia.

"What did Katrin do? She ditched me. She stopped calling, stopped visiting, I no longer existed. I was never a real person to Katrin. That's why she could tell me everything. It was like telling a dog. But even more anonymous and insignificant. When I suddenly started speaking when spoken to, when I made demands of her, questioned what she was doing, she dropped me. Actually, she threw me as far away as she possibly could. She had definitely not signed up for anything like that. I'm not stupid. I understood what she was doing. Everyone assumed I had done something. Or actually, I suppose they didn't give a shit. I never said anything to the school nurse. Talking to her parents wasn't an option, but the school nurse, I should have...she asked me how I was, one time, but I didn't speak up then either. I was just so hurt that Katrin dissed me like that, and then she died, and it was too late."

Eija took a ragged breath, stood up, and left the kitchen. Sophia let her go.

On the fridge were two pieces of paper, schedules of some sort. There were freshly ironed red curtains in the window. In one corner stood a box. There were various Christmas decorations on a chair right next to it. *It's actually quite neat here*, Sophia thought.

Eija returned. On her way through the door she raised one hand to gesture at the half-decorated tree in the next room.

"The kids and I are taking down the tree. It's early, but they bring over a container to start collecting large items tomorrow, already. If we wait until after New Year's, it will be too full. And I took the opportunity to do one of those clean-outs that you always plan but never do. Most of the stuff is already on the balcony."

Sophia blushed. Eija blew her nose.

"Katrin wasn't...I'm making her sound like a hell of a snob, and sometimes she was, but I liked her anyway. She was scared. Or scared isn't the right word. She did all that stuff, she got stuck in it, and once you're stuck you feel like you don't have any right to say no, to get out of it. You think it's fucking disgusting, but you keep doing it anyway. It sounds crazy, but that's how it is. And she shouldn't have been murdered, she really shouldn't have."

"Why didn't you tell the police about that guy?"

"Who? That first dude?"

Sophia nodded.

"Why would I have?" Eija blew her nose again. "Katrin was nothing to him. He hardly knew who she was. Plus, I didn't know his name. I never met him. No, it wasn't him. Everyone knows that. It was that creep. Professor Death. I'm totally sure…it's obvious he's the one who did it."

Sophia looked down at her mug. Surely she wasn't obliged to drink any more.

"It must have been tough for you."

Eija considered Sophia. Her eyes narrowed. The fridge hummed, and a door slammed in the stairwell. Eija didn't take her eyes off Sophia.

"You probably had someone like me too. Although I'm sure you've forgotten her. Because she didn't mean anything."

"Maybe," Sophia said cautiously. She met Eija's gaze.

Never, she thought. *Anna and Carl are my family. And I've never had friends besides them.*

"Have you ever known someone who does absolutely everything no one should ever do?" Eija asked. "Have you ever hated yourself so much you only want it to hurt, hurt so bad you can't feel anything else? No, you haven't."

Sophia loosened her cashmere scarf. She had left it on, wound around her neck. Eija seemed to be waiting for her to take over. Sophia couldn't think of anything to say. Her shirt bunched awkwardly around her waist and her skirt felt too tight.

"Well, I've stopped feeling like that," Eija said at last. "And it doesn't hurt all that much anymore."

Sophia had planned to stroll for a bit. But after just a few hundred yards, she realized she didn't even know which way the city was. She found a metro station and traveled to T-Centralen downtown. Black ice glistened under the streetlights. She walked quickly, eyes on the ground and hands in her pockets, all the way across Vasagatan, up Tegelbacken and Jakobsgatan, down Malmtorgsgatan. As she reached the Ministry for Foreign Affairs she glanced toward the opera house, where a taxi was letting off a woman in an ankle-length mink coat. A man wearing only shirtsleeves was waiting to be let into Bakfickan, the small restaurant attached to opulent Operakällaren. Sophia hurried on, down to Strömgatan.

They were fuzzy, those memories from her own teen years. The feeling that her hair was always greasy, her pants always too tight, and that her makeup never quite stuck. She recalled sorting all her records in alphabetical order, making mixtapes and sitting in her room listening to the same song over and over again. She remembered copying down English song lyrics in her diary, daydreaming about boys now long forgotten, and crying herself to sleep a few times because she was convinced she wasn't quite good enough. Still, she'd had a decent time of it. Because there was also the joy, closeness, kisses, the first time someone gazed into her eyes, touching her, the completely stunning sensation of wanting more, of not being able to stop for anything in the world.

She guessed she'd done well, as a teenager. Making it through had helped her feel stronger, better equipped for life. She had been lucky somehow.

Sophia walked up onto Norrbro, grabbed the railing of the bridge, and gazed down at the dark water. The current flowed down, away, out to the archipelago. The sea smelled stagnant and stuffy here. Dirty gray scum swirled around the abutments. She stood there for a moment, perfectly still.

The seabirds weren't around this time of year; they wintered at the garbage dumps outside the city. Only the pigeons and house sparrows were left. They huddled in bushes and alleys, near air vents and exhaust fans. The ice had already formed at Årstaviken, a layer the thickness of a fingernail, as dark as the night in which it was created. But it was getting colder now. With every degree below freezing, it would thicken and brighten. Spring seemed so far off. The ice-out and her boat, shrink-wrapped for the winter, its mast dismantled. It was something to look forward to, she supposed. The feeling a little too big, a little too hasty; these weren't things she put into words. Not emotions she would admit to, if someone asked.

The snow began to fall in large flakes, down toward the black water; the white bits disappeared in the darkness. Sophia lifted her face, closed her eyes.

When she was a child, she had climbed trees, a book stuffed in her waistband, up, high, close to the trunk. Once she lost her grip, the bark crumbled into dust in her hand, she broke a nail straight across the middle and fell to the ground. Ten feet or perhaps only seven; she landed on her back and got the air knocked out of her. It felt like her lungs were collapsing. She spent a few seconds waiting to die, then had to force herself to open her mouth, expand her chest, force the air back into her body. She remembered sitting up, leaning against the trunk, and concentrating on inhaling and exhaling. In. Then out. She must not feel — not her back, not her foot, not her head, nowhere that might hurt. She must only concentrate on that one thing. Breathing. In and out.

Katrin had been fifteen years old. Sophia's client had slept with her, had undressed her, touched her, taken her. Even if he hadn't killed her, he was one of the ones who had destroyed her. Who had made her impervious to help.

Sophia stared hard at the black water. She swallowed. Sour, watery bile gathered in her mouth and she had to concentrate.

I don't need to defend the rest of it, she thought. But that didn't make her feel better.

Breathe. In and out. Don't feel. Sophia turned her face up to the snow. The sound had vanished; the wind had died down and the streets were empty. Never was the city as quiet as under new-fallen snow. *If I don't focus on my client, no one will. I'm the only one he has.*

Sophia began to walk home. It was getting colder and colder. The snow melted against her cheeks, but not on the ground; it muffled her steps.

She walked faster, pulling her hands up into the sleeves of her coat and hugging herself.

I don't need to contact Stig's daughter. That has nothing to do with this. Breathe in, breathe out. Nothing more.

26

Whose ridiculous idea was it to have a party the day before New Year's Eve?

"It's not a party," Anna had responded when Sophia asked. "I just thought we could get together at a time when people can actually get babysitters. To eat and chat and have a nice evening. Without taking a Russian firecracker to the eye."

Not a party, Sophia had thought as the taxi turned off at Anna's house. The driveway was lined with lit torches. There were two-foot snow lanterns on either side of the front stairs. The glow from the lanterns flickered against the wood paneling and rowanberry branches at the front door. When she walked into the dining room, she thought it again: *Just a simple dinner.*

The table was set for sixteen, with ceramic plates, each a different color. They looked like they had been kneaded into shape by an amateur. Although she certainly couldn't rule out the possibility that Anna had made them, Sophia assumed they were by some famous Danish designer and insanely expensive. Each guest had also been supplied with a set of glasses: a dimpled water glass and three different types of crystal wineglasses, all scored at an antiques fair in Brussels. The napkins were of the same natural linen as the thick tablecloth and had been placed into rings of braided leather along with a sprig of myrtle and a tiny, dark red Christmas rose. In the center of the table stood a row of thick red candles, of various lengths, linked together with braided leather to match the napkin rings. In one of the corners stood the twenty-foot Christmas tree, one of Anna's four decorated trees, if you didn't count the two in the yard. The dining room tree was ornamented with hand-painted glass balls, red velvet ribbon, and actual lit candles.

Sophia found her place. Sᴀꜰɪᴀ, it read on the place card, in handwritten letters with a backward ꜰ.

So humble, Sophia thought. *Letting the kids help set the table.*

The other guests were also on their way in. Anna hurried by, her youngest daughter on her hip. She was in her sock feet; she'd left her five-inch heels on the floor by her chair. Her eyes were frantic, but she looked happy. Then Anna found her husband, handed their daughter to him, and returned to the dinner table. She stood by Sophia, placing an arm around her and pressing a hand to her cheek. Sophia smiled and hugged her back.

The appetizers were already on the table, along with six full breadbaskets. Sophia set down the champagne glass she'd been instructed to bring to the table and looked at her plate: three grilled oysters.

"Naturally," Sophia whispered in Anna's ear, "we're having oysters and champagne. You have to, when you're celebrating having a babysitter."

The wine was already open on one sideboard; on another stood an enormous cheese plate, a gigantic bowl of salad, and three Pavlova tarts with fresh passion fruit. The buffet of entrees was laid out in the attached kitchen, resting on the warmers of Anna's ten-foot stove. Grilled chicken thighs, warm lentil salad, and mashed sweet potatoes with Västerbotten cheese.

Before Anna could respond, one of the male guests approached them.

"So much effort you've put in here."

Sophia didn't recognize him. He had full lips and a small chin. He'd already taken off his tie; it was sticking out of his jacket pocket like a balled-up sock. His hands were on his waist.

"Or should I say, has been put in here?" He coughed. "Truly impressive."

Anna laughed in response. She gestured vaguely with one hand and vanished into the kitchen.

The man watched Anna go.

"Women really are skilled," he said. "At hiring services, that is."

He chuckled in self-satisfaction. Sophia bit her cheek. She was just about to turn around and head for the kitchen to see if she could be of help when she discovered Anna's oldest son Emil rushing after his mother with an apron around his waist.

If only you knew, Sophia thought. *What Anna can do.*

"Sebastian," said the man with the sock-tie, extending a thin hand. "But everyone calls me Sibbe."

"Sophia Weber."

"Aha!" Sibbe pulled the tie from his pocket and slowly began to roll it up. "Anna's famous lawyer friend. I read an article about you in the paper today. Stig Ahlin's lawyer, eh? Interesting. Nothing but strong women this evening! I'll have to watch it, so I don't get affirmative-actioned out of here."

The chuckling started up again. Sibbe took his seat and crossed his arms. He eyed her thoroughly. Up and down. Taking his time.

Don't say anything, Sophia thought. *Smile instead. Just smile.*

But Sibbe didn't remain seated long. A skinny woman with duck lips, a sequined dress, and waist-length hair had approached the table. Sibbe bolted up. He conscientiously pulled out a chair for her.

At the same time, Sophia felt someone put an arm around her waist. She looked to her left. It was Ludwig Venner. For a brief time, he had lived in the same student corridor as Sophia and Anna, back in Uppsala. As far as Sophia remembered, he had also studied law, although she didn't think he had sat exams in any subjects. Instead he had run a radio station from an empty basement laundry room in one of the student housing units. These days he was the CEO of the Venner Group's six largest commercial TV channels.

"Ludwig!" Sophia cried happily.

"Mmm," he breathed into her ear. "I've been waiting so long."

"Oh, that's right," Sophia said, placing a hand on Ludwig's shoulder and pushing him away. "I heard she finally kicked you out. She did the right thing."

"Yes," Ludwig nodded. "She really did. But now, here I am. The only single person here this evening. Only male single one, that is. And that means it's my turn to escort you to the table. I'd almost started to lose faith."

"Proof that time passes, if nothing else."

"Proof, my dear Sophia, that we have one foot in the grave. Or that you've slept with everyone else."

Sophia smiled. She let him kiss her on the cheek and then took her seat.

"If we're being honest, I've slept with you too," she said. "But don't worry. I have to get up early tomorrow. You'll get your eight hours of sleep and be well rested for the new year. I imagine you have tons to do. I heard you've made an offer to the Norwegians."

The man across from them had caught sight of Ludwig and was leaning across the table. He kept his balance with one hand; the other was extended as far as he could reach.

"Sibbe," he gasped out. "Everyone calls me Sibbe."

Ludwig took the man's hand and gave him a brief nod.

"Sebastian," he declared, turning to Sophia again. "We didn't sleep with each other. Not for real. I don't want you to think that that night . . . I have to protest. You don't know me. Not as you should. In a biblical sense, 'know' is synonymous with — "

Sophia shook her head. "We won't be sleeping together again. Not tonight, and not any other night."

She caught sight of Anna across the table. They made eye contact and Anna raised her glass.

Fantastic party, Sophia mimed.

Anna gave her a big smile and shook her head firmly. She always had known what Sophia was thinking, even before Sophia admitted it to herself.

No, Anna mimed back. *Bad idea. Really bad idea.*

. . .

Sophia had known it would come. It always did, especially from people like Sibbe. Sooner or later, in various ways. But tonight it had taken much longer than usual for the question to come up. Sophia and Ludwig had managed to get all the way through the appetizer and two helpings of the main course.

Sibbe had taken off his jacket. The woman in the sequined dress had turned to the man on her right. Sibbe's only company was his glass of wine.

"Hey you!" he spat. "Anna's bestie. The hotshot attorney. I read about you in the paper. There was an article about you in one of those incredibly serious evening papers. You're the one who decided to get Stig Ahlin out of the slammer. Damn straight, that's you, isn't it?"

Sophia nodded. He had obviously forgotten that he'd mentioned it when they first said hello.

"I have a question." His voice was far too loud. "I wanna know something."

Sophia nodded again. It was best to get this over with.

"How the hell can you live with yourself? Would you defend any old pervert at all? Or do you only spend time on celebrities like Stig Ahlin?"

This had little to do with today's article. Sophia was frequently faced with versions of this question when she was at parties and was forced to converse with her neighbors at the table. When she said she was an attorney who specialized in criminal cases, there it was. Could she defend what the Nazis did during World War II? Could she work for Charles Manson, or that Austrian guy who'd locked his own daughter in the basement and fathered a bunch of children with her? And how did she manage? Did she laugh all the way to the bank, or was she just generally bananas?

"Would you..." Sibbe didn't rack his brains long. "Would you be able to defend someone who raped your little sister? What if Stig Ahlin had attacked your sister, would you still think it's so important to get him out then? Huh?"

Sophia had had this discussion so many times that she could rattle off her responses in her sleep.

Ludwig pulled her close.

"You have a little sister?" he mumbled into her ear, a little too loudly. "God in heaven, that sounds fantastic. And you never told me. Can she join us tonight? I swear I'll pay you the most attention. But while you're resting? Please? I'll be extra obliging and I won't get tired and fall asleep."

"Well?" Sibbe was almost shouting by now. It was becoming very difficult for the rest of the dinner guests to pretend they hadn't noticed him.

Sophia turned to him.

"No," she said curtly.

Ludwig shook his head in concern and pointedly shifted to the side. He was no longer mumbling in her ear.

"Just as I suspected. If you had a sister, obviously I would have slept with her already. And my wife would have found out. And then you, your sister, and my wife would have started a book club together, gone off on vacation with the kids, and blocked me on Facebook."

Sibbe started laughing. There was no way of telling whether it was at Ludwig's joke or because Sophia had admitted that there were people she couldn't imagine defending. But he leaned across the table toward Ludwig and raised his hand for a high five. Ludwig aimed a measured look at him and refused the offer.

"I don't have a little sister," Sophia said. "But I would, without a doubt, defend someone who had raped your little sister, Sibbe."

Sibbe's face changed color and he began to squirm in his chair. It was silent around the table now. But no one was looking at Sophia or Sibbe. The woman in the sequined dress left her place to stand farther away. Her eyes were darting here and there; she was doing everything she could not to look at her table escort. No one was looking at Sophia or Sibbe as they did their utmost to pretend they hadn't heard anything.

"Oh, I see." Sibbe raised his voice. "You like rapists. Men who kill little kids. And I bet you think pedophiles can make terrific day care teachers. Because they deserve the opportunity to do any kind of work they like once they've served their time. And you'd be happy to see that time shortened as much as possible. Because..." He raised his voice even more. "Did you know that only one out of every five rape charges leads to a conviction?"

"Well," Sophia hesitated. She didn't want to discuss statistics with someone who wouldn't listen. "That depends on..." Sophia was trying to speak in muted tones. "Should we take this to the kitchen? Have a nice, quiet conversation? To keep from ruining dinner for..."

Sibbe's face was beginning to turn purple. Now he was shouting. The other guests glanced around uneasily. Anna's husband had vanished from the table; he was putting their youngest daughter to bed.

"Do you think those numbers are good? Do you think that's right? Jesus, you're even stupider than you look. Do you know how many people are too afraid to report assault because they're afraid no one will believe them? Do you know how many rapes never even lead to charges? Do you think that's the way it should be? Is that the just society we want? Is that the kind of country we want to live in? And while people like you whine about how we should reduce sentences and raise the standard of evidence, we men have to take the blame for people like Stig Ahlin."

Sophia sipped her wine. From across the room, Anna met her gaze. She looked nervous.

I'm trying, Anna, she thought. *I'm trying to get him to calm down. But I'm no good at this. Can't I cuff him one instead?*

Anna wiped her mouth with her linen napkin. It could be her imagination, but Sophia thought Anna's hand was trembling. Could that be Sibbe's girlfriend sitting across from her?

"It's a goddamn disaster," Sibbe howled. "A failure of unbelievable dimensions. That we can't punish people who commit that kind of crime. What is it going to take? Gang rapes, where the rapists go free because it's impossible to prove who was watching the door and who was doing the raping? Why don't we just lock them up and throw away the key?"

Ludwig shook his head and stood up. Sophia tugged at his arm.

"Hold on," she said quietly. "Don't mind him. Let's have dessert instead. He'll tire himself out soon."

"Attorney Sophia Weber!" Sibbe was spitting with rage. "It's thanks to you, you and your colleagues, that we can't afford to take care of our elders. That we have drug dealers selling just outside our children's schoolyards. How can you live with yourself?"

Then it was quiet. When Sibbe realized that Ludwig Venner was standing, he lost his train of thought. He watched in surprise as Ludwig bent down, picked up his dessert fork, and tapped his glass.

"You remind me of someone...," Ludwig mumbled, still facing Sibbe. "Or something. I can't quite recall what it is..." He looked away from Sibbe and focused his attention on the other guests instead.

The gathering looked up at him. Their relief at the interruption was so obvious that it was palpable.

"I'm not the one who escorted our hostess to the table this evening," Ludwig said at last. He was speaking slowly, almost drawling, and he turned to Anna, who had returned to her chair and was smiling broadly. "So, I'll only give a short speech. Much shorter than I'm accustomed to. Definitely not longer than forty-five minutes."

Ludwig nodded at Anna's dinner escort, who raised his glass in understanding. After waiting for the other guests' chuckling to die down, Ludwig continued.

"I'm sure it's a violation of good etiquette, but I'd really like to thank you, Anna. For finally allowing me to escort Sophia Weber to the table. If you had any idea how long I've been begging...I hadn't realized that I just had to be unhappy and recently divorced first. But anyway, thank you."

The guests laughed in relief. Sophia exhaled.

"Right?" Ludde turned to Sibbe, who gave a reluctant nod. "We're having a pleasant time, we're incredibly grateful that we were invited and can spend a fantastic evening in the company of some pretty incredible people."

Ludwig paused. He observed his glass, letting the dark red wine slide up to the edges, letting the crystal glitter in the candlelight.

"Tomorrow is New Year's Eve," he said. "Which raises a number of thoughts. You might think I'm joking, but I do occasionally think about something other than what makes good TV. Not often, but still." He looked at his glass again. "Aw...I don't really know what I want to say. I'm mostly just standing here because the alternative would have been to take this out to the yard and start throwing punches."

The guests laughed again and allowed him to go on.

"Fighting for a woman's honor. That usually makes good TV, of course. Although Sophia is much better at fighting than I am. Honestly, I couldn't even ward off a mosquito. Sophia Weber, on the other hand..." Ludwig lifted Sophia's hand and kissed it melodramatically. Sophia shook her head. "This woman sees to it that we can live in a better society."

Ludwig looked at Sibbe again. Then he raised his eyes and his glass toward Anna. "Anna. I want to thank you, your husband, your children, your mother, your fantastic mother...and my own mother, of course, I want to thank her too. And the jury, my producer, MGM, CBS,..." Anna laughed. "...the Academy...everyone who called in and voted for me. Thank you. And Anna, if you're thinking of closing up shop and making room for the rest of us on the stock exchange, I'd suggest you chain yourself to the stove. Because damn, your cooking..."

They all raised their glasses. The mood was calm once more. Anna pantomimed a thanks and blew a kiss to Ludwig. The buzz around the table resumed. The woman across from Sophia had returned to her seat.

Before Ludwig sat down, he leaned across the table, touched his glass to Sebastian's, and hissed, "You remind me of one of those cracked, brown pieces of soap my grandmother used to have, out in the country. You pass yourself off as someone who works for the common good, but it soon turns out you just leave a layer of paraffin all over everything. What a cowardly bastard you are. Smarmy and shameless. All at once. Let's get one thing straight, little Sibbe. My family owns four of Sweden's biggest daily papers, and we control 80 percent of the commercial Swedish-language TV channels. I can't keep track of how many gossip rags, publishing companies, and radio channels we own. If you don't shut your mouth right now, I'll assign some of my best journalists to make sure your pathetic life is ruined. It doesn't matter which line of business you happen to pollute with your presence...if I want to destroy you, I can, before we ring in the new year." He looked at his watch. "I have just over twenty-four hours. Shouldn't take more than half that."

Then he leaned back toward Sophia and whispered, "You'll have to excuse me. That wasn't one of my better speeches. Far too emotional and grandiose. I didn't have time to call in my speechwriter. But still, I think I've done my part, foreplay-wise. May I suggest we go home to your place?"

"I want dessert first."

"Of course, we'll have dessert. Two helpings each. You're going to need all the calories you can get. If you like, we'll have coffee as well. Not that I think you'll have trouble staying awake, but I can get you some. Milk and sugar, Attorney?"

27

Twenty-four hours until the new year. One thousand, four hundred and forty minutes. This would be his fourteenth calendar year behind bars.

Before Stig Ahlin began to work out again, there had been a six-month period during which he could hardly get out of bed. That, in combination with the cheap, energy-rich, taste-deficient food they served, had caused him to gain weight. He managed to put on forty pounds before he started running and reversing the trend and regaining control over his body.

But there had been something refreshing about letting his body swell. The fat transformed him, turning him into someone else. A tired blob of lard whose body ached in places it never had before. And it was oddly freeing. The man he became was able to get through the baffling days; the man he had recently been would never have survived.

During his fat months, he devoted every spare minute to watching TV, meaningless TV, entertainment TV. No news, no live debates, no documentaries. Preferably nothing that was even in Swedish. Only empty images.

One day, an American legal drama series was on. In one scene, the prosecutor was trying to convince the members of the jury that the defendant was guilty of intentional homicide rather than manslaughter. The defendant had stabbed the victim, and the prosecutor directed the jury to count.

"Count silently to yourself, count to twenty-four, and with each second that passes, imagine carefully how you must pull the knife from the woman's body and take aim again: one stab, two stabs, three stabs, four stabs, five, six, seven, eight. Think quietly to yourself all the way up to twenty-four stabs of the knife, and then go out and decide how this ongoing, drawn-out, senselessly repetitive lethal violence should be categorized."

This would never happen in a Swedish courtroom. Not even in Stig's own trial would the prosecutor have dared to say such a thing. It was theatrics, pure and simple.

Stig watched the entire show. When the arguments were over, the TV jury handed back their sentence: life in prison, no parole. Life in prison.

As the credits rolled, Stig stood up. The next day he began to work out. And then Stig began to count.

He counted the days that had passed since he was arrested. He counted the days that had passed since he was jailed. The nine months that had passed before the appeals court sentenced him to prison for homicide. The two weeks it had taken before he was moved from the jail to Kumla Prison. And the four months he'd had to wait before arriving at the facility that had become his home. He counted every day. Every morning when Stig woke up, he measured the time that had passed.

Because whether you believed time was linear, dynamic, or even circular, it could be sorted. Into days, hours, weeks, and years. Stig found a certain comfort in that. That time was the same for everyone, even if it might be experienced in different ways. Now. Four thousand, eight hundred and sixty-seven days. When Stig went to jail, Ida was not yet five. Now she would soon be eighteen, legally an adult. But when he thought of the day he had been arrested, it felt like yesterday.

Time flies, even when you're not having fun. In reality, it was only the individual days that dragged on for an unbearable eternity. Those were the ones he'd been robbed of. One at a time. And he kept counting.

One, two, three, Stig thought as he ran. *Four, five, six...*

28

Sophia was the first to wake. She stole into the kitchen. In the fridge, which was still well stocked from Christmas, was a carton of eggs and half a carton of cream. Sure, the cream was a few days past its best-by date, but it smelled okay. She emptied it into a bowl and whisked it along with the eggs and a few drops of white truffle oil. From the freezer she took a package of bacon, which she laid in a cast-iron skillet. Her Italian coffeemaker only took a few minutes. She fried the omelet in extra-salted butter.

"You have to marry me."

Ludwig propped himself up in bed and pulled Sophia toward him. Once she'd set down the tray, he stuck his hands up under her T-shirt.

"Never," she said. "And stop that right now. I told you yesterday. My breasts are not stress balls."

"But I can't imagine a life without these. I mean, you. And I'd forgotten you can cook too. How, how, how could I forget that? How is it possible? Oh!"

He stuck his hands back under her shirt. Sophia smiled.

"I like you too. But we're not getting married. We're not going to do this again, either. Even though it was nice."

Sophia wormed away from him and sat down on the bed, handing him one mug of coffee and downing half the other. Then she stood up. Ludwig grabbed her arm and pulled her back down.

"Why not? And what are you doing? This kind of coffee should be enjoyed, not bolted down like a shot. Are you in a hurry?"

"If I had to guess, you would manage to remain faithful to me for two days," she said. "And only if it was a weekend and I didn't let you out of sight the whole time. After that you would sleep with absolutely anyone, and then I'd be forced to have a chat with one of my old clients, someone who knows what to do with guys like you, and then your mom would be very sad because there wouldn't even be enough left of you to give you a proper burial, and I like your mom. I really like your mom an awful lot. So, no. The answer is no. We're not getting married. We're not going to have a relationship, not as a joke and not for real, and yes, I am in a serious hurry. I have to be at Grandpa's in an hour. But first I have to pick up the car and I should swing by the office too."

Ludwig took a bite of omelet, moaned softly, and took another.

"But Sophia. Please. What about how I'm filthy rich, honestly for real totally loaded, like Scrooge Mc-Fucking-Duck. Couldn't you marry me for my money?"

He extended a forkful of eggs. Sophia opened her mouth and allowed herself to be fed.

"I'm not interested in money. I'm an idealist. Didn't you hear that Sibbe guy? I'm completely obsessed with my firm belief that everyone must be able to rape and do drugs and sex-murder tiny, tiny babies without being punished for it."

Ludwig shook his head and ate a few more bites. Sophia followed suit.

"Professor Death. Stig Ahlin." It sounded like he was talking to himself. "Even just that name. Old Professor Stig, disgusting killer pig. That's a life sentence in itself. It's practically a goddamn nursery rhyme."

Then he set his fork on the tray and took Sophia's hand.

"Honestly now. I have to ask. Do you really believe that Stig Ahlin is innocent? I mean, forget reeling off all that crap about how it's important you don't worry about innocence, I get it, really, but do you seriously believe he didn't do it? I understand why you'd take it on even if you don't believe that, but I want to know."

Sophia swallowed. She had the sudden urge to thank him. And not just for salvaging Anna's dinner last night.

"I don't know how to answer that," she said at last. "I'm sure he never should have been found guilty. There simply wasn't enough for a conviction. But what I believe? Do I believe he's innocent? I suppose I do. The more I read, the stranger it gets. So, yes. I believe there's a considerable risk he's been locked up for thirteen years for something he didn't do. It's horrible, almost unbearable to think about, but I don't think he's the one who killed Katrin Björk. I never would have spent so much time on him if I thought otherwise."

It's true, she thought, almost surprised. *I actually believe he's innocent.*

Ludwig nodded. Sophia went on.

"But it also feels like I'm the only one who believes that. Getting a new trial is a hopeless task even in typical cases. But this case is...everyone knows who Stig Ahlin is, and everyone believes he's guilty. How am I supposed to fight that? I've gotten myself into something I'll never manage to pull off. If I were the only one who's going to suffer for it, I suppose that would be fine. But I'm not. Stig Ahlin is going to be stuck where he is."

Sophia took a bag from the wardrobe. Ludwig remained in the bed. Now he was eating bacon with his fingers.

"Do you really eat pork?" she wondered. "Doesn't your mother get awfully upset?"

"Fuck, why do you keep bringing up my mother?" He swallowed and took another bite. "Only on very special occasions. Fateful ones. Like when I've met my future wife. Or on Sundays. Then I eat pork. And on Christmas Eve. But not otherwise. Even though, between us, it's much tastier than carp. And much more effective than cholent when you're hung over."

Sophia laughed.

"But, Sophia? If you don't want to keep sleeping with me, I mean, marry me..." — Ludwig licked his thumb — "...couldn't you still come work for me? You can come to my defense in case I happen to beat my wife's new boyfriend to death, or in case his shitty firm suddenly goes bankrupt."

Sophia took three dresses from the wardrobe and carefully folded them. She would choose one later.

"Why would you need a lawyer if his business goes under? We're in a recession. Lots of people are losing their jobs. You can't be held legally responsible for being a megalomaniac and thinking you can influence the stock market."

"You see!" Ludwig Venner leaned out of the bed as far as he could and tugged at Sophia, who was digging through a drawer for a pair of tights. His hand slid down her back and landed on her ass. "Hear that? You said that without even having a charge sheet in front of you. Fuck, that's sexy. It's like I've always said: there's no way I can manage without you."

Sophia smiled and slapped at Ludwig's hand. She shoved a bundle of nylons and some underwear into her bag, then fetched her toiletries from the bathroom. Anyway, she was only celebrating New Year's with Grandpa and Carl and his parents. They'd seen her without makeup before.

"Lock the door behind you when you leave," she said. "And do me a favor. Start going to therapy. You need tons of help. But not from a lawyer. Stay away from lawyers." She kissed him on the cheek and zipped the bag. "Put the keys in the mailbox. There is no way you are keeping my keys, because we are never doing this again."

. . .

"I Googled your friend." Sture gave a contented laugh. "I Googled Stig Ahlin."

They were in the car Sophia had rented for the weekend. It had started to snow as they turned out of the parking lot at Fjärilsgården. Even though Sophia had turned the wipers and the defrost on high, the windshield was fogging up.

"I didn't know you did that stuff," Sophia said. *I didn't even know you had the Internet,* she thought.

"My dear Sophia. Everyone uses the Internet. Except Hans Segerstad. Surely, he still writes on his old Remington. Even though he could benefit from a spell-check program. And why wouldn't I use Google? There's a lot to learn. And besides, everything is perfectly true. Very practical. 'Wikipedia is Minerva's own abode,' as Mark Twain said. You have no idea how much I've learned about Ahlin. The symbol of patriarchal oppression in our society; one of Sweden's most abominable sex offenders ever. I Googled you too. Know how many hits there were?"

Sophia shook her head and wiped the windshield with the sleeve of her coat. It barely made a difference.

"Around seventy thousand. I had nine hundred. Thousand, that is. Stig Ahlin got seven hundred and ninety thousand." Sture smacked his lips in satisfaction. "He's very famous. I also found a couple of entertaining Web sites. Forums, they're called. Kids these days get all their knowledge from them. I read the most hair-raising stories there. A whole lot of honorable citizens, the journalists of the future, provide information. And they use aliases too. Good old-fashioned journalists would consider such things beneath them. But here! The real entertainers are on these forums. Signed Cousin Cocaine, Zulu Zumba, Shopping Cart Klutz, Litigashunner, Jeezus, and The Illiterate, what hard-hitters! Armed with nuclear weapons.

They fear nothing in the battle against evil. The stories they tell...how Stig Ahlin arranged parties with prostitutes in the morgue at Karolinska, and how even as a child he was suspected of rape but couldn't be convicted since he wasn't yet fifteen. Did you know that about your client?" Sture laughed.

"Yes." Sophia wasn't laughing. "I'm familiar with those stories."

Sophia hadn't only read them; she had to some extent fact-checked as well. Naturally, there was no evidence to back them up in the least. But they were combined with reports on the two crimes Stig Ahlin had actually been accused of. And they existed online. Along with the convictions, along with the events the justice system had determined really happened. And they were part of the public image of Professor Death, her client. In some ways, this was the battle she had to fight.

"He really is popular, your pedophile. And they're all in agreement. Stig Ahlin ought to be locked up in the toughest of all prisons, and back when he was imprisoned our dear prime minister Göran Persson should have swallowed the key along with his breakfast Danish. By the way, have you been out there to see how he's doing?"

"Have I been out to Göran Persson's house to see how he's doing?"

"No, to Emla, obviously. I've been there a few times. I've been to Göran's place too, but I won't go back. The food he offered was inedible. You'd never believe it, considering how food seems to be one of his interests, in contrast to politics. Furthermore, that man is unbearable. He's incapable of talking about anything but himself."

"Right," Sophia said, refraining from pointing out the obvious. "I have been to Emla. I've even seen how they live." She turned the heat on high. "I was surprised to find I thought it was awful."

At last she could see through the windshield without too much trouble. They had reached Uppsalavägen. The snow was sticking; there were no plows in sight.

"I wouldn't have lasted fifteen minutes," she said. "If they locked me up in there I would collapse into a fetal position and stop breathing."

"No, you wouldn't," Sture snorted. "You may think you would, but that's only because you're spoiled. We could perform a simple experiment. I'll take you to a motel. We'll get you a single room and I'll lock the door on you from the outside. You can lie in your clean bed and stare at the TV and chow down on candy all night, and then I'll come let you out the next morning. That's prison life. You will survive."

Sophia shook her head.

"You've never been inside one of those cells, Grandpa. They're nothing like a hotel room."

She recalled the narrow bed, the rubber mattress, and the yellow blanket with the logo of the Prison Service. Sture drew a handkerchief from his pocket and blew his nose.

"Three square meals a day, education, free-time activities — what else do you think the taxpayers should be financing?"

"They wash their own clothes and sheets. And they prepare food themselves."

"Of course." Sture raised his eyebrows. "Poor and misunderstood." He blew his nose into his hand and wiped it on the seat. "Why don't we give them a medal? For years of meritorious service to the Kingdom of Sweden. Perhaps the Order of the Seraphim?"

Sophia didn't bother to respond. Sture turned on the radio, channel-surfing for a while before he turned it off again. On a straightaway, just after Sophia exited the highway, Sture pushed back his seat, turned his face toward the window, and dozed off. He was snoring when Sophia's phone chirped. She picked it up and glanced at the screen. It was a text from Ludwig Venner.

"Primetime 60 min is doing your trial pet. Airs feb 20. My loyal subjects will call jan 9. Be prepared."

She read it half a second at a time; she didn't want to take her eyes from the road. She read. Looked at the road. Read some more. Looked at the road.

"Yikes," she whispered, putting her phone in her lap. She held tight to the wheel and tried to catch her breath. Deep, deep into her lungs. It felt like she needed oxygen.

Primetime 60 Minutes was not just any program. It was TV4's greatest investment ever. They'd moved their most respected reporters to the show and supplied them with a nearly unlimited budget. February twentieth was the premiere. The program was expected to reach an enormous number of viewers, and her petition for a new trial would be part of it. If Channel 4 stuck to the format of the

American original, 60 Minutes, there wouldn't be more than three stories per show, four tops.

And it wasn't just your average reporting. 60 Minutes presented only scoops, only sensational stories. They were always looking for new angles on old truths. It seemed obvious that if they addressed the Stig Ahlin case, they would question the conviction; otherwise there would be no point in bringing it up.

Her mind was spinning.

Be prepared. How could she prepare herself? What had she found, really? An analysis from the National Board of Forensic Medicine that had been relegated to the slush pile when it should have been part of the preliminary investigation file. But that wasn't enough for a new trial. Nor would it be good enough for sensationalist reporters. They would want a great deal more.

And when the program was broadcast, Katrin's parents would be watching; presumably they would refuse to participate, but even so they would find out what Sophia had learned. About their daughter's mental state before she was killed.

Would they speak with Stig's ex-wife, Marianne? Would they have to bring up the incest allegations as well, even if those weren't part of the indictment? Everyone wanted to know what Stig Ahlin had done to his daughter. They wanted to know how she was doing in the present day. And what she thought of her father.

Sophia clung to the wheel. Suddenly it felt like the curves were coming too fast.

Many years had passed since Katrin's death. The wounds she'd left behind must have healed, to some extent. But now they were about to be ripped open again. And Sophia was going to contribute.

The road was quiet; the forest flashed by outside the windows. The sun was low in the sky, and the road seemed to sparkle. The snow was blinding, so she pulled down the visor and squinted. She glanced at Sture. He was still asleep, his mouth agape. His face looked different. She swallowed.

Damn you, Ludwig, she thought. *I'm not ready for this.*

29

Stig would have appreciated it if his attorney, that Sophia Weber, had prepared him. He knew she would have to speak to them, but he would have liked to have been informed before it happened.

The prisoners couldn't buy newspapers on the day before New Year's Eve. The commissary wouldn't open again until January fourth. But one of the guards had left the paper out, open. Forgotten in the common room.

It wasn't a long article. Only half a page, on page 7. The photograph of him had been taken during the district court trial. He'd seen it before. In it he was smiling. He couldn't remember having smiled a single time during the trial, but he must have. Because it was by far the most used photograph when they wrote about him.

It was a smile of great pleasure. He was like a clown in face paint, a stiffened death mask. The photo of Sophia Weber wasn't even half as large. She was posing at a desk. But Stig didn't recognize her hairstyle; it was much shorter than when she had visited him. It must have been taken on an earlier occasion and was lying around in the newspaper archives, ready to be used for this sort of occasion. Because the article was no interview. "Attorney Sophia Weber confirms that she is preparing Stig Ahlin's petition for a new trial." That's what it said. If they'd interviewed her, it would have said so.

Maybe she hadn't been aware, either, that this article was going to be published. But she did know she'd spoken with a journalist. And she should have told him. Even if it wasn't as important to her as it was to him.

Stig Ahlin took the newspaper into his room. He read the article four times. He paged through the paper three times, back to front and front to back, but he couldn't find anything more.

Slowly his heart rate went back to normal. *I could be exaggerating*, he thought. *It doesn't matter. This is only a petition for a new trial. Not something they're likely to care much about. It doesn't mention that there's any doubt it was me. Quite the opposite, in fact.*

Another journalist — to be safe, it was one employed by the same newspaper — had agreed to be interviewed about the case. He commented on Stig Ahlin's chances of being granted a new trial. This skinny man with the neck of a vulture stated that the chances were about equal to his own chances of scoring the lead role in the next Scorsese film.

Stig Ahlin wiped the sweat from his palms. He took a deep breath. Why did this upset him? The journalist was right.

Stig didn't put the paper back where he'd found it. He didn't toss it in the common room wastebasket. He tore it into tiny strips and put it in his own wastebasket. Each time he went to the bathroom, he would take a fistful along and flush it. There was no reason for anyone else but him to read it. The fewer people who knew what he was up to, the better.

He began by tearing up the page with the article. He and Sophia Weber weren't the only ones whose pictures had been printed. She was there too. Katrin Björk. Her class photo. No makeup, smiling. One eye slightly narrower than the other, freckles and tiny pimples on her forehead. By now he had seen it many times, but he never got used to it. The person in that photo was a child, and that's not how he remembered her.

Katrin
1997

In *Pretty Woman*, Julia Roberts had a stash of multicolored condoms and did everything but kiss; Katrin had seen the movie tons of times. Katrin didn't have condoms, a wig, thigh-high boots, or, really, rules. She just did whatever Stig wanted.

Katrin and Stig seldom went to his place. Not after that first time. They ended up at different spots. Hotels. A colleague's overnight apartment; Stig was allowed to borrow the keys. The backseat of his car.

She didn't care where they were. She came along. Didn't ask questions. Did as she was told. The place didn't matter to her.

Stig was allowed to French kiss her. His tongue met hers; it was thick at its root, moving around, going back and forth. Kissing wasn't hard at all.

A few times, he paid her. Smooth, new bills in white envelopes. He was the only one who paid her. She wasn't the only one Stig paid; she knew that. But she was special, he said. Not like the others. He paid her because he wanted to give her something, not because he had to.

She took the envelopes.

She said thanks.

And threw the money away as fast as she could. She didn't even count it.

30

The last four kilometers were a private drive. In the summer it was a narrow gravel road with a grass strip down the middle, but now it consisted of two deep, unsanded tracks in the snow.

Sophia skidded gently through the open gates. She parked the car. The walk had been shoveled, and she helped Sture out of his seat. This was the fourth year in a row they'd been invited to spend New Year's with Carl Bremer and his parents Carl Johan and Adrienne. At their "place," as Carl Johan called it.

She'd met Carl at a party at Stockholm's Nation in Uppsala back when Carl was studying medicine and Sophia was in her second year of law school. It had been an early-summer evening, the fresh air easy to breathe. Sophia had been working at the student bar. She liked it there. Behind the protection of the counter she dared to laugh at bad jokes. She might even allow someone to lean over and touch her arm.

She and Carl had struck up a conversation toward the end of the night. She was playing her own music on the bar's sound system; she'd turned up the volume and was singing along so loudly that she became hoarse and picked up a large glass carafe to serve herself a drink she'd mixed herself. Carl stuck around until after closing time and then they went out dancing at a club none of Sophia's friends knew about. She'd fallen asleep in Carl's bed, but never thought he wanted anything from her but the bright laughter that flowed from her when they were together.

Uncomplicated. But never shallow or unimportant. When Anna started her first company and spent her weekends getting it going rather than hanging out with Sophia, she and Carl began to see each other even more. It was the first time Sophia hadn't felt lonely when Anna didn't have time for her.

Even after just a few months of friendship, she'd accompanied Carl to the countryside. He had taken her hunting, and with Carl she got to slit the belly of a freshly shot moose, empty it of entrails, stand in the hot steam, and let the heat melt the snow all around what had so recently been alive. Carl wasn't the type to be intimidated. Not by death, not by blood, and definitely not by her. It made her feel oddly safe.

Later Sophia had also come along to feed new families of deer; he settled the two of them downwind, so they could observe the fawns undisturbed. And she knew that when he was younger he'd succeeded in taming a hare. He'd given it food and water and made a bed for it under the front steps.

It was a given for Carl. Death one day, caring for life the next.

The family's "place" was a yellow manor house. On the first floor was the hall; the library, with its grand piano; the dining room, with a table that seated thirty; the kitchen, with its open hearth where they'd grilled one New Year's Eve when the power was out; and the billiard room, with the family's collection of Zorn etchings.

The first time Sophia got to visit Carl there, she had felt so welcome that she'd had to ask if his parents thought they were a couple. They didn't, said Carl, who by the next year had brought his boyfriend along. Carl and his boyfriend had stayed together on the third floor, where only the family slept. Sophia never went up there.

There were nine guest rooms and space for seventeen guests in all. She and Sture each had a room. Sophia's was more than three hundred square feet and had silk wallpaper, parquet floors from the century before last, silk-edged velvet curtains, a six-foot mahogany headboard, Persian rugs, a tile oven with dark-blue pansies painted on the topmost tiles, and an enormous oil painting above the bed, depicting someone whom Carl claimed was the first gay in the family.

She always got to sleep in the same room. It almost felt like her very own. At each visit, she began by hanging up her clothes in the Dutch wardrobe of cherrywood, opening the door into the adjoining bathroom, and running a bath.

By the third time she was invited to spend the weekend with them, Carl Johan and Adrienne made sure she brought her grandparents. And they always set a silver tray in the room, bearing mineral water, a few mandarins, and almond biscotti. At dinner they would sit at their usual places, always the same ones.

By the time Sophia was finished bathing, the evening meal wasn't far off. Darkness was already waiting for her in the bedroom. She turned on the light and looked at the book she'd borrowed from the library. If she started reading it now, she would only fall asleep. It was time to dress for dinner.

As she rubbed her legs with lotion she'd found in the bathroom, she turned on the small TV that stood on a narrow table along one of the long walls. It didn't receive any channels, so she turned it back off. She buttoned her dress halfway up the back before wrangling it over her head; otherwise she couldn't get it buttoned the rest of the way. Outside, the snow was still floating to the ground.

. . .

Sophia was standing on the manor house steps in her thin, high-heeled shoes, so cold she was shaking. Someone had hung a fur on her; it smelled like an old cabinet and didn't do anything for her ice-cold feet. Carl and his boyfriend had run off to ignite some firepower whose magnitude equaled that of a ground assault in the final, decisive attacks on the Belgian lowlands in World War I.

"Fireworks. Obviously, we have to have fireworks."

Sophia had never understood why. But she'd stopped protesting years ago.

Sture stood a few yards away, stamping his feet. He'd brought along a cigar and a snifter of brandy and didn't seem to feel the cold. But he was sneezing so hard his knees bent. He was allergic to brandy, he liked to say. And cigars.

Carl Johan and Adrienne were standing beside Sophia. Adrienne had hooked her arm through Sophia's and her dainty feet were stepping lightly in place. She, too, was cold. Carl Johan had the family's foxhound, Wallis, on a leash. The dog was darting in figure eights around their feet and whining.

The other hunting dogs howled from the kennel.

"Well, she's not gun-shy, anyway," said Carl Johan, reeling in the dog. "Isn't that right, Wallis honey, this is nothing, is it?"

The dog was trembling harder than Sophia. Lifting one paw at a time, putting it back down again, putting her nose in the air and howling. She looked as if she wanted to cry. Or as if that was exactly what she was doing already.

"She's a real hunter. Used to it." He turned to Wallis again. "But you'd very much like to know what it is we're hunting, wouldn't you? Wouldn't you, girl?"

The first rockets launched into the air. And as the red and yellow sparks spread across the sky, the foxhound went bananas. Sophia could see the whites of her eyes. Carl Johan swore as the odor of the gunpowder reached them. His hand was bleeding; he had let go of the hound's leash.

"She bit me," he said.

"Not gun-shy at all," Adrienne snorted, adjusting her thin, fur-clad arm under Sophia's. She raised the glass of champagne she'd brought out and pressed her lips together.

"Happy New Year," said Sture, stomping off toward the snowbank where the dog was huddled with her head between her front legs. He put out his foot and stepped on the leash. The brandy sloshed over the rim of his snifter and he dropped his cigar in the snow.

Sophia stared at Carl Johan's hand. Another shell flew into the air and the dog let out a howl. Everyone else looked at the sky, but Sophia couldn't take her eyes from Carl Johan's bleeding hand.

Could it be that simple? She thought. *No, there's no way.*

Carl Johan had taken out a silk handkerchief and was pressing it to his wound. He didn't seem to be in pain. Sophia walked up to him, took his hand, moved the handkerchief, and looked at the marks. Four dots of unequal sizes, all right next to each other. A few centimeters farther down, the skin was pierced. It looked like an abrasion.

"Excuse me," Sophia whispered, letting go of Carl Johan. She felt like she needed to sit down.

"Are you okay, honey?" Adrienne asked. She was gazing at Sophia in concern. "Don't worry about Carl Johan." She leaned the other direction and tugged at Carl Johan's coat sleeve. She, too, lifted his injured hand, glanced at it without much interest, and let it go again. "You see? He'll be just fine. His vaccinations are up to date and anyway, he has only himself to blame. No reason to look so upset, Sophia. I've told him a hundred times."

A fresh swarm of rockets ascended into the sky. The hound howled in unison with the whistling. Adrienne went on.

"I point out to him every year that he should give the dogs sedatives, but he refuses on the grounds that they're hunting dogs, for goodness' sake. This year Carl Johan can bandage himself up. And by the way" — she turned to Carl Johan — "you need to go shut Wallis up in the kitchen. She can't be here."

Sophia jumped, let go of Adrienne's arm, went over to Sture, and took the dog's leash.

"I can take her in." She looped the leash over her hand and nodded eagerly. "I'm happy to take her in. I have to make a call anyway."

She pulled the dog over and walked off. Adrienne didn't protest.

Hans Segerstad didn't answer until the fourth ring. He didn't even say hello.

"Sophia Weber. The woman herself...Are you calling to wish me a happy New Year? Are you drunk?"

"There was a dog at the crime scene, right?"

"Oh please, please...Sophia? If you think I'm sitting here paging through the Ahlin file at ten minutes past midnight on New Year's, you are mistaken."

"But there was, wasn't there? When the neighbor called the emergency number, it was because the dog was making such a racket. It's in the printouts. The neighbor wanted...that's why it took so long. Because he only complained about the dog."

"When the neighbor called? What do you mean? Oh right…the emergency call. Sure, that's what happened."

Sophia stood by the window. Wallis had lain down under a chair by the wall. At every sound, she got up, hit the seat above her, and lay back down. The winter night was illuminated by the thick snow. The fireworks flashed.

"It was the dog that bit her," she said. "Dogs do that when they're frightened, they can bite anyone. Even their master. Or mistress."

"What are you talking about?" Hans Segerstad sounded annoyed. "You mean the dog bit Katrin to death?"

"What's wrong with you?" Sophia suddenly wondered why she'd called Hans. She should have known he'd be too drunk to talk any sense. "Of course that's not what I'm saying. But I think it might have been the dog that bit her. No one has claimed that those bites were the cause of death. But the court believed Stig bit her for sadistic reasons. I don't think he did. I think it was Katrin's dog that bit her, and if that's true there's nothing to link Stig Ahlin to Katrin at the time of the murder. Do you hear me? Nothing!"

"Would they have mistaken a dog bite for a human one? Do you really think those Englishmen were that hopelessly stupid?"

"I think so, yes."

"Hmm." Hans sounded completely uninterested and far from convinced. "We have to find an expert who will agree with you."

"Well, if that's what we have to do, then let's do it."

"Sounds good, Sophia." The buzz in the background had increased. She could barely hear Hans. "That sounds excellent. We'll talk later."

Sophia hung up. Her phone still in hand, she brought up Ludwig's text and read it one more time.

Primetime 60 Minutes. She locked the phone, stuck it in the evening bag in her hand, and left the kitchen. Wallis could stay put.

It sounded like the fireworks were over. The others had gone down to clean up. She stood on the stairs to wait for their return.

It shouldn't be impossible to get a new opinion. Couldn't money buy anything?

In the meantime, I'll talk to that evening paper guy, she thought. *I'll give him what I've found on Katrin. Then I'll give Primetime 60 Minutes the results of the analysis. And tell them there was a dog at the crime scene. They've got money. They might find someone who wants to be on TV. And they can talk to Katrin's parents, Eija Nurmilehto, Ida. No reason for them to meet Stig. Not yet. How many minutes are we talking about? A ten-minute report? They'll have to settle for stock footage. As for me. I should have bought that suit. If worse comes to worst, I'll borrow clothes from Anna.*

Sture climbed the steps, panting, and handed her his brandy snifter. She waved it off, instead accepting a glass of champagne from Adrienne. How they had managed to clean up the hill with all these glasses in hand, she had no idea. But Carl Johan stuck a freshly opened bottle into a snowbank alongside Sophia's car. Sophia took her grandfather by the arm and looked at him.

There weren't many ways to work on a petition for a new trial. A typical case was like a living organism; there were a variety of tactics one could use. A weak indictment could be quashed until it went away; a matter of civil law could be delayed; an application to sue could be buried in paperwork. But a petition for a new trial was based on something that was already settled. Dead. The only remaining option was to beg. Beg the Supreme Court justices for mercy. And resurrection. Some used the media to their advantage. Sophia had never tried that; she thought there was too great a risk it might backfire. It was impossible to predict how a journalist would elect to describe her problems. But now it was time. She was ready.

"Happy New Year," she said, raising her glass to Sture. Once they'd toasted, she kissed him gently on the cheek. "How many Google hits did you say you had, again?"

31

The stroke of midnight on New Year's Eve passed almost unnoticed at the sex crimes unit at Emla Prison. The sounds of a nearby town's celebrations were faintly audible outside the facility. Inside, it was quieter. The guards drank a quick toast with amber-colored soda. One of the prisoners turned the volume up as high as it would go to watch the New Year's greetings on TV. Someone else banged on a wall. No one responded.

Stig Ahlin had turned off his TV and rolled up the blinds. He opened the air intake as far as he could.

Ida would turn eighteen on the fifth of January. It had been almost six years since they'd seen each other, and fourteen years since he got to spend his daughter's birthday with her. He didn't know where she celebrated New Year's. Probably with her friends, tipsy on champagne she wasn't allowed to drink. He didn't know what she looked like anymore. When he tried to picture Ida as a young woman, it was Marianne's face that appeared. He recalled the way Marianne had leaned toward him, mildly drunk, breathing into his neck. Happy New Year!

He had given Ida a dollhouse for her fourth birthday. He'd installed lighting and purchased tiny furniture. In the morning, before she woke up, he had placed the illuminated house next to her bed and covered it with a sheet. She had awoken and sat up in bed, her back ramrod straight and her mouth wide open, the faint light of the shrouded dollhouse glittering in her dark eyes.

Back then, they still knew each other. She missed him when he was gone and was happy when he returned. A few years ago, Stig had written a long letter to Ida. But he'd known even while writing it that he would never be able to send it. There were far too many reasons not to.

One of the countless shrinks Stig had spoken with during his years in prison said after a few months of work that he accepted that Stig considered himself innocent. And in that case, Ida's mother must be considered just as much a victim of circumstances as Stig was. It took some time for Stig to understand what he meant: that Marianne couldn't be blamed for wanting to protect her daughter. And that a mother always takes her child's side.

Stig stopped speaking during those sessions. After four months, he was no longer summoned for treatment. Instead he was allowed to spend that time in the workshop. He had been offered the chance to further his education, of course, even though priority was given to those without previous higher education. But unless he could do research, it was pointless. He preferred to build tables and chairs.

Sometimes Stig dreamed that he had murdered Ida's mother. He fell asleep and was suddenly sitting on a bare floor with Marianne's head in his hands. She was looking at him with dark, shiny eyes. She was powerless, breathing through her mouth. Then he crushed her skull, felt it give way like layered hardboard. Her skin tore away; her hair matted with blood. Or else he pressed his hands to her throat, his thumbs digging into her thin skin until her eyes bulged out and the blood vessels there burst like the glass in an old windowpane.

The next psychiatrist, a short, almost dwarf-sized woman with black bug eyes, also tried to get Stig to consider what it must have been like for Marianne when she was confronted with all the suspicions surrounding Ida, about Ida's injuries and Ida's stories.

So Stig told her about his dreams.

"It's not a nightmare," he said. "More like just a regular dream."

Then he stopped speaking during those appointments and soon that treatment, too, was terminated. "Incapable of feeling remorse," the psychiatrist wrote in the file. That information would be saved for the future; it was important to record. In case he ever applied to have his sentence time-limited.

It had been a long time now since Stig Ahlin was forced to undergo treatment. They left him alone. In solitude. It was just as well.

Misery isn't contagious, Stig's father used to say. But that wasn't true. Misery was epidemic, a flare of wild cancer cells spreading in every direction. Airborne infection. It was contagious if you talked about it. It was contagious if you thought about it. Or it could be spread by physical contact. It was impossible to vaccinate oneself against misery. And it was incurable. So Stig preferred to be alone. Ida was better off without him.

Stig left the blinds up and lay down on his bed. He couldn't hear anything outside any longer. It was the start of a new year. He tapped cautiously on the wall. Then a little harder. In the next room was a family man, a mechanic by trade, convicted of seven rapes. Stig let his hand rest against the painted wall; it was chilly and vibrating slightly — the neighbor's TV was on. He wanted to wish someone a happy New Year. He knocked one last time but received no response.

32

Sture and Sophia only spent two nights at Carl Johan and Adrienne's. For three days, they had lunch and dinner and took long walks, and Sophia tried to relax. Whenever there was a short break in the game of social intercourse, she sat on the sofa in the library under layers upon layers of blankets that smelled faintly of tobacco. She read the first few pages of a book, dozed off, paged through a newspaper, built a fire in the tile oven. Slept, played billiards, made tea, baked a cake, ate it up.

After lunch on January second, she could stand it no longer. It was time to leave.

"Stay," Adrienne pleaded.

But Sophia shook her head and mumbled something about work. She wanted to go home, to a functional Internet connection, to a phone she could use without standing in a very particular position, leaning slightly to the right to keep from dropping coverage. She wanted to go home to her apartment, to the file and her office.

She felt better as soon as she got in the car. The sun was low, glaring off the white fields; it took effort to keep from driving too fast. First, she drove Sture home, helped him into his apartment and out of his shoes; she brought him his slippers. Then she drove into the city to return the car.

The snow was starting to fall as Sophia walked through the afternoon gloom, from the rental office to the Mörby Centrum metro station. The escalator wasn't moving; she walked down. Three people were waiting for the train. At the other end of the platform, a man was asleep on a bench, his back facing out, using a lumpy bag as a pillow.

In a few days, Sophia would have to return to her usual work. There wouldn't be much time left over for Stig Ahlin. She knew the risks: if she didn't do all she could now, the file would lie untouched; it would end up buried under other tasks. To the best of her ability she must try to finish, or else she never would. Once Sophia took a seat on the train, she sent an email from her phone.

"I need to ask a few questions about destructive teenagers. Can you help me?"

That was all she wrote. She didn't close with "xoxo." No way. But she didn't write "best wishes" either. She just couldn't. She signed with an "S."

If only I were the emoji type, she thought. *I could have added a smiley. A breezy, impish, smiling little face. A flourish that could have conveyed everything.*

It's-all-forgotten-let's-turn-the-page-obviously-I'm-not-spending-every-waking-moment-thinking-about-you.

Then she changed her mind. First, she wrote "Sophia Weber." Then she tried "Sophia." Sophia. Not just "S." He could know lots of S's. But Sophia would do. She settled for that.

And she was going to send this to his work email. This wasn't a private communication. It wasn't a way to start something, just a move she was making to help the case take a step forward. That was it. She needed to talk to a police officer; he was one. It would be useful for her to speak to an officer with his expert knowledge. She hit Send and turned to face the window. The tunnel outside was passing in brief flashes. The fluorescent lights snapped and popped.

He's off for Christmas break, she thought. *He won't read it until after Epiphany at the earliest.*

It must have been three minutes before she checked her email for the first time. She managed to bring up her in-box four times before she arrived at her stop. An hour later, when she opened her computer in her apartment, she found he had responded.

"Call me tomorrow and we'll find a time."

That was all. Not his name. Not even an initial. And certainly, no smiley.

Sophia's heart was racing.

33

At five minutes to six on January third, Stig Ahlin sat on the edge of his bed, waiting, fully dressed, for his time to run. The blinds were up, but the darkness outside was as dense as dull cloth. He could usually hear them approaching, their steps outside, the sounds as the key entered the lock were familiar; he knew them by heart. Sometimes he could tell which guard it was just by the sound of the click. But no one had come to let him out.

Stig checked the time on his TV. Then he let ten minutes go by. In the meantime, he looked at his bookcase. On it were four books. *The Sense of an Ending*, the collected works of Tomas Tranströmer, Haruki Murakami's book about running, and the Bible. It could have been an arrangement in a Spanish boutique hotel. If every single other detail were different.

No one came. But he didn't ring the bell. The other prisoners hated the racket. If you had to take a piss, you did it in the sink. Only emergencies or the stomach flu warranted unnecessary ringing.

He had never had to wait this long. In the end, he couldn't stop himself. He heard the ring from beyond his door, dully, coming from the guards' room. Like a typical doorbell. He heard steps. The key. The door opened. Quickly, efficiently.

"Do you need to pee?" the guard asked. His face was impassive. As if he cared.

Stig shook his head. The air from the corridor felt damp and raw. Stig shivered. *He knows why I rang the bell.*

"You have to wait until quarter past seven like everyone else."

The door closed again. Slowly, each sound drawn out to its maximum limit.

Stig watched the closed door and raised his hand to ring the bell again. *I have to run,* he thought. *You have to take me to the gym, damn it. You can't just change your minds, change your attitude, punish me. Not without a reason. You have no right to treat me this way. You have no right.* He lowered his hand.

They might just be understaffed. The holidays weren't over yet. It could go back to normal as soon as the holidays were over.

Stig didn't ask, just pulled off the prison athletic wear. Changed into his regular clothes. The winter pants and sweater, beige, the same color as the athletic wear, the same color as the summer pants and summer shirt. Then he sat down on his bed.

■ ■ ■

A moving box stood on the floor in the lobby. Sophia noticed it right away as she entered. At first, she wondered what it was doing there, but then she remembered that Anna-Maria was packing up her belongings.

She would be off on leave now, for a year. Sophia picked up the box, placed it behind the desk instead, and went to her office.

Once she sat down, she took a piece of paper from her pocket. It was awkward to fish it out; the note was all crumpled. She knew what was on it — how could she forget? Four names, not hard to remember. Four names, their phone numbers all entered in her phone, and an email was written on the note. Yet she smoothed the paper out and placed it on the desk in front of her. She brought up journalist Tor Bengtsson's number on her phone but called it from the landline. He answered on the first ring.

"Speak. Or forever hold your peace."

Jesus, Sophia thought. *What kind of dumb ass is this?*

"Sophia Weber," she tried. "Stig Ahlin's attorney."

Tor Bengtsson coughed. "Sorry. I thought it was someone else. I apologize. But, hey there! Hey, girl. Nice of you to call, did you miss me?"

Girl? Sophia shook her head. *Could this get any worse?*

"I'm calling because I promised to contact you today. And because you wanted to meet with me."

"That's absolutely right. Have you talked to Stig? Does he want to meet with me?"

"No. But I can tell you I contacted that friend of Katrin Björk's you tipped me off about. And I'm going to use the information she gave me in our petition. Which will be submitted sometime in the next two months."

You'll know why, she thought. *You'll watch the program, curse me for not telling you what I'm going to tell them, and you'll know why.*

"Is he going to give an interview to someone else? You didn't forget your promise, did you?"

"I didn't promise you an interview with Stig Ahlin — quite the opposite. He's not going to give any interviews to the evening papers. He refuses to."

"I understand." Tor suddenly sounded glum. "TV came calling."

Sophia didn't respond. Let him suck on that for a while. It would only make the article about her petition for a new trial more interesting. He would devote even more space to her. Let her explain, tell the story, be visible. Tor cleared his throat before speaking again. Now he sounded more serious.

"I spoke to Eija too. And I'm going to publish a long piece on Katrin. We're doing a special insert about teenagers and self-harm, including a lengthy interview with a girl who asked for help back then and a girl who's caught up in our sorry excuse for a mental health system as it is right now. I actually contacted Katrin's parents as well."

He sighed.

"They didn't want to be involved, I assume."

"No. I had almost hoped the mom would be dead by now. I thought...but she wasn't. She seemed fine. And she's still married to Katrin's dad. She didn't even hang up on me. She listened to what I had to say. Was going to talk to her husband later on."

How could he bring himself to tell her? Sophia wondered. *Did he really share everything?*

"I told her everything. At least, all of what I'm going to publish. Some of it I read out loud. There was quite a bit of sobbing, but it almost felt like…" He changed his mind and started over. "No. Most of that is just in my head. I guess I wanted her to be happy I was telling her. That she wanted to hear. But she did listen, anyway. And I promised it wasn't going to be just a trashy gossip piece. Katrin was a good kid. A little girl too. I'm not going to make her out to be a whore who only had herself to blame. I promised her mother. That it wouldn't be like that. And now she knows. For when the next journalist calls. Who was it you talked to, from television? Someone at SVT?"

"You can come see me at my office, if you like." *Might as well get it over with.* "I'll be here all day."

"I'll be there in half an hour. May I bring a photographer?"

Sophia looked at her dirty jeans. *I can wash my hair in the sink,* she thought. *Anna-Maria might have some makeup at her desk.*

"In that case, give me an hour." She looked at the clock. *No, I'll never make it. That'll never work.* "No, wait. Half an hour, that's fine."

It doesn't matter if I look overworked. Unglamorous, exhausted, and ugly. It's even a good thing. Stig Ahlin's idealistic attorney. No silk tie or helmety Dallas hair for folks at home to get worked up over for lack of anything else.

Her next call was to the forensic odontologist. She would be able to visit late the next week. The dinner she had promised to buy was rescheduled as a coffee break in the staff cafeteria. The doctor had a lot to do, she explained. Sophia thanked her.

After that, Sophia called Stig Ahlin. It didn't take more than fifteen minutes for him to return her call. Their conversation lasted no more than five minutes.

He seemed off, she thought once they'd hung up. Certainly, he was never long-winded on the phone, but this had to be a new record. *Stig has to understand we need these journalists. If he can't turn public opinion around a little, drive a wedge of doubt into the general consciousness, he'll end up staying put in prison. And this story on Katrin is problematic as well. Because even if it does end up demonstrating that there are alternative perpetrators, it's hardly going to cast him in a sympathetic light.*

Patting the note in front of her, she let her thumb follow each crease in the paper. One item left. Just one. And Tor would be arriving with his photographer at any moment.

She knew the last phone number by heart. She hadn't tried to memorize it, and yet it was impossible to forget.

She got a cup of coffee and read the news online for a few minutes, without really absorbing anything. She emailed Anna. Sent another to Carl and his parents to thank them for the visit. When those emails were done, she filled in the lines she'd already made, crossing out items on her brief list. There was only one thing left to do.

Instead she rested her hand on the phone receiver.

The journalist is going to be here any second. He should already be here. I have to call now.

She lifted the receiver. The dial tone echoed urgently. *I have to call this minute. Right now. I can't be on the phone when they arrive; that will only make a mess of everything.* She stared straight ahead for a minute, hung up the phone, and then lifted it again.

Couldn't I talk to someone else? Why does it have to be him? He doesn't know anything about this suit. I could try to get in touch with one of the officers who actually worked on this case. Then she picked up the note. The phone number wasn't on it, but it didn't matter.

When I sent that email he answered right away, she thought. *It hardly took an hour for him to respond, so that must mean something.*

Her heart was pounding by now, and she could feel sweat tickling under her arms. The dial tone roared, and she hung up. *I'll call after Tor leaves, when we're done with the interview. That'll be better, I won't have to stress out so much.*

Then the phone rang. Sophia jumped out of her skin and grabbed the receiver. It was him.

It really was Adam. His voice sounded short, as if he were speaking in Morse code or staccato, biting off each word and editing his sentences to be as brief as possible.

"Come by tomorrow. Not a soul at work. The holidays, and all. We'll talk. After the holidays will be difficult. To find time. Just as well. To get it done. So? Can you? Or? Are you busy?"

They spoke for under a minute. When she hung up, she stared at the phone in suspicion. They were going to meet at two o'clock. If something came up, they would call. But otherwise they would be seeing each other. Her and him. Alone in his office. She would see Adam.

Sophia pressed her forearm to her ribcage. Her lungs felt knotted up; her lips were dry and chapped. Her head was pounding.

We're going to see each other tomorrow at his office. Just as well we see each other right away, he'd said. Is it really? Why? Doesn't he have even more on his plate than usual, during the holidays, when the people he's meant to protect are gulping down glögg and draining boxes of wine nonstop in order to go to work? Isn't his team under a lot of pressure right now? Don't kids call in more around this time of year than any other? Wouldn't it be better to see each other in a week or two?

We're going to be alone. Why would he say that? Why would he point out that we'll be alone? What does that mean? Why would he say so? Does he want us to be alone? Does he think I want to be alone with him?

Her head swirled with questions; she felt dizzy.

It has to mean something, she thought as the doorbell rang. She buzzed Tor and his photographer in and went out to the lobby to greet them. Once they'd lugged in all their equipment, Tor put out his hand.

"Hey girl. Nice to meet you. What a cozy little spot you've got here."

34

"So it's true. You're representing Stig Ahlin?"

Adam Sahla was sitting on a chair that seemed far too small for him. He leaned back, tilting the chair with his legs spread wide and his arms crossed over his chest. He was wearing short sleeves. Then he dropped the legs of the chair to the floor again. They banged against the laminate floor.

"You'll have to excuse me," he said. "But he's an asshole."

Sophia was still standing. They'd let her through the security checkpoint and told her to go right on up. Adam hadn't come down to meet her. Instead he had greeted her in the corridor. They ended up standing there, and he put his arms around her and she'd had to take a step back in order to get away, in order to breathe.

Sure enough, the place was deserted. Aside from Adam, she hadn't seen a single person since she'd left the lobby. But obviously Adam still didn't think they should sit in his office; instead he had led her to a conference room. There were eight chairs around the table. He hadn't invited her to take a seat.

He smiled. "Gonna stand there long?"

Sophia swallowed, cast her eyes down, regretted it, and looked back up again.

I never should have come here, she thought.

"It's not against the law to be an asshole."

Sophia pulled out the chair farthest away from Adam. She sat down and put her bag on the table. It fell open and her phone slid out.

"Tell me where you got this stupid idea," he said. "Please tell me. And then you'll have to explain how I can help."

It's winter. He should be wearing a sweater. Why isn't he? And what kind of weird hug was that, in the corridor? Are we friends now? Friends who hug because we're relaxed around each other?

Sophia tossed her phone back in her bag and took out a notepad instead. Her cheeks flushed, and she swallowed.

Calm down, she thought, paging to her initial notes from her meeting with Katrin's friend Eija. Then she clicked the nib out of a pen. And clicked it back in. *It can't be normal for my chest to hurt this much. I should go to the doctor and get a chest x-ray.*

"I'll start by telling you about Katrin," she said. Her voice felt steady. "Then I can explain the basic pillars of justice in our society. A police officer really ought to be aware of them, but it's never too late to learn."

Adam swallowed.

I never should have agreed to this, he thought. *What am I doing here? Norah and I are fine. Why is Sophia sitting here flipping through her notepad as if her life depends on it?*

She was angry; he could tell. He always made her angry, no matter what he did. *Just like with Norah,* he had time to think.

She's the one who wanted to see me. Why? If she's so upset with me she can barely sit still? Offering her hand to shake, what was that?

Adam shifted on his chair, trying to find a position that didn't make his body feel too big. He hugged himself, rubbing his arms for warmth. It was too cold in there. It had been like a sauna in his office. The radiator was broken, stuck on high; his office was hardly inhabitable. But now he was freezing, and he really should go get his sweater, but he couldn't walk past her; couldn't get near her again.

She wasn't looking at him. It was more than anger; she hated him. Her entire being signaled that she wanted to get out of there. Away from him. He never got used to her chilliness, her distance, as soon as he tried to get close. *It will never work.* He repeated the mantra. *Sophia's not the one I want; Norah and the kids are my life.*

That pen — she was clicking it in and out, staring down at her notepad. He could see the back of her neck under her sloppy ponytail; her ever-present ponytail. Her hair grew downward and resisted being put up; she had a cowlick by one ear, he knew what it felt like to follow it with his index finger, with his mouth.

He shifted in his chair again. Thank God he'd spent the morning reading up on this. He'd known what she wanted to talk about. And he had read in the newspaper that she was representing Stig Ahlin.

Could he have said no? Could he have said *I don't think it's a good idea to see each other?* Presumably. When he tried to get hold of her, she never returned his calls. All those times he'd tried, after that night — he'd even gone to her workplace. Planted himself in the lobby since she refused to answer when he called, refused to call back when he left messages. He'd wanted to talk to her; she had refused. Of course, he could have decided not to call her back. Yet the thought had never occurred to him, not until now. And now here he was, and she was talking and talking, but he didn't hear what she was saying.

Her mouth — he couldn't look at her mouth. He must absolutely not think about her mouth — anything but that.

He already knew everything he needed to know to help her. She wanted to talk about the victim. Defense attorneys usually did. And she wanted to prove that the girl had had it rough, that her life choices placed her in risky situations. It didn't take a PhD to figure out what Sophia was after.

"That's about it." Sophia put her notepad on the table. She wiped her sweaty palms on her jeans. "But given that this isn't part of the preliminary investigation material, I believe these must be considered new facts. And I would like to supplement Eija's witness statement with an opinion on what it might imply. You know, to the extent that there are statistics, psychological interpretations, I want to include those. Anything that could help the court understand the bigger picture."

Sophia tried to think of a way to conclude. Adam had raised his arms over his head again. His skin was much paler on the undersides of his arms; she caught a glimpse of the dark, curly hair under the sleeves of his T-shirt.

"I don't have much more to tell you," she went on. "Just…I'm going to include Eija's story in my petition, but I'd like to place that story in a context, I need to make the court understand her, how they lived, what they did. And why."

I'm repeating myself, she thought. *Shut up. If he wants to help me, he will. If he doesn't, I can leave. I never should have come. I never should have contacted him. What was I thinking? I need to leave. Now.*

"And this story suggests that your client is innocent?" Adam spat the word. He had his arms crossed now. "I don't understand. He still confessed to having sex with her. As I see it, this only explains why Stig Ahlin was able to exploit her. Not why he didn't kill her."

Sophia looked back down at her documents. *Those eyes — I don't want him to look at me, it looks like he hates me. Why did he agree to meet with me if he loathes me so much?* She cleared her throat.

"Stig Ahlin was convicted of murder. The fact that he slept with Katrin doesn't make him a murderer. There's no question that if it turns out there were a lot of other potentially violent men in her life, this would be extremely pertinent to the court's decision."

Adam shook his head and didn't say anything for a moment. Sophia leaned across the table to pull her bag closer and was about to stand up and leave when he began to speak again.

"Back then, not much was known about teenage girls and their problems," he said. "We knew about anorexia, but that was about it."

"You accept that she might have lived like this?" Sophia dropped her bag again.

"Without a doubt." He nodded.

"Saw lots of men? Allowed herself to be used? Because everything that has come out about Katrin up to this point suggests that she was the responsible type. The *most* responsible. Is it really likely that her life was like this? That she did that sort of thing? Just tell me what you believe."

"You have no idea how many girls in lamb's wool sweaters and pearl necklaces I've listened to. Who have sat there primly, knees together, and told me the most incredible stories." Adam's gaze was steady on her. "I think this sounds like a pretty classic example. And even if my colleagues made a hell of a mistake in not digging deeper, I understand why. On a human level, at least."

Sophia let him continue.

"But if we stick to Katrin. This kind of self-harm often begins with an assault. A rape, or a sexual game that goes off the rails."

"If that's what happened, why do you think it never came out? It would have been pivotal. If she had been raped previously. The guy that raped her..." Sophia didn't finish her sentence. She wasn't out to find the killer. All she wanted to do was prove that Stig Ahlin wasn't the only one who could have killed Katrin.

"Probably because the people who should have known didn't know that she had been subjected to something, and because those who did know didn't think it was important. Her parents..." Adam cleared his throat. "She probably didn't mention anything to them, because if she had they would have told the police, at least after she was murdered. But why would Katrin have told them? There are a hundred reasons for a child not to say anything, and only one reason to tell the truth. It doesn't mean they're bad parents — sometimes it's even the opposite, in certain respects. But there could be something else going on. Another sibling who isn't doing well or who dies, someone's sick and gets overlooked. Or a divorce. Dad is unfaithful, and he and Mom are having a shitty time, what do I know?"

Silence. Sophia cast her eyes down. Adam cleared his throat.

"She seeks out other adults," he said. "Ones who see her. Who tell her that she's good, that's she's sexy, damn good at fucking, anything. Of course, it's easy for us to see that this makes the girls feel even worse in the long run, but it's not so simple for them."

"But she was so young. Isn't it — "

"Fourteen. If I were to generalize, I'd say this is more or less the age of debut for these girls. I met one girl who was twelve. In her case, not a single person believed her. Not even me. She had a mild mental handicap and I thought, sometimes that can…there are examples…it can be a reason…I was wrong. We made a hell of a mistake. One of my colleagues had to go to her house and cut her dead body down from the shower rod in her parents' bathroom. She hanged herself when the prosecutor closed the investigation into one of her friends' dads. She was twelve. Had just had a birthday."

"How do they find these men? Where do they find each other? How do they meet?"

"Here and there. The Internet wasn't too widespread yet in 1998. *Aftonbladet* had some site where they hung out, but it wasn't very common. I guess it was still doable, though. Where did you say she met your client? At her after-school job? That sounds like a place they might have met, to me. Otherwise, at school, at training camp, at the stables, at the grocery store. You can't just ban them from going online and assume that's enough. The only thing that might help is making sure that the kids are mentally all right."

Sophia was quiet. Adam stared at her. The water bottle in front of him was empty. He laid it on the table and spun it around.

"And what are you planning to do with this information?" he wondered. "Conveniently leak to a handy journalist that Katrin Björk was a slut and Stig Ahlin was just a poor bastard who thought he would get to have uncomplicated sex with a girl who was up for anything? Consensually, of course. How was Stig Ahlin supposed to understand that she didn't want to, if she didn't say no? I'm guessing that's how you see it. That Stig Ahlin can't be blamed and now her parents just have to take this blow too. As if they didn't already have quite a bit to deal with."

Sophia shook her head. She clenched her jaw so hard that pain shot through one of her molars.

"It's not about blaming Katrin or her parents." She stood up. "I don't know what I'm going to do with this information, other than use it in my petition for a new trial." Her phone fell out of her bag again. Sophia snatched it up. "What do you think I should do? Ditch Stig Ahlin because he's a creep? Because he has a horrible view of women? I'm sorry you dislike him, and excuse me for repeating myself, but he was convicted of homicide, not of sleeping with Katrin. You don't get life in prison for having consensual sex with a woman who has reached the age of consent, even if she is young."

Adam was standing now as well. They stood there on either side of the oblong table, Adam with his legs planted wide and one hand clenched in a fist.

"What do I think you should do?" he wondered. "Nothing, I guess. That bastard deserves to rot in jail. He should never be allowed out."

He walked across the room, approached Sophia, and took her arm. She stared at her arm. At his hand. That broad, soft, warm hand was just as she remembered it. He was touching her. *What is he doing?* she had time to think. Her skin was burning. She yanked free and walked out of the room.

"You can't just take off," he called. "I have to escort you to the lobby. You can't go by yourself."

Sophia heard Adam, but she stalked off anyway. As fast as she could, without turning around. He didn't come after her, not right away. The elevator was still where she'd left it; the doors opened as soon as she pushed the button. She made it inside before he caught up with her. But he didn't follow her. The doors closed, and he hadn't tried to get in. He didn't touch her again. Then he was gone.

35

Sophia and the forensic odontologist, Maria Larsson, met in the cafeteria at the National Board of Forensic Medicine. They were each sipping a mug of coffee, and Maria Larsson was speaking at a rapid pace. She had a job to get back to, and far too much to do.

"I don't actually agree with the practice of obtaining expert opinions in crime investigations like this one," she said, "or at least I very seldom do. My job is to identify dead people. In cooperation with the National Board pathologists I try to find out who died, not who killed whom. Fire victims, big disasters. The tsunami — we were very busy after that."

Sophia nodded.

"But naturally I remember the Stig Ahlin case very well." The forensic odontologist had put down her coffee and taken off her glasses. She polished them intently with a handkerchief that smelled strongly of eau de cologne. "And I've taken a look at the pictures you sent. I wasn't here then; that was my predecessor, but he's dead now." She stopped polishing and aimed a grave look at Sophia.

"He was Sweden's first forensic odontologist. A real legend, just brilliant. A pioneer. He taught me — well, he was..." She paused to put her glasses back on. "But we're not here to talk about me. So, the analysis in the Stig Ahlin case."

"I'm truly grateful," Sophia began, but she was interrupted by the odontologist, who waved an annoyed hand in the air.

"What can I say besides the obvious? I agree completely with that analysis. The marks on Katrin Björk's body are far too inconclusive, far too superficial. That Englishman who performed the examination that was used at the trial..." She laughed. "Actually, I know who he is, met him once at a conference a year or so after the murder. Enthusiastic, eloquent, disturbingly popular among investigators. But naturally, he's an idiot."

Sophia nodded.

"You don't believe that the marks match Stig Ahlin's teeth?"

"Definitely not." Maria Larsson seemed almost amused. "And I'm prepared to swear to it. For my part, there is nothing in those pictures that shows with any certainty that the marks on her body came from teeth. If the pathologists confirmed they were, that would change things, but just going on the image of the marks, and disregarding how the girl died, some of them could be insect bites, or a rash."

She picked up one of the photographs of Katrin Björk's dead body that Sophia had placed on the table. She pointed.

"This irregular, half-moon-shaped mark, for example — when it comes to this one and a few of the others I can at least understand how someone thought they saw an impression left by teeth. In those pictures it undeniably looks like the wound could be a bite mark. But the others? And to go from there to deciding those teeth belonged to Ahlin and no one else? Can you explain that to me?"

She looked urgently at Sophia, then went on.

"Oh well. But I seldom get excited for no reason. Especially not when a police officer has stated exactly the results he hopes for beforehand. Because we get to...well, I'm sure you know, our specialty is unique among forensic analysts in that we find out quite a bit about the presumed perpetrator before we start working. We are given a lot of prior information, too much, if you ask me. We are supplied with dental molds and images of what are alleged to be bites, and we're expected to put those two puzzle pieces together. We're often held to rather low standards in these examinations. It's unusual for the odontologist to receive more than one dental cast to compare. Imagine if the police arranged a lineup, but only allowed the witness to see the main suspect. It's kind of like that. Even when the assumptions are better thought out, though, lots of people are happy to embellish to be accommodating. It's human nature, and sometimes it's even necessary. Nothing to get worked up about. Unless you're Stig Ahlin, that is."

"You're prepared to swear to it, you say? What does that entail?"

"That I'd be happy to write a brief opinion. It will look more or less like my colleague's. You can include it in your petition."

Sophia squeezed her hands in her lap. This was good, but would it really be enough? She needed more.

"I mentioned on the phone that there was a dog at the scene of the crime."

"Right." The odontologist drank the last of her coffee. "I know what you're getting at. But you won't get me to state that it was a dog. Not even if you provided me with a dental cast of that pooch. Which is dead anyway, I assume? The marks are still too incomplete, no matter what you want me to compare them to. I can't swear it was the dog, not with a clear conscience. My reputation is on the line here."

Sophia's heart sank. Maria Larsson glanced at her watch.

"It's a tricky area. But you should know that after a few decades of slavering uncritically over any complex notion that arrived bearing an official stamp, we scientists have become more and more skeptical toward... Let's say that there's an enormous difference in what can be scientifically proven, and exercises in which the results of an analysis depend solely on an expert opinion. I think you should have a decent chance of getting your new trial."

"Unfortunately, the courts aren't equally skeptical," Sophia said.

One time, she thought. *Only one single time did a Swedish court go against an expert opinion from the National Board of*

336

Forensic Medicine. I need a new opinion from the board, one that clearly points away from Stig Ahlin. That would increase my chances for a new trial tenfold.

"We'll hope that the legal world catches up soon. Because the thing about experts — what can I tell you?" The odontologist looked at her watch again. "There are about three hundred people in the world who have as much experience in this arena as I do. In the world. Not even those of us in this limited group agree. When we meet, we're more inclined to disagree about everything. Attorneys who deal with the same sorts of things you do — you're not on the same page all the time, are you?"

Sophia shook her head in acknowledgment.

"You spend half your time arguing and ratting each other out, and the rest of it explaining to each other how many idiots are in your profession?" Maria Larsson grinned. "No one raises a glass for absent friends?"

"Not exactly."

"That's what specialists are like. It's something you learn at university. It's as if that's the only way to make a name for yourself. And furthermore, there's no shortage of dentists who'd love to make an extra buck working for the police. Not here in Sweden, but abroad."

I have to get her to say this on tape, Sophia thought. She already knew that forensic odontology was one of the most hotly debated arenas in the forensic sciences, and that it wasn't a specialty recognized by the National Board of Health and Welfare. But she'd hardly expected to hear it from one of the top experts in Sweden.

"These sorts of problems are well known in the United States," said Maria Larsson. "There are tons of notorious cases. You've heard of them, I expect?"

"A few."

"The most famous one is the Ray Krone case."

Sophia nodded. She'd read that one.

"Received the death penalty after some guy somehow managed to match his snaggle-toothed dental impression on a Styrofoam cup to the bite marks on the breasts of a woman who was raped and murdered." She sighed. "He spent ten years in prison before they managed to free him. And what got him out was the new DNA technology. I don't suppose Stig Ahlin will be that lucky?"

Sophia shook her head. It seemed important to say as little as possible and let Maria Larsson speak.

"If you ask me...forensic odontology is indispensable when it comes to identifying a dead body or figuring out how old the deceased is. But it should not be used to finger murderers and rapists."

She stood up, pushed her chair in smartly, and picked up her empty mug. She'd promised Sophia fifteen minutes. Thirteen of them had passed. Sophia felt her stomach knotting. She needed to keep talking to Maria Larsson.

"I know you're very busy. I really appreciate this. But..." She didn't know what she should say. "But you did say that it could have been the dog," she said. "Couldn't you say so in court too, that it could have been?"

"No. I'm not going to put it that way. But I will say that the marks are too incomplete to conclude that they were made by human teeth, much less Stig Ahlin's teeth. I think that should be convincing enough."

Sophia was reluctantly putting out her hand to say goodbye when Maria Larsson went on.

"There's just one part I don't quite understand."

Sophia nodded.

"The reason we seldom do this sort of analysis is that bites often have traces of DNA left by saliva. What did the DNA analysis say in this case? Was there saliva but no usable DNA, or too little DNA to test? Or was there no saliva at all? Because if they didn't find any, that might indicate that those aren't bite marks."

"Uh..." Sophia hesitated.

"We're not the ones who analyze potential bodily fluids; they do that at SKL, as you know. First the pathologists examine the body. They send samples to SKL and we typically aren't involved until after that."

"The DNA test showed no results. They found the victim's own DNA...but..." *All those tests, I can't keep them straight*, Sophia thought. *How did they put it? I've read the autopsy report and the prosecutor's case notes, which were attached to the forensic odontologist's analysis, and they said that neither that analysis nor the DNA test could link Stig Ahlin to the crime scene.* As she thought, Maria Larsson continued.

"I understand that. But why didn't it show anything? That could be a point of interest."

Sophia felt her mouth go dry. The odontologist was beginning to sound irritated. A crease had appeared on her forehead. She spoke more slowly.

"Normally our analysis is only supplementary or is needed only if there isn't reliable DNA. Was that the case?"

Sophia bit her lip. Her mind was racing. "It appears from the preliminary investigation that they were not able to retrieve usable DNA. They tried, but they didn't find any..." Sophia felt her cheeks flush. "There's nothing in the autopsy..." Sophia cleared her throat, trying to keep her voice steady. She had been sloppy.

"You should talk to SKL. They can explain exactly what their analysis entails. Have you done that?"

"You're absolutely right," Sophia said. "You don't suppose you could...you have those results here as well, right? Don't you keep them? Archive them?"

It took effort for Sophia to remain calm. Maria Larsson sighed. Her entire body was signaling reluctance.

"Archived somewhere. Yes, you can bet on it. But I doubt you want to tackle that. Ordering something from the archives can take months."

Almost eighteen minutes had passed. Sophia had gone well beyond her allotted time.

"I'm not even sure the archives are still here in Solna," said Maria. "They may have outsourced the entire operation, shipped the documents to a for-profit company in Far-Offistan."

"But I could go to the office and search for it. If I fax it to you, would you be able to explain it to me, what it would mean for your assessment? Don't you need it to write your opinion?" Sophia could hear the way she sounded, as if she were begging on her knees. "You said so yourself, that it might be decisive in your opinion."

"No," Maria said. "I didn't say that. I said that it's for the best if the odontologist can work without already knowing the results ahead of time…that's what I've been trying to explain. That we know too much. We should know as little as possible when we begin our work. The fact that we usually have access to those results is a different matter altogether."

The odontologist tapped her watch. She was weighing her options. If she left without helping Sophia, she would have her on the phone half an hour later. Sophia would hardly give up before getting exactly what she wanted. If, on the other hand, she dealt with this right away, it would be over faster.

"Let's go up to my office," Maria Larsson said decisively. "I can make a call to SKL for you. They'll know who performed the analyses in the Ahlin case. It's not the sort of thing you forget in a hurry. Professor Death — we all remember that."

■ ■ ■

Sophia was already in the ticket line at Central Station by the time she called her office's contracted receptionist to instruct her to cancel all Sophia's meetings. This couldn't wait. She had to travel to SKL right away.

Fresh ticket in hand, she dashed to the platform, and when she stepped off the train at Linköping Central Station, only delayed by an hour and fifteen minutes, her calves ached from pressing her feet to the floor the whole way.

The taxi driver didn't even look at her as she threw herself into the backseat and coughed out the address. Instead he got out of the car, opened her door, and gestured her out.

"That's less than two hundred yards away. Walk. And take an extra lap around the block if you can. You look like it would do you good to get your heart rate down."

The apartment was on the fourth floor of a five-story building. It was poorly lit, poorly maintained, and even more poorly ventilated. In the hall stood three pairs of rubber boots, all the same size, and four more pairs of men's shoes.

He lives alone, Sophia observed, stepping in a place for a moment before realizing that he was waiting for her to take off her shoes. Embarrassed, she kicked them off and thanked him for letting her visit on such short notice.

Olof Westlin, the retired head biologist for the former SKL, hummed in response. He seemed amused. They went to the living room.

Sophia politely declined coffee but accepted water; she tried to sit still on the sofa, drank a sip of water, put down her glass, picked it up again. Westlin was carefully munching on a thick slice of store-bought sponge cake. It was perfectly silent in the room. The windows were closed; the weak afternoon light filtered through the drawn curtains. In only a few minutes it would be dark. Sophia's train back to Stockholm would leave in an hour and thirty-two minutes.

At last he appeared to be done chewing. He used the back of his hand to wipe a few crumbs from his clean-shaven chin, then stood up and left the room. A minute later he returned with a plastic folder.

"I have copies of my most important cases. In the basement. It might be against the rules, but I don't care. Folks can never keep track of things, and I'm sure as hell not about to let people like you show up and claim I was the careless one. I'm not careless. Never have been."

Sophia's hands were shaking as she accepted the folder.

"No," she said as firmly as she was able. "Of course not. I certainly don't mean to suggest you were careless. Not you. But — "

Olof Westin cut her off. "Like I said. We could have dealt with this over the phone. It would have been much faster. And you wouldn't have had to buy a train ticket."

He sounded upset, almost angry. Sophia swallowed and let him go on. She put the folder on the table and rested her shaking hands on top.

"The only human DNA found on Katrin Björk's body was her own. You must know that already."

"The only *human* DNA?" Sophia hardly dared to breathe. "But you found something else too?"

"Yes. I damn well did." Westlin threw out his hand and accidentally hit the sponge cake. It flew across the table, crashed to the floor, and left behind a cloud of crumbs. "I honestly cannot believe these questions. I've never tried to hide that fact." He really was angry now, as he leaned down, grabbed the top of the cake, and put it back on its plate.

"I made my opinion perfectly clear in my analysis. What's more, I discussed it with the investigator, to make sure it didn't end up in the hands of one of the many indifferent illiterates on the police force. I talked to that officer, Bertil was his name, Lundberg, Lundgren, something like that."

"What did you tell him?"

"That a dog must have disturbed the body somehow."

"You told the officer that?"

"Yes. As I recall, he wasn't surprised in the least. There was a dog at the crime scene. The police wondered if the dog had licked his mistress clean. I responded that it was possible. And that the dog might have done more than that. Tried to move her. Drag her away from the scene of the crime. What the hell do I know? But why you look so shocked about this, I have no idea. Everyone knew this. Everyone."

Not the court, Sophia thought, taking the folder from the table. *Everyone but the court knew this.* She had to swallow before she could speak.

"Would you be prepared to say this in court?"

"Why couldn't I?" Westlin shook his head in suspicion. "Damn straight I can."

"Thank you," she said. "I don't know how I can..." She took his hand and pumped it furiously. She couldn't let go. "Thank you so, so much."

Katrin
1998

Bertil Lundberg had said he would pick Sara up at work, so they could drive to the clinic together. But he hadn't had time. They'd had to meet there instead. When he finally arrived, she was annoyed. But she didn't say anything. The waiting room was full. In one corner, a woman was perched on the edge of a chair and crying. Next to her, a man was leafing through a magazine. Page after page, loudly and firmly.

It wasn't Bertil's fault he was late. How could he have predicted that a batch of results would arrive from SKL? He had to go through them before he could leave and ended up needing further information on certain points. He'd called SKL to discuss one of the results. It had taken some time to reach the right person.

The dog, said the guy at SKL. It was the dog that destroyed the evidence. That mongrel had disturbed the body too. There was nothing to be done about it — it was what it was. No traces of Stig Ahlin were left.

When Bertil hung up, he threw away the notes he'd jotted down. They didn't have to become part of the investigation.

He didn't have to annotate everything. All the pointless analyses would be sufficient. Plus, he was in a hurry.

Just a few minutes after Bertil rushed into the prenatal clinic, Sara's name was called. Now they were in an exam room. The midwife smelled faintly of sweet perfume and Sara had taken off her shirt and unbuttoned her pants. She was lying on the paper sheet of the slightly inclined table and breathing nervously. Her shoes were still on, covered in blue shoe protectors identical to the ones Bertil was slipping around in.

The midwife raised a plastic bottle over Sara's taut abdomen. Sara took Bertil's hand. When the pale blue gel landed on her belly she jumped. Her hand was warm and damp.

Using something that looked like a fat razor, the midwife spread the gel across the lower part of Sara's belly and then pointed at the screen.

The image was grainy, but Bertil could make it out perfectly clearly. It was the head of a child, already too large to fit on the small screen in its entirety. The midwife pressed a button and the room filled with the sound of a steady drumroll, the rapid heartbeat of his child.

It's going to be okay, Bertil thought. *We'll get Stig Ahlin anyway. That goddamn whoremonger. He bit his wife. He bit his daughter. He bit Katrin and he's the one who killed her. We don't need any DNA. We will not let those science types in their ivory towers ruin this. The rest of what we know will be enough. Stig Ahlin is guilty. The court will realize it too. No one wants that man running loose on our streets.*

"And you're sure you want to know the sex?" the midwife asked.

Sara nodded. She was already crying. Bertil leaned toward her, placing his lips alongside her cheek.

"Then I'd like to congratulate you both," the midwife said, smiling. She pressed a button on the machine. The image froze. "On your perfect, beautiful little girl."

36

TV host, journalist, columnist, and author Lasse Wilander stepped through the door, gathered momentum across the threshold, and seemed to wind up, swinging his arm in a half circle before slapping Sophia's hand with his own palm, remarkably enthusiastic. Four journalists shared the role of host, but *Primetime 60 Minutes* was his baby.

"I want to thank you for agreeing to talk to us."

Sophia smiled tentatively.

"What a story," he went on. "Just incredible. This is the greatest judicial scandal in Sweden's history. No one else has been exonerated after spending such a long time in prison. No one."

Sophia hesitated. The *Primetime* team had been working on the case for just about four weeks exactly. It was reasonable to assume that most of their material was made up of her own information, of the work she had done and shared with them.

"He's not free yet," she attempted.

A crease appeared between Lasse Wilander's eyebrows. He observed Sophia for a moment before sitting down beside her and gazing into the mirror that covered one wall of the room.

"A minor detail, given the situation," he declared.

"Can you close your eyes for a sec?" The makeup artist gently laid a finger on Sophia's forehead. Sophia leaned her head back and complied.

"Have you gotten a chance to watch the tape?" Lasse Wilander leaned toward the mirror, carefully inspecting his own face. He gently pinched the skin under his eyes with two manicured fingertips and turned to the makeup artist. "You'll fix that, won't you, Nettan?"

The woman, who had just introduced herself to Sophia as Helena, nodded.

"No." Sophia took the opportunity to respond as Helena dabbed her forehead with a rubber sponge. "Not the new one. I just got here — I haven't had time to look at anything yet. Did you find lots?"

Helena took hold of Sophia's chair and spun her halfway around so her back was facing the mirror. Lasse replied.

"You're probably already aware that we've decided to devote the entire pilot episode to this. I don't under-stand how we managed, given the time crunch, but we have a ton of material. Their British expert — all we had to do was call Scotland Yard. And what's more..." Lasse turned around and scanned the room, as though looking for something. "...I haven't got my notes here, but, well, a court of appeals in Wales made him eat humble pie. I'll show you what they wrote."

Sophia had already heard this.

"You've done a fantastic job," she said.

"I'd say so. The pedophile Stig the Pig, Professor Death himself, is innocent. Who would have thought?"

"I'm sorry." A sudden jab of pain in Sophia's eye and the makeup artist grabbed a cotton swab to wipe away the mascara that had ended up on Sophia's eyelid. "That was an accident."

"No problem," Sophia whispered back.

"I actually need to wash my hair," said Lasse. "But you usually have that stuff... freshly washed hair isn't optimal either. You could get me some of that dry shampoo, right?"

The makeup artist nodded, annoyed. "Did anyone talk to Stig's daughter?" she wondered. "Or are you not bothering with that? Don't people care how she feels?"

Sophia had seen the segment about the incest allegations. It was brief. One of the hosts read aloud from the decision to close the investigation, sounding matter-of-fact and distant. A psychiatrist discussed the failings of the investigation and pointed out that Ida had never said her father sexually abused her, not explicitly. Nor had she said he'd done anything that couldn't also be interpreted as normal contact between parent and child. A doctor had been interviewed about alternative factors that could have caused the swelling and marks that had been found around Ida's genitals.

"He was never charged for that crime," Sophia said quietly. "It was a mistake from the start to make the general public aware of it. You are innocent until found guilty by the courts. That's the way it has to be."

The makeup artist shook her head. She went over Sophia's face with a soft brush. This time her motions were more abrupt and firm. "I don't know," she mumbled. "If there's going to be an hour-long program about how innocent her dad is, someone should ask how she's doing. How she is nowadays."

Lasse cleared his throat. "There are two kinds of journalists," he said. "The great majority are charlatans who think it's in society's best interest to publish the names and photographs of anyone suspected of being a sex offender, those who believe the most important thing is to make sure no guilty person goes free. If you were a journalist, Nettan, we would find you among those people."

The makeup artist still hadn't corrected him about her name. Lasse went on.

"Then there's a minority of journalists who have come to understand the basics of what we call 'the rule of law.' We, my lovely girl, believe the most important thing is that no one is convicted of a crime they didn't commit. That is more important than anything else. Even if it means a pedophile is set free. Do you understand? But of course, this isn't popular in homes across Sweden. Or even among the majority of journalists. To find awards for this sort of journalism, one must look abroad. The Pulitzer. The Peabody Award. Because Stig Ahlin is innocent. Of the pedophilia allegations as well, no doubt. His crazy ex-wife — why would anyone believe that cow?"

"Tell me what I'm about to see." Sophia wanted to change the subject. Helena was going through her hair with the curling iron and Sophia could swear she already had three burns on her scalp. "I understand you interviewed Katrin's mother."

Lasse Wilander spun on his chair and leaned toward Sophia.

"Made for unbeatable TV. She spills all. She talks a lot about her regrets. What a tough time Katrin had. What she should have done. I interviewed Katrin's mother along with Eija, that little friend. It was their idea. A stroke of genius, I must say. When Eija talks about how her friend's parents let her down and her mother is sitting there blowing her nose all over the place — shit, it's so good. We're all sobbing. Even me. Like I said, good TV."

"How her parents let her down?" *I don't follow*, Sophia thought.

"Yeah, maybe her mother most of all. We don't put the blame on her, nothing like that. But she had quite a bit to deal with. What was she supposed to do? She had to. You can see it for yourself. I asked them to play it for you while I'm in makeup. That gives you something to do. It's all set up, out in the studio."

"You're done now," said the makeup artist, spinning Sophia around. She looked at her reflection in the mirror.

Jeez. Sophia blinked in disbelief. *Is that what I look like?*

A beige easy chair and a pale gray sofa were facing each other in what looked like a cross section of a living room. Sophia declined a cup of coffee and sat on one side of the sofa.

"Do you want to watch?" The studio gal shot Sophia a questioning look. When Sophia nodded, the woman started the VCR on the cart. "It's not fully edited, but Lasse thought you should see it anyway."

On the TV screen, Sophia watched a woman in her fifties enter the studio, the same studio she was in right now. She was shown to a seat and given a microphone. Eija Nurmilehto was already seated, but it was the older woman who spoke first.

When she was finished, the camera zoomed in on Lasse. He was leaning forward slightly in his chair. His eyes were shiny.

"Why didn't anyone notice how Katrin was feeling?"

Eija responded. "Because she didn't say anything."

Lasse still hadn't taken his eyes from Katrin's mother. He had moved so close that he was almost brushing her knee.

"She didn't mention anything to you either?"

Katrin's mother was clutching a tissue in one hand. But she wasn't crying. Instead she just shook her head.

"I wasn't there," she said at last.

Katrin
1997

Katrin wasn't actually all that worried. She didn't spend all her time thinking about it, definitely not. Because her mother would get well. The doctors had said so. They were almost certain of it. And anyway, Dad was, a hundred percent. Absolutely sure, no doubt at all. They didn't even have to talk about it, because they knew it would all be fine.

Katrin had a cup of tea with her dad before she left. She would put on her makeup at a friend's house.

"It's important for you to have fun," Dad said as they put their mugs in the dishwasher. "Mom wants you to enjoy yourself. To be happy. For life to go on as usual."

Katrin gave him a kiss. She liked this about Dad. That he didn't worry.

In her bag was some brown liqueur her parents never drank anyway, and a few splashes of port, whiskey, and vodka. Not much of any one sort. but altogether the mixture filled half a plastic bottle. She'd watered it down with mixed-berry juice. Dad never kept track of the liquor cabinet in the first place, but it was even easier now. Mom at least used to get suspicious. Once she had been cleaning out Katrin's backpack after a field trip and when she unscrewed the top of the empty thermos she could tell from the smell that Katrin hadn't exactly been drinking hot chocolate while orienteering with her classmates. But Mom was gone — all weekend and four days after that.

When they arrived at Gården he was already there. He had dark blue eyes and thick eyebrows and had told Helen's brother that he thought Katrin was cute. He was two years older but didn't care about that sort of thing. He didn't consider her just a little kid.

First, they danced. He held her, his hand on her waist, and she laid her cheek against his chest. He was tall.

Next to him, she was light, soft. She felt her waist become thinner as he placed his hand there, and when his other hand slid down toward her butt it was like it became rounder all on its own. He thought she was sexy as hell, she could feel it, he couldn't resist her and pressed her to him, kind of hard.

She finished the bottle and he took her by the hand and they went outside together. None of the adults had noticed she was drunk. That was good, but it was even more important that she get out, she couldn't throw up indoors or someone would call her house.

It was cold outside. The night was black and the sky endless. Katrin held onto him; he held onto her. She kissed him. She took his hand again, his large hand, and brought it inside her jacket, inside her shirt. Then she had to stop. She couldn't keep her eyes closed any longer. Her head was spinning. She didn't want to throw up. She wanted to feel his cold hands on her breasts, his tongue in her mouth.

But the bus arrived. And he got on and Katrin followed him and passed out in the back. When she woke up she was lying down and he was all over her, and Katrin realized that his friend was there as well, on the other side of the same seat. The friend pretended to be looking out the window, but she met his gaze in the reflection. Katrin didn't remember the friend's name anymore. But she could see in his eyes that it wasn't like before. The look told her how bad it was. What was being done to her.

She should have screamed, but that didn't occur to her until much later. Another person than Katrin would have screamed. Another person than Katrin would have sat up and battled her way free. But instead Katrin lay where she was. She let him do what he was doing and she looked at his friend's eyes in the window.

The driver didn't notice a thing. He couldn't have. Because the bus drove and drove and when it was finally over, she was allowed to put on her pants again. Her underwear was gone, the zipper got caught on her pubic hair, and when the bus stopped he stood her up, with the help of his friend; she had to lean on his shoulder, he pulled her close as they hauled her down the steps and off the bus. They sat her on a bench, and only then did she throw up.

He got back on the bus before it left the stop and the friend did too, and she said, "Don't go. Please. Don't leave." But both of them left. Then she threw up until it turned dark red and she could tell she had a nosebleed, or she was puking blood. And she didn't know where she was, but he and the friend had disappeared, and she knew she had to get home.

Katrin didn't cry when she lost her virginity. She didn't even close her eyes. She couldn't, because her head was spinning too fast, whirling, zooming down and out into something that was gone forever. Was it rape? Did she want it? She didn't know. How could she? She didn't say anything; what would she have said?

When she arrived home, she went to the bathroom, locked the door, and got into the shower, on the floor under the boiling-hot water. Dad was asleep. He didn't wake up when the hot-water heater came on. Mom would have; Mom would have woken up, but she wasn't there. Katrin showered until she ran out of hot water and then she went to her room and Dad didn't wake up, or else he was just letting her be. Dad left her alone.

The next morning, she ate breakfast with Dad. He read the paper and she lay down in front of the TV. She didn't say anything, because she had nothing to say.

He asked, "Did you all have fun last night?"

What did she say to that? She didn't remember.

Mom came home four days later. She was tired. She spent most of each day sleeping. When Katrin went to school, when she returned home, when it was time for dinner, when they were going to watch a movie on TV. The exhaustion never let up.

Sometimes she came up to eat with Dad and Katrin, her robe open and her hair greasy. But she just picked at her food and left the table after a few minutes. Sometimes she wrapped herself in a blanket and lay down on a chair on the balcony. She fell asleep there too, even though it was cold.

Katrin went into her room, crawled into bed next to her mother as she had when she was younger, cuddling up to her angular back. Her nightgown smelled like sweat.

But Mom got so warm; the covers were too thick. She told Katrin that soon, but not now, they could talk, later, she just had to sleep for a while first. She was awfully tired.

37

Adam Sahla bolted up from the sofa, startled. He wiped saliva from his chin with the back of his hand. What time was it? *Bolibompa* was over and the kids were no longer in front of the TV. Norah wasn't home yet, but she would be soon — at nine, she'd said. He should get the kids to bed.

He heard his daughter's shrill voice from the children's room. She wasn't crying, but his son was protesting about something. Adam struggled to get up. He found the remote, which was stuck between the cushions, and changed the channel. He could catch a few minutes of the news before it was time to deal with the kids.

"Go put on your pajamas," he called, but there was no response. Instead his son started screeching. Adam couldn't tell what he wanted. Then it was his daughter's turn to start howling. Adam surfed through the channels and turned up the volume. *Soon*, he thought. *I'll go in there soon.*

"Quiet," he tried again. Not as sharply this time. And not very convincingly — in any case, they didn't listen.

It seemed the news hadn't started yet. Instead, Sophia Weber was on the screen, wearing a navy-blue suit and high-heeled shoes. Her hair was down and her eyes were sparkling. She finished a sentence, listened to the reporter's commentary, and brushed a lock of hair from her cheek. Then she was gone. Up came blurry images of a dead body. More blurry pictures: naked women, a girl photographed from behind. They flashed by, all but the little girl. That image froze on the screen. She was wearing a backpack and her hair was plaited into two skinny braids.

What had Sophia said? That no other man was so hated. That we were prepared to do anything to get him convicted. She was talking about Stig Ahlin. This was a teaser for a documentary on Stig Ahlin.

Sophia was back on-screen. Her voice was just as he remembered. She wasn't apologizing; she didn't demand attention, but she attracted it anyway. When Sophia spoke, you had to listen to her. Adam swallowed and turned up the volume some more to hear what she was saying.

"A man who goes to prostitutes, who sleeps with a fifteen-year-old girl, whom we have heard subjected his daughter to sexual abuse. We want to do all we can to get him convicted. Locked up. To make him disappear. But...lowering the standard of evidence doesn't mean we are able to convict more guilty people. Some claim this makes the law more effective. Effective sounds like a good thing. But when we lower the standard of evidence, only one thing is certain: more innocent people are convicted. It's as simple as that."

Cut to Lasse Wilander, that channel's star reporter. He was standing in front of a plain background and looking urgently into the camera. Next to him, a clock was ticking.

Without taking his eyes from the lens, his voice steady, he rattled off his lines.

"Stig Ahlin. A cold-blooded killer? Or the victim of the greatest judicial scandal in modern Swedish history? We will spend our entire premiere episode on the case of Stig Ahlin and the murder of Katrin Björk. We have scrutinized the actions of the police, the prosecutor, the court, and the correctional system. Hear the story of Professor Death. A man who has been subjected to injustice at every step of the judicial process: from the day he was labeled a suspect to the moment the sentence was handed down. Life in prison for a murder he didn't commit."

Adam Sahla found himself standing in front of the TV. Just as the news began, he heard a crash. It had come from the kids' room. He had to go see what it was. It sounded like someone had thrown the bed at the wall.

When he walked into the bedroom, his son was standing there with a phone in hand. His daughter was flat on the floor, sobbing.

"Mom! Come hooooome now!" His son shouted into the receiver. "I hate her. She broke my Legos."

"What are you doing? Why are you on the phone?"

Adam took it from the boy, who kept shouting.

"You never come when I call for you. I hate you, Dad. You just sleep and sleep and then you watch TV and you never hear. You never hear, Dad. Never, never, never. I want my mommy!"

Adam spoke into the phone. "We'll talk later."

He hung up.

Adam had thought the kids would never calm down, but surprisingly enough his son fell asleep almost immediately. His daughter, however, was less cooperative. After an hour of trying to settle her, he lay down in her bed. He had already tried reading a story, bringing her water, singing a song so softly it made his throat sting, and swearing up and down that he would stay until she fell asleep.

His daughter had placed one sticky palm on his cheek to make sure he wouldn't disappear, and she was looking intently at him, her eyes wide open. Adam closed his own eyes, peeking now and then to watch as she slowly gave in to sleep. It took half an hour before her eyelids began to droop and her breathing slowed. Yet he didn't dare move.

It was past ten, and Norah still wasn't home. They hadn't spoken since their son called her, and Adam knew why she wasn't back yet. This was another of her punishment strategies. His penalty for being unable to care for the children, for not doing as she wished and in the exact way she would have done it. But he didn't have the energy to think about that right now. He hoped it would be some time before she came home, that he could fall asleep first. That way she couldn't talk to him until tomorrow night at the earliest. He could work late.

Instead he thought about Stig Ahlin. When Sophia had first contacted him to ask for advice, Adam had assumed she wanted to talk about the investigation into the sexual abuse of Stig Ahlin's daughter. That was Adam's specialty, what he worked with most frequently. He'd had the case file sent up and had browsed through it in preparation. It had made him feel as despondent as usual. Stig Ahlin's daughter had shown physical signs of abuse; she had demonstrated odd behaviors and had been interviewed by a skilled person who allowed her to speak without urging her on or putting words in her mouth. Several things the girl said had raised question marks. In Adam's opinion, it had been a well-managed investigation with multiple strong indicators of abuse.

He had also glanced through the interviews with Stig Ahlin's wife. She had appeared trustworthy. Not out for revenge — sad and shocked rather than angry and bitter.

Yet the investigation had been closed. This wasn't unusual, of course. It was often the case. The girl hadn't been able to share any clear and explicit account of abuse. Whether this was because of her age or some other reason was hard to say. Nor were there any unambiguous medical indications that she had been exploited. To be sure, such clear indications were extremely unusual, but their existence or lack thereof still played a role in determining the priority of a case. Stig and his wife had just gotten divorced. She was not financially secure, and she was fighting her ex for alimony. It would have been difficult, to say the least, to file charges against him based on her information.

Adam stroked his daughter's silky-smooth arm. She had refused to go to bed unless he let her put on a white lace sundress. She had kicked the covers off, and her dress had slid up over her bare hip.

He carefully removed the child's hand from his cheek. His little girl was asleep now, exhaling right into his neck, and when he turned to face her he could smell her breath.

When she was a baby he had enjoyed all the ways she smelled — the warm cardamom scent of her powdered skin, her soft hair that reminded him of Nutella. But what he loved most of all was her toffeelike breath.

These days, those scents had changed. A faint whiff of bitter almond reached him as he kissed her as gently as possible to keep from waking her. They had forgotten to brush their teeth.

Adam shouldn't let himself get worked up over the Stig Ahlin case; it had been long before his time. But he couldn't help it. The investigation had been closed when it should have been given priority. So many measures should have been taken, but instead the case had been buried in closure forms. It was still the same; little had changed in the years since Stig Ahlin went to prison. Some things never did. The onus was placed on little kids. Wispy, terrified girls and boys who didn't even know what was expected of them.

Adam cautiously wiggled his way out of the bed and sneaked to the door. He wanted to go to his own bed. Norah could clean up the kitchen when she got home. He needed sleep. In the doorway, he turned around to look at his children. His son was battling with his covers; his daughter sighed and muttered in her sleep.

Stig Ahlin is not a victim of a miscarriage of justice, Adam thought. *Stig Ahlin is exactly where he should be.*

38

In some ways, this felt like rowing across a lake. At this stage the analysis was over; only routine and habit were left. Sophia was drained of emotions, ideas, strength. The petition for a new trial would soon be complete. Collected into binders, boxes. Marked and copied. The document itself would be physically delivered from her office to the registrar of the Supreme Court. And Sophia was rowing: slowly, rhythmically, with no real thought but of arriving. On the other side.

Physical labor, she thought. *The type lawyers do at night, once your brain stops cooperating.*

The petition wouldn't get any better than this. There were no further arguments to add or refute. Everything had been composed, proofread, corrected, and read again. Now she was sitting on the floor in the lobby with her legs out in a V and binders and attachments spread out before her. Before she could drag herself and the petition to Riddarholmen, where the court was located, she must check one last time to make sure the original and the copies matched exactly, that no pages were missing or mislabeled.

She always did this part on her own. Otherwise she would lie awake at night and wonder if something was missing. And it seemed so improbable that Hans Segerstad would agree to lick the tip of his finger and slowly page through each document that she hadn't even bothered to ask.

He's busy giving interviews, she thought, setting yet another binder aside. *Or eating dinner with Lasse Wilander. They're celebrating all my amazing success, since they're taking credit for it.*

Soon she was done. Sture had wanted her to come out to dinner with him. But she didn't have the energy to deal with him right now; she had no strength left over to worry about him or give him all the attention he needed. She'd told him she had already promised to have dinner with Anna. This wasn't true. Yes, she had tried calling, but Anna was on a business trip and when her oldest son answered the phone he was still so upset about her appearance on *Primetime 60 Minutes* that he hung up on her. Sophia realized he thought she had done something he needed to rebel against, something as upsetting as long and environmentally harmful morning showers, human trafficking, and hamburger meat.

Carl wasn't in Sweden, or she would have gone to see him. He would have understood. He could have told her convincingly that she'd done a fantastic job. But she would have to manage without him too.

She picked up her cell phone. The registrar's office wouldn't open for another forty minutes. But if she headed over now she would miss the worst traffic. She called a cab and meticulously taped up the box that contained the petition and copies.

It was time. There was nothing more to do. It was time to go to the Supreme Court.

. . .

Today that attorney would be sending in his petition for a new trial.

"We'll deliver it on Friday," Sophia had said last time they spoke. That was exactly how she'd put it: we'll deliver it. As if he had agreed to pretend this were a joint project.

"Would you like to read it first?" she had asked. But he could hear it in her voice, that she didn't want him to say yes. Sophia Weber wasn't a fan of listening to others. Even if she claimed to do her utmost to make her clients feel like a part of the process, she wanted to be in charge.

Still, Stig had demanded to see the petition. Afterward he had shared his thoughts. She had thanked him without sounding particularly grateful.

But Sophia Weber was a good lawyer. Stig could tell. She was a skilled writer, thorough — she was good for him.

He'd certainly been wrong about that sort of thing before. There had even been a time when he'd thought the same of Marianne. That she was good for him.

Back when they got to know each other, Marianne worked at the information desk at Karolinska Hospital. She greeted visitors and called queue numbers. Answered questions with a cautious smile on her thin lips — not too forward, not too withdrawn or shy. Just reassuring. There was something about her voice. It wasn't too loud or too soft. She made people believe she would help them, set things right, show them the way. No one blamed Marianne for long wait times, incorrect diagnoses, or canceled consultations. If they wanted to shout or make demands, they turned to her colleagues.

Stig had thought it was her personality. Not something she had practiced; she might have been born that way. And from the very first day they spent time together, he couldn't shake the feeling that she was the type of woman he should marry. That she would make his life easier, more orderly. Not too much. Not too little. Better.

But he was wrong. He realized as much during the birth. As Marianne sweated, began to smell, as feces and blood came from her body, as her hair stuck to her head and she demanded water and nitrous oxide and took his hand to squeeze it in order to ease her own pain. That was when he understood that she was not good for him at all.

Marianne came home from the hospital a different person. With a personality change. From the shell of what had once been a competent woman, stable and dependable, crept a timid, catlike animal. Marianne became sloppy, inattentive, and distant. Her sleep patterns changed; her eyes became restless and her hands were always nervously busy. Gathering and folding, wiping and patting. Her anxiety took over every movement. She had lost control.

Stig assumed Marianne had a hard time handling Ida. It seemed like she didn't know what to do, and that terrified her. Initially Stig had assumed it would get better in time, once her hormone levels stabilized and Marianne had settled into the baby's routines. But instead Marianne began to make demands of Stig. About how he should be and what he should do.

Now it was Friday morning. Sophia Weber had delivered Stig's petition, and all that was left to do was wait.

There were no rules about how long it could take. Sophia Weber had explained this. The Supreme Court could, in principle, consider the petition for as long as they wished. Three weeks or four years. And no one had any way of knowing what decision the court might reach.

Stig shouldn't be too optimistic. The program on TV had presented the issue as obvious, but the justices on the Supreme Court were no easily-swayed viewers. They would not be convinced by anything other than jurisprudence. There were any number of miscarriage-of-justice cases in which the huge media attention actually led to the opposite outcome.

Sophia had explained all of this to him. She had done so in her usual competent manner. Stig had not found it difficult to understand what she was saying or why. But that didn't necessarily mean anything either. He would have to wait and see.

39

Sophia was let into the stairwell by the postal carrier. Once inside, she stopped and stared at the ceiling, at the decorative stucco and the murals. She was already regretting this. It was a terrible idea. She turned to head back out to the street, but she ran into Ludwig Venner at the door. He was carrying a Styrofoam coffee cup and a sticky paper bag.

"Sophia," he declared.

"I shouldn't," she said hesitantly.

Ludwig looked puffy, half-asleep, and surprised. But not surprised in a good way. Sophia raised her hands.

"I'm going back home," she said. "Let's pretend this never happened. It was a dumb idea. But I was on Riddarholmen and I wanted...I wanted to thank you for your help."

She felt her voice betraying her. It wasn't true, and Ludwig knew it. Ludwig wasn't part of her life; she'd made that decision on her own. She looked up at him and swallowed.

"So, thanks. Thanks for arranging *Primetime 60 Minutes*. It made my petition an awful lot better, and I never could have done that on my own. I just delivered it, and I wanted...but I should have called instead, I don't know, I never would have...it was nice of you. I'll be going now."

Ludwig stood in her way and handed her the coffee and sack of pastries. Then he dropped a set of keys in Sophia's coat pocket.

"You're not going anywhere. Now that you're here, let's have breakfast together. Take the elevator to the sixth floor. You'll need the key to go up. Let yourself in, I'm just going to get another cup of coffee and I'll be right back."

. . .

Adam was sitting on the bathroom floor. Norah's nude-colored slip was hanging in the bathtub to dry. The moisture dripped from the slippery fabric and onto the enamel. It would be an hour or two before she got home. Then they would wake up the kids, and he had to get up before it was time.

He was all packed. Three suitcases. It was all he would need for now.

"If you forget something, you can always drop by," she had assured him. And in a week, he would come home again. Then it would be her turn to pack the suitcases and disappear.

"I don't want them to have to live in two places," she had added. "Not until we know what we're going to do."

So she had said. But she had already made up her mind. He could tell by looking at her; he could hear it in her voice. It was only a matter of time before he would have to find a new apartment. Before they would have to do all of that. Go through their belongings. Buy new beds. Divide up books,

CDs, memories. Buy double sets of rubber boots and gym clothes for the kids. He and Norah hadn't done it yet; they hadn't even talked about it, not properly. But it already felt so trite.

The tile was cold. He was holding his daughter's pajamas in his hand. He'd been trying to straighten up the bathroom and was planning to put her jammies in the hamper. Now he wanted to take them with him.

He had packed three suitcases. But this was his home. His children lived here. And his wife. He lived here with his family.

. . .

The elevator opened directly into Ludwig's penthouse. The hall, living room, office, library, and kitchen were combined into one huge room; it must have been over two thousand square feet. The ceiling was rather low, and one of the walls was covered in a gigantic oil painting, black cranes against a dark blue sky, the style was almost Japanese. But the artist wasn't Japanese; it had been painted by Bruno Liljefors. The short walls gave way to four bedrooms with adjoining bathrooms, and beyond one long wall was a seven-hundred-square-foot terrace where she had stood years ago, gazing out across Stockholm. Back then this had been Ludwig's bachelor pad; as she assumed it was once again, although the clothes and shoes in the hall and the toys scattered all over the place suggested that these days, he had regular visits of a different sort from when she used to be invited to parties here.

This was a terrible idea, Sophia thought, sinking onto one of the three sofas in the living room area.

When Ludwig walked in with coffee and a sack of pastries the size of an IKEA bag, Sophia began to cry.

"Sorry," she sobbed. "I'm just a little tired."

Ludwig sat down and put his arms around her. She drew in his scent as deeply as she could; he smelled like tobacco and, faintly, sweat. She shifted closer and let him stroke her back. When her sobs had abated she turned her face to his and slipped her hand around to the back of his neck. But Ludwig put a finger to her lips and shook his head.

"Stop," he said. "Let's just eat breakfast. Because you clearly need to eat. Then you can go grab a few hours of sleep in my bed. Alone. Because you clearly need to sleep."

Sophia rose from the sofa as fast as she could. Ludwig reached for her, but she slapped his hand away and headed for the door. As she shoved her feet into her shoes he pressed the pastry bag into her hands. When she tried to give it back, he handed her the coffee as well. He took her by the shoulders.

"Sophia," he tried. "This is just silly. Come in and sit back down. Don't be angry. You know I'd love to sleep with you. But not when you're worn out and overtired. We can wait until you're well rested and horny. Otherwise it won't be any fun. And I do want you to find it fun. Really, I would have preferred that you liked me back, a little. That would have made me happy. But you don't. So, don't be angry with me, Sophia. It doesn't happen so often, that I care about women this way. Don't punish me for it. My therapist would be very displeased with you if you were to do that when I'm finally doing something kind. Mom too."

Sophia shook her head. Her throat ached, but she wanted to stop crying.

"No, no," she mumbled. "I'm not angry, not at you, anyway, but I never should have...I'm sorry."

"Stop. Don't apologize. And definitely don't thank me. That would just be silly."

Her tears dripped to the floor. Ludwig wiped them away with his thumb and pulled her close. He hugged her as hard as he could without squashing the coffee cup and the pastries.

"If you want," he mumbled into her hair, "we can have dinner next week. I have the kids from tonight until Sunday, but after that I'm available."

She nodded against his chest and wriggled out of his grasp. When the ancient elevator showed up she opened the door as fast as she could and closed it hard behind her.

The coffee was gone before the elevator made it to the ground floor. She tossed the cup in a bin just outside the front door, shoved the pastries into her purse, and jogged all the way down to the Royal Dramatic Theater. There, she stopped and sat on one of the steps leading to the main entrance. Slowly her pulse returned to normal and she caught her breath. Once her chest stopped burning she turned her face to the sun.

The archipelago ferries were resting at the edge of the water. A group of gulls were arguing loudly over a forgotten sandwich. It was a typical workday, too early in the year for tourists or recreational boats. In the lee of the building behind her it was surprisingly warm; the snow had melted a few weeks back. And the archipelago was iced out, she'd heard on the radio.

It might just be possible, she thought.

As she walked up Sibyllegatan, she called the marina.

The director at Rådmansö answered on the first ring. Sophia introduced herself and explained what she was after. She heard him place his hand over the receiver.

"It's that lawyer girl with the Shipman," he said. "She's gotten it into her head to go sailing."

The phone crackled. It sounded like a small crowd had burst out laughing.

"Hello," she tried. "Are you still there? Can you arrange that?"

The director uncovered the receiver. Someone wolf-whistled.

"Slow down there, missy. You know it's only forty degrees in the water? At the shore. Just a few yards out and as soon as it gets deeper it's even colder. The ice may be gone, but once you get out on the water you'll hardly be able to tell."

"I know," she said. "Could you bring over the gear in storage as well, and check the batteries? I'd like to get moving right after lunch."

The director snorted.

"So no cleaning or waxing. How about propane and gas? A thermos and warm socks, have you got those? Because you may have been enjoying coffee out on your little balcony, but you can hardly order a latte at sea."

The laughter in the background was renewed. This time they applauded as well.

"I don't know how far I'm going," said Sophia. "But I need to be back on Sunday night."

The man stopped laughing.

"Are you out of your mind, girl?" Now he sounded upset. "You're going to sack out on the boat? Do you have any idea what that involves? This time of year, there's no such thing as a breezy little jaunt on the sea. But there is such a thing as freezing to death. If you fall in the drink it'll be over in a few minutes. And you'll just stay there. You might wash up on land around Midsummer, but you won't look pretty, I can promise you that."

"I understand it's cold." Sophia crossed the street to her front door. "Could you please include the items from the storage area as well?"

"You're a stubborn one. I hope you have a fellow with you. For warmth, if nothing else."

"I have propane." Sophia clamped the phone between her shoulder and ear and fished out her keys. The keypad lock seemed to be broken again. "The bottle's almost full and I have an extra in the boat. You tuned up the engine in the fall. The batteries are still in the boat, and as I said, if you have time to check them that would be great. And say hello and thanks to your noisy colleagues whom I can hear in the background — it's so kind of them to offer to share my sleeping bag, but I'll manage on my own."

She headed straight to the basement. *If I kept the rest of my life as organized as my boating equipment, I would never have any problems.*

40

It took some time for Sophia to get from the bus stop to the pier. Although she'd done her best to pack practically, it was hard to transport everything. Lined boots, gloves, scarf, long johns, a thick and wind-resistant hat, two sleeping bags, sheets, the nautical charts she'd had at home to use for desk-sailing over the winter, binoculars, a bearing compass, and a GPS. The lined survival suit that wouldn't help in the least if she fell overboard, because she would freeze to death long before she had time to drown. And food. She'd brought way too much food.

Titteli was waiting for her in the water when she arrived, looking lonely. Sophia had taken over the care of Grandpa Sture's old boat. A line of empty buoys bobbed along the piers; there were only four boats in the harbor, and none was a sailboat like hers. The sun was still shining, but you could tell by looking at the water how cold it was; it was winter-shiny, like a metallic gray sheet of ductile steel.

The boatyard director and three men in their twenties were on board her boat. They turned to look as she walked onto the pier. The sun was still warm; the boatyard guys had taken off their jackets. They observed her in silence as she approached.

Sophia nodded curtly and put down her bags. It smelled like tar here, and seawater, diesel, and coffee. The director turned off the engine; he'd been warming it up for her. The boat's bumpers were out, and the flag was at the stern. The spray shield had been installed, the main-sail was on the boom, the battens were in, the furling jib was attached, and all sheets were in place. One of the men took her bags from the pier; another held out his hand to help her on board. The heater was on. Sophia peered below deck. They'd even put the cushions and rugs in place.

She offered her hand. The boatyard director shook it. With his other hand he removed a packet of snuff from his lip and tossed it overboard.

"I sent one of the boys out to pick you a bouquet of flowers. I thought you should have a vase in the cockpit," he said, spitting. "But he claims nothing's growing yet."

Sophia smiled, opened one of the bags she'd brought, and handed over two bottles of Russian Standard Vodka.

"You sure aren't the typical Stockholmer," the director declared, a smile blossoming over his face. His upper teeth were still black from the snus. "Sture's kid, makes sense. Totally fucking nuts."

Sophia took her time stowing everything she'd brought along. She turned on the radio; it was already tuned to P1. The weather promised westerly winds.

She gazed out at the water. The sunlight was glittering here in Gräddöviken and the possibilities were endless. She didn't want to sail to Åland; if the wind held that would mean a headwind all the way back and she didn't need that. The cold would be bad enough as it was. She could head north through the Väddö Canal toward Grisslehamn, but the bridges at Bagghus and Älmsta weren't yet open for the season. That only left one good option: she should sail for Tjockö, Långskär, and the open sea.

All the outer archipelago was open to the south, but the question was whether the more sheltered inlets were iced out yet. Sophia ran her finger along the nautical chart she had unfolded across the seat next to her. Gålgryte, Mjölkö, Vidingsöra. Fejan, Mysingen, Svartlöga, Sunnansund, Vattungarna. Huvudskär.

I'll make it work, she thought.

The director called out to her as she began to loosen the rope at the stern. He was sitting on the pier with his colleagues, not far away. They'd opened one of the bottles she'd brought and were raising their glasses to Sophia.

"Totally nuts," she heard him shouting as she started the engine. It didn't sound like he was laughing any longer. But the men were full of smiles. One of them placed two fingers to his temple in a salute; another waved.

She raised her arm to wave back. Then she turned the boat seaward. How far she traveled, exactly where she ended up — it really didn't matter.

Once she had put Gräddöviken behind her, she sailed into the wind, turned on the autopilot, and raised the mainsail. Up on deck she turned her face into the breeze and let the icy air shock her lungs. After unfurling the jib, she turned off the engine. She settled in at the rudder, pulled up the hood of her down jacket, and tied the drawstring tight so only a small opening remained.

A white-tailed eagle glided on outstretched wings just above the mast. From the foggy coast came the faint odor of metal and freshly sawn timber. Two gray gulls shrieked, coasting over the foaming water; they veered away and were gone.

She passed south of Lidö, island of the wide-faring, without encountering a single boat. The farther out she got, the harder the wind blew.

The hull burst through the swells. Each time *Titteli* met a wave, water was tossed over the deck and a cascade of icy drops hit her face like tiny nails. Despite her thick mittens, Sophia's hands ached with cold and her fingers were stiff around the rudder. Now and then she had to put her mouth to the gap at her wrist and blow her mitten full of warm air. When that didn't help, she shoved her hand under her bottom to get her circulation going.

But Sophia didn't want to slow down. Three tons of boat roared beneath her body, rollicking, and she let the sails out even more.

She rounded Fejan at beam reach from the starboard side; she passed south of Botveskär sailing downwind; she headed east into the waterway. At some points, the snow was still visible on the northern slopes.

The wind rushed across the sea; each time the water grew dark ahead of the boat, Sophia's body tensed. She planted both feet against the footwell as the boat tilted another few centimeters to the side. Then she sat down. Two or three hours, time disappeared. Sweat broke out over her back.

When dusk caught up to her, she had reached Idskär. The bay was on the leeward side. Sophia furled the jib, brought in the mainsail, and started the engine.

By the time she'd set the anchor and moored the boat ashore with a rope and spike, her clothing was glued to her skin with sweat. She went belowdecks and turned up the heat. She boiled a pot of water on the stove and tossed in half a box of bow-tie pasta and four lamb sausages.

The propane heater had been on throughout the journey, yet she was shaking with cold. When the food was ready she drained the water and added two large pats of butter. She pulled the sleeping bag from its cover, crawled into it fully clothed, and began to eat straight from the saucepan. By the time she'd finished eating, the worst of the stiffness in her joints had eased. Her hands had softened up a little and when the berth felt a little warmer she shuffled up and peed in a bucket, which she then set on deck. Then she closed herself in and gazed through the porthole. In the summertime she liked to climb up the rocks to the range marker on top and sit there while the sun went down. She wasn't about to do so today, but she did watch the last of daylight filter across the island. Sea smoke had settled on the bare cliffs.

She pulled the curtains and put the pot back on the stove. As the water boiled for tea, she made up the berth with sheets and extra blankets. Then she changed into dry underlayers and warm wool socks and drank the tea so fast that she burned her tongue and the roof of her mouth. As she crammed herself into the berth, a gull cried forlornly. Otherwise, it was silent. Perfectly silent. She fell asleep immediately.

THREE

41

What was wrong with people? On Midsummer's Eve? Sophia swore. A clicking sound was coming from the fax machine. The alarm was already set, and she was holding the front door to the office. Typical. Of course, she would be the one who had to follow up on this, whatever it was coming out of that machine. She was the only one left at the office; all her colleagues were already stuck in traffic or standing in line at the state liquor store. It was Midsummer, for God's sake. Even Sophia was supposed to get some time off.

Since her solo sailing trip in March, Sophia hadn't had time to take the boat out more than twice. Now she was finally about to have the chance, and in only two hours she was supposed to pick up Grandpa Sture. After a few disastrously rainy and cold June weeks, the weather was decently warm at last. The rental car was illegally parked down on the street. She really didn't have time for any surprise faxes.

Sophia sighed. One minute. If only it had come in one minute later. Then she would have been gone already.

The alarm was beeping faster and faster. And the fax was still making sounds. The alarm would be armed any second now. She had to have locked up and left by then. Who used a fax anymore? She hadn't received a fax from a client in years. Who would be sending anything to Gustafsson & Weber on the morning of Midsummer's Eve? Was it a foreign client? Were there any active cases that might necessitate a message from abroad? Did Lars have clients like that? Or was it one of Björn's deportation cases? Some foreign authority?

The realization hit her suddenly, and full force. She let go of the door and it closed behind her. Her bags dropped to the floor.

There was only one thing it could be. As incredible and unexpected as this was, it had to be. They'd even joked about it, she and Hans Segerstad, that they were expecting word on Christmas Eve.

Because what did the Supreme Court do if they wanted to avoid publicity and lots of questions? They handed down decisions on a day when no one was reading the paper and all the journalists were on vacation. The last time Thomas Quick had been granted a new trial, the court had announced the decision on Maundy Thursday. As little attention as possible. And today was Midsummer's Eve.

Sophia's heart was pounding. The alarm box had started its incessant beeping to announce that it was armed. She turned it off as quickly as she could and headed straight for the reception desk. The fax machine was right next to it.

The Supreme Court. Of course, the justices would use the fax. They probably still wrote their decisions by hand.

Or used Dictaphones with cassettes you could no longer buy at a regular store. Let the secretaries type them out. Corrected their spelling errors with Wite-Out. But why would they hand down the Ahlin decision so soon?

Sophia felt her palms grow damp. It was stuffy in the cramped area behind the reception desk. She could hear her own breaths coming like quick pants — she sounded like a frightened animal.

Could they really have decided already? In only three months? And if they had, what did it mean?

She picked up the phone, searched for Hans Segerstad's number, and placed the phone in front of her on the table. The sheets of paper were fed out of the fax front side up, last page first. But she didn't look at them; she couldn't look yet. No reading until it was all there.

She might be wrong. It could be something else entirely. Anything but Stig Ahlin's petition for a new trial. She might be getting all worked up for nothing. An advertisement? A mistake? The Migration Board, a district court, some client or attorney who was out in the countryside where the Internet didn't work very well. She glanced quickly at the stack of paper. Nope, she recognized the seal of the Supreme Court. It was unmistakable.

But why did the Supreme Court want to avoid attention? Which criticism were they afraid of? Did it mean a new trial had been granted, or did it indicate the opposite? What was their reasoning? Sophia squeezed her eyes shut as hard as she could. White dots danced inside her eyelids.

The pages kept chugging out. Her head began to swim, and she opened her eyes again, staring at the wall, at the bulletin board that hung there.

It's too many pages to be anything else, she thought. Her heart pounded even faster. An icy drop of sweat made its way from her armpit to her waist. It was followed by two more. *It can't be, it has to be — it's the only possibility, isn't it?*

The machine clicked one last time, then fell silent. It was done. Sophia picked up the pile of paper, gasped for breath, and began to read.

Her knees went weak just a few lines in. She steadied herself against the wall and slid to the floor, sitting with the papers in her lap. After five minutes she took her phone from the table and woke it up to call Hans Segerstad. Her hands were shaking too hard to hold the phone, so she placed it on the pile of fax paper and turned on speakerphone.

When Hans Segerstad answered, she couldn't produce a single word. It was impossible.

Hans Segerstad allowed for her silence. For a long time they just sat there, he in Uppsala, she in Gamla Stan, on the floor beside the fax machine, her phone in her lap and her trembling hands next to it, palms up.

He had to be the first to speak.

42

"Congratulations," Sophia said when she called to share the news.

"Thanks," Stig responded.

Now he and his fellow prisoners were eating lunch.

Before they sat down in the unit cafeteria, someone had glanced up from the laminate floor, gazed at a point just past Stig, and mumbled, "No fucking way." Someone else had raised a hand to thump him on the back. As if they were friends, as if they had anything in common. But that hand had changed its mind halfway there. The thump had turned into a skewing blow, a pat glancing off Stig's shoulder.

Stig had said thanks to them too.

The kitchen team had managed to score near-beer for their Midsummer lunch without going over budget. But there was no appreciable improvement to the general mood. One of the guards tried to raise a glass and sang half a verse of a dirty song before he realized it might not be the best choice of mealtime entertainment, if you were celebrating Midsummer in the sex crimes unit of Emla Prison.

They ate their herring in the ensuing silence. Someone got up to turn on the TV. The lead guard came in and said that Stig would be allowed to call the journalist at TV4. The administration was going to let Stig give the extended, recorded interview the editorial staff at *Primetime 60 Minutes* had requested.

"Have you been given a date for trial?" one of the guards wondered.

They hadn't. The newly appointed prosecutor had asked for an extension period to get acquainted with the case. But according to Sophia Weber, it shouldn't be too long. The Supreme Court's decision to grant a new trial had been formulated in such a way that the trial itself should happen quickly. There were extraordinary reasons to grant the trial, it had said. "Extraordinary reasons" was strong wording.

When it was time for dessert, Stig suddenly felt nauseated. He excused himself and went to his room, where he lay down on his bed.

He knew he should be happy. He knew he should celebrate. He knew that if all went as expected, he would soon be free, in two or three months. That was sensational. A judicial miracle. A new chance, a window to a new life.

Maybe. He couldn't be certain. Because he'd been to the court of appeals before. That was almost fourteen years ago, but his memory was crystal clear. He recalled the evasive glances of the judges, the lead judge's rapid blinking, the feeling of paralysis that had come over Stig when it was all over and his attorney explained the final costs.

Stig Ahlin had been granted a new trial. His case would be heard once more. But nothing was a given, not yet. As part of the petition Sophia Weber had demanded that the Supreme Court free Stig Ahlin immediately. This request hadn't been granted, only the new trial. It was hard to speculate what that might mean. Sophia Weber said it didn't mean a thing. But Stig wasn't sure he believed that. Nothing was certain.

Never knowing — not when, not how, not where. That terror had settled in his body. This wouldn't make it go away. It would always be with him, like chronically aching joints.

■ ■ ■

"I'm sorry."

Stig wasn't listening. He dug through his pockets for his debit card. He had it somewhere; he'd put it there before leaving his room. He found it and handed it to the man who ran the canteen. But the man didn't accept it; he just shook his head.

"I'm sorry. It hasn't arrived yet."

"Excuse me?"

"Was there anything else? Were you going to purchase anything? Or was that all?"

"But..."

Stig was in line at the canteen. Behind him stood eleven of the sixteen inmates in his corridor. The whole group had only thirty minutes to select and pay for their goods. If they didn't manage in time, they would have to wait until next week. Stig Ahlin waved his debit card urgently.

"I don't understand. I received confirmation that it was delivered. Early last week. It must be here. You'll have to check again."

"That's too bad. But unfortunately, I can't..."

The canteen owner glanced quickly to the left. Stig followed his gaze. There stood one of the guards, who refused to look at him. Instead he turned his whole body away. The owner looked back at Stig. He raised his voice, steadier now.

"I'm sorry," he said. "But I don't see a package for you here. And you know you have to show the delivery slip; how else could I check? There must have been a mistake."

"A mistake?"

Stig lowered his hand and the card. The inmates were only allowed to have ten CDs. When he'd gotten the delivery confirmation he got rid of some of the discs he already had. But the slip was back in his room. The prison canteen was only open once a week, Stig visited it each time, and it was always the same man working on their day. He never had a substitute, aside from the five weeks of vacation he got a year. Stig didn't need to show a slip. He'd never had to before. Why should he now? Why today, all of a sudden, when he'd never had to do so?

"It must have been delayed."

The man didn't as much as blink. All the hesitation in his voice was gone. He straightened a bundle of newspapers instead.

"Is there anything else you'd like? Otherwise I'll have to ask you to — "

"Are you sure that's not it?" Stig pointed past the man. There, on a shelf behind the counter, was a package. Of the very size his CD orders usually were.

"Absolutely sure."

The canteen man didn't look at it. But he whirled around, picked up the flat package, and placed it in a drawer in front of him without looking at the address, without giving it to Stig. He closed the drawer again.

"It will probably arrive next week. You'll have to come back then. The mail can be slow during vacation season. And some things just get lost."

The canteen man turned his eyes on the next man in line. It was Anders, one of Stig Ahlin's pedophile neighbors, who was just over forty and had been convicted of sexually abusing boys so young they didn't yet have pubic hair.

Pedophile Anders looked like a caricature of himself. Fat, bad teeth, eternally greasy hair. He bought a toothbrush. When the canteen man turned his back, Anders pulled two more toothbrushes from the shelf and stuck them up his sleeve. Stig noticed but didn't say anything. The canteen man turned to Stig while he accepted Anders's payment.

"We'll have to see what happens with your package." He smiled. As if this was funny.

"Right," said Stig.

The canteen man glanced at the guard again. Was he smiling too?

"But naturally I can't be certain. I can't promise anything. If worse comes to worst I suppose you can file a formal complaint. I'm sure your amazing lawyer can help you out."

. . .

The TV crew from *Primetime 60 Minutes* was allowed to come into the daytime unit. They'd been promised two hours. When they offered him makeup, Stig declined.

"This is how I look," he said. They would have to settle for that.

Ten minutes were spent readying the gear: a camera, sound-recording equipment, a spotlight, and a reflector screen. But then the interview began. It was important for Stig to get into the swing of things, to start talking. For as long as possible.

Stig felt remarkably relaxed. This was the building in which some of his fellow inmates devoted themselves to painting or furthering their education. He came here himself, now and then, to pick up one of the books that had been moved after they'd had to close the library. This was where the food team prepared their meals. The atmosphere was homey. But it was something else that caused him to relax.

Lasse Wilander had said hello to him. He had squeezed his hand and looked him fully in the eye. It was his manner in doing so that Stig recalled faintly, from another time. The photographer had done the same. And the woman they had with them.

They all greeted him in the same way. With something resembling respect. It wasn't with hatred, in any case.

"My past experience with the media hasn't exactly been positive," Stig managed to say when Lasse Wilander sat down across from him and took a stack of small notes from his pocket; they were covered in cramped writing.

Lasse Wilander nodded and turned to his photographer.

"We'll take the shots of me afterward," he said. "Back home, if we have to."

Then he turned to Stig.

"I understand. A large portion of our program is going to revolve around that very thing. Self-critical examination of the media's role. What sort of impact it had on what happened to you. I mean, what befell you. Not least, how it influenced the justice process."

Then the interview began.

A green light glowed on the front of the camera. The words flowed from Stig Ahlin. Not quickly, but astonishingly easily.

"I was picked up at my place of work on a Monday in October, thirteen years and eight months ago. I had brought a gym bag to the office. I wasn't allowed to take it with me to jail. Nor did they let me have my outerwear. My cell phone was in my coat pocket, so I didn't have it with me. I haven't been back in my apartment since that October day in 1998. When the decision was handed down by the court of appeals, I put it up for sale. My attorney at the time paid a moving company to empty it, since I no longer had any friends who would pick up the phone when I called. For four years I rented a storage unit, but later I gave that up as well. Some of my belongings were donated to charity, and practically everything else was thrown out. I have a safe-deposit box with a few personal documents. A couple of pieces of jewelry that belonged to my mother. I'd been planning to..."

Stig fell silent, letting the sentence remain unfinished. The camera operator had placed a plastic bottle of sparkling water on the table before him. Stig unscrewed the cap, filled the provided glass, and took a drink.

"I've never even seen the key to that safe-deposit box," he said at last. "It's held by the prison. I left detailed instructions for what should be kept and put aside. But naturally I don't know...How could I have checked to make sure it was done right?"

Stig blinked into the lamp the cameraman had set up to provide more light in the squat building. He wiped his forehead with a paper napkin. Lasse Wilander nodded in encouragement.

"I have been robbed of my life," said Stig. "Even if I am freed, even if I am given redress, even if this is all over someday. I will never be able to get my life back."

"It's hard to understand," said Lasse Wilander. "How you've managed to survive. That hatred hasn't destroyed you."

"It's been many years since I hated anyone," Stig heard himself say.

I'm lying, he thought at first. But then a realization struck him. His dreams of revenge and longing were something different. Hatred was clear, metallic, unambiguous. It was an expression of a comprehensible emotion.

Everything would have been much simpler if he was in fact full of hatred.

"Something happened to me when I was convicted," said Stig Ahlin. "I believe it's been many years since I've been able to feel."

That was what he said. It might even have been true.

43

"We're making history." Hans Segerstad's face dipped forward; his head had become too heavy for his neck, so it drooped like a three-day-old tulip. "We're making history, you and me. My dearest Sophia. Fourteen years after Stig Ahlin was locked up, almost to the day. Almost to the day."

If, by "almost to the day," you mean he will have been imprisoned for fourteen years in almost three months, Sophia thought, digging a painkiller out of her pocket.

"Fourteen years after the murder," she said, taking a sip of champagne and washing down the pill. "A little longer."

They were sitting at a round table; Hans's treat. At least, so he'd said. But Sture had appeared extremely skeptical when Sophia invited him to come too. If she knew Sture, he would have brought his own credit cards along.

"I remember it so well," Hans said, refilling his glass. "When I first decided to have a look at Stig Ahlin's case. No one asked me to, but I did it anyway. And I thought I might have gone and become sentimental in my old age. But I felt, *he's innocent, that man is innocent, I have to do something about it.* So I did."

He smiled in satisfaction. His eyes flashed in the dim light of the dining room as he swirled the wine around in his glass.

"Solely based on that gut feeling. I've become an old man. A romantic."

Sture groaned out loud. Sophia frowned. But it seemed Hans Segerstad hadn't heard.

It wasn't the fault of old age that Hans Segerstad was sentimental. Every decision he made came from the heart; he'd always been like that. True, he often spoke about the necessity of objectivity in law, that lawyers must not allow themselves to be controlled by emotion, but those were only words. Segerstad had been married three times. Not a single one of those marriages had lasted longer than it typically took for one of his doctoral students to write the introductory chapters of a middling dissertation.

Jurisprudence was the closest to true love Hans had come in his life. Sophia wasn't surprised in the least that he had taken on Stig Ahlin because he believed in the man's innocence. What did surprise her was that he would admit it.

"You?" Sture muttered, annoyed. Hans Segerstad still hadn't heard him. "*You* haven't done a whit to get Stig Ahlin freed, have you? You've been far too busy giving lengthy interviews. It's thanks to someone else entirely that Stig Ahlin will have a new trial. A toast to you, Sophia."

Sophia shook her head but still clinked glasses with her grandfather. She didn't have the energy to argue. With either of them. Hans Segerstad's gaze had drifted out across the dining room again, landing on a table of particularly noisy teenagers. He was ignoring both Sophia and Sture. Soon he would disappear from their table and find someone who would treat him the way he thought he deserved. It wouldn't be difficult: Hans Segerstad had gotten to give all the victorious interviews while Sture and Sophia were out sailing. Hans was the man of the moment, and the crowd at Teatergrillen kept up with that sort of thing.

When she'd received the decision, Sophia had thought at first that she should stay home. That this incredible news demanded her complete attention. But then she'd spoken with Stig Ahlin and her euphoria subsided. It had been replaced by worry, and a sense of emptiness. Stig Ahlin was not in the least inclined to start celebrating. It wasn't over yet; the court of appeals loomed ahead and Stig Ahlin was still at Emla. And there he would remain unless the court freed him.

She had decided to stick to her plans. Delayed only by an hour and a half, she and Sture had boarded the boat. They'd just returned after three days of sailing in a drizzle. The temperature had never climbed above fifty-seven degrees, and she hadn't turned her phone on again until she was back in her apartment and lying in a scalding hot bath.

The only journalists whose calls Sophia had returned were Tor Bengtsson and Lasse Wilander. All she would tell them was that she was very happy with the decision and was now preparing for the proceedings, which she hoped would take place as soon as possible.

The very next day, Tor Bengtsson had made her statement a headline, as an exclusive interview. He succeeded in blowing up her brief comment, along with a few photos and old quotes, into an entire two-page spread. Lasse Wilander, on the other hand, hadn't seemed very keen when they spoke. He'd done a lengthy interview with Hans Segerstad while she was still out at sea. It had complemented the exclusive chat with Stig Ahlin. He didn't need more than that.

"Hans Segerstad praised your effort," Lasse had assured her. "A very generous and magnanimous man. So strange that he never became a Supreme Court justice."

But it wasn't only Hans Segerstad who'd given interviews while Sophia was sailing against the wind up by Huvudskär. The case was receiving enormous attention, even though the decision had been handed down on Midsummer's Eve.

The prosecutor-general had been forced to hold a press conference. He stated that he didn't see any reason whatsoever to reconsider the indictment. According to him, it remained strong despite the new information. He expected the court of appeals to agree. Stig Ahlin would remain in prison.

Tor Bengtsson had spoken with the new chancellor of justice. She said she had no plans to become involved in the matter.

"You mean you're waiting to see what the court of appeals decides?" Tor Bengtsson had wondered.

"No, that's not what I mean," the chancellor insisted. "It's deeply unfortunate that this has happened, but I don't expect it to become a matter for the office of the chancellor of justice. Our justice system in Sweden has a consistently high degree of legal security. I don't consider there to have been any mistakes made during the investigation."

Those positive reactions that did appear were not aimed at Sophia.

"A victory for legal security and investigative journalism," claimed author and journalist Jan Guillou, who also named Lasse Wilander "peak of the week." A similar take was on offer in Johan Hakelius's editorial "Injustice Is So Not Fair."

In the legal journals, Hans Segerstad was the hero of the hour. *Legally Yours* planned to put him on the cover; *Jurist-tidningen* was going to publish a special issue on his career, and *Juridisk Tidskrift* had launched a massive effort toward a belated Festschrift in his honor.

The criticism, though — Sophia got to enjoy that all on her own. It wasn't necessarily to be found in the newspapers, but Sophia Weber and her lack of moral compass were a hot topic in the comments below each online article.

Sophia received almost all of these reactions via anonymous email. She'd never experienced the like. Hundreds of missives full of threats, more or less explicit, more or less offensive. Once she'd labored her way through twenty of them, she decided to stop reading. There was no point. Why waste her energy on it?

She decided to ask her law partner Lars Gustafsson for help. He had a summer intern — a male one, for a change. This man could sift through her emails. Lars had offered the help, after all; he'd almost insisted. Asked her to keep the intern busy while he himself was on a last-minute charter trip to Greece. This time of year, there was relatively little to do. And what else were summer interns for, if not scut work?

Sophia tried to find a comfortable position on the restaurant chair. Her five-inch heels were still in her handbag. Just as well; the soles were coming loose. She wiped her forehead again. *Makeup*, she thought. *Next time I'll at least put on makeup.*

Sture caught her eye.

"What's wrong, honey? Do you think it's too early to celebrate?"

Sophia shrugged. He was right, of course. That was exactly what she was thinking. She couldn't escape from her spiraling thoughts. Sure, she was drinking champagne Hans Segerstad had ordered and Sture, in all likelihood, would have to pay for. It would have been impolite for her to do anything else. But she didn't feel particularly happy. Stig Ahlin had been granted a new trial. It was thanks to her, and that was fantastic. But it didn't necessarily mean Stig Ahlin would be freed. It *should* mean that. But nothing was for certain.

The court of appeals could still arrive at the decision that Stig Ahlin was guilty. Certainly, Stig was starting from a better position now, but it wasn't over yet. There were tons of people who were convinced Stig Ahlin was guilty. It would only take three of them serving in court on the day this matter would be retried.

I have to get out of here, she thought, *get away before it's time to socialize with this herd. People crowding in, newly discovered intimacy that only gets more intense as blood alcohol concentrations rise.*

Sophia leaned toward her grandfather to whisper.

"I'm going to head home. Do you want me to drop you off first, or will you get a cab on your own?"

Sture frowned. "I'll stay." He observed Hans Segerstad. "This clown is going to forget to pay the tab any moment now. And I want to be here to keep from ending up in the papers as a simple fraudster."

Sophia kissed Sture's forehead and made her way to the bar, where she'd hung her coat upon arriving. Now it was crowded and noisy and she pushed through to the bar counter to ask what had become of her coat. As she tried to get the bartender's attention, a man she'd never seen before leaned toward her. She tried to back up, but there were too many people behind her. She was stuck; the man steadied himself against her shoulder, raised his glass, and slurred into her ear.

"Cheers to Professor Death," he hissed. The man's saliva sprayed across her cheek. "Cheers, you fucking cunt! I hope you're happy."

The man let his hand slide from her shoulder down her back and toward her waist. He pulled her close as someone passed behind Sophia, forcing her even closer to him. She felt his heavy breath against her neck.

"Excuse me," she managed. She tore herself from his grip and shoved her way through the wall of people and away from the bar. The exit was only a few yards on; she could retrieve her coat tomorrow. She skidded out to the street, past the bouncer and a pair of smoking patrons. She stumbled, regained her balance, and jogged up Grev Ture-gatan. Only when she was a few hundred yards away did she turn around. No one was following her.

44

"What exactly do you want me to do with them?"

The summer intern was standing in the doorway to Sophia's office. He was holding a stack of email printouts four inches high. Sophia had asked him to go through her in-box. He'd made a face as if she'd asked him to scrub the bathroom on his knees. But he hadn't dared to refuse.

"I'd like you to pass on the ones I need to answer," Sophia said with as much calm as she could muster.

"And how am I supposed to know which ones those are?"

"If it comes from another law firm, a government authority, a client, or the courts, I want it right away."

He handed over six sheets of paper.

"Thanks," she managed to say. "Is the rest about Stig Ahlin?"

"Uh-huh. And quite a few ads too."

"Did you read the ones about Stig Ahlin?"

He nodded and handed that bundle to her. Sophia shook her head and pushed it aside.

"Can you give me a summary, please?" she asked. "If I wanted to read them myself, I would have."

"'How the hell could you, you goddamn witch?'" The intern curled his upper lip. His capacity for empathy was impressive. Reluctantly, he went on. "In summary, that is. And you got the occasional congratulations. And a few that say they know who really murdered Katrin."

"Did they seem credible?" Sophia took the opportunity to glance through the six emails that didn't have to do with Stig Ahlin.

The intern snorted. "Two of them claim they killed Katrin Björk themselves. Because they were possessed by evil spirits. Or because Katrin Björk was possessed by evil spirits. One claims Breivik did it. Another said it was the prime minister. The rest are in a similar vein."

"Okay." Sophia looked at her watch. "Thanks. You can set them there." She pointed at the pile of unread material on her visitor's chair. "And delete the emails from the server, please. Otherwise it won't be long before it crashes."

The young man gave a stiff nod, put down his printouts, and walked off. He closed the door behind him, only a little too fast and a little too hard. He didn't quite dare to slam it.

The summer intern returned to the reception desk. He plunked himself down in the parental-leave secretary's seat at the main computer.

She was so bossy, that Sophia Weber. So smug that half as much smugness would have been enough for at least five female assistants. She didn't look at him when she spoke, and she cut him off anytime he used more than three words per sentence.

This was definitely not how he'd imagined a summer job at a law firm. They hadn't even given him an office. People who visited the firm thought he was a receptionist. That he sat there answering the phone, watering the flowers, opening the door, and booking appointments for the partners. Him. A guy who'd received an A on every exam since he started his legal studies, who was scheduled to go on an Erasmus exchange program to King's College in London. Who certainly had no intention of wasting two years of his life clerking in the lower courts but could have done it if he'd wanted to. His grades were good, really good — he could have gotten a clerking position anywhere in Sweden. It was just those high-end business law firms who sent back his applications without even bringing him in for an interview.

"Criminal law," he'd said to his classmates to explain why he wouldn't be working on Norrmalmstorg that summer. "That's real law, what real lawyers do. The only ones who go to the business firms are people who couldn't get jobs at Goldman Sachs."

But clearly he had ended up at the wrong place.

Each morning when he arrived at the office, he was assigned a fresh batch of pointless tasks. First, he'd had to write a couple of case briefs for Lars Gustafsson. Presumably no one would ever even read them. Then they'd asked him to write a lecture on legal ethics for Lars to give at the Swedish Bar Association. And now this. Going through Sophia Weber's email account and cleaning out crap from nutjobs. And he wasn't even earning anything at this stupid gig. Flipping burgers at McDonald's paid better.

Never again, he thought, opening Sophia Weber's email account. *Never again*.

He clicked through quickly. But only one at a time; he better not delete an important work email by accident, that woman would probably go mad. Because you could tell by looking at her she was unbalanced. She was clearly the type to shout and go on rampages if something didn't go her way. Not that he'd seen this for himself, but it was obvious that she was capable of it. He clicked on. It was incredible that people had time to sit around writing this sort of thing.

At least he'd increased his vocabulary. If it was, in fact, a perk to learn a ton of innovative words for sex organs — it wasn't as if he could include it on a CV.

He felt his heart growing lighter as the number of emails in the in-box decreased.

How does Sophia Weber stand it? he thought. *No wonder she's so grumpy*. It couldn't be easy to be the attorney who managed to land a dream case like Stig Ahlin's and then receive these sorts of reactions. Tinfoil-hat types who said they knew who shot Olof Palme or who had killed Katrin Björk. Those clowns. How had they even learned how to turn on a computer? But Gustafsson & Weber should have a secretary for this stuff. They should be using him for real tasks, important tasks.

Anyway, he was almost done. He could call that girl he'd met out at Sturecompagniet last night. She'd been decently impressed when he told her he was working at a law firm over the summer. He'd also told her why he preferred criminal law instead of that fill-in-the-blanks jurisprudence they did over at Norrmalmstorg. He could tell her he was working on the Stig Ahlin case, but they'd decided to finish early for once. She would like that.

The in-box was almost empty when he clicked on an email from Ida Sörensson.

"I need to meet with you," the brief note said. "There's something I want to tell you, it's really important. I know things about Stig Ahlin and the murder of Katrin Björk."

She had included her phone number and address.

The intern hesitated. Had he noticed that email before? The name didn't mean anything to him.

Whatever, he thought. *Who killed Palme? I know! I was possessed by the devil, and he told me.* Naturally, whatever she wanted to share would be along those lines. Fuck it. A copy of the email was in the pile he'd given to Sophia too. She had a copy of all the crazy emails. They couldn't accuse him of being careless. So he clicked the trash symbol. The computer made a crunching noise.

That's that, he mumbled to himself, pleased. It was only five o'clock — time for a beer. Or a drink, if the girl from yesterday wanted to tag along. If she did, it would have to be drinks. Although in that case he'd have to go home first to put on a tie. Lawyers wore ties. He would make a date with her, hurry in a few minutes late, and loosen his tie as he sat down. And he would tell her how they were in the process of preparing Stig Ahlin's case for the court of appeals. But no details — she would understand, client-attorney privilege and all. She would definitely like that.

He scrolled through the in-box, selected the rest of the emails and erased them as well. Then he turned off the computer.

Law. A noble occupation.

45

It took a few days, but daily life went back to the way it had been.

Planned out. Every hour.

Short walk. Long walk. They were let out like dogs, and each activity had a name. They were herded in various directions like livestock and fed like lab rats. Even their free time was scheduled. If they wanted to sit in their rooms between activities, the door had to remain open. It could only be locked from the outside.

Stig Ahlin still wasn't allowed to run alone in the mornings before the general wake-up call. Now they were saying it was out of concern for his security. He was a high-risk inmate. But Stig knew the real reason.

They hated him. The inmates. The staff. All of them. Stig knew it. It hadn't mattered before. He used to persuade himself he didn't care about them anyway. But Lasse Wilander had changed that fact. He made Stig see them for what they were. Paltry. Small. Pathetic. They refused to let him run alone because they wanted to demonstrate their power, that they controlled him. Also, they were afraid that someone on the outside would find out he had received special privileges.

But Stig's petition for a new trial had been granted. For extraordinary reasons. And even if Sophia Weber wouldn't say it out loud, Stig was starting to realize that this meant he would soon be out of here. Lasse Wilander had taken it for granted. Had even said it, more than once. He allowed Stig to believe it, to talk about it. When the program aired, Stig sat on his bed and realized that Wilander was right. And with that insight came the flood of contempt.

Stig wanted them to see who he was. For them to speak to him the way he deserved. He wanted to look them in the eyes and see that they knew they were wrong. See the shame. He wanted to make them feel ashamed. About everything, but especially for having believed they could break him by refusing him his solitary exercise time, by delaying his mail, by pretending to have misplaced his packages. Such small people. Worthy only of contempt.

He still woke up at the same time. But these days he didn't remain in bed. He had put together an exercise program instead. Push-ups, sit-ups. All the drills he could think of. For weights he used books. When the door opened he was drenched with sweat and the oxygen in his cell was nearly depleted. He headed straight for the showers; these days he never had to wait his turn.

After breakfast he went to the workshop, where he sat down and got to work. The machines immersed everything in flashing metal. The blade whined; the plane shrieked like a madman; the band saw howled. The heat was almost unbearable. Outside it was a cool summer day, unusually rainy and chilly. But in here it was hot. Still, he put on his work coveralls and ear protection and safety goggles. Thick gloves and special shoes.

As soon as it was exercise time, he ran. None of the other inmates bothered him anymore. He still counted, but now he was counting down. One day at a time. Soon he would be out of here. And they would be ashamed. He would make them regret their actions. And pay for what they had done to him. At least a million kronor per year in damages. Money for a life abroad.

And he made his way through the days. He knew now that they couldn't stop him anymore. Soon it would all be over.

■ ■ ■

A red cottage with white trim, in the middle of the forest. In the yard was a swing hanging from a knobby apple tree. White roses climbed the facade and in the outhouse was a rag rug, a washing pan made of floral porcelain, and moisture-swollen royal postcards in frames on the wall. Inside was all oiled wood floors, plaster walls with wainscoting, and a wood-burning stove. There were two small bedrooms, one with a pair of twin beds, the other with a view of the lake.

Adam had been renting the place for two weeks, the two weeks he was supposed to spend alone with the children.

They were three days in and the weather was getting better and better.

Adam had put up a tent in the yard. They'd gathered bark in the woods and started to whittle a boat each. He'd also built a herd of cows out of pinecones and matches, filled egg-carton stalls with lush clover, and unpacked beads and watercolors in the kitchen. In the shed he had found a tangled net and two fishing poles. There were worms in the overgrown herb garden on the east side of the house.

"Dad," his son whined while Adam was lying in the hammock after lunch. "There's nothing to do."

On the first night they ate tacos. On the second night he made homemade meatballs and French fries. On the third night they had pancakes for dinner. Served with ice cream, warm raspberries, and lightly whipped cream.

"Dad," his daughter cried. "I want lingonberry, why didn't you get any lingonberry jam?"

He had brought his favorite books from when he was a boy and filled one of the shelves with them. So far, neither his son nor his daughter had read a single one. The two magazines they'd bought before the trip were unread as well, but they had played with the accompanying plastic toys until they fell apart. It had taken twenty minutes.

Tomorrow would be hamburgers. The shed was full of charcoal for grilling. Or should they get out the sleeping bags and flashlights and sleep in the tent tonight?

How bad could the mosquitoes really be?

46

It was a struggle for Sophia to keep from screaming uncontrollably. They'd been at it for over three hours. The sun was blazing outside. Thunder was in the air and she was starting to think that Hans Segerstad was crazy.

He said he wanted to argue the case.

They didn't yet have a date for the hearing, to be sure, but it wouldn't be long, and it wasn't likely to be far in the future once they received it. They had to be prepared. So she had said when she asked Hans to come by her office. Sophia was the one who wanted them to meet, at least once before Hans took off on vacation. To divide up the work, to the extent there was any work to divide up.

There was no way she could have predicted that Hans would be struck by delusions of grandeur.

Hans Segerstad knew next to nothing about the practicalities of a trial. He didn't have her detailed knowledge about the case, nor did he have any intentions of putting in the work it would take to learn. Yet he had just casually thrown out that he felt he should give the closing arguments in the case.

Sophia could hardly believe her ears. This was her case. She had Segerstad to thank for getting in contact with Ahlin, but now he had to live with the consequences of asking Sophia to handle the petition for a retrial. Anything else was unthinkable.

Hans Segerstad didn't understand the gravity of this situation. He thought his reputation as a renowned academic was exactly what this court of appeals hearing needed, and that his age and merits were of more import than what he called her "impeccable preparatory work."

With each word that came from his mouth, Sophia became angrier. *Preparatory work.* Now she was almost afraid to say anything, afraid she would lose control. Hans had taken a chair on the other side of her desk. Next to him towered her unread pile of guilty-conscience material. At the top was the collection of nutjob emails the summer intern had printed out and dropped off at her office.

She tried to calm herself before speaking.

Along one side of her office ran the timeline of the Stig Ahlin case. She turned her back to Hans Segerstad and gazed at it instead. She ran a hand along the very first sheet, the one that showed the emergency call made near the time of Katrin Björk's death.

No matter what he says, Hans Segerstad knows he's not the one who got Stig Ahlin that new trial, she thought. *I did. He can give as many interviews as he wants, I don't care. He can go on every TV channel in Sweden and claim that I played an important part in his petition and not vice versa. But he will not take my work away from me. That is out of the question.*

She kept looking at the timeline. It covered an entire wall. The case files were in piles beneath it.

Everything from the preliminary investigation and all the other material I could find on the inquiry. I know it by heart and Hans doesn't. He doesn't know anywhere near as much as I do.

Hans Segerstad has gotten what he needs. He's been celebrated; he has gotten to feel immortal. The trial is my turn. I need to argue it. And if he is freed, I'll know I did the right thing. I'll know he's innocent. Then he will be innocent.

"Not on your life," she said at last. "I'm Stig Ahlin's attorney, not you. There is no need to discuss this any further. If you insist, I'll tell Stig Ahlin that he has to choose one of us. And if that happens, you won't even get a seat in the gallery. Because even if you manage to convince everyone else the opposite is true, Stig Ahlin knows which one of us did the work."

"What's all of this?"

Hans Segerstad had picked up the stack of printouts. He read the top one, frowning.

"Those came from some of the many wackos who write to me," Sophia replied. "To me. I'm the one they want to tell off. Because I'm Stig Ahlin's attorney, I'm the one who was appointed, and I'm the one who will handle his defense — his whole defense, including the closing arguments."

"This is insane," said Hans Segerstad. "Where do people get the time? Where do they get the energy to write this sort of crap?"

The professor slowly paged through the stack.

"Never mind," he said suddenly, putting down the documents. "Let's get lunch. If you're doing the trial, you're buying."

. . .

Stinging nettles. Mosquitoes. Wasps. Vipers. Spanish slugs. No Internet, no TV. Rain. Every day. Each time he thought, *Surely today the weather will be nice,* another downpour broke out.

They had driven to Heron City mall, where the children got Happy Meals and they watched two movies. Adam slept through the first and woke up with a strand of saliva dangling from his lower lip and his lap full of popcorn. In the middle of the second film, his daughter dozed off. Adam made a lame attempt to wake her, but soon gave up.

He let his son sit in the front as they drove back to the cottage. Even so, he got carsick and puked cascades into his Happy Meal box. It only leaked a little.

When they returned home, the hot water was out. Adam heated three pots of water on the stove and bathed the kids in a plastic tub on the kitchen floor.

Then he went out and sat on the kitchen stairs and cried.

· · ·

The tasks Stig performed in the workshop were monotonous, but they took a certain amount of concentration. Still, he could see from the corner of his eye how his neighbor at the wide-belt sander rose as smoke began to pour from his machine. Just a few seconds later, sparks were flying across the stone floor. The dust in the exhaust vent had ignited. It was burning like a propane flame.

It didn't occur to Stig to help. Instead he took a step back from his workbench.

His fellow inmates did the same. None of them had a mind to try to stop this.

Stig took off his safety goggles and observed the chaos.

The guards panicked. One of them ran in one direction and yanked the fire extinguisher from its rack. The other shouted about dust explosions and opened the sliding doors into the adjacent hall, then turned around and yelled something at his colleague.

The whole room filled with smoke from the burning motor and a thick haze from the extinguisher.

Suddenly only one guard was left in the room. The other had taken off, leaving the sliding door wide open. Was he getting help? Stig moved a little farther away from the remaining guard, who was busy putting out the fire; he could hardly be seen in the cloud of powder and dust.

Stig looked at the door, which was now wide open. Open, unguarded, a gaping wound. On the other side was an identical workshop. The entire job annex was made up of workshops, side by side, separated by well-sealed doors. But now the isolated sex crimes unit was no longer isolated. Nothing separated their team from the other work teams.

In all his years in this prison, Stig had never seen a unit besides his own. He had never seen those who worked there, what they looked like, the people he was supposed to be protected from.

But now he did. There they stood. Twelve men. Side by side. Gazing in, at the tumult. At him. Two of them began to move toward the opening. They pulled off their visors and safety goggles, dropping them on the floor. Coming closer.

Stig looked over at the guard. The extinguisher was empty, and he called for someone to bring one from the other workshop. But the guard wasn't looking in Stig's direction.

The two inmates from the next room had seen Stig. Recognized him. They looked at one another. No discussion was needed — each knew what the other was thinking, what they must do. They simply separated from their group as if on command. Now they were heading for him.

Stig knew what was about to happen. The guard was turned away. He was busy with the fire and wasn't watching Stig.

47

Sophia and Hans Segerstad had gone out for lunch, and then Hans strolled toward Central Station; he would be heading home to Uppsala. In a few days he would take off for three weeks in Italy.

"You can do this," he declared just before he left. There were no hints of their earlier conversation about who should argue the case in court. He didn't mention it. His voice was breezy, not accusatory or wounded. It didn't seem like he was angry about what Sophia had said, or even slightly upset.

Sophia lingered in the sidewalk seating and gazed at Kungsträdgården. The park was crowded: blemished legs, unshaved armpits, fungus-ridden feet. Bare skin where there should have been clothing. Lemminglike streams of a different sort of people than were usually found here. The Stockholmers had fled when the city seethed beyond recognition. Now it was the city of country folk, of Germans and Norwegians, of sandals, sweat, and shorts.

She looked down at her empty coffee cup. Was it time to go, or should she have a refill? Treat herself to that extra cup of coffee? She was relieved that she'd avoided an argument with Hans. Relieved, but also, in some sense, abandoned. The oppressive heat had made her feet swell. Her shoes hurt, but she couldn't take them off — she'd never get them back on. Her T-shirt stank; she stank.

It didn't sound appealing, going back to the office. She could call Grandpa. They could go out sailing for a few days. No one would miss her. She had time. There was no reason for her to stress out as long as they hadn't been given a date for the proceedings. Furthermore, she knew the case file by heart. There was no way she was going to forget it, and if she had trouble relaxing she could start writing her arguments out in the archipelago.

"Extraordinary reasons," the Supreme Court had said. That was a strong statement.

The appeals court trial is just a formality, she thought. *In truth, I know that. There's no reason for me to worry. He'll be released. Soon.*

She took her phone from her bag to call Sture. He would want to come along.

. . .

Stig Ahlin was drenched in a helpless sweat even before the two men made it through the open sliding door. The first thing they did was shove him into a corner. He didn't know who they were, but he knew they hated him.

The first blow landed before Stig could put up his hands, his arms, to protect himself. He was struck in the back of the head and he stumbled, blood flowing down the narrow valley on the back of his neck. The dizziness was worse than the pain.

Stig was in good shape, more athletic than most. But the blows came one after another. While one of them was striking him the other took his mark, finding a new angle of attack. Stig tried to fend them off, keep his abdominal muscles taut, but it didn't help. When he tried to brace himself he slipped, moaning in pain, flailing helter-skelter in vain, in the wrong direction. He fumbled in the empty space between his own helplessness and the other men's fists.

His eyebrow split, a rib cracked, one eye swelled shut, and his nose was bleeding like a fountain. Stig felt his knuckles hit someone, or something, and pain radiated up his forearm. It was quickly replaced by pain from somewhere else. Someone kicked him, and he fell hard on the concrete floor; he spat out a splinter, a piece of tooth; he tried to curl into a ball but was kicked again.

Stig looked up from the floor. At last the guard had turned around. He took out his walkie-talkie and brought it to his mouth.

Help is on the way, Stig managed to think. But then he saw the hesitant movement. What the guard wasn't doing. He hadn't clicked the walkie-talkie. He was holding it. Breathing on it. But he wasn't calling for help.

The fire was out now. The other inmates were standing in a semicircle around Stig. Watching him. The guard looked on. It took ten seconds, fifteen max.

Then Anders the pedophile took half a step forward. There was a white plastic object in his hand. When the inmates from the neighboring workshop saw what it was, they interrupted their assault and let him pass, let him approach Stig Ahlin. Two toothbrushes taped together and sharpened like an awl at one end. Plastic didn't set off metal detectors.

Anders fell to his knees alongside the prone Stig, bent slowly over him, and sank the plastic into the soft gap between Stig's ribs. It was astonishingly easy. As the weapon slid into his body he could feel the pedophile's hand on his skin. Blood rushed across the workshop floor and under his own back; it was warm, almost hot. Then Stig faded into unconsciousness. By the time the guard finally called for help, it was all over.

■ ■ ■

This isn't happening, Sophia thought in the cab. *It's not possible.*

They had flown Stig to Karolinska Hospital by helicopter. He would undergo surgery.

It was completely unnecessary for her to go to the hospital. They had insisted. Any information she needed could be given over the phone. They had assured her of it. Yet Sophia wanted to be there.

No one else will be, she thought. *I'm all he has.*

Even before she stepped out of the taxi, she realized her error. There was a crowd of people who wanted to know what was happening to Stig Ahlin.

It wasn't chaos; there weren't that many journalists. No one was shouting, there were no hysterics. They spoke in low voices, no one running back and forth. They posed kind questions, introduced themselves, spoke one at a time in calm tones. And she responded. They let her finish, no interruptions.

As she walked through the hospital doors she found herself looking into a silent camera, straight into its lens; she saw the shutter close. She blinked back.

This isn't happening, she thought again. *It's not possible.*

The journalists were still waiting when she exited the hospital again. Sophia shared what she knew. For everything else she referred them to the press conference the hospital director would be holding in cooperation with the police.

It was scheduled to take place immediately, so Sophia stayed to watch.

An investigation had been launched to find out what had happened and why security had failed.

The three suspects had been isolated from the other inmates. Two of them were serving lengthy sentences for violent crimes. The third was a man who had been convicted of sexually abusing children. A knifelike stabbing implement had been involved.

"It's a statistical fact," said the chief of police, "that brawls are very unusual in Swedish prisons."

An initial interrogation had been performed. The suspects had confessed to their crime and claimed it had been necessary. The chief of police did not want to give further comment on their statements. But it was clear that this was not a case of self-defense.

It was an execution, Sophia thought. But she didn't say it out loud.

48

Sophia had no conscious plan to take a walk. She just did it. She could hear noise around her: cars, an ambulance, music from an open window, gravel beneath her feet. But she didn't think about them. The odors: exhaust and melting asphalt, her own sour sweat — they didn't trouble her.

When she came to Östermalmstorg and Hedwig Eleonora Church, she stepped through the open church doors. Just inside, in the cool air, a father and a child were standing before a rack of postcards. The souvenir shop was open. A handwritten sign urged visitors to stop by the summer café just beyond the second church door. Sophia caught a glimpse of a few round tables and white china. A woman laughed. It was a beautiful day, sunny with a pleasant breeze and scattered clouds.

A man was tuning the organ at the front of the church. A group of Germans had gathered below the pulpit. In one of the side chapels Sophia read the words on the stone wall: WHOEVER DOES NOT RECEIVE THE KINGDOM OF GOD AS A LITTLE CHILD WILL NEVER ENTER IT. Sophia turned and left the church.

Back home in her apartment, she kicked off her shoes. She stood there in her hall, at a loss, unsure of what to do. She had turned off her phone. To be safe, she unplugged her landline. Locked the door. Went to the kitchen and opened the fridge. Closed it again. Opened the pantry. Closed it again. She kept linens in the next cupboard over. Mangled tablecloths and other items she never used. She took out a worn, blue-checked kitchen towel, so smooth, its embroidered monogram as soft as silk. She brought it to her nose. It smelled clean, like childhood and her grandmother. It made her feel tired.

Don't think.

Sophia just wanted to rest awhile. She hated oversensitive people, like her mother. People who cried and broke down and forced others to steel themselves and take responsibility. Forced others to be strong because they felt their own feelings were more important, more worthy.

To Sophia, being sensitive had never seemed like a virtue; it was a sign of egoism.

What did Sophia have to cry about? Stig Ahlin was her client, not her friend. She worked for him. It was a job. It wasn't her fault that he was dead; it wasn't even her responsibility. She brought the kitchen towel to her face again, breathing in its scent. Letting the memory of her grandmother drown out everything else.

When the tears came, Sophia bent forward, pressing her fist into her mouth to keep from making any noise. But the sounds came out of her anyway. The strain was too much, she couldn't stop it, she couldn't handle it. Her body shook with convulsions.

"There, there...," her grandmother would have said.

Sophia sat down on the floor, stroking her own cheek with the fabric. She closed her eyes.

"There, there...," her grandmother would have murmured. Droning, like a lullaby, the same word again and again. "There, there...Just get it out. There, there...Cry as much as you can."

FOUR

49

The kitchen was clean, the fridge turned off. The phones were forwarded to an answering service and the email autoreplies were set. The lobby was empty, the hallway was empty, and all the offices besides Sophia Weber's were locked.

Sophia, Lars, and Björn had decided to close the office for two weeks. There was no reason for it to be staffed; that only cost money. Soon even Sophia would be on her way.

She had brought two empty boxes into her office. But as she looked at the rows of binders on Stig Ahlin, and all the documents stacked on the floor, she realized two boxes would never cut it.

Pulling the first binder off the shelf, she opened it, pried open its rings, took out the papers, and dropped them in the wastebasket. It was immediately overfull. She found a garbage bag in the kitchen and repeated the process for the second binder.

She lacked the energy to page through the documents first, to see if she ought to save anything. She really should be sorting everything, but she didn't have the energy for that either. She didn't even have the strength to find more boxes to put the case in. All she could manage was to throw it out. And she had to get this case file out of her office. It could not be there when she returned from vacation.

When the doorbell rang, Sophia had filled the garbage bag with documents to be shredded. She dragged it to the lobby and looked at the entry phone. The image wasn't especially clear, so she turned on the speaker to let the visitor identify themself.

"My name is Ida...," a young woman said hesitantly. "Sörensson." She looked down, toward what she must have thought was the camera. "Stig Ahlin's daughter. To see Sophia Weber."

Sophia greeted Ida in the lobby. As Ida hung her denim jacket in the coatroom, Sophia sneaked a look at her in profile. Those blond curls the media had been so fond of when she was younger — she still had them. But she seemed to be trying to tame them now. Her hair was waist-length and only curled at her temples. Did she resemble her father? It was hard to say. Something about her eyes, the way her forehead wrinkled.

Ida rubbed her hands together. It had to be eighty degrees in here — the ventilation system was off, and the poorly insulated top floor always got too warm this time of year, even in bad weather. But Ida looked like she was freezing.

"Please," Sophia said as they entered her office. She pointed at the visitor's chair. "Have a seat. I'll just grab something to drink."

When Sophia returned from the kitchen Ida was still there, standing among the documents that formed the remains of Stig Ahlin's case file. She was looking at the timeline that was still tacked up on the wall. Her index finger was tracing the line where Sophia had noted all the important events in the murder of Katrin Björk. It appeared that she was reading everything carefully.

Emla Prison had shipped Stig Ahlin's belongings to Sophia, whom Stig had listed as his next of kin. Sophia had been planning to send the items to Ida by messenger, but Ida was insistent. She very much wanted to come and pick them up at Sophia's office.

"Of course," Sophia had said. "Just come on by." But inside, she knew. *I don't want to*, she had thought, even then. *I don't want to talk about that. Don't think you can just come by and ask me anything, because I'm not about to answer.*

"Have you decided on a date for the funeral?" Sophia took a glass of water from the tray and handed it to Ida.

"We're not having one," Ida replied, accepting the glass. She drank it greedily. "Only an interment. I've told the funeral director I want to do it. We don't need a pastor. If they'll just show me the spot, I'll do it myself."

"Do you need help? With anything else?" Sophia took back the empty glass and set it on the tray.

"No. Thank you, but it's not necessary."

Ida pointed at the very first event on the timeline, the one that signified the night of the murder.

"Did you know that on the night Katrin Björk was killed, I was brought in for observation?"

"No." Sophia rearranged the coffee cups, the thermos, and the water she'd placed on the tray along with a plate of cookies. It was mostly for decoration; in some instances, it could have a calming effect. Putting something in your mouth, sipping at a glass. "No," she said again, steeling herself, preparing herself to be the target of Ida's accusations. "I didn't know that."

"They were supposed to examine me, a whole team of investigators. Psychologists, social workers, police, doctors. And they wanted to observe how I acted when Mom and...Stig weren't there. To determine whether he'd abused me or not. I guess that's how they do it. They place the child in a different environment. I had to stay at a special home for two nights."

Sophia picked up the plate of cookies and offered it to Ida. She shook her head.

"I don't remember much about those days. But I remember crying when I was supposed to go to sleep. They let me come to the kitchen. Sit on the counter and drink warm milk. Then the woman sang, I think she was a psychologist, or a social worker, she sang me a lullaby, and I pretended to fall asleep. But at some point, I must have fallen asleep for real, because I couldn't have been awake all night."

"That's an odd coincidence," Sophia said.

She went to her desk and sat down. From the top drawer she took a white envelope, also sent from the staff at Emla. In it was the key to Stig Ahlin's safe-deposit box. She set it on the desk.

"That it was the same night as the murder? Yes, very odd."

Ida ran her hand along the paper on Sophia's wall. Petting the timeline, stroking it as if it were a living being. Her finger stopped at the point that showed the weeks before the district court trial began.

"And here," Ida said, tapping her finger. "Exactly three weeks before the murder trial began, the police informed Mom they were closing the incest investigation. The investigation hadn't turned up anything, or not enough. Those days at the home, all the interviews, all the doctor's examinations. They didn't believe me. Or, wait. That's not exactly how they put it. They said they thought I seemed like a good girl. Mature for my age. Something like that. But it wasn't enough to bring charges. What I had to say wasn't enough. I wasn't clear enough. The investigation was closed."

Sophia could hear the gulls calling from the quay. She was holding the envelope with the key in her hand now. The boxes were already in the lobby. As soon as Ida had her belongings, she would go. Sophia could get back to cleaning. Ida turned to Sophia, her eyes perfectly clear.

"What is it that they want you to provide? What evidence does it take? Can you tell me? What should we have done? What should Mom have done?"

Sophia didn't respond. Stig Ahlin may have been dead, but he was still Sophia's client. Nodding sympathetically as Ida explained why she hadn't wanted to see her father — she really couldn't do it.

"They told Mom not to worry. It didn't matter that the investigation was closed. It was no problem. She shouldn't worry. Because they were going to get him for murder. He had killed Katrin Björk and would be locked up for it. That's what they said. They would lock him up. For so long that I would be a grown-up before he got out. As long as he was convicted of homicide, Mom didn't have to worry. He would never get to be alone with me again."

"Ida," Sophia attempted cautiously, "I understand this is difficult for you. But I don't think I'm the person you should be talking to."

Ida cut her off.

"My mom…" She raised her voice and her eyes were gazing steadily into Sophia's. "You have to understand that Mom…I have tried to imagine what it was like for her. Stig was her husband for many years. He touched her. She slept beside him, night after night. I assume she loved him, that she wanted him to touch her, listen to her, love her. I assume she wanted all of that. But…she never met anyone new. I'm all she has."

"I haven't looked at the incest allegations," Sophia lied. "You shouldn't ask me about that, because I don't know anything."

Sophia stood up and walked around the desk to Ida. She held out the envelope.

Take it now, Sophia thought. *Go home. Open your dad's safe-deposit box, go through his things, get to know him a little. As much as you can. That will help you move on.*

"Unfortunately, I can't help you with your questions," Sophia said. "There's nothing I can do."

Ida looked down at her hands. She shook her head as if in protest. She raised her voice; it trembled slightly. "Did I ask you for anything? I wrote to you. An email. But you never responded."

Sophia frowned. She glanced at the stack of documents with the nutjob emails.

Shit, she thought.

"There was something I wanted you to know," Ida went on. Suddenly she looked very young. Not a woman anymore. She wrung her hands, licked her lips, tugged at her long hair and pushed it back. "About Stig. About my mother. I thought that...you should have known...something important. But I guess it wasn't important for you. My life. Whatever my mom had to deal with and whatever she had to do..." Ida stopped talking. She shook her head. "I don't know what I thought. Maybe I thought you could tell me if you knew...if you knew what he did, if he told you, but, why would he do that? Why would he tell the truth? And why would you care?"

Sophia slowly shook her head. "I'm sorry I didn't get back to you. I would have, if I'd known you wanted that. But your email must have gotten lost. You see, so many people wrote to me after the murder. I never got yours."

She tried to catch Ida's eye, but Ida was still staring intently at her own hands. She sounded as if she were talking to herself. "My mom, how could she do anything else? I was only two years old. I couldn't tell her what to do. I still don't know." Suddenly, Ida looked up. "You know. If he did do it, it saved my life that I can't remember. But if he didn't, I killed him. And I will never know which it is. No one will know. All I know is that it isn't my mom's fault."

"But you know, what happened to you, Ida..." Sophia wasn't sure what Ida was trying to tell her. "The fact that your father was convicted of murder, you couldn't have done anything about it. Even if it feels like you could have. I have a hard time believing... they were two different things."

Ida snatched the glass of water again. She filled it to the brim, gulped it down, and looked up at Sophia. At first she looked like she might protest, but then she changed her mind. She set the glass back on the tray.

"You're right," Ida said at last. "I couldn't... it doesn't matter anymore." She took the envelope from Sophia's hand and turned it over a few times. Then she shoved it into her handbag. "Anyway, it's too late. It's too late now."

Once Ida left, the silence returned. Sounds that usually couldn't be heard indoors were faintly audible in the background. The tourists, the gulls, the street musicians. Kids crying, cars honking, a church bell.

Sophia stood in her office for a while, looking at the timeline. There was nothing on it about what had happened to Ida. It wasn't legally relevant. She didn't want to have to think about it. Especially not right now. She tore the papers off the wall and crumpled them into her overflowing wastebasket.

The remaining binders went into the empty boxes and Sophia dragged them out to stow them behind the reception desk. When she returned she would ask the temp receptionist to finish sorting them, file what needed to be filed, and toss the rest. The important thing was that shelves in her office were empty once more. The case file was put away. She closed and locked the office door. It was time for vacation.

50

It was tradition. Every year they spent a weekend in Sörm-
land, at the home of Norah's best friend and her husband.
This year he hadn't wanted to think about it. He'd intended
to plan something else, to do one of the many things he
used to wish, as a married man with small children, that
he could still do. But when Norah asked if he wanted to
come along anyway, for the kids, and because they were his
friends too, he said yes. Breathlessly, as though the chance
might vanish if he was too eager.

"Just like always, Dad," his daughter said in the car,
looking at him in the rearview mirror.

Anxious — his daughter sounded anxious, and he said,
"Of course, it's just like before," and glanced at Norah. She
gave him a tentative smile, leaned into the backseat, and
stroked her daughter's cheek. Not even Norah wanted to
protest.

As usual, Adam, Norah, and the kids stayed in the
guesthouse. When they said it would be perfect, that they
were happy to stay there, their friends had looked relieved.
Still, their hostess offered him the sofa up in the house, but
Norah shook her head silently, and that was the end of that.

No one had expected Adam to say what he wanted. Everyone knew Norah was in charge here. She was the one who'd asked Adam to move out. It was all up to her — every decision about what they would do from now on.

They had dinner down by the dock. The warmest evening of the summer. They'd laughed at the same stories, the same memories they'd been telling and retelling for years now. And the children had fallen asleep an hour ago. Adam had put them to bed; Norah had stayed behind, had looked up at Adam and mimed a *thank you*.

As night fell, the air became chilly. Norah had drawn a blanket over her shoulders and Adam had wriggled into his sweater. But they stayed where they were. A fresh bottle was uncorked; a thermos of tea was put out on the table, and each time someone rose Adam was afraid Norah too would say, *Good night, time for me to hit the hay.* He was afraid because he didn't know what he would say then, whether he should rise to join her or wait until she was ready to get in bed before he followed.

But the minutes passed, the sea grew dark, and the shore vanished into the dusk. The moon rose above the water and then the two of them were the only ones left.

Norah flailed angrily at the mosquitoes swarming around her. Adam took a newspaper from the table and rolled it up, front side in, and waved it in her direction. He never had as much trouble with mosquitoes as she did. Norah took the paper from him and smacked him on the shoulder.

"Did you get it?" Adam wondered.

Norah smiled, shook her head, and looked down at the paper.

It had been lying there all night, on the edge of the table, with its black headline and large photo. They'd discussed it, of course, how could they keep from talking about Stig Ahlin?

"Was he guilty?" someone had asked Adam.

"I don't know," he'd heard himself say. "But regardless, he shouldn't have been killed."

They agreed about that. Beaten and stabbed to death on a concrete floor by three fellow inmates. No one deserved that. Not even Stig Ahlin.

There was a picture of Sophia inside the paper, but they hadn't said much about her. She wasn't important to them.

"I've worked with her," Adam had said. But no one had paid attention. There had been a big interview with Sophia. She'd looked like her normal self, her ponytail at the back of her neck, a white T-shirt, those piercing eyes. Adam had looked at the photo, but not for long.

"She's a good attorney," he had mumbled. No one had reacted to that either.

Adam had written Sophia an email. That was only two weeks ago, but it felt like an eternity. Two days after the decision on the new trial was handed down, he had walked off, just before he was supposed to eat lunch with the kids in that cottage he'd rented. It had taken him ten minutes of walking to find a spot with coverage enough to send an email. That had felt less intrusive than a text. Not as personal. But she had never responded.

Had what he had written been unclear? He hadn't wanted to congratulate her, but he had said that she had done an important thing. Last time they saw each other had been so strange. He'd sounded like he was accusing her of something. He had upset her.

But most of all he'd just wanted to have contact with her, any way he could. To see her. He had thought a lot about her, out there in the forest. But Sophia hadn't responded. She never responded.

Norah whacked him on the shoulder with the paper again. More gently this time.

"I can't take it anymore," she whispered. "They're everywhere. I'm going up to bed."

Adam placed his hand over hers; he took the paper and set it on the table, front page down.

"Come on," he said. "Let's go for a swim instead. They can't bite us in the water."

At first, she said nothing. And he could hardly breathe. Because she was in charge now. These decisions lay with her, and her only. Then she stood up. She pulled off her shirt and stepped out of her pants and underwear.

Just before she dove in, Norah's eyes flashed. He followed her.

The water was warm and silky, but he was shivering as if with fever. Norah's bare skin shimmered under the surface. She swam four strokes away from him before turning around to let him catch up. As he took her by the waist and pulled her close, the surface rippled. He stood on the soft bottom to put her legs around him.

As she took his head in her hands, he kissed her. Her fingers in his wet hair, her chest against his. The water lilies turned away from them as he pressed into her, and everything was just like always.

51

Sophia let Sture take the rudder. Her grandfather knew all the islets and skerries out here, the labyrinth of sea and islands. He knew them by heart, the way you know an irregular verb. He could rattle off the locations of treacherous underwater rocks; he knew how to find a narrow inlet deep enough to sail into. She still needed the nautical maps. Grandpa teased her about it anytime he got the chance.

Instead she went up and lay down on the foredeck. They had a tailwind, the breeze from the stern, and the sails unfurled like butterfly wings on either side of the bow. The boat was flush, with the wake gurgling behind.

"How are you feeling?" Sture asked.

Sophia groaned.

"Oh no, my little Fia. None of that. No more of your teenage behavior. Even if I do happen to be the country's foremost professor of psychiatry through the ages, I must be allowed to pose a relatively simple question to my granddaughter."

Sophia squinted into the sun. *How am I feeling? Do I even know?*

"There are lots of people who think it's a good thing Stig Ahlin is dead," she said instead. "Even if he wasn't guilty of the murder. They say that in a greater sense, it's still good that he was punished. For what he did to his daughter."

Sophia felt the boat lurch. She steadied herself with her elbow and glared at Sture. One time he had tipped her overboard when she was lying there like this.

"That doesn't answer my question."

Sture set the boat back on its original course. The sails filled quickly, and Sophia cautiously lay back down.

"I'm afraid it's the best answer I can give you."

"So, you're not feeling so hot," Sture muttered. "It's still eating at you." He looked up at the top of the mast. "Is it important to you? To know whether Stig Ahlin was guilty or not?"

"What do you mean?" Sophia sat up. She took the pillow she'd been using from under her head and placed it under her bottom instead. "No, not really. It's not a question I typically ask myself in my work. If I did, I couldn't be an attorney."

"But it was different with Ahlin," Sture declared.

Sophia nodded. "I thought that was why I was doing it. Because I was going to get an innocent man freed. But then he was murdered. Because his fellow prisoners wanted to keep me from getting him out. And to be honest, I don't know if Stig Ahlin was innocent. I don't even know what that means. To be innocent."

"I dug up those interviews with Ida when she was little." Sture had engaged the autopilot and was about to open a pilsner. "I know you said it wasn't necessary, but I was still interested."

Sophia drew up her knees.

"And I don't know," Sture went on. He paused. "That kid, she said things that don't make me entirely comfortable with what happened later. You know, there are certain things it's easy to overanalyze when you listen to children. At least, if you already suspect they have been victimized somehow."

The wind whipped a little and the leech began to flutter. Sophia came down off the deck and took over the rudder. Sture shuffled off a bit, leaning back and taking big gulps of his beer.

"Your grandmother always touched you," Sture said. "As if she owned you."

Sophia smiled.

"No man can touch his kids that way."

Sophia adjusted the sail and their course. Sture put down his beer and helped her sheet in the jib.

Grandma touched me like I was a part of her, she thought. *As if she owned me. Always, constant, close. Touching my bottom, stroking my belly. Lifting my hair and kissing the back of my neck. Helping me with ointments when my bottom stung. Checking that the birthmark in my groin hadn't started to grow. Way into my teens, she crawled into bed with me and cuddled up close when I was crying. Looking extensively at my changing body. Scanning me when I showered to see how my pubic hair was growing, asking me about discharge and periods, contraceptives and masturbation.*

She accepted a fresh beer from Sture and drank it slowly.

"I don't understand what you mean," she said. "Do you think Grandma did something she shouldn't have?"

Sture just looked at Sophia. His eyes darkened. Slowly he shook his head. Then he swallowed and shook his head once more.

"Definitely not. I just mean that there are ways of being with your children that can be obtrusive, but still perfectly correct. And when little kids talk about stuff like that, it's not a given that we can interpret what they're saying the right way. And I should have been better at hugging you when you were little. More like Grandma. But when I was a child, parents didn't hug as much. At least not in my family."

"But there's no comparison here," Sophia said. "There was still something strange about Ida's stories. I didn't go to day care and say that I slept naked in Grandma's bed. Because with Grandma I was always safe. Everything she did was obvious and right. Ida's stories were..." She swallowed. "I should have let Ida say what she wanted when she was up in my office. It was clear there was something she wanted me to know. Something she would have told me, if I'd given her the chance. She wanted to ease her conscience in some way I wasn't expecting. We should have talked about options for moving forward in the judicial process."

"Do you really think she'd want to?"

"No, not a chance. But the thing about Ida," Sophia went on. "It's not just what she said. She did such strange things too. A four-year-old playing sexual games, in that odd way she did, doesn't that suggest something had happened to her?"

"Maybe," said Sture. He drank the last of his beer. "But what? And does it mean it had to be her dad who did it? I have no idea."

Suddenly the evening breeze died down. The wind was fickle. The boat nearly stopped short and the sails collapsed to the mast. Sophia went up on deck to bring them down; there was no point in sailing any more today. Sture started the engine. Time to head to harbor for the night.

"Don't worry about what Stig Ahlin did or did not do," said Sture. "You'll never find out whether he was guilty. Of one thing or the other. But what you did for Stig Ahlin was really...you have to allow yourself to feel, my lovely Fia. It was a damn good job. You should be pleased with yourself, as fantastically proud as I am."

Up on land, Sophia found early blueberries and a few chanterelles. They ate the mushrooms fried in butter along with smoked herring, fresh spinach, and boiled new potatoes. She served the berries with whipped cream.

Now they were sitting on either side of the cockpit and drinking coffee. The last of the daylight clotted over the water and fog blew toward the outer skerries in gauzy bands. A mink dove from a rock into the inky water and swam off like furry quicksilver under the surface.

"I remember," Sture said quietly, "when you sat on my lap and held the rudder, you couldn't have been more than six. I heard you counting. 'What are you counting?' I wondered. Do you remember what you said?"

Sophia shook her head. *No,* she thought. *I never remember that sort of thing.*

"'I'm counting the colors of the sea,' you said. 'Do you think anyone can count that high?'"

52

"I'll wait in the car," Marianne had told her daughter on the way to the cemetery. "I'm happy to drive you there, but you'll have to bury him yourself."

Ida hadn't reacted.

"I didn't say anything to the lawyer," she'd said instead. "I went up to her office. But I didn't tell her. Because I don't want you to be charged with perjury."

Marianne couldn't help but smile. Her clever daughter with her complicated words. She meant well, but she knew nothing about that stuff. Marianne would not be convicted of perjury; she had never lied. Not to the court, not in interrogations. She had never said anything she didn't know to be true. Because no one had asked her. Why would they have?

Yet she was glad Ida hadn't said anything. Because now Ida believed she had rescued her mother from prison and dishonor. Marianne thought this might make Ida feel better. As if she were guilt-free. Because she was — Ida and everyone else. No one knew what Marianne knew. Not even Marianne herself, at first.

That night. Marianne remembered it all in great detail. The early-summer light. And the hatred. It had settled in her body and infected her blood.

Ida was picked up right after lunch. Marianne had taken a sick day and had packed Ida's bag the night before. Ida had her own backpack as well, with her blankie, a doll's baby bottle, and her favorite puzzle. It was missing four pieces.

When the social worker rang the doorbell, Ida began to cry; she usually did, when they had guests. Marianne couldn't bring herself to comfort her. She just handed her daughter over, prying her sweaty little hands from her body.

"Bye, sweetie," she had said. "See you very soon. You're going to have a nice time. And Mommy will pick you up in two days. Two days will go by very, very fast."

Ida would be away for two nights, and once the social worker had strapped her into the car and driven off, Marianne was struck by rage. A fury that resembled nothing other than, possibly, birthing pains. With that rage coursing through her body she got in the car to see Stig. She wanted to confront him. She would force him to confess. And if he didn't confess what he had done to her daughter, if he didn't take responsibility, she would kill him.

This was the first time she had hated another person. And the consequences were self-evident.

But Stig hadn't been home. Instead she sat outside his house, on the street. She stared straight into his apartment with its large picture windows. When they divorced, he'd gotten himself a showpiece apartment. Twice the size of the one Ida and Marianne lived in.

When Stig got home from work she allowed him to park in the garage and go into the building and up the stairs and into his apartment. He didn't see her. *I'll go in in a minute,* she had thought. But that's as far as she ever got. Her body betrayed her. Her hatred didn't make her brave, only weak.

As if paralyzed, she stayed in the car, watching Stig turn on the ceiling lights, watching him as he sat in front of the TV, as he went to bed and turned out the lights. Filled with contempt at her own fear, she stayed there until after six in the morning, when the bright summer night turned into a brand-new day. Then he woke up. When he left the building to get in his car and go to work, she too started her car and drove off.

Marianne had sat in her car, just like now, watching Stig. She hadn't slept; how could she have slept? She hadn't dozed off. Not for a second. She was there the whole time. And Stig never left. He ate in front of the TV and went to bed early.

The second night Ida was gone, Marianne slept like a log. The sleeping pills she'd been prescribed suddenly worked, and then she picked up Ida and the investigation went on. The night outside Stig's apartment faded to an uncomfortable reminder of her own weakness.

Each week it was something new. Conversations with the police. Doctors' visits. Talking with the psychologist. Talking to the day care. Nothing else mattered. In Marianne's world, this was all there was.

But it didn't help. One day when she was called to the station, it wasn't to be questioned. She was told the police would not be devoting any further resources to her daughter. The investigation would be closed. But Marianne shouldn't worry, because they would make sure Stig was sent away for murder, that he would never be set free.

Marianne understood what they meant. It didn't matter that they couldn't throw him in jail for what he'd done to Ida. But as long as he was convicted of murder, he would never be able to harm Ida again and she would be spared more interrogations, more examinations. Their new life could begin.

Only then did Marianne take an interest in the murder of Katrin. Because what the police didn't say was that if Stig couldn't be convicted of killing Katrin Björk, he would be a free man, and no one would be able to stop him from demanding joint custody.

It took a few days for Marianne to understand. For her to put the two events together and realize what they meant.

Why would the police have wondered, *What were you doing when Katrin Björk was killed? What was your husband doing that night? Tell us what you witnessed. Tell us how you happen to know that there is no way your husband could be responsible for that murder.*

Of course, no one asked Marianne. No one knew. Not even Stig knew what she'd seen.

But they did ask Stig.

"What were you doing the night Katrin Björk was murdered?"

"I was at home," he replied. "Home alone in my apartment, watching TV. Eating leftovers. I went to bed early."

The police didn't believe him.

Marianne stepped out of the car. Tall cumulus clouds dotted the sky. A breeze whistled through the treetops and everything smelled like freshly mown grass. She sat down on a bench farther on that afforded a view of the cemetery. The neat lines of gravestones, arranged like mathematical tables, tidy paths, raked smooth.

The prim and proper organization of the cemetery reminded her of a grid-patterned city, the city where she grew up. That evident sterility. With rules everyone could understand. When Marianne was a child there were no accidents, no crimes, no dirty old men. Until one day, when Marianne was thirteen. A girl was found dead in the basement of the apartment building where they both lived.

Marianne had played with her a few times, even though the other girl was younger. Before she was found she had been reported missing. It was in all the papers, along with a photo of the girl. And a description of her clothing. She was wearing red jeans from Gul&Blå at the time of her disappearance, the very same ones Marianne had asked for for her birthday. When the girl was found, it said in the paper that she had been violated. Marianne understood only vaguely what this meant. A few days later, the girl's father was arrested. He had done it.

Marianne stood up. The cemetery was large, the biggest in Stockholm. She couldn't even see where it ended. Gently sloping rises, flowers gathered in identical vases, stuck in the ground so they wouldn't blow over. Each gravesite was marked by a granite headstone. Dark gray, red, black, blue. Polished, raw, matte, smooth. Marianne couldn't see the open grave where Ida would put Stig's urn.

So many people had told her Stig had abused Ida, that they'd found signs of assault. Ida said things to suggest it was true. And Marianne had felt like it could be so.

Had she known for sure? No. Had Ida begged her, *Mama, save me*? No. But the possibility, the risk, had determined each action she took moving forward.

Yet she wasn't ashamed; how could she be ashamed of this? There was no way she could have done anything different.

The other part, though — that haunted her. This was her punishment. Because when Marianne closed her eyes, it wasn't Ida's body she saw but Katrin's. The girl Marianne had sacrificed. And the unknown man who had taken her life. The killer could still be alive; he could have harmed someone else. And Marianne was the one who'd made that possible.

A hole in the ground. Lined with plastic so it wouldn't collapse. A pile of symbolic earth beside it. Ida would place Stig's remains there. An employee would fill the hole with dirt, cover it with grass, mask the opening. No stone had been ordered for Stig. The grave would be marked with a number. It hadn't been said out loud, but both Marianne and Ida understood what it would mean if they wrote out his name.

No one had asked Marianne what she'd been doing while Katrin Björk was dying. Why would they have? And she had no choice. It was not an option to tell them what she knew.

Katrin
1998

The nurse inhales the chilly morning air. It's twenty to six and she's waiting at the ambulance bay. Bay. That's what it's called. This is where Katrin Björk's body will be delivered to the National Board of Forensic Medicine in Solna. Here she will be received and admitted.

The board's own vehicle slowly approaches the doors. It stops right in front and the driver and his colleague say a brief hello to the nurse before lifting down the stretcher and rolling the body inside.

The examination room is the size of a small gym. The ceiling is high. The early summer morning sun finds its way into the room through the frosted glass and the half-drawn blinds. Everything smells faintly of chlorine and an odor few people recognize. The already spotless room has recently been cleaned again. Everything has been rinsed away; all traces of the previous examination have been washed down the drains; the grates have been rinsed and cleaned. This is done before each new autopsy.

The nurse puts on a pair of gloves and opens the body bag. She clears her throat mildly and asks for help transferring the girl onto one of the imperceptibly tilted autopsy tables of shiny steel. Then she signs the delivery confirmation as required by the ambulance service and begins to fill in the first form.

The girl was fifteen years and eleven months old; her body weighs 115 pounds and is sixty-five inches tall. The nurse has to write carefully; the ink pen is messy.

Katrin will be weighed, measured, opened up, photographed, turned over, and sewn back together again. This is where they will go through her body, square inch by square inch. They will sample her coagulated blood, the remains of what was once her saliva and secretions. Someone will scrape under her nails; someone else will open her mouth. They will take samples from her vagina and use a special shiny metal tool to hold it open. Her pubic hair will be combed with a special implement made for this very purpose. They will cut tissue from her body, microscopically thin slices. She will be placed under extra bright lights to undergo a quality-assured and accredited evidence-collection protocol. A flake of skin, a fingerprint, a defensive injury that left marks. Laboratories, instruments, techniques for analysis.

The instruments have already been prepared, laid out in straight rows on a cart. Another cart full of sterile packages, cotton balls, tweezers, pipettes, test tubes, small beakers, slightly larger beakers, litmus paper, everything that will store the samples, is also ready for use. The camera is charged, all the old images deleted.

Preparing Katrin for the autopsy will be quick, the nurse thinks. The girl's body is already naked, and she is not to be washed. The clothing that was found at the crime scene, a pair of panties and a cotton dress, have already been packaged up to be sent to the Division for Forensic Toxicology in Linköping.

Then the woman stops what she's doing and looks at her hands. They feel stiff; her joints are suddenly achy. Her heart is pounding, and her tongue is hot and swollen in her mouth.

She breathes in deeply, pressing her fist to her sternum. *Is it because of my own little girl?* she wonders. *Is it because of that hollow under the collarbone that she has too? Or is it because the dead girl's hair has curled at her neck, as if she only fell asleep and got a little sweaty?*

Then the woman squeezes her fists, opens her hands again, blinks her eyes clear, forces her shoulders down. It's a body. There's no other meaning to this tale.

The two doctors who will perform the autopsy step through the door, their hands up, wearing the department's protective blue gowns and white plastic aprons.

"I'm almost done," the nurse says quietly.

They nod. There's no real hurry, not in that way. One of the doctors goes to browse through the police documents, to look at the crime-scene photographs. Not much time has passed since they left the scene, but they still want to remind themselves of what they saw.

They have written preliminary notes of their own and discussed in low voices how to go about this job, what they should look for first, what they must absolutely not forget. Nothing will be left to chance; they don't want to risk unnecessary mistakes.

Katrin is on her back, her palms up and her legs slightly apart. Around her neck is a pearl necklace. A single strand of sticky, yellowish, freshwater pearls. The nurse leans over her, feeling as gently as she can for the clasp.

How strange that it didn't break, she has time to think, just before the necklace snaps in two. The pearls dance on the floor. The doctors stop speaking, look at one another.

The room is filled with the sound of clattering pearls as they vanish under counters and cabinets, side tables and desks. It sounds like more pearls than it actually is.

And then everything is quiet again.

Malin Persson Giolito was born in Stockholm in 1969 and grew up in Djursholm, Sweden. She holds a degree in law from Uppsala University and has worked as a lawyer for the biggest law firm in the Nordic region and as an official for the European Commission in Brussels, Belgium. Now a full-time writer, she has written four novels including *Quicksand,* her English-language debut. Persson Giolito lives with her husband and three daughters in Brussels.

Rachel Willson-Broyles holds a bachelor's degree in Scandinavian Studies from Gustavus Adolphus College in St. Peter, Minnesota. She started translating while a graduate student at the University of Wisconsin-Madison, where she received a PhD in Scandinavian Studies in 2013. Her translation of Malin Persson Giolito's *Quicksand* was published in 2017. Willson-Broyles lives in St. Paul, Minnesota.

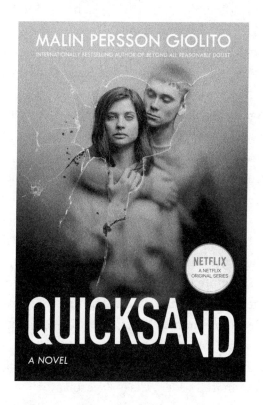

Lying next to the left-hand row of desks is Dennis; as usual he's wearing a graphic T, ill-fitting jeans, and untied tennis shoes. Dennis is from Uganda. He says he's seventeen, but he looks like a fat twenty-five year old. He's a student in the trade school, and he lives in Sollentuna in a home for people like him. Samir has ended up next to him, on his side. Samir and I are in the same class because Samir managed to be accepted to our school's special program in international economics and social sciences.

Up at the lectern is Christer, our homeroom teacher and self-described social reformer. His mug has overturned and coffee is dripping onto the leg of his pants. Amanda, no more than two meters away, is sitting propped against the radiator under the window. Just a few minutes ago, she was all cashmere, white gold, and sandals. The diamond earrings she received when we were confirmed are still sparkling in the early-summer sunshine. Now you might think she was covered in mud. I am sitting on the floor in the middle of the classroom. In my lap is Sebastian, the son of the richest man in Sweden, Claes Fagerman.

The people in this room do not go together. People like us don't usually hang out. Maybe on a metro platform during a taxi strike, or in the dining car on a train, but not in a classroom.

It smells like rotten eggs. The air is hazy and gray with gunpowder smoke. Everyone has been shot but me. I haven't got even as much as a bruise.

■ OTHER PRESS

www.otherpress.com